Writings in the United Amateur, 1915-1922

H. P. Lovecraft

Writings in the United Amateur, 1915-1922

ISBN: 978-1-63637-370-6

CONTENTS

UNITED AMATEUR PRESS ASSOCIATION:

EXPONENT OF AMATEUR JOURNALISM

ITS OBJECT

The desire to write for publication is one which inheres strongly in every human breast. From the proficient college graduate, storming the gates of the high-grade literary magazines, to the raw schoolboy, vainly endeavoring to place his first crude compositions in the local newspapers, the whole intelligent public are today seeking expression through the printed page, and yearning to behold their thoughts and ideals permanently crystallized in the magic medium of type. But while a few persons of exceptional talent manage eventually to gain a foothold in the professional world of letters rising to celebrity through the wide diffusion of their art, ideals, or opinions; the vast majority, unless aided in their education by certain especial advantages, are doomed to confine their expression to the necessarily restricted sphere of ordinary conversation. To supply these especial educational advantages which may enable the general public to achieve the distinction of print, and which may prevent the talented but unknown author from remaining forever in obscurity, has arisen that largest and foremost of societies for literary education The United Amateur Press Association.

ITS ORIGIN

Amateur journalism, or the composition and circulation of small, privately printed magazines, is an instructive diversion which has existed in the United States for over half a century. In the decade of 1866-1876 this practice first became an organized institution; a short-lived society of amateur journalists, including the now famous publisher, Charles Scribner, having existed from 1869 to 1874. In 1876 a more lasting society was formed, which exists to this day as an exponent of light dilettantism. Not until 1895, however, was amateur journalism established as a serious branch of educational endeavour. On September 2nd of that year, Mr. William H. Greenfield, a gifted professional author, of Philadelphia, founded The United Amateur Press Association, which has grown to be the leader of its kind, and the representative

1

of amateur journalism in its best phases throughout the English-speaking world.

ITS NATURE

In many respects the word "amateur" fails to do full credit to amateur journalism and the association which best represents it. To some minds the term conveys an idea of crudity and immaturity, yet the United can boast of members and publications whose polish and scholarship are well-nigh impeccable. In considering the adjective "amateur" as applied to the press association, we must adhere to the more basic interpretation, regarding the word as indicating the non-mercenary nature of the membership. Our amateurs write purely for love of their art, without the stultifying influence of commercialism. Many of them are prominent professional authors in the outside world, but their professionalism never creeps into their association work. The atmosphere is wholly fraternal, and courtesy takes the place of currency.

The real essential of amateur journalism and The United Amateur Press Association is the amateur paper or magazine, which somewhat resembles the average high-school or college publication. These journals, varying greatly in size and character, are issued by various members at their own expense, and contain, besides the literary work of their several editors or publishers, contributions from all the many members who do not publish papers of their own. Their columns are open to every person in the association, and it may be said with justice that no one will find it impossible to secure the publication of any literary composition of reasonable brevity. The papers thus published are sent free to all our many members, who constitute a select and highly appreciative reading public. Since each member receives the published work of every other member, many active and brilliant minds are brought into close contact, and questions of every sort, literary, historical, and scientific, are debated both in the press and in personal correspondence. The correspondence of members is one of the most valuable features of the United, for through this medium a great intellectual stimulus, friendly and informal in nature, is afforded. Congenial members are in this way brought together in a lettered companionship, which often grows into life-long friendship, while persons of opposed ideas may mutually gain much breadth of mind by hearing the other side of their respective opinions discussed in a genial manner. In short, the United offers an exceptionally well-proportioned mixture of instruction and fraternal cheer. There are no limits of age, sex, education, position, or locality in this most complete of democracies. Boys and girls of twelve and men and women of sixty, parents and their sons and daughters, college professors and grammar-school pupils, aristocrats and intelligent labourers, Easterners and Westerners, are here given equal advantages, those of greater education helping their cruder brethren until the common fund of culture is as nearly level as it can be in any human organization. Members are classified according to age; "A" meaning under sixteen, "B" from 16 to 21, and "C" over 21. The advantages offered to those of limited acquirements are immense, many persons having gained practically all their literary polish through membership in the United. A much cherished goal is professional authorship or editorship, and numerous indeed are the United members who have now become recognized authors, poets, editors, and publishers. True, though trite, is the saying that amateur journalism is an actual training school for professional journalism.

ITS PUBLISHING ACTIVITIES

Members of the United may or may not publish little papers of their own. This is a matter of choice, for there are always enough journals to print the work of the non-publishing members. Youths who possess printing presses will find publishing an immense but inexpensive pleasure, whilst other publishers may have their printing done at very reasonable rates by those who do own presses. The favorite size for amateur papers is 5×7 inches, which can be printed at 55 or 60 cents per page, each page containing about 250 words. Thus a four-page issue containing 1000 words can be published for less than $2.50, if arrangements are made, as is often the case, for its free mailing with any other paper. Certain of the more pretentious journals affect the 7×10 size, which costs about $1.60 for each page of 700 words. These figures allow for 250 copies, the most usual number to be mailed. Mr. E. E. Ericson of Elroy, Wisconsin, is our Official Printer, and his work is all that the most fastidious could demand. Other printers may be found amongst the young men who print their own papers. In many cases they can quote very satisfactory prices. Two or more members may issue a paper co-operatively, the individual expense then being very slight.

ITS CONTRIBUTED LITERATURE

The United welcomes all literary contributions; poems, stories, and essays, which the various members may submit. However, contribution is by no means compulsory, and in case a

3

member finds himself too busy for activity, he may merely enjoy the free papers which reach him, without taxing himself with literary labour. For those anxious to contribute, every facility is provided. In some cases negotiations are made directly between publisher and contributor, but the majority are accommodated by the two Manuscript Bureaus, Eastern and Western, which receive contributions in any quantity from the non-publishing members, and are drawn upon for material by those who issue papers. These bureaus practically guarantee on the one hand to find a place for each member's manuscript, and on the other hand to keep each publisher well supplied with matter for his journal.

ITS CRITICAL DEPARTMENTS

The two critical departments of the United are at present the most substantial of its various educational advantages. The Department of Private Criticism is composed exclusively of highly cultured members, usually professors or teachers of English, who practically mould the taste of the whole association, receiving and revising before publication the work of all who choose to submit it to them. The service furnished free by this department is in every way equal to that for which professional critical bureaus charge about two dollars. Manuscripts are carefully corrected and criticised in every detail, and authors are given comprehensive advice designed to elevate their taste, style, and grammar. Many a crude but naturally gifted writer has been developed to polished fluency and set on the road to professional authorship through the United's Department of Private Criticism.

The Department of Public Criticism reviews thoroughly and impartially the various printed papers and their contents, offering precepts and suggestions for improvement. Its reports are printed in the official organ of the association, and serve as a record of our literary achievement.

ITS LITERARY AWARDS

To encourage excellence amongst the members of the United, annual honours or "laureateships" are awarded the authors of the best poems, stories, essays, or editorials. Participation in these competitions is not compulsory, since they apply only to pieces which have been especially "entered for laureateship." The entries are judged not by the members of the association, but by highly distinguished litterateurs of the professional world, selected particularly for the occasion. Our latest innovation is a laureateship for the best home-printed paper, which will excite keen rivalry among our younger members, and bring out some careful specimens of the typographical art. Besides the laureateships there are other honours and prizes awarded by individual publishers within the United, many of the amateur journals offering excellent books for the best stories, reviews, or reports submitted to them.

ITS OFFICIAL ORGAN

The association, as a whole, publishes a voluminous 7×10 monthly magazine called The United Amateur, which serves as the official organ. In this magazine may be found the complete revised list of members, the reports of officers and committees, the ample reviews issued by the Department of Public Criticism, a selection of the best contemporary amateur literature, together with the latest news of amateur journalists and their local clubs from all over the Anglo-Saxon world. The United Amateur is published by an annually elected Official Editor, and printed by the Official Publisher. It is sent free to all members of the association.

ITS GOVERNMENT

The United Amateur Press Association is governed by a board of officers elected by popular vote. The elections take place at the annual conventions, where amateurs from all sections meet and fraternize. Those who attend vote in person, whilst all others send in proxy ballots. There is much friendly rivalry between cities concerning the selection of the convention seat each year. The principal elective officers of the United are the President, two Vice-Presidents, the Treasurer, the Official Editor and the three members of the Board of Directors. There are also a Historian, a Laureate Recorder, and two Manuscript Managers. Appointed by the President are the members of the two Departments of Criticism, the Supervisor of Amendments, the Official Publisher, and the Secretary of the association. All save Secretary and Official Publisher, serve without remuneration. The basic law of the United comprises an excellent Constitution and By-Laws.

ITS LOCAL CLUBS

The United encourages the formation of local literary or press clubs in cities or towns containing several members. These clubs generally publish papers, and hold meetings wherein the pleasures of literature are enlivened by those of the society. The most desirable form of club activity is that in which a high-school instructor forms a literary society of the more enthusiastic members of his class.

ITS PLACE IN EDUCATION

During the past two years, as it has approached and passed its twentieth birthday, the United has been endeavoring more strongly than ever to find and occupy its true place amongst the many and varied phases of education. That it discharges an unique function in literary culture is certain, and its members have of late been trying very actively to establish and define its relation to the high-school and the university. Mr. Maurice Winter Moe, Instructor of English at the Appleton High School, Appleton, Wisconsin, and one of our very ablest members, took the first decisive step by organizing his pupils into an amateur press club, using the United to supplement his regular class-room work. The scholars were delighted, and many have acquired a love of good literature which will never leave them. Three or four, in particular, have become prominent in the affairs of the United. After demonstrating the success of his innovation, Mr. Moe described it in The English Journal, his article arousing much interest in educational circles, and being widely reprinted by other papers. In November, 1914, Mr. Moe addressed an assemblage of English teachers in Chicago, and there created so much enthusiasm for the United, that scores of instructors have subsequently joined our ranks, many of them forming school clubs on the model of the original club at Appleton. Here, then, is one definite destiny for our association: to assist the teaching of advanced English in the high-school. We are especially eager for high-school material, teachers and pupils alike.

But there still remain a numerous class, who, though not connected with school or college, have none the less sincere literary aspirations. At present they are benefited immensely through mental contact with our more polished members, yet for the future we plan still greater aids for their development, by the creation of a systematic "Department of Instruction," which will, if successfully established, amount practically to a free correspondence school, and an "Authors' Placing Bureau," which will help amateurs in entering the professional field. Our prime endeavor is at present to secure members of high mental and scholastic quality, in order that the United may be strengthened for its increasing responsibility. Professors, teachers, clergymen, and authors have already responded in gratifying numbers to our wholly altruistic plea for

6

their presence among us. The reason for the United's success as an educational factor seems to lie principally in the splendid loyalty and enthusiasm which all the members somehow acquire upon joining. Every individual is alert for the welfare of the association, and its activities form the subject of many of the current essays and editorials. The ceaseless writing in which most of the members indulge is in itself an aid to fluency, while the mutual examples and criticisms help on still further the pleasantly unconscious acquisition of a good literary style. When regular courses of instruction shall have been superimposed upon these things, the association can indeed afford to claim a place of honour in the world of education.

ITS ENTRANCE CONDITIONS

The only requirement for admission to the United is earnest literary aspiration. Any member will furnish the candidate for admission with an application blank, signed in recommendation. This application, filled out and forwarded to the Secretary of the association with the sum of fifty cents as dues for the first year, and accompanied by a "credential," or sample of the candidate's original literary work, will be acted upon with due consideration by the proper official. No candidate of real sincerity will be denied admittance, and the applicant will generally be soon rewarded by his certificate of membership, signed by the President and Secretary. Papers, letters, and postal cards of welcome will almost immediately pour in upon him, and he will in due time behold his credential in print. (Unless it be something already printed.) Once a member, his dues will be one dollar yearly, and if he should ever leave the United, later desiring to join again, his reinstatement fee will be one dollar.

ITS REPRESENTATIVES

The United Amateur Press Association is anything but local in its personnel. Its active American membership extends from Boston to Los Angeles, and from Milwaukee to Tampa, thus bringing all sections in contact, and representing every phase of American thought. Its English membership extends as far north as Newcastle-on-Tyne. Typical papers are published in England, California, Kansas, Wisconsin, Ohio, Illinois, Alabama, Mississippi, North Carolina, District of Columbia, New York, and Rhode Island.

In writing for entrance blanks or for further information concerning the United, the applicant may address any one of the following officers, who will gladly give details, and samples of amateur papers: Leo Fritter, President, 503 Central National Bank Bldg., Columbus, Ohio; H. P. Lovecraft, Vice-President, 598 Angell St., Providence, R. I.; Mrs. J. W. Renshaw, Second Vice-President, Coffeeville, Miss.; William J. Dowdell, Secretary, 2428 East 66th St., Cleveland, Ohio; or Edward F. Daas, Official Editor, 1717 Cherry St., Milwaukee, Wis. Professional authors interested in our work are recommended to communicate with the Second Vice-President, while English teachers may derive expert information from Maurice W. Moe, 658 Atlantic St., Appleton, Wis. Youths who possess printing-presses are referred to the Secretary, who is himself a young typographer.

ITS PROVINCE SUMMARIZED

If you are a student of elementary English desirous of attaining literary polish in an enjoyable manner,
If you are an ordinary citizen, burning with the ambition to become an author,
If you are a solitary individual wishing for a better chance to express yourself,
If you own a printing-press and would like to learn how to issue a high-grade paper,
If you are a mature person eager to make up for a youthful lack of culture,
If you are a professor or teacher seeking a new method of interesting your English class, or
If you are an author or person of ripe scholarship, anxious to aid your cruder brothers on their way, then

YOU ARE CORDIALLY INVITED TO BECOME A MEMBER OF THE UNITED AMATEUR PRESS ASSOCIATION.

H. P. LOVECRAFT
Vice-President

8

THE UNITED AMATEUR

OFFICIAL ORGAN OF THE UNITED AMATEUR PRESS ASSOCIATION OF AMERICA

Volume XIV GEORGETOWN, ILL., JANUARY, 1915. Number 3

DEPARTMENT OF PUBLIC CRITICISM

THE BADGER for January is the first number of a strikingly meritorious and serious paper published by George S. Schilling. We here behold none of the frivolity which spoils the writings of those who view amateur journalism merely as a passing amusement. The Badger shows evidence of careful and tasteful editorship, combined with a commendable artistic sense in choice of paper and cover.

The leading article, an essay on the minimum wage, is from the pen of the editor, and shows both literary ability and a sound knowledge of economics. "Sister to the Ox", by A. W. Ashby, is an excellent short story whose strength is rather in its moral than in its plot. The editorials are certainly not lacking in force, and seem well calculated to stir the average amateur from his torpor of triteness and inanity.

THE INSPIRATION for November is an "Official Number", containing the work of none but titled authors. Rheinhart Kleiner contributes the single piece of verse, a smooth and pleasing lyric entitled "Love Again", which is not unlike his previous poem, "Love, Come Again". As an amatory poet, Mr. Kleiner shows much delicacy of sentiment, refinement of language, and appreciation of metrical values; his efforts in this direction entitle him to a high place among amateur bards.

One of the truly notable prose features of the magazine is Walter John Held's delightful sketch of Joaquin Miller's home and haunts. This artistic picture of Californian scenery exhibits a real comprehension of the beauties of Nature, and stirs to an unusual degree the imagination of the reader. Mr. Held's prose possesses a fluency and grace that bring it close to the professional quality, and its few faults are far less considerable than might be expected from the pen of a young author. However, we must remark some rather awkward examples of grammatical construction. The correct plural of "eucalyptus" is "eucalypti", without any final "s", the name being treated as a Latin noun of the second declension. "Slowly and dignified—it pursues its way" is hardly a permissible clause; the adjective "dignified" must be exchanged for an adverb. Perhaps Mr. Held sought to employ poetical enallage, but even so, the adjective does not correspond with "slowly"; besides, the use of enallage in prose is at best highly questionable. "This free and rank flowers and brush" is another bad clause. But it is not well to dissect the sketch too minutely. A youth of Mr. Held's ability needs only time and continued practice to raise him to the highest rank in prose composition.

INVICTUS for January, the first number of Mr. Paul J. Campbell's new individual paper, is one of those rare journals concerning which it is almost impossible to speak without enthusiasm. Not one of its twenty-six pages fails to delight us. Foremost in merit, and most aptly suited to Mr. Campbell's particular type of genius, are the three inspiring essays, "The Impost of the Future", "The Sublime Ideal", and "Whom God Hath Put Asunder". Therein appears to great advantage the keen reasoning and sound materialistic philosophy of the author. "The Sublime Ideal" is especially absorbing, tracing as it does the expansion of the human mind from a state of the narrowest and most violent bigotry to its present moderate breadth.

The three pieces of verse, "Inspiration", "The Larger Life", and "Down in Mexico", are all of smooth construction and musical metre, though not exhibiting their author's powers as well as his essays. "Down in Mexico", a virile poem in Kipling's style, is unquestionably the best of the three.

Mr. Campbell's comments on amateur affairs are well-written and entertaining, especially his reminiscent article entitled "After Seven Years".

OUTWARD BOUND for January is an excellent journal edited by George William Stokes of Newcastle-on-Tyne, England. It is gratifying to behold such a paper as this, one of the links between America and the parent country which the United is helping to forge.

Herbert B. Darrow opens the issue with a short story entitled "A Lesson". The tale is of conventional pattern, containing a sound though not strikingly original moral. The language is generally good, except in one sentence where the author speaks of "the vehicles in the street and buildings about him". Surely he does not mean that the vehicles were in the buildings as well as in the street. The use of the definite article before the word "buildings" would do much toward dispelling the ambiguous effect.

"The Haunted Forest", a poem by J. H. Fowler, is almost Poe-like in its grimly fantastic quality. We can excuse rather indefinite metre when we consider the admirably created atmosphere, the weird harmony of the lines, the judicious use of alliteration, and the apt selection of words. "Bird-shunned", as applied to the thickets of the forest, is a particularly graphic epithet. Mr. Fowler is to be congratulated upon his glowing imagination and poetical powers.

"A Bit o' Purple Heather", by Edna von der Heide, is a delightful piece of verse in modified Scottish dialect, which well justifies the dedication of the magazine to this poetess.

Mr. Stokes' editorial, headed "Ships that Pass", sustains the nautical atmosphere of his periodical. We wish he had given his thoughts a larger space for expression.

THE PIPER for December comes as a surprise to those who have known Rheinhart Kleiner only as a master of metre, for he is here displayed as the possessor of a pure and vigorous prose style as well. In this, the opening number of his individual journal, Mr. Kleiner provides us with a pleasing variety of literary matter; two serious poems, two rhymes of lighter character, an essay on the inevitable topic of Consolidation, and a brilliant collection of short editorials and criticisms.

"A Carnation", which begins the issue, is an exquisite piece of sentiment couched in faultless verse. The odd measure of the poem is one peculiarly suited to the author's delicate type of genius; an iambic line of only three feet. The other lyric, "Heart, Do Not Wake", is likewise of excellent quality, though the succession of "again" and "pain" in the first line might suggest to some ears an unnecessary internal rhyme.

"The Rhyme of the Hapless Poet" is very clever, and can be truly appreciated by every author of printed matter. Perhaps the misfortune of which the poet complains is the cause of the extra syllable in the first line of the second stanza; we hope that the following is what Mr. Kleiner intended:

"I wrote a poem, 'twas a prize".

Otherwise we are forced to believe that he pronounces "poem" as a monosyllable, "pome". "My Favorite Amateur" is a good specimen of light, imitative verse.

The article on Consolidation is cynical in tone, but eminently sensible. It is only too true that our greatest intellectual stimulus is found in controversy and antagonism; we are really quite bellicose in our instincts, despite the utterances of the peace advocates.

Mr. Kleiner concludes his journal with a sparkling epigram on a rather obvious though regrettable tendency in amateur circles.

The Piper is in general a paper of satisfying merit, to whose future issues we shall look forward with eagerness.

THE RECRUITING FEMININE for 1914-1915 is a publication

of unusual worth. "The Rose Supreme," by Coralie Austin, is a delicate little poem in which we regret the presence of one inexcusably bad rhyme. To rhyme the words "rose" and "unclosed" is to exceed the utmost limits of poetic license. It is true that considerable variations in vowel sounds have been permitted; "come" makes, or at least used to make, an allowable rhyme with "home", "clock" with "look", or "grass" with "place"; but a final consonant attached to one of two otherwise rhyming syllables positively destroys the rhyme.

Mrs. Myra Cole's essay on "The Little Things of Life" is well written and instructive.

"The Dirge of the Great Atlantic", by Anne Vyne Tillery Renshaw, is a grim and moving bit of verse, cast in the same primitively stirring metre which this author used in her professionally published poem, "The Chant of Iron". Mrs. Renshaw possesses an enviable power to reach the emotions through the medium of written words.

"Two Octobers—A Contrast", by Eloise N. Griffith, is a meritorious sketch ending with the usual appeal for the cessation of the European war. We fear that the author cannot quite realize the ambitious passions, essential ingredients of human nature, which render necessary a final decision.

Miss Edna von der Heide, in an able article, rallies to the defense of Mr. W. E. Griffin's now famous "Favorite Pastime". The Modern Lothario is fortunate in having so competent and experienced a champion. However, we cannot wholly endorse the sentiments of these excellent writers. The statement that "all amateur journalists are flirts, more or less", is a base and unwarranted libel which we are prepared completely to refute.

"The Audience", by Mrs. Florence Shepphird, is a masterly defense of those inactive amateurs whom we are all too prone to consider as delinquent. It is indeed true that authors would be useless were it not for some sort of a reading public.

TOLEDO AMATEUR for December is a wholesome juvenile product. The typography still leaves something to be desired, but the evidences of care are everywhere visible, and we may reasonably expect to see it improve from month to month, into one of the leading amateur papers. Credentials form the keynote of the current issue, and a very promising assortment of recruits are here introduced to the members of the United. Miss Sandborn, who is fortunate enough to be one of Mr. Moe's pupils at Appleton, contributes an interesting school anecdote, narrated in simple fashion. Miss Thie gives information concerning the "Campfire Girls". Some new members of adult years are also represented in this number. Mr. Jenkins shows an admirable command of light prose, and will undoubtedly prove one of the United's most entertaining writers. Misses Kline and McGeoch both exhibit marked poetical tendencies in prose, the latter writer having something of Mr. Fritter's facility in the use of metaphor. Mr. Porter's editorials are refreshingly naive and unaffected. His grammar is generally good, except in the one sentence where he speaks of the Toledo Times. He should say, "the newspaper which has given me much experience, and to whose publishers I owe a great deal of experience gained."

THE UNITED OFFICIAL QUARTERLY for November marks the beginning of a laudable enterprise on the part of the official board. The magazine is of artistic appearance in cover, paper, and typography alike, while the contents show considerable care in preparation.

Ira A. Cole's essay on "The Gods of Our Fathers" is the leading feature and, though not of perfect perspicuity nor faultless unity, is none the less noteworthy as a sincere expression of Pantheism. Mr. Cole keenly feels the incongruity of our devotion to Semitic theological ideals, when as a matter of fact we are descended from Aryan polytheists, and his personification of the Grecian deities in the men of today is a pleasing and ingenious conception. We are inclined to wonder whether the author or the printer is to blame for rendering the poet Hesiod's name as "Hesoid".

The metric art is represented by three contributions. Paul J. Campbell's lines on "The Heritage of Life" are smooth in construction and proper in sentiment, though they are far from showing their author at his best. Mr. Campbell is a supreme master of the philosophical essay and of pointed, satirical prose, being a very "Junius" in bold, biting invective; but is placed at something of a disadvantage in the domain of conventional poetry. Rheinhart Kleiner and ourselves revel in heroic couplets of widely differing nature. Our own masterpiece is in full Queen Anne style with carefully balanced lines and strictly measured quantities. We have succeeded in producing eighteen lines without a single original sentiment or truly poetical image. Rev. Mr. Pyke, the object of the verses, deserves a better encomiast. Mr. Kleiner, on the other hand, uses an heroic metre of that softened type which was evolved at the close of the eighteenth century from the disruption of the more formal style. In this sort of verse the stiff, classic expressions are discarded, and the sense frequently overflows from couplet to couplet, giving the romantic poet a greater latitude for expression than was possible in the old models. "Vacation" is not distinguished by any strikingly novel idea, but is in general a very clever piece of light work. The only substantial defect is in the eighth line, where the word "resort" is so placed, that the accent must fall wrongfully upon the first syllable.

Leo Fritter's article on criticism is timely and sensible. As he justly contends, some authorized amateur critics deal far too roughly with the half-formed products of the young author, while most unofficial and inexperienced reviewers fairly run mad with promiscuous condemnation. The fancied brilliancy of the critic is always greatest when he censures most, so that the temptations of the tribe are many. We are at best but literary parasites, and need now and then just such a restraining word as our counter-critic gives us. Mr. Fritter's style is here, as usual, highly ornamented with metaphor. One slight defect strikes the fastidious eye, but since split infinitives are becoming so common in these days, we shall attend the author's plea for gentleness, and remain silent.

H. P. LOVECRAFT,
Chairman, Department of Public Criticism.

THE UNITED AMATEUR MARCH 1915

DEPARTMENT OF PUBLIC CRITICISM

THE BLARNEY STONE for November-December is dedicated to its contributors and wholly given over to their work. "Did You Ever Go A-Fishin'?," by Olive G. Owen, is a vivid poetical portrayal of that peculiar attraction which the angler's art exerts on its devotees. While the whole is of high and pleasing quality, exception must be taken to the rhyming of "low" with itself at the very beginning of the poem. It may be that the second "low" is a misprint for "slow", yet even in that case, the rhyme is scarcely allowable, since the dominant rhyming sound would still be "low". Miss Edna von der Heide, in "The Christmas of Delsato's Maria", tells how an Italian thief utilized his questionable art to replace a loss in his family. "To General Villa" is a peculiar piece of verse written last summer for the purpose of defying those who had charged its author with pedantry and pomposity. It has suffered somewhat at the hands of the printer; "Intrepido" being spelled "Intrepedo", and

14

the word "own" being dropped from the clause "your own name can't write" in the third line of the second stanza. Also, the first of the Spanish double exclamation marks around the oath "Santa Maria" is right side up instead of inverted according to Castilian custom. Having been hastily written, the piece is wholly without merit. "Senor", in the second line of the third stanza is placed so that the accent must fall erroneously on the first syllable. The changes of time and revolutions have rendered the last stanza sadly out of date.

The issue is concluded with a beautiful editorial on "The Service With Love", wherein is described the ideal spirit of brotherhood which should pervade amateur journalism. We regret the two blank pages at the back of the magazine, and wish that some talented Blarney had seen fit to adorn them with his work.

THE BROOKLYNITE for January is of unusual merit, fairly teeming with features of a well-written and substantial character.

The short story by Mrs. Carson is developed with admirable simplicity and ease; the plot not too strained, and the moral not too pragmatically forced upon the reader. The conversation, always a difficult point with amateur authors, is surprisingly natural.

Mrs. Adams' essay on ghosts displays considerable literary knowledge, though the anecdote at the end is rather ancient for use today. We last heard it about ten years ago, with a Scotchman instead of a negro preacher as the narrator, and with the word "miracle" instead of "phenomena" as the subject.

Mr. Goodwin's "Cinigrams" are delightful, and we expect soon to hear the author heralded as the Martial of amateur journalism. "Ford, Do Not Shake", Mr. Goodwin's parody on Kleiner's "Heart, Do Not Wake", is actually side-splitting. The metre is handled to perfection, and the humor is extremely clever.

"Consolidation", by George Julian Houtain, is a fair example of the manner in which some of the less dignified National politicians try to cast silly aspersions on the United. The elaborately sarcastic phrase: "United boys and girls", seems to please its author, since he uses it twice. There is unconscious irony in the spectacle of a National man, once a member of the notorious old Gotham ring, preaching virtuously against the "unenviable record" of the United.

Mr. Stoddard's brief essay, composed at a meeting of the Blue Pencil Club, is excellent, and his concluding quatrain regular and melodious. We wish, however, that he would give us some more of the serious fiction that he can write so splendidly, and which used several years ago to appear in the amateur press.

"Music Moods", by Charles D. Isaacson, is an emotional

sketch of great power and delicate artistry. Mr. Isaacson has an active imagination and a literary ability which makes his readers see very vividly the images he creates.

Mrs. Houtain's poem shows great but as yet undeveloped talent. The repeated use of the expletive "do" in such phrases as "I do sigh", or "I pray and do pine", mars the verse somewhat. As Pope remarked and humorously illustrated in his Essay on Criticism:

"Expletives their feeble aid DO join."

Mr. Ayres' jocose epic is clever and tuneful. The climax, or rather anticlimax, comes quite effectively.

Mr. Adams, in his brilliant verses entitled "Gentlemen, Please Desist", exposes in a masterly way the fatuity of our loud-mouthed peace workers. Miss Silverman's lines on the same subject are very good, but scarcely equal in keenness of wit. It is all very well to "keep industry booming", but industry cannot take the place of military efficiency in protecting a nation against foreign aggression.

As a whole, the January Brooklynite is the best number we have yet seen.

THE COYOTE for March is not a revival of Ex-President Brechler's well-known amateur journal of that name, but a semi-professional leaflet edited by Mr. William T. Harrington, a rather new recruit. The leading feature is a sensational short story by the editor, entitled "What Gambling Did". In this tale, Mr. Harrington exhibits at least a strong ambition to write, and such energy, if well directed, may eventually make of him one of our leading authors of fiction. Just now, however, we must protest against his taste in subject and technique. His models are obviously not of the classical order, and his ideas of probability are far from unexceptionable. In developing the power of narration, it is generally best, as one of our leading amateurs lately reiterated, to discard the thought of elaborate plots and thrilling climaxes, and to begin instead with the plain and simple description of actual incidents with which the author is familiar. Likewise, the young author may avoid improbability by composing his earliest efforts in the first person. He knows what he himself would do in certain circumstances, but he does not always know very exactly what some others might do in similar cases. Meanwhile, above all things he should read classic fiction, abstaining entirely from "Wild West Weeklies" and the like. Mr. Harrington has a taste for excitement, and would probably thrive on Scott, Cooper, or Poe. Let him read the Leather Stocking Tales if he loves pioneers and frontier life. Not until after he has acquired a familiarity with the methods of the best authors, and refined his imagination by a perusal of their works, should he make attempts at writing outside his own experience. He will then be able to produce work of a quality which would surprise him now.

We are sorry to note that the Coyote's editorial columns are occupied by a mere condensed copy of the United's standard recruiting circular. This space might have been filled much more profitably with brief original comments by the editor on the numerous exchanges which are listed in another part of his paper. The paid advertising and subscription price are not to be commended. Such things have no place in a truly amateur paper. But continued membership in the United will doubtless fill Mr. Harrington with the genuine amateur spirit, and cause The Coyote to become a worthy successor to its older namesake.

DOWDELL'S BEARCAT for October is a modest but very promising little paper, mostly composed of amateur notes and brief reviews. The editor has interest in his work, and fluency in his language, foundations on which a more elaborate structure may some day be erected. One feature open to criticism is Mr. Dowdell's sudden change in his editorial column from the usual first person plural to the third person singular. It would be better to save "The Old Bear" and his interesting chat, for a separate column. The typography of Dowdell's Bearcat is not perfect, but may be expected to improve from issue to issue.

THE EMISSARY for July is a National paper, but contains the work of several United members. Of the publication itself we need not stop to speak. Mr. Reading, though only eighteen years of age, is an editor and printer of the highest grade, and has produced an issue which will be long remembered in the amateur world.

"Ausonius, the Nature-Lover", by Edward H. Cole, is a pleasing and judicious appreciation of a later Latin poet, showing how a bard of the decaying Roman Empire approached in certain passages the spirit of modern romanticism. Mr. Cole's translated extracts are beautifully phrased, and his comment upon the subject well exhibits his wide and careful scholarship. Articles of this quality are rarely found in the amateur press, and it will be interesting to note what effect their more frequent appearance would have upon the literary tone of the associations.

"To Sappho", by Olive G. Owen, is a lyrical poem of much merit, yet having a defective line. Why, we wonder, did the author see fit to leave two necessary syllables out of the third line of the opening verse?

"Lamb o' Mine", by Dora M. Hepner, is probably the most attractive bit of verse in the magazine. The negro dialect is inimitable, and the consoling spirit of the old black "mammy" fairly radiates from the lines. Metrically, the piece is faultless, and we wish its author were a more frequent contributor to the amateur journals.

Miss von der Heide's two poems, "The Mill Mother", and "Greeting", express admirably the sentiments of pathos and natural beauty, respectively. Personally, we prefer "Greeting".

Mr. Campbell's lines on "Huerta's Finish" are distinctly below the usual standard of this talented writer's work. The metre is satisfactory, but the humor is somewhat strained, and the pun in the last line based on a mispronunciation of the old Indian's name. "Wehr-ta" is probably the correct sound, rather than "Hurt-a".

THE INSPIRATION for January must be judged strictly by its quality; not its quantity. Pinkney C. Grissom, a very young amateur, cheers us greatly with his article on "Smiles", while Miss von der Heide's microscopic story, "A Real Victory", is indeed a literary treat. We trust that the editor's threat of discontinuance may not be realized.

THE KANSAN for July reaches us at a late date through the kindness of Mr. Daas. In this magazine the Sunflower Club of Bazine makes its formal debut, being ushered into amateur society by means of a pleasing and well-written article from the pen of Miss Hoffman. The informal "Exchange Comment" is a charitable and generally delightful department, whose anonymity we rather regret. The Editorial pages are brilliant in their justification of the United's sunny spirit, as contrasted with the National's forbidding frigidity.

THE OLYMPIAN for September-February well sustains the lofty traditions of that magazine. Mr. Cole defines with considerable precision his latest editorial policy and his true attitude toward the United, revealing only the more strongly, however, his remarkable and ineradicable prejudice against our association in favor of the National. "Evening Prayer", by Rheinhart Kleiner, is a poem of great beauty and real worth, couched in the alternating iambic pentameter and trimeter which this poet seems to have made his own particular medium of expression. Mr. Kleiner is rapidly assuming a very high rank among amateur poets.

"The Public Library", by Eloise N. Griffith, is a delightful and appreciative reminiscence of quiet hours of lettered joy.

"The Play Hour", consisting of two clever bits of metre dedicated to a very young amateur, appears in a collection of short and sprightly pieces signed by the Senior Editor himself. It is difficult, nevertheless, to imagine the dignified Olympian Zeus as the author. Though the second of these tuneful rhymes is apparently written in the "simplified" spelling now so popular among certain amateur editors, a closer inspection reveals the fact that the spelling is merely made juvenile to suit the subject. After all, however, simplified spelling and baby-talk are but little removed from each other. The Reviewers' Club is in this issue represented by both editors, whose criticisms are as usual just and illuminating.

PROMETHEUS for September-November is a journal of unusual literary and artistic value, edited by our poet-laureate, Miss Olive G. Owen. The paper well lives up to its sub-title, "A Magazine of Aspirations Dreamed into Reality". Mr. William H. Greenfield, the honored founder of the United, claims the first page with a graceful Pindaric ode, "To My Friend". "The Weaver of Dreams", by Edna G. Thorne, is a strikingly well-written short story pervaded with a delicate pathos and expressing a beautiful Christian philosophy. George W. Macauley, continuing to concentrate his narrative powers on the Oriental tale, presents a pleasing fable of old Moorish Spain, entitled "Ali Ahmed and the Aqueduct". "The Ethics of Stimulation", by Maurice W. Moe, is an eminently sound exposition of the relative evil of coffee and alcoholic liquor as stimulants. "Partners", by H. A. Reading, exhibits great ability on the part of its author, and is well calculated to arouse the emotions of affectionate fathers and sons.

Miss Owen's work, scattered here and there throughout the magazine, is naturally of the very first quality. It is hard to choose between the two poems "Atthis, I Love Thee", and "To Elizabeth Knopf", but we incline slightly toward the former. The sketches "The Visitor" and "Some Things I Like in New York" are both delightful in their artistic simplicity.

Critically analyzed, Prometheus may be classed as one of the most varied and generally readable magazines of the season.

RED LETTER DAYS for October is the first of an informal individual paper by George W. Macauley, representing the most purely personal phase of amateur journalism. This issue is almost completely devoted to an animated account of the "Red Letter Days" spent by Mr. Macauley last summer with the amateurs who stopped to see him while on their way to the various conventions. The author's style is familiar and pleasing, though rather careless, and slightly marred by defects in spelling and grammar. For instance, we are told of the caution which he and Mr. Stoddard exercised in changing seats in a boat, since neither "could swim, had the boat DID the usual thing." We are sorry that Mr. Macauley has adopted "simplified" spelling, but it is an evil in which he is by no means alone.

Red Letter Days, broadly considered, is a highly commendable paper; its simplicity and lack of affectation are alone sufficient to win general approval.

STRAY LEAVES for May-June is another paper which has arrived late and indirectly. In this publication we note with disapproval some evidence of pseudo-professionalism, such as a subscription rate and advertisements, but we trust that Miss Draper will ere long acquire the perfect amateur spirit. "Love Proved To Be the Master of Hate", a short story by Frances Wood, is handicapped by its unwieldy title. "The Triumph of Love", or some heading of equal brevity, would better suit it. Indications of immaturity are here and there perceptible, and at the very beginning there is an inexplicable mass of hyphenation. However, the tale is undeniably of considerable merit, conveying a pleasing picture of jealousy overcome.

The Editorial department might be improved by a judicious copying of the best amateur models. The reference to anti-Suffrage and Suffrage as "two vital questions" is hardly permissible; these are the two sides of only one question.

"Thinkers", by G. D., is really excellent as an essay, despite the awkwardness of style.

The Bermuda letter is highly interesting in its descriptions, but painfully unscholarly in its phraseology. We here behold a case of real talent obscured by want of literary polish, and hope that F. A. B., whoever he or she may be, will profit by his or her connection with the United.

Stray Leaves has great possibilities, and will doubtless prove one of the leading papers of amateur journalism in times to come.

THE UNITED OFFICIAL QUARTERLY for January hardly lives up to the artistic standard set by the first number, though it contains much valuable matter. Herbert B. Darrow pleads very ably for the personal acknowledgement of amateur papers received, while Paul J. Campbell writes convincingly on the true value of amateur journalism. Pres. Hepner, in the concluding article, opposes with considerable vigor the Hoffman policy of issuing co-operative magazines. We are not, however, inclined entirely to agree with our executive's conclusions. The co-operative journal is practically the only adequate medium of expression for the amateur of limited means, and most of the later journals of this class, of which the Official Quarterly is itself an example, have been of excellent quality. It is perhaps too much to expect the average President, encumbered with a host of other duties, to conduct this work, but in any event some suitable official should be delegated for that purpose. The association should not lightly abandon a policy which made the preceding administration one of the most brilliant and successful in years.

THE WOODBEE for January exhibits amateur journalism at

its best. Mrs. Anne Tillery Renshaw opens the magazine with a pleasing poem, dedicated to the Woodbees, which combines simplicity of diction with regularity of metre. Those decasyllabic quatrains are a decided departure from Mrs. Renshaw's usual style, which explains the slight lack of fluency. The last line of the third stanza contains a redundant syllable, a defect which might be corrected by the removal of the article before the word "louder", or by the poetical contraction of "sympathy" into "symp'thy". The third line of the fourth stanza possesses only four feet. This may be an intentional shortening to give rhetorical effect, yet it mars none the less the symmetry of the verse.

"The Spiritual Significance of the Stars", by Leo Fritter, is the leading feature of the issue. The inspiring influence of astronomical study on the cultivated intellect is here shown to best advantage. Mr. Fritter traces the slow unfolding of celestial knowledge to the world, and points out the divinity of that mental power which enables man to discern the vastness of the universe, and to comprehend the complex principles by which it is governed. In the laws of the heavens he finds the prototype of all human laws, and the one perfect model for human institutions. Mr. Fritter's essay is eminently worthy of a place among the classics of amateur journalism.

"A Morn in June", by Harriet E. Daily, is a short and dainty poem of excellent quality, though marred by a reprehensible attempt to rhyme "grass" with "task". As we mentioned in connection with another amateur poem, a final consonant on one of two otherwise rhyming syllables utterly destroys the rhyme. "We Are Builders All", by Elizabeth M. Ballou, is a graceful allegory based on the temple of Solomon. Edna Mitchell Haughton's character sketch, "The Family Doctor", is just and well drawn.

"A Dog for Comfort", by Edna von der Heide, is a meritorious poem of gloomy impressiveness. We cannot quite account for the defective second line of the fourth stanza, since Miss von der Heide is so able a poetess. Perhaps it is intentional, but we wish the line were of normal decasyllabic length. "My Grandmother's Garden", by Ida Cochran Haughton, is a truly delightful bit of reminiscent description which deserves more than one reading. "A Little Girl's Three Wishes", by Mrs. R. M. Moody, is entertaining in quality and correct in metre. It is a relief to behold amidst the formless cacophony of modern poetry such a regular, old-fashioned specimen of the octosyllabic couplet. "Two Little Waterwheels", by Dora M. Hepner, is an exquisite idyllic sketch. In the second paragraph we read of a channel "damned" up by a projecting root of

21

a tree; which somewhat surprises us, since we did not know that tree-roots are accustomed to use profane language. Perhaps the author intended to write "dammed".

The editorials are brief. In one of them it is stated that the paper is submitted without fear to the critics AND Eddie Cole. In view of Mr. Cole's scholarly and conscientious critical work, we hope that no reflection upon him is there intended.

H. P. LOVECRAFT
Chairman, Department of Public Criticism

MARCH

Let other bards with nobler talents sing
The beauties of the mild, maturer spring.
My rustic Muse on bleaker times must dwell,
When Earth, but new-escap'd from winter's spell,
Uncloth'd, unshelter'd, unadorn'd, is seen;
Stript of white robes, nor yet array'd in green.
Hard blows the breeze, but with a warmer force.
The melting ground, the brimming watercourse,
The wak'ning air, the birds' returning flight,
The longer sunshine, and the shorter night,
Arcturus' beams, and Corvus' glitt'ring rays,
Diffuse a promise of the genial days.
Yon muddy remnant of the winter snow
Shrinks humbly in the equinoctial glow,
Whilst in the fields precocious grass-blades peep
Above the earth so lately wrapt in sleep.
What sweet, elusive odor fills the soil,
To rouse the farmer to his yearly toil!
Though thick the clouds, and bare the maple bough,
With what gay song he guides the cumbrous plough!
In him there stirs, like sap within the tree,
The joyous call to new activity:
The outward scene, however dull and drear,
Takes on a splendor from the inward cheer.
Prophetic month! Would that I might rehearse

22

Thy hidden beauties in sublimer verse:
Thy glorious youth, thy vigor all unspent,
Thy stirring winds, of spring and winter blent.
Summer brings blessings of enervate kind;
Thy joys, O March, are ecstasies of mind.
In June we revel in the bees' soft hum,
But March exalts us with the bliss to come.

H. P. LOVECRAFT

THE UNITED AMATEUR

OFFICIAL ORGAN OF THE UNITED AMATEUR PRESS
ASSOCIATION OF AMERICA

Volume XIV GEORGETOWN, ILL., MAY, 1915. Number 5

DEPARTMENT OF PUBLIC CRITICISM

THE BLARNEY STONE for January-February is replete with good literature, amidst which may particularly be mentioned Arthur Goodenough's harmonious poem, "God Made Us All of Clay". The theme is not new, but appears advantageously under Mr. Goodenough's delicate treatment.

M. W. Hart's short story, "The Redemption", is intended to portray a righteous transformation from conventional false morality to true Christian life, but in reality presents a very repulsive picture of bestial atavism. The meaner character was not "reformed by mercy", but merely withheld from wholesale vice by isolation. Mr. Hart is so plainly in earnest when he relates this dismal tale as a sermon, that we must not be too harsh in questioning his taste or condemning his free standards of civilized morality; yet we doubt seriously if stories or essays of this type should appear in the press, and especially in the amateur press. Two or three technical points demand attention. The word "diversified" on page 2 might better be "diverse", while "environment" on page 4, could well be replaced by "condition" or "state". On page 5 occurs the sentence "All intelligence ... were ... instinct". Obviously the verb should be in the

23

singular number to correspond with its subject. Mr. Hart is developing a prose style of commendable dignity, unusually free from the jarring touch of modern frivolity.

H. B. Scott is proving himself a finished scholar and a thoughtful editor in his conduct of The Blarney Stone; his able essay on "Personality" is eminently worthy of more than one perusal.

THE BOYS' HERALD for May presents us with a highly interesting account of Robert Louis Stevenson's career as an amateur journalist, together with a facsimile reproduction of the cover of "The Sunbeam Magazine", Stevenson's hand-written periodical. The column of reminiscences, containing letters from various old-time amateurs, is extremely inspiring to the younger members, showing how persistently the amateur spirit adheres to all who have truly acquired it. "Nita at the Passing Show" is a witty and entertaining parody by Mr. Smith, illustrating the theatrical hobby of Miss Gerner; one of the latest United recruits. The Boys' Herald discharges a peculiar and important function in the life of the associations, connecting the present with the past, and furnishing us with just standards for comparison.

DOWDELL'S BEARCAT for December opens with a Christmas poem of great beauty and harmonious construction from the pen of Dora M. Hepner. The thoughts and images are without exception lofty and well selected, and the only possible defect is the attempt to rhyme "come" with "run" in the last stanza. Edward H. Cole's review of a recent booklet in memory of Miss Susan Brown Robbins, a former amateur, is more than a criticism. It is a rare appreciation of the bonds of mutual esteem and respect which grow up amongst the congenial members of the press associations. Mr. Cole is peculiarly well fitted to deal with his subject, and no praise is needed beyond the statement that the review is characteristic of him.

DOWDELL'S BEARCAT for January marks the metamorphosis of that periodical into a newspaper. With youthful ambition, Mr. Dowdell is resolved to furnish the United with the latest items of interest concerning amateurs. While the general style of the paper is fluent and pleasing, we believe that "Bruno" might gain much force of expression through the exercise of a little more care and dignity in his prose. For instance, many colloquial contractions like "don't", "won't", or "can't" might be eliminated, while such slang phrases as "neck of the woods", "make good", "somewhat off", or "bunch of yellow-backs" were better omitted.

DOWDELL'S BEARCAT for March is notable for an increase in size. "A Visit to Niagara Falls", by Andrew R. Koller, is an intelligent and animated piece of description, which promises well for the development of its author. What looseness of construction exists may be charged to youth. "An Ambition and a Vision", by Nettie A. Hartman, is a neat and grammatically written little sketch, probably autobiographical, describing the evolution of an amateur. Greater cultivation of rhetorical taste would improve Miss Hartman's style, and we are certain that it possesses a fundamental merit which will make improvement an easy matter. With the usual regret we observe an instance of "simple spelling", which Mr. Dowdell, who does not fall into this vice himself, has evidently overlooked in editing. The news items this month are timely and vivacious, exhibiting "Bruno" at his best.

THE LAKE BREEZE for March inaugurates a very welcome revival of the United's foremost news sheet, now to be issued monthly. Mr. Daas is so active an amateur, and so closely connected with the development of the association, that his ably edited journal has almost the authority of an official organ.

The editorial entitled "Ashes and Roses" is a powerful and convincing reply to a rather weak attack lately made on the United by a member of a less active association. Mr. Daas uses both sense and sarcasm to great advantage, leaving but little ground for his opponent to occupy.

"The Amateur Press" is a well conducted column of contributed reviews, among which Mrs. A. M. Adams' eulogy of Mrs. Griffith's essay in Outward Bound is perhaps the best. "What is Amateur Journalism?", by "El Imparcial", is a sketch of the various types of amateurs, with a suggestion of the ideal type. While free from glaring defects, the essay gives no really new information, and brings out no strikingly original ideas. "Some Objections to Moving Pictures", by Edmund L. Shehan, presents a strong array of evidence against one of the most popular and instructive amusements of today. We do not believe, however, that the objections here offered are vital. The moving picture has infinite possibilities for literary and artistic good when rightly presented, and having achieved a permanent place, seems destined eventually to convey the liberal arts to multitudes hitherto denied their enjoyment. Mr. Shehan's prose style is clear and forceful, capable of highly advantageous development.

LITERARY BUDS for April is the first number of a paper issued by the new Athenaeum Club of Journalism, Harvey, Ill. Though the text of most of the contributions has suffered somewhat through a slight misapprehension concerning the editing, the issue is nevertheless pleasing and creditable.

"A la Rudyard", a poem by George A. Bradley, heads the contents. While hampered by some of the heaviness natural to authors of school age, Mr. Bradley has managed to put into his lines a laudable enthusiasm and genuine warmth. The editorial column is well conducted, the second item being especially graphic, though the "superdreadnought" metaphor seems rather forced. Clara Inglis Stalker, the enthusiastic and capable educator through whose efforts the club was formed, gives a brief account of her organization, under the title "The History of an Eight-Week-Old", and in a prose style of uniformly flowing and attractive quality. "A Love Song", Miss Stalker's other contribution, is a poem of delicate imagery and unusual metre. "Our Paring Knife", by Gertrude Van Lanningham, is a short sketch with an aphorism at the end. Though this type of moral lesson is a little trite, Miss Van Lanningham shows no mean appreciation of literary form, and will, when she has emerged from the "bud" stage, undoubtedly blossom into a graphic and sympathetic writer. "Co-Education", by Caryl W. Dempsey, is an interesting but only partially convincing article on a topic of considerable importance. The author, being enthusiastically in favor of the practice, enumerates its many benefits; yet the arguments are decidedly biased. While the advantage of co-education to young ladies is made quite obvious, it remains far from clear that young men receive equal benefit. A desirable decline of cliques and hazing might, it is true, result from the admission of women to men's universities, but the young men would undoubtedly lose much in earnest, concentrated energy and dignified virility through the presence of the fair. The experiment, radical at best, has failed more than once. The style of this essay is slightly wanting in ease and continuity, yet possesses the elements of force. "The Traitor", by Agnes E. Fairfield, is a short story of artistic development but questionable sentiment. The present fad of peace-preaching should not be allowed to influence a writer of sense into glorifying a socialistic, unpatriotic fanatic who refuses to uphold the institutions that his fathers before him created with their toil, blood, and sacrifice. It is not the right of the individual to judge of the necessity of a war; no layman can form an intelligent idea of the dangers that may beset his fatherland. The man is but a part of the state, and must uphold it at any cost. We are inclined to wonder at Miss Fairfield's mention of a king, when the name Phillipe La Roque so clearly proclaims the hero a Frenchman. France, be it known, has been a republic for some little time. "Penny in the Slot", by Vaughn Flannery, possesses a humor that is pleasing and apparently quite spontaneous. We should like to behold more of Mr. Flannery's efforts in this field.

Viewed in its entirety, allowance being made for its present essentially juvenile nature, Literary Buds may be regarded as a pronounced success. That it will mature in consonance with the club which it represents is certain, and each future issue can be relied upon to surpass its predecessor.

OLE MISS' for March, edited by Mr. and Mrs. J. W. Renshaw, easily falls into the very front rank of the season's amateur journals. In this number Mr. Joseph W. Renshaw makes his initial appearance before the members of the United, producing a very favorable impression with his pure, attractive prose. The introduction, credited in another column to Mr. Renshaw, is of graceful and pleasing character, recalling the elusively beautiful atmosphere of the Old South which is too soon passing away.

"The Humble Swallow", an anonymous essay, praises with singularly delicate art a feathered creature whose charms lie not on the surface. The concluding paragraph, condemning the wanton slaughter of this winged friend to mankind, is especially apt at a time of hysterical peace agitation. While the well meaning advocates of peace call wildly upon men to abandon just warfare against destructive and malignant enemies, they generally pass over without thought or reproof the wholesale murder of these innocent little birds, who never did nor intended harm to anyone. "A Higher Recruiting Standard", by Mrs. Renshaw, is an able exposition of the newer and loftier type of ideals prevailing in the United. Our association has never lacked numbers, but would undoubtedly be the better for an increased standard of scholarship such as is here demanded. Mrs. Renshaw's work as a recruiter is in keeping with her policy, and this, together with Mr. Moe's work amongst the English teachers, seems destined to raise the United far above its lesser contemporaries. "An A. J. Suggestion", by Mr. Renshaw, deals ingeniously and logically with the always difficult problem of selecting a printer. Though evidently written quite independently, it ably seconds Paul J. Campbell's original suggestion in the UNITED AMATEUR. The advantages of having one printer for all amateur work are many, and the well presented opinions of Mr. Renshaw should aid much in securing this desirable innovation.

The poetry in Ole Miss' is all by Mrs. Renshaw, and therefore of first quality. "Some One I Know" is a lightly amatory piece of tuneful rhythm. "Night of Rain" gives a peculiarly pleasing aspect to a type of scene not usually celebrated in verse. The only jarring note is the rather mundane metaphor which compares the trees to a "beautiful mop". Though Mrs. Renshaw holds unusual ideas regarding the use of art in poetry, we contend that this instance of rhetorical frigidity is scarcely permissible. It is too much like Sir Richard Blackmore's description of Mount Aetna, wherein he compares a volcanic eruption to a fit of colic; or old Ben Johnson's

27

battle scene in the fifth act of "Catiline", where he represents the sun perspiring. "Man of the Everyday" is a noble panegyric on the solid, constructive virtues of the ordinary citizen, portraying very graphically the need of his presence in a world that heeds him but little.

Considered in all its aspects, Ole Miss' is a notable contribution to amateur literature, and one which we hope to see oft repeated.

THE PASSING SHOW for February is the "second annual production" of an excellent though informal little paper by Nita Edna Gerner, a new member of the United, and the daughter of an old-time amateur. Miss Gerner is an enthusiast on all matters pertaining to the theatre, and has impressed her hobby very strongly on the pages of her publication.

The dominant theme of the current issue is that of amateur romance, exhibiting the press associations in the role of matrimonial agencies. "The Twos-ers", by Edwin Hadley Smith, is a long list of couples who became wedded through acquaintanceships formed in amateur journalism. This catalogue, recording 26 marriages and engagements from the earliest ages to the present, must have cost its author much time and research. "A Romance of Amateur Journalism", by Edward F. Daas, is a very brief statement of facts in unornamented style. "An 'Interstate' Romance", by Leston M. Ayres, is more elaborate in treatment, and displays an easy, colloquial style.

The editorial column, headed "Through the Opera-Glasses", is bright and informal. We note with regret that Miss Gerner has seen fit to adopt the popular mutilated orthography of the day, a fad which we trust she will discard in time.

PEARSON'S PET for April is a bright and attractive little paper throughout. "Burnin' Off" is a delightful specimen of dialect verse which conveys a graphic image. We have never witnessed such an agricultural function as Mr. Pearson describes, but can gain from his clever lines a vivid idea of its weird impressiveness. "How I Met Elbert Hubbard" is narrated in commendably easy prose, which same may be said of the sketch or editorial entitled "Broke Loose Again". Mr. Pearson is assuredly a competent exponent of amateur journalism's lighter and less formal side.

THE PIPER for May is as pleasing and meritorious as the first number, both in its verse and its prose. "The Modern Muse", exhibiting Mr. Kleiner in a somewhat humorous mood, is very forceful in its satire on the altered ideals of the poetical fraternity, but is marred by the noticeably imperfect rhyming of "garret" and "carrot", it is barely possible that according to the prevailing New

York pronunciation this rhyme is not so forced as it appears, but we are of New England, and accustomed to hearing the sounds more classically differentiated. The defect is trivial at most, and mentioned here only because Mr. Kleiner professes such a rigid adherence to the law of perfect rhyming. "The Books I Used to Read" is the most delightful appreciation of juvenile literature that has appeared in amateur journalism within our memory. There are few of us in whom this poem will fail to arouse glad reminiscences. "Spring" is a pleasing poem on a subject which though not exactly new, is nevertheless susceptible to an infinite variety of treatment. The four stanzas are highly creditable, both sentimentally and metrically. Apart from the poetry, criticism seems the dominant element in The Piper, and it would be difficult indeed to find a more lucid and discerning series of reviews. Mr. Kleiner's unvarying advocacy of correct metre and perfect rhyming is refreshing to encounter in this age of laxity and license. Perhaps he is a little stern in his condemnation of the "allowable" rhymes of other days, especially in view of his recent "garret-carrot" attempt, yet we admit that there is much to be said in favor of his attitude.

THE PLAINSMAN for February contains a gruesome moral tale by Ricardo Santiago, entitled "The Bell of Huesca". It is proper to remark here, that an important sentence was omitted at the top of page 3. The passage should read "'Sire, thy bell has no clapper!' 'Thy head shall be the clapper'; said the king, and he sent him to the block" etc. Whatever may be said of the aptness of the allegory, it is evident that Mr. Santiago possesses the foundations of a pure and forcible prose style, and a commendable sense of unity in narration and development of climax. This story is undoubtedly worthy of its distinction as winner in The Plainsman's post-card contest.

THE SPECTATOR for June-July, 1914, though somewhat trite in title, is the first number of a magazine notable for its quality. Walter John Held is without doubt one of the most enterprising youths who have ever joined the ranks of the association, though his views on paid subscriptions and advertisements show his still imperfect acquisition of the true amateur spirit. Mr. Held mistakes commercial progress for artistic development, believing that the aim of every amateur in his ascent toward professional authorship is to write remunerative matter. He therefore considers a publisher's advancement to be best shown in ability to extract an odd penny now and then from a few subscribers who really subscribe only out of courtesy. We wish that Mr. Held might come to consider amateur journalism in its higher aspects; as a medium for improvement in literature and taste; an aid to the cultivation of the art for its own sake in the manner of gentlemen, not of cheap tradesmen. The selection of commercial prosperity as a goal will ruin any true literary progress, and dull the artistic aspiration of the student as soon as his mercenary instincts shall have been satisfied. Besides, there is really no sound business principle in the so-called "sale" of little papers. No youth could ever found or sustain a real magazine of substantial price and more than nominal circulation. The various ten-cents-a-year journals which some "amateurs" try to edit are no logical steps toward actually professional publishing. The latter comes only after literary skill has been attained, and literary skill must at first be developed without regard for immediate monetary profit.

But the merit of Mr. Held's work is none the less unusual. "The Frank Friend" gives evidence of considerable critical ability, despite the touch of arrogance, apologized for in a latter issue, shown in imperfect appreciation of Mr. Edward H. Cole's phenomenally pure English. Mr. Held, in his enthusiasm for "local color", forgets that all the English-speaking world is heir to one glorious language which should be the same from Cape Colony to California or New York to New Zealand.

The only poem in this issue is Olive G. Owen's "How Prayest Thou?", a piece of true sentiment and artistic beauty. The only fault is metrical; the use of the word "trial" as a monosyllable. This tendency to slur over words appears to be Miss Owen's one poetical vice, as exemplified in the imperfect rendering of "jewel", "realness", and "cruelness" elsewhere.

THE SPECTATOR for August-September is marred by a resurrection of the ever odious topic of Consolidation, but is otherwise of remarkable merit. Elbert Hubbard, a professional advertiser and writer of considerable popularity in certain circles, relates in an interesting way the history of his most widely known literary effort. Mr. Hubbard's prose style is direct and pointed, though rather abrupt and barren. "The Midnight Extra", by Dora M. Hepner, is a humorous short story of unusual merit, leading from a well created atmosphere of terror to a clever and unexpected anticlimax.

THE SPECTATOR for October-November contains much matter of very substantial worth. "Creation", by Edward R. Taylor, Dean of the University of California, is a beautiful bit of poetical sentiment and harmonious metre, while "Half-past-twelve", by Miss von der Heide, is likewise of great merit, both in thought and in structure. We have lately been told that many apparent metrical defects which we have noted are really no more than typographical errors, wherefore we will here content ourselves by expressing the belief that the third line of the second stanza of "Half-past-twelve" was originally written thus:

30

"Across the dark their shrilling laughter floats".

This rendering would do away with two seeming errors in the printed copy. Olive G. Owen's "Battle-Prayer" is powerful in its appeal and faultless in its construction. Of marked interest is "Divine Self-Tower", a brief essay by Takeshi Kanno, the Japanese philosopher. These words, in a tongue foreign to the writer, contain material for more than a moment's thought.

"The Frank Friend" is in this number as interesting a critic as before. The passage of four months has tempered his undue severity; indeed, we fear that he has in certain cases veered a little too far toward the other extreme. The most ambitious review is that of "Pig-pen Pete", by Elbert Hubbard, which gives Mr. Held an opportunity to display his powers to great advantage. Of the two editorials, that entitled "Life" is the more notable. Though its philosophy must necessarily be rather artificial, considering Mr. Held's age, it is none the less a very artistic and generally creditable piece of composition. The cover of The Spectator would be less Hearst-like if the fulsome announcements were eliminated.

TOLEDO AMATEUR for April greets us in altered form, as a two-column paper. Having given over the previous issue to the credentials of new members, Mr. Porter very justly claims a goodly space for himself this month, commenting ably on the affairs and activities of the associations.

"Camp Columbia", by James J. Hennessey, gives an interesting outline of the American army routine in Cuba during the years 1907 and 1908. "Observations of an Outsider", by Mrs. Porter, mother of the editor, sheds light on amateur journalism from a hitherto unusual angle. We note with pleasure that Toledo Amateur remains immune from the destructive bacillus of deformed spelling.

THE WOODBEE for April contains "The Cycle Eternal", a lucid philosophical article by Samuel James Schilling, wherein is described the dispersal and new combinations of the organic cells that compose the body of mankind. By the perpetual reincorporation or reincarnation of these cells in all other forms of matter, man is shown to be immortal, and in the closest degree akin to every natural object surrounding him. His outward form is merely one transient phase of a ceaseless rearrangement of atoms; he is simply one aspect of infinite and eternal Nature. Save for a few slight traces of rhetorical awkwardness, Mr. Schilling's expository style is remarkable for its force and clearness; the arrangement of the essay into Prologue, Body, and Epilogue is especially favorable to comprehensiveness.

While Mr. Schilling deals with mankind in the abstract, Miss

Mabel McKee, in "A Gift from the City", presents a concrete example of the workings of the human heart. Her subject and treatment are not startlingly original, but such themes lose very little when repeated in pure English and attractive style. The story is distinctly pleasing, and artistically developed throughout.

A notable feature of the April Woodbee is Miss Hepner's fervent and unstudied tribute to Mr. Leo Fritter, candidate for the United's Presidency. Though the editorial is bestrewn with slang and distinctly familiar in construction, it produces upon the reader an impression of absolute sincerity and intensity of feeling which more elaborate rhetoric might fail so forcibly to convey. Great as is the tribute, however, we feel that Mr. Fritter is worthy of it, and must congratulate him on having such support. Our own efforts for his election, appearing in The Conservative, seem slight in comparison. The only verse in this number is "My Shrine", by Harriet E. Daily. Though containing an attempt to rhyme the words "time" and "shrine", this ethereal little poem of spring is of great attractiveness.

ZEPPELIN for March, a publication emanating from the pen of Mr. O. S. Hackett of Canton, Pennsylvania, is scarcely as formidable and menacing as its name, being distinctly friendly and fraternal in its general tone. Mr. Hackett's prose has obviously not received its final polishing, but it is so filled with aspiration, ambition, and enthusiasm for the cause of amateur journalism, that it evidently requires only such development as is obtainable from a closer study of grammar and rhetoric, and a wider perusal of classic English literature. In one matter Mr. Hackett seems to harbor a wrong impression. The name "credential", in the language of the amateurs, is not applied to all literary productions, but only to those which are submitted by the new recruits as evidence of their educational fitness for membership in the association they seek to enter.

Joseph R. Schaffman's poem, "Think of Times Yet Coming", shows the same innate sense of rhyme and metre that has distinguished his earlier work. Only the conclusion lacks perfect ease and naturalness. Mr. Schaffman has so far confined his Muse to optimistic opinions and moral maxims; we hope that in the near future he will vary his efforts and attempt to reflect more of his general reading in his poetry. The field is large for one so happily favored with the gift of song.

H. P. LOVECRAFT,
Chairman

THE UNITED AMATEUR

Official Organ of the United Amateur Press Association

Volume XV ELROY, WIS., SEPTEMBER, 1915 Number 2

DEPARTMENT OF PUBLIC CRITICISM

The Alabamian for Spring is a magazine unique amongst the publications of the United. Devoted wholly to poetry, it contains some of the finest short verses to appear this season, whilst even the crudest part of its contents possesses some undoubted merit. The opening poem, a delightful and ornate nature sonnet entitled "The Brook," professes to be a translation from the Spanish, a claim borne out by the use of the word "jasmine" in a place where the metre throws the accent anomalously on the last syllable, as in the corresponding Spanish word "jazmin." The sentiment of the whole is exquisite, and every image exhibits striking beauty. It is to be regretted that both author and translator are suffered to remain unrevealed. "A Poet's Songs," by Miss Owen, is a powerful and well-written tribute to her fellow-bards both ancient and modern. In Coralie Austin's "Tribute to Our President," dedicated to Miss Hepner, we may discern the native talent of the true poet, slightly obscured by the crudities of youth. The opening line appears to lack a syllable, though this may be due only to the printer's omission of the article before the word "laurel." In stanza 1, line 2, the trisyllabic word "violets" appears as a dissyllable. This contraction is a rather natural one, and must not be criticised too sternly. Indeed, there is here a sort of middle zone betwixt error and allowableness, wherein no decisive precepts may be laid down. Words like "radiant," "difference," and so forth, are nearly always slurred into dissyllables, and we were ourselves guilty of an even greater liberalism when we wrote that line in "Quinsnicket Park" which reads:

"The bending boughs a diamond wealth amass."

But in Miss Austin's second stanza occur two errors of graver nature. "For only her alone" is a lamentably tautological line which requires the omission either of "only" or "alone," and the substitution of some word to carry on the flow of metre. The attempted rhyming of "alone" and "home" is obviously incorrect.

33

The dissimilar consonantal sounds render agreement impossible. This "m-n" rhyme, as we may call it, is becoming alarmingly frequent in careless modern verse, and must ever be avoided with utmost diligence. In the third stanza we discover a marked error in maintenance of number. We are told that the "years go" and that at "its end" we will lay trophies, etc. This mistake may be obviated with ease, by changing "years go" to "year goes." Miss Austin's poetic talent is great, but shows the want of precise cultivation. "Mother o' Mine," by Miss von der Heide, is a beautiful piece of anapaestic verse whose metre and sentiment alike attract the reader. "Parsifal," by Miss Owen, shows satisfactory depth of thought, but is rather modern in metre. From the conformation of the last line of the first stanza, we are led to believe that the word "viol" is contracted to a monosyllable, or, to make a rather reprehensible pun, that "vi-ol" has here a "vile" pronunciation. "Frailties of Life," by Editor Baxley, shows a remarkable system of extended rhyming, coupled with a noticeable lack of metrical harmony. Mr. Baxley's technique is such that we believe his improvement would be best effected by a repeated perusal of the older poets, whose classical exactitude of form would teach him rhythm by rote, so to speak. Let him cultivate his ear for metre, even though forced to acquire it through nonsensical jingles. We believe that many a child has obtained from his "Mother Goose" a love of correct rhythm which has later helped him in serious poetical efforts. "Paid Back," a short, powerful poem by Miss von der Heide, concludes an excellent and praiseworthy issue.

Aurora for April is a delightful individual leaflet by Mrs. Ida C. Haughton, exclusively devoted to poetical matters. The first poem, "Aurora," is truly exquisite as a verbal picture of the summer dawn, though rather rough-hewn metrically. Most open to criticism of all the features of this piece, is the dissimilarity of the separate stanzas. In a stanzaic poem the method of rhyming should be identical in every stanza, yet Mrs. Haughton has here wavered between couplets and alternate rhymes. In the opening stanza we behold first a quatrain, then a quadruple rhyme. In the second we find couplets only. In the third a quatrain is followed by an arrangement in which two rhyming lines enclose a couplet, while in the final stanza the couplet again reigns supreme. The metre also lacks uniformity, veering from iambic to anapaestic form. These defects are, of course, merely technical, not affecting the beautiful thought and imagery of the poem; yet the sentiment would seem even more pleasing were it adorned with the garb of metrical regularity. "On the Banks of Old Wegee" is a sentimental poem of considerable merit, which suffers, however, from the same faults that affect

"Aurora." Most of these defects might have been obviated when the stanzas were composed, by a careful counting of syllables in each line and a constant consultation of some one, definite plan of rhyming. We must here remark an error made in the typewritten copy of the original manuscript, and reproduced in the finished magazine, for which, of course, neither the poetical art of the author nor the technique of the printer is to blame. In the second stanza, lines 6 and 7 were originally written:

"How oft I've essayed to be
A fisherman bold, but my luck never told."

"Anent the Writing of Poetry" is a short prose essay, in which many valuable truths are enunciated. Mrs. Haughton has evidently taken up the poetic art with due seriousness, and considering the marked talent shown in the first issue of her paper, we may justly expect to behold a wonderfully rapid development in the near future.

The Badger for June fulfills the promise of January, and shows us that the present year has given the United a new and serious periodical of satisfying quality. In the "Introductory," Mr. George Schilling discusses in lively fashion the latest topics of the day, thereby atoning for our own tedious "Finale." "Ready Made," by Samuel J. Schilling, is a thoughtful presentation of a lamentable fact. The evil which he portrays is one that has rendered the masses of America almost wholly subservient to the vulgar press; to be led astray into every sort of radicalism through low tricks of sensationalism. Our own poetical attempt, entitled "Quinsnicket Park," contains 112 lines, and spoils three and a half otherwise excellent pages. It is probable that but few have had the fortitude to read it through, or even to begin it, hence we will pass over its defects in merciful silence. "What May I Own?" by A. W. Ashby, is an able sociological essay which displays considerable familiarity with the outward aspects of economic conditions. Mr. Ashby, condemning the present system practiced in the coal and iron industries, declares that on moral grounds he had rather be a brewer or purveyor of liquor than a coal magnate or an ironmaster. In this statement, evidently born of hasty fervour, Mr. Ashby forgets the basic character of the two types of industry which he contrasts. Beneath the liquor traffic lies a foundation accursed by decency and reason. The entire industry is designed to pander to a false craving whose gratification lowers man in the scale of mental and physical evolution. The distiller and vendor of rum is elementally the supreme foe of the human race, and the most powerful, dangerous and treacherous factor in the defiance of progress and the betrayal of mankind. His trade can never be improved or purified, being itself a crime against Nature. On the other hand, the coal and iron industries are, in their fundamental forms, desirable and necessary adjuncts to an expanding civilization. Their present evils are wholly alien to their essential principles, being connected only with the uneasy industrialism of this age. These faults are not confined to coal-mining and iron-working, but are merely those possessed in common with all great industries. Joseph E. Shufelt's article on the European war is an amazing outburst of socialism in its worst form. The idea that this shocking carnage is the result of a deliberate plot of the ruling classes of all the belligerents to destroy their labouring element is wonderfully ludicrous in its extravagance. We are led to infer that those best of friends, der Kaiser and his cousins George and Nicholas, are merely pretending hostility in order to rid themselves of a troublesome peasantry! We do not know what Mr. Shufelt has been reading lately, but we hope that time may modify his ideas to such a degree that he will turn his dignified style and pure English to some object worthy of their employment.

Dowdell's Bearcat for July marks the beginning of an unprecedented era of improvement in the quality of that periodical. Having settled down to the conventional 5×7 size, it has now acquired a cover and an abundance of pages which the editor informs us will never be lessened. The influence of The Olympian is perceptible in the Bearcat, and for his taste in the selection of so worthy a model Mr. Dowdell is to be commended. "When the Tape Broke" is the first article of the editorial column, and well describes an example of collapsed activity which the United should avoid. "A Runaway Horse," by Mrs. Ida C. Haughton, is a brief and vivid sketch of a fatal accident. "Tragedy," an exquisite poem by Emilie C. Holladay, deserves very favourable notice for the delicate pathos of its sentiment, and perfect adaptation of the measure to the subject. We may discern a few traces of immaturity in the handling of the metre and in the presence of "allowable" rhymes. As elsewhere stated, we personally approve and employ the old-fashioned "allowable" rhyming sounds, but the best modern taste, as exemplified in the United by its Laureate, Rheinhart Kleiner, demands absolute perfection in this regard. As to the metre, we respectfully offer the following amended second stanza as an example. It is absolutely uniform with the original first stanza, which, of course, furnishes the model.

> The summer rains
> And autumn winds

The snowdrop find yet standing;
A petal gone,
And all alone,
Her tender roots expanding.

The remarkable poetical talent exhibited by Miss Holladay deserves a cultivation that shall invest her productions with a technique of the highest order. "The Dignity of Journalism," by ourselves, may be taken by the reader as a sort of supplement to this Department. We there enumerate in the abstract some of the precepts which we shall here apply to individual writers. There are several misprints, which we hope will not be taken as evidences of our bad spelling, and at the conclusion the word "even" is omitted from the phrase which should read: "the necessity, or even the expediency." "June Journals" is an excellent set of short reviews which display very favourably the critical ability of Mr. Dowdell. The concluding notes on "Amateur Affairs" are brief, but very interesting. The general excellence of Dowdell's Bearcat excuses the instances of imperfect proof-reading, which fault we are sure will soon be eliminated.

The Blarney Stone for March-April contains "Thoughts," a meritorious poem by Chester P. Munroe. The tone of the piece is that of sentimental and almost melancholy reverie, hence the metre is not quite uniform; but a commendable absence of rough breaks lends a delightful flow to the lines. We hope to behold further efforts from Mr. Munroe's pen. "The Amateur's Creed," by Mrs. Renshaw, is written in the style of this author's previous and now well-known poem, "A Symphony," and should do much toward lifting the United upward to the highest literary ideals.

The Blarney Stone for May-June has cast off all undue seriousness, and teems with light and attractive matter concerning the recent Rocky Mount convention. Some of the displays of wit and cleverness are very striking and entertaining indeed, while no page departs so far from merit that it may be justly adjudged as dull.

The Boys' Herald for August is an issue of unusual elaborateness, announcing the engagement of its editor, Mr. Edwin Hadley Smith, and Miss Nita Edna Gerner of New York. Excellent portraits of the happy couple follow the formal announcement, and Miss Gerner, now Associate Editor, describes in an excellent prose style the romance which culminated in the engagement. "Gerneriana," consisting mainly of a reprint from an earlier issue, is an interesting account of the late Richard Gerner, an old-time amateur, and father of the prospective bride. This article is well supplemented by the reproductions of parts of old amateur papers which adorn the back cover of the magazine. The remainder of The Boys' Herald is wholly statistical, dealing with the amateur career of Mr. Smith. Few members of the association could produce superior records of activity.

The Brooklynite for April maintains the high standard set by the previous number. "A Miracle," the opening poem, was composed by Alice L. Carson during the course of a meeting of the Blue Pencil Club, yet exhibits all the grace and harmony expected in a carefully planned and laboriously polished work. "Spring Thoughts," by A. M. Adams, is a humorous prose masterpiece by the National's new Critic. Seldom is the amateur press favoured with such a well-sustained succession of brilliant epigrams. Miss Owen's "Ode to Trempealeau Mountain" is a noble specimen of heroic blank verse, containing some very striking antithetical lines. The title, however, is a misnomer, since a true ode is necessarily of irregular form. "Some Late Amateur Magazines," by W. B. Stoddard, is a series of brief, informal reviews. As a critic, Mr. Stoddard shows considerable discernment, though having a rather unpleasant air of conscious superiority in certain places. A little more stateliness of style would add to the force of his criticisms. "Spring" reveals Rheinhart Kleiner in his favourite domain of amatory verse. Mr. Kleiner's tuneful numbers and pure diction render his poetry ever a delight. "Rebellion," by Miss von der Heide, is a metrically perfect piece of verse whose artistry is marred only by the use of the unpoetical philosophical term "subconscious" instead of "unconscious."

The Brooklynite for July is of especial interest as the first paper to print an account of the Rocky Mount convention. This description, from the facile and versatile pen of Miss von der Heide, is of distinctly informal character, yet is none the less interesting as an animated chronicle of an enjoyable event. Rheinhart Kleiner's account of the National convention is more dignified, and may be considered as a model for this sort of composition. Mr. Kleiner shines as brightly in prose as in verse, and each day surprises us with revelations of excellence in various dissimilar departments of literature.

The Conservative for July is notable for Mr. Ira Cole's delightfully pantheistic poem, "A Dream of the Golden Age." The unusual poetic genius of Mr. Cole has been revealed but recently, yet the imaginative qualities pervading some of his prose long ago gave indications of this gift. The pantheistic, Nature-worshipping mind of our author lends to his productions an unique and elusive atmosphere which contrasts very favourably with the earthy tone of some of our less fanciful bards. Metrically, Mr. Cole adopts instinctively the regular, conservative forms of a saner generation. In this specimen of heroic verse he inclines toward the practice of Keats, and does not always confine single thoughts to single couplets in the manner of the eighteenth-century poets. We believe that Mr. Cole is commencing a successful career as a United poet, and await the day when he shall be accorded the honor of a laureateship.

The Coyote for July reveals a wonderful improvement over the March number, both in the literary quality of its contributions and in general editorial excellence. Never before have we seen the perfect amateur spirit acquired so quickly as in Mr. Harrington's case. "Night Fancies," by Helen H. Salls, is a sonnet of exceptional power and artistry, whose faultless metre is equalled only by its bold and striking images. Amidst this profusion of excellent metaphor, it is difficult to select individual instances for particular praise, but we might commend especially the passage:

"... the stars still keep
Afloat like boats that black sky-billows ride."

Miss Salls is clearly an amateur poet of the first rank, and it is to be hoped that she will be a liberal contributor to United magazines. "The Rebirth of the British Empire," by William T. Harrington, is a clear and concise exposition of the virtues whereby Old England maintains her proud position as Mistress of the Seas, and chief colonial empire of the world. The style of the essay is admirable, and well exhibits the progressive qualities of Mr. Harrington. "An Ideal," by Nettie Hartman, is a short poem of pleasing sentiment and harmonious metre. The notes on amateur affairs are interesting and well composed, revealing Mr. Harrington's increasing enthusiasm for the cause.

Dowdell's Bearcat for May is another striking illustration of the improvement which can affect a paper within a very short time. Since last October Mr. Dowdell has been progressing swiftly toward journalistic excellence, and even this cleverly conceived and uniquely shaped issue fails to mark the limit of his ambition. "Knowest Thou?" by Mrs. Renshaw, is an expressive tribute to a nation whose recent infamies can never wholly becloud its rugged virtues. "With Nature I Rejoice" is probably the best poem which Joseph R. Schaffman has yet written. As his remarkable talent matures, the didactic element in his verse is gradually giving way to the more purely poetic, and this latest effort is one of which he may be justly proud. Concerning Mr. Dowdell's own spirited prose, we need only repeat the previous suggestion, that a little less slang would add much to its force and dignity.

Dowdell's Bearcat for May 26 contains another poem by Mrs. Renshaw whose national tone is not likely to be popular just now outside the country to which it refers; in fact, Editor Dowdell has deemed it wise to make an apologetic statement concerning it. However, if we call "Ein Mann" Col. Theodore Roosevelt, and shift the scene to San Juan Hill, we may be able to appreciate the real patriotism delineated.

Dowdell's Bearcat for June is wholly given over to notes of the amateur world. Mr. Dowdell is indeed a pleasing young writer, and leaves none of his topics without a characteristic touch of light adornment.

The Lake Breeze for April is distinguished by James L. Crowley's poem entitled "April," a brief lyric of marked merit, highly expressive of the season. "Writing Poetry," an essay by Dora M. Hepner, is a clear and tasteful analysis of the poet's art and inspiration. "The Norwegian Recruit," a dialect monologue by Maurice W. Moe, is the leading feature of this issue. This exquisite bit of humor, recited by Mr. Moe at the United's 1913 convention, is a sketch of rare quality. "The Amateur Press," now firmly established as a column of contributed reviews, is this month of substantial size and fair quality. It is needless to say that the news pages are interesting, and that the paper as a whole well maintains the high reputation it has ever enjoyed.

The Lake Breeze for June apparently opens an era of unprecedented improvement, being of distinctly literary rather than political nature. The plea for a Department of Instruction is a just one, and ought to meet with response from some of our pedagogical members. "Broken Metre," by Mrs. Renshaw, is an attempt at defending the popular atrocities committed in the name of freedom by the modern poets. While the article is superficially quite plausible, we feel that the settled forms of regular metre have too much natural justification thus to be disturbed. The citation of Milton, intended to strengthen Mrs. Renshaw's argument, really weakens it; for while he undoubtedly condemns rhyme, he laments in the course of this very condemnation the lame metre which is sometimes concealed by apt rhyming. "Some Views on Versification," by Clara I. Stalker, is an essay written from a sounder and more conservative point of view. The middle course in poetical composition, which avoids alike wild eccentricities and mechanical precision, has much to recommend it, and Miss Stalker does well to point out its virtues. However, we do not see why even the few irregularities which are here said to be inevitable, cannot be smoothed out by the bard without destroying the sense of his poetry. "Disappointment," by Mrs. Maude K. Barton, is a clever

40

piece of light verse whose sprightly humour makes up for its slight metrical roughness. The imperfect but allowable rhyming of "bear" and "appear" in the first stanza is entirely correct according to the old-time standards which we ourselves follow, but we fear that the delicate ear of a precise metrical artist like Rheinhart Kleiner would object to its liberalism. "The Amateur Press" is distinguished by an excellent review from the pen of Mrs. Renshaw. The style is satisfactory, and the criticism just, making the whole well worthy of the prize book it has secured for its author. "'Pollyanna,' the Glad Book" is a meritorious and entertaining review by Mrs. Griffith. "Hope," by Marguerite Sisson, is commendable for its use of that noble but neglected measure, the heroic couplet. Mr. Daas' concluding editorial, "Literature and Politics," is admirable for its concise exposition of the United's new ideals, and its masterly refutation of the common fallacy that political quarrels are necessary to stimulate activity in the press associations.

The Looking Glass for May is a journal unique in purpose and quality. Edited by Mrs. Renshaw in behalf of her many gifted recruits, it reveals a condition absolutely unexampled; the acquisition by one member of so many high-grade novices that a special publication is required properly to introduce them to the United. "To a Critic of Shelley," by Helen H. Salls, is a long piece of beautiful blank verse, marred only by one accidental rhyme. Miss Salls is evidently one of those few really powerful poets who come all too seldom into Amateur Journalism, startling the Association with impeccable harmony and exalted images. The present poem grows even more attractive on analysis. The diction is of phenomenal purity and wholly unspoiled by any ultra-modern touch. It might have been a product of Shelley's own age. The metaphor is marvellous, exhibiting a soul overflowing with true spirituality, and a mind trained to express beautiful thought in language of corresponding beauty. Such unforced ornateness is rarely met in the domain of amateur poetry. We feel certain that Miss Salls has already become a fixed star in the empyrean of the United. Exalted poetry of quite another type is furnished by the work of our new Director, Rev. Frederick Chenault, whose two exquisite lyrics, "Birth" and "The Sea of Somewhere," appear in this issue. With little use of formal rhyme and metre, Mr. Chenault abounds in delicate conceptions and artistic renditions. "Retrospection," by Kathleen Baldwin, is likewise a poem of high order, and of fairly regular metre, evidently following comparatively recent models in technique. "The Faithful Man," by I. T. Valentine, shows growing poetical talent, but is cruelly injured by the anticlimactic line. Not that there is any anticlimax of sentiment, but the colloquial mode of expression shocks the reader who has been perusing the more dignified lines which go before. "The Stonework of Life" is an excellent prose sermon by Joseph Ernest Shufelt, which displays great ability in the field of metaphor and allegory. Mr. Shufelt possesses an admirable style, unusually well fitted for didactic matter of this sort; indeed, it is regrettable that he should ever depart from such congenial themes and turn to the wild sensationalism which he shows in The Badger. In demonstrating the beauties of morality and religion, he has few superiors, and a task so appropriate to his genius ought to claim his whole attention. True, his thoughts may follow strange courses in their quest for truth and beauty, but were he always to curb them within the bounds of probability and conservatism, as here, he would never lose the confidence of his public, as he has done with his strange war theories. "The Autocracy of Art," by Anne Vyne Tillery Renshaw, is the leading article of the magazine. Herein the author proclaims the supremacy of spiritual utterances over all restrictions created by the mind, and urges the emancipation of the soaring bard from the earthly chains of rhyme and metre. That the inward promptings of the poetic instinct are of prime value to the poet, few will dispute; but that they may give final form to his soul's creations without some regulation by the natural laws of rhythm, few will agree. The metric sense lies far deeper in the breast of man than Mrs. Renshaw is here disposed to acknowledge. After this article, the perfectly regular stanzas of "Fellow Craftsman," by the same author, are refreshing. The typography and form of The Looking Glass leave something to be desired, but the riches within make ample compensation for outward crudity.

The New Member for May, edited by William Dowdell, contains but one credential, yet doubtless paves the way for a resumption of the enterprise so ably conducted by Miss Hoffman last year. "Melancholy," a poem by I. T. Valentine, shows traces of the beginner's crudeness, yet has about it a quality which promises much for the future of the poet. "Lock-Step Pete," by Miss von der Heide, is an unusual poem with a thoughtful suggestion embodied in its concluding stanza.

The New Member bound with the May Official Quarterly is a model that should henceforth be followed as the nearest approach to perfection yet beheld. Credentials, lists of prospective members, news of recruits, and accounts of local clubs are here given in just and pleasing proportion. "Bluets and Butterflies," by Carolyn L. Amoss, is a poem of great delicacy and ethereal atmosphere. The solitary, tiny flaw is the attempted rhyming of "Miss" and "yes." "War in America," by Annette E. Foth, is a pleasant juvenile story.

E. Ralph Cheyney's extract from his essay on "Youth" is in many ways remarkable, and shows us that we have another recruit of choice quality. His rather peculiar ideas are well expressed, though their soundness is quite debatable. A few abnormal characters like Byron and Shelley doubtless experienced all the adolescent phenomena which Mr. Cheyney describes, but we believe that the average youth is a copyist, and for the most part reflects his environment. Radicalism and novel ideas arise just as much from blasé, elderly cynics, who are tired of sane and sober conservatism. We have been reflecting on Life for about twenty years, ever since we were five, and have consistently believed that the wisdom of the ancient sage is the true wisdom; that Life is essentially immutable, and that the glorious dreams of youth are no more than dreams, to be dissipated by the dawn of maturity and the full light of age. "Flowers on the Grave," a poem by J. D. Hill, has a commendable sentiment, and is remarkable for its possession of only one repeated rhyming sound. Whether or not the latter feature be monotonous, all must admit that the versification is attractive. "We Are All Desperate!" is a striking philosophical fragment by Melvin Ryder, which first appeared as an editorial in the Ohio State Lantern. The conjectures are plausible, and the precepts sound. The news items in this paper are all fresh and interesting, concluding an issue uniformly excellent.

The Pippin for May displays very favourably the high-school club whose founding and maintenance are due entirely to the genius of Mr. Maurice W. Moe. "The Coasters," by Esther Ronning, is the only poem in the issue, but its quality atones for the absence of other verse. The pleasures and perils of coasting are here portrayed with wonderfully graphic pen, whilst the metre is, so far as technical correctness is concerned, all that might be desired. However, we wish that Miss Ronning were less fond of unusual rhyming arrangements. The lines here given are of regular ballad length. Were they disposed in couplets, we should have a tuneful lay of the "Chevy Chase" order; but as it is, our ear misses the steady couplet effect to which the standard models have accustomed us. "With the Assistance of Carmen" is a clever short story by Gladys Bagg, derived from the same plot nucleus by Mr. Moe which likewise evoked Miss Moore's story in the March United Amateur. The structure of the narrative is excellent, but we do not like the use of the plebeian expression "onto" on page 3. There is properly no such word as "onto" in the English language, "upon" being the preposition here required. Webster clearly describes "onto" as a low provincialism or colloquialism. "Little Jack in Fairyland," by Ruth Ryan, is a well written account of a dream, with the usual

43

awakening just as events are coming to a climax. The style is very attractive, and the images ingenious. "Getting What You Want," by Mr. Moe, is a brief one-act farce illustrating the subtle devices whereby the sharp housewife bewilders the good-natured landlord into the granting of extraordinary favours. Had the heroine kept on to still greater lengths, she might have secured an entire new house. The present number of The Pippin is, save for the absence of photographs, quite as pleasing as the previous number. We trust that Mr. Moe's editorial prophecy may be fulfilled, and that we may soon behold another issue which shall make us familiar with the new faces brought by revolving time into the congenial Appleton circle.

The Plainsman for July is the best number yet issued, the two eleventh-hour contributions being very cleverly introduced. "Revised Edition," by Mrs. Jeanette Timkin, is a versified piece of keen humour and good metre, well illustrating the opening of the third or aerial element to human travel. "To Bazine, Kansas" is a sprightly prose account by James J. Hennessey of his journey from Boston to Bazine. "An Incident of Early Days," by Mrs. John Cole, is presented in the same attractive reminiscent style which makes her article in The Trail so readable and interesting. We are here told of the times when herds of bison were common sights, and are given a pleasing account of the formation of the Bazine Sunday-School. The articles by Mr. and Mrs. Ira Cole show their appreciation of the amateurs who have visited them, and conclude an issue of thoroughly entertaining quality.

The Providence Amateur for June introduces to the United another local press club of great enthusiasm. Owing to some unauthorized omissions made by the printer, this first issue is scarcely representative of the club's entire personnel, but that which still remains affords, after all, a fair index to the character and ideals of the new organization. The editorials by John T. Dunn are both frank and fearless. We detest a shifty club whose allegiance wavers betwixt the United, the Morris Faction and the National, and so are greatly pleased at Mr. Dunn's manly and open stand for the one real United. The editor's opinions on acknowledgment of papers is certainly just from one point of view, though much may be said for the opposite side. When an amateur journal has been prepared with unusual labour, and mailed conscientiously to every member of the Association, the publisher has substantial reason for resenting any marked display of neglect. We do not blame The Blarney Stone for its attitude on this question, and shall probably follow its custom by mailing the next Conservative only to those who have acknowledged one or both of the previous issues.

44

The Reflector for June is a British amateur magazine, transplanted on American soil by its able editor, Ernest A. Dench. "Crossing the Atlantic in War Time" is a pleasing account of Mr. Dench's voyage from Liverpool to New York. "Chunks of Copy" forms the title of an excellent though informal editorial department, while "A Brain Tank at Your Service" teems with witticisms concerning various members of the Blue Pencil Club. This magazine has no connection with any former journal of like title, but seems likely to prove a worthy successor to all its namesakes.

The Trail for Spring is a new and substantial illustrated magazine of 20 pages and cover, issued by our well-known Private Critic, Mr. Alfred L. Hutchinson. At the head of the contents are the reminiscences of the editor, which prove extremely interesting reading, and which are well supplemented by the lines entitled "The Tramp Printer." Also by Mr. Hutchinson is the well written and animated account of Mr. Nicholas Bruehl, whose artistic photographical work adorns the inside covers of this issue. "Pioneer Life in Kansas," by Mrs. John Cole, is a delightfully graphic picture of the trials and adventures of the early settlers in the West. Being written from actual personal experience, the various incidents leave a lasting impression on the mind of the reader, while a pleasing smoothness of style enhances the vividness of the narrative. "Memory-Building" is the first of a series of psychological articles by our master amateur, Maurice W. Moe. It is here demonstrated quite conclusively, that the faculty of memory is dependent on the fundamental structure and quality of the brain, and may never be acquired or greatly improved through cultivation. "Evening at Magnolia Springs," by Laura E. Moe, exhibits the same type of literary talent that her gifted husband possesses; in fact, this sketch may be compared with Mr. Moe's well-known "Cedar Lake Days." The use of trivial incidents gives an intense naturalness to the description. "Caught," by Ruth M. Lathrop, is a brilliant short story whose development and climax are natural and unforced. Fiction is generally the amateur's weakest spot, but Miss Lathrop is evidently one of the few shining exceptions. So thoroughly excellent is The Trail, that we hope to see not merely a second issue, but its permanent establishment as one of the United's leading magazines.

The Tryout for June belongs to the National, but contains much matter by United members. "Tempora Mutantur," a very meritorious short story by Marguerite Sisson, affords an illuminating contrast between the solid culture of 1834 and the detestable shallowness of the present time. This prevailing frivolity and unscholarliness is something which the United is seeking to remedy, and we are thankful indeed for stories such as this, which expose modern levity in all its nauseousness. It is evident that Miss Sisson is emulating the appreciative Anne Carroll of 1834, rather than her obtuse and indifferent descendant. "The District School," by Edna R. Guilford, describes very vividly the many petty annoyances that beset the average teacher. While the picture is extremely well presented as a whole, certain roughnesses of diction nevertheless arrest the critical eye. "Onto," in the first paragraph, is a provincialism which should be superseded by "to." Further on we hear the teacher admonishing a youth to wash up some ink, and "wash it good"! Would a teacher thus express herself? "Well" is the adverb here needed. "Too tired to hardly stand" is a seriously ungrammatical phrase, which should read: "almost too tired to stand." We note that one of the pupils' names is given as "Robert Elsmere." While it may not be essentially a fault thus to use the name of a famous character of fiction, we feel that the exercise of a little more originality might have avoided this appropriation of Mrs. Humphry Ward's celebrated hero. Miss Guilford's fundamental talent is unmistakable, but needs cultivation and practice before it can shine out in full splendour.

The Tryout for July contains "Cripple George," a beautiful short story by Mrs. Rose L. Elmore, commendable alike in plot and technique. "A Day in the Mountains," by Harry H. Connell, is a very interesting sketch whose style exhibits considerable promise.

The United Amateur for March contains a literary department which will, we hope, remain as a regular feature. "Tobias Smithers, Leading Man" is Miss Ellen Moore's prize-winning attempt at constructing a story from a very brief nucleus given by Mr. Moe. Miss Moore here exhibits a facile pen and a just appreciation of humorous situations. "Ghosts," by Mrs. Renshaw, well illustrates the vague superstitions of the negroes, those strange creatures of darkness who seem never to cross completely the threshold from apedom to humanity. "March," by ourselves, is a gem of exquisite poesy, etc., etc., which we have here praised because no one else could ever conscientiously do so. Line 10 apparently breaks the metre, but this seeming break is due wholly to the printer. The line should read:

"The longer sunshine, and the shorter night."

"The Unknown Equation" is a love story by Mrs. Florence Shepphird. Though the major portion is quite polished and consistent, we cannot but deem the conclusion too abrupt and precipitate. Perhaps, being a frigid old critic without experience in romance, we ought to submit the question to some popular newspaper column of Advice to the Lovelorn, inquiring whether or not it be permissible for a young lady, after only a few hours' acquaintanceship with a young gentleman, to encourage him to "put his arm around her yielding form and kiss her passionately"!!

The United Amateur for May is graced by "Reveille," a powerful and stirring poem written in collaboration by our two gifted bards, Mr. Kleiner, the Laureate, and Miss von der Heide. "Nature and the Countryman," by A. W. Ashby, is an iconoclastic attack on that love of natural beauty which is inherent in every poetical, imaginative and delicately strung brain. In prose of faultless technique and polished style, Mr. Ashby catalogues like a museum curator every species of flaw that he can possibly pick in the scenes and events of rustic life. But while the career of the farmer is assuredly not one of uninterrupted bliss, it were folly to assert that Nature's superlative loveliness is not more than enough to compensate for its various infelicities. No mind of high grade is so impervious to aesthetic emotion that it can behold without admiration the wonders of the rural realm, even though a vein of sordid suffering ran through the beauteous ensemble. Of all our personal friends, the one who most adores and loves to personify Nature is a successful farmer of unceasing diligence. Mr. Ashby errs, we are certain, in taking the point of view of the unimaginative and unappreciative peasant. This sort of animal interprets Nature by physical, not mental associations, and is unfitted by heredity to receive impressions of the beautiful in its less material aspects. Whilst he grumbles at the crimson flames of Aurora, thinking only of the afternoon rain thus predicted, the man of finer mould, though equally cognizant that a downpour may follow, rejoices impulsively at the pure beauty of the scene itself, a scene whose intellectual exaltation will help him the better to bear the dull afternoon. Is not the beauty-lover the happier of the two? Both must endure the trials, but the poet enjoys compensating pleasures which the boor may never know. The personification and deification of Nature is a legacy from primitive ages which will delight us in an atavistical way till our very race shall have perished. And let Mr. Ashby remember that those early tribes who placed a god or goddess in every leafy tree, crystal fount, reedy lake or sparkling brook, were far closer to Nature and the soil than is any modern tenant farmer.

The United Official Quarterly for May has resumed its former attractive appearance, and contains a very creditable assortment of literary matter. "Atmosphere," by Mrs. Shepphird, is a thoughtful and pleasing essay, whose second half well describes the individuality of the various amateur authors and editors. "The Kingly Power of Laughter," by Louena Van Norman, is no less just and graphic, illustrating the supreme force of humour and ridicule.

Leo Fritter, in "Concerning Candidates," points out some important details for office-seekers, whilst Ira A. Cole, in "Five Sticks on Finance," gives some interesting suggestions for economy. "Opportunity," an essay by Mildred Blanchard, concludes the issue, and successfully disputes the noxious old platitude, that "Opportunity knocks but once at each man's door." With the Quarterly is bound The New Member, reviewed elsewhere, the two forming a tasteful and meritorious magazine.

The Woodbee for July is an issue of unusual interest, revealing the more serious and substantial activities of the prosperous Columbus Club. The opening feature is a sonnet by Alma Sanger, "To Autumn Violets," which exhibits some poetical talent and a just sense of metrical values. We are sure that the defective second line is the fault of the printer rather than of the author. "The Blind Prince," by Henriette Ziegfeld, is an excellent juvenile tale involving a fairy story. The only serious objection is the undercurrent of adult comment which flows through the narrative. Particularly cynical is the closing sentence: "'And here's Mother,' finished poor Auntie with a sigh of relief." The ordinary fairy stories told to children are bits of actual Teutonic mythology, and should be related with a grave, absolute simplicity and naivete. However, as a psychological study of the typical childish auditor, the sketch as a whole is highly meritorious. We are inclined to wonder at the possible meaning of the strange word "alright," which appears more than once in Miss Ziegfeld's tale. It is certainly no part of our language, and if it be a corruption of "all right," we must say that we fail to perceive why the correct expression could not have been used. "What's in a Name?" by Irene Metzger, is a clever sketch concerning the silly modern practice of giving fancy names to helpless infants. Glancing backward a little through history, Miss Metzger would probably sympathize with the innocent offspring of the old Puritans, who received such names as "Praise-God," and the like. Praise-God Barebones, a leading and fanatical member of Cromwell's rebel parliament, went a step further than his father, naming his own son "If-Jesus-Christ-had-not-died-for-thee-thou-hadst-been-Damned"! All this was actually the first name of young Barebones, but after he grew up and took a Doctor's degree, he was called by his associates, "Damned Dr. Barebones"! "Moonlight on the River," by Ida Cochran Haughton, is an exquisite sentimental poem, each stanza of which ends with the same expression. The atmosphere is well created, and the images dexterously introduced. The whole piece reminds the reader of one of Thomas Moore's beautiful old "Irish Melodies." That Mrs. Haughton's talent has descended to the second generation is well proven by Edna M. Haughton's "Review of the

Literary Work of the Quarter." Miss Haughton is a polished and scholarly reviewer, and her criticisms are in every instance just and helpful. The editorial on "Miss United" is very well written, and should be carefully perused by those in danger of succumbing to the autumnal advances of that sour old maid, Miss National.

Howard P. Lovecraft
Chairman

LITTLE JOURNEYS TO THE HOMES OF PROMINENT AMATEURS

Among the many amateurs I have never met in the flesh and realness of Life, Howard Phillips Lovecraft, poet, critic and student, appeals to me as no other recent "find" in the circles of amateuria has ever appealed. And Lovecraft is a distinct "find." Just why he holds a firm grip on my heart-strings is something of a mystery to me. Perhaps it is because of his wholesome ideals; perhaps it is because he is a recluse, content to nose among books of ancient lore; perhaps it's because of his physical afflictions; his love of things beautiful in Life; his ardent advocacy of temperance, cleanliness and purity—I don't know. We disagree on many questions; he criticises my literary activities; he smiles at my suffrage theories, and disapproves of my language in Chain Lightning. But I like him.

Howard Phillips Lovecraft has an interesting history, and this fact was known to Official Editor Daas when he asked me to take a little journey to the study-home of the Vice-President. "Don't stint yourself for space" was noted on the assignment tab, and after glancing over the biographical notes before me—I am sure that Daas has again exemplified his quiet humor during a serious moment.

Lovecraft was born at 454 Angell St., Providence, R. I., on August 20, 1890. His nationality is Anglo-American, and under British law he can claim to be a British subject, since he is a grandson in direct male line of a British subject not naturalized in the United States. His ancestry is purely English. On the paternal side he is a descendant of the Lovecrafts, a Devonshire family which has furnished a great many clergymen to the Church of England,

and the Allgoods of Northumberland, a history-honored family of which several members have been knighted. The Allgoods have been a military line, and this may account for Lovecraft's militarism and belief in the justice of war. On the maternal side he is a typical Yankee, coming from East English stock which settled in Rhode Island about 1680. Lovecraft is a student of astronomy—it is a domineering passion with him—and this love was apparently inherited from his maternal grandmother, Rhoby Phillips, who studied it thoroughly in her youth at Lapham Seminary, and whose collection of old astronomical books first interested him. Lovecraft came from pure-blood stock, and he is the last male descendant of that family in the United States. With him the name will die in America. He is unmarried.

As he was about to enter college at the age of eighteen, his feeble health gave way, and since then he has been physically incapacitated and rendered almost an invalid. Being thus deprived of his cherished hope to further his education and prepare himself for a life of letters, he has contented himself with his home, which is just three squares from his birthplace, and where he lives with his mother. And his home life is ideal. His personal library—his haven of contentment—contains more than 1500 volumes, many of them yellowed with age, and crude examples of the printer's art. Among these treasured books may be found volumes which have passed through the various branches of his family, some dating back to 1681 and 1702, and methinks I can see Lovecraft poring over these time-stained bits o' bookish lore as the monks of old followed the printed lines with quivering fingers in the taper's uncertain, flickering light. For Lovecraft appeals to me as a bookworm—one of those lovable mortals whose very existence seems to hang on the numbered pages of a heavy, clumsy book!

His connection with organized amateur journalism is of recent date. On April 6, 1914, his application for membership in the United Amateur Press Association of America was forwarded to the Secretary. Like a great many of the recruits, Lovecraft was completely ignored for several months. In July of last year he became active, and he has proven to be an invaluable asset to the literary life of the Association. He is not a politician. However, his literary activities had been prosecuted many years before he had ever heard of the United. At the age of eight and one-half years he published the Scientific Gazette, a weekly periodical, written in pencil and issued in editions of four carbon copies. This journal was devoted to the science of chemistry, which was one of his earliest hobbies, and ran from March, 1899, to February, 1904. As in most cases, my knowledge of chemistry was acquired after I had spent four years in high-school, and the fact that any boy should be interested in that study at the age of eight and one-half years appeals to me as something out of the ordinary. But Lovecraft was not an ordinary boy. His second and more ambitious venture was the Rhode Island Journal of Astronomy. This was at first published as a weekly, and later changed to a monthly publication. This was carefully printed by hand and then duplicated on the hectograph and issued in lots of twenty-five copies. The Journal was issued from 1903 to 1907, and contained the latest astronomical news, rewritten from the original telegraphic reports issued from Harvard University and seen at the Ladd Observatory. It also contained many of his original articles and forecasts of phenomena. He owns a 3-inch telescope of French make, and aside from amateur journalism, his one great hobby is astronomy. At the age of sixteen he commenced writing monthly astronomical articles for the Providence Tribune, and later changed to the Evening News, to which he still contributes. During the present year he has contributed a complete elementary treatise on astronomy in serial form to the Asheville (N. C.) Gazette-News. Besides contributing a great many poems and articles to the amateur press, editing The Conservative and assisting with the editorial work on The Badger, the appearance of Mr. Lovecraft's work in the professional magazines is of common occurrence. During the past year he has had charge of the Bureau of Public Criticism in The United Amateur, where he has proven himself a just, impartial and painstaking critic. That he will achieve a great popularity in the world of amateur letters is a foregone conclusion, and I do not think that I am indulging in extravagant praise in predicting a brilliant future for him in the professional field.

I am acquainted with Howard Phillips Lovecraft only through correspondence; I have never felt the flesh of his palm, and yet, I know he is a man—every inch of him—and that amateur journalism will be enriched and promoted to its highest plane through his kindly influence and literary leadership.

Andrew Francis Lockhart

The Teuton's Battle-Song
"Omnis erat vulnus unda
Terra rubefacta calido
Frendebat gladius in loricas
Gladius findebat clypeos—
Non retrocedat vir a viro
Hoc fuit viri fortis nobilitas diu—
Laetus cerevisiam cum Asis
In summa sede bibam
Vitae elapsae sunt horae
Ridens moriar."

—Regner Lodbrog

The mighty Woden laughs upon his throne,
And once more claims his children for his own.
The voice of Thor resounds again on high,
While arm'd Valkyries ride from out the sky:
The Gods of Asgard all their pow'rs release
To rouse the dullard from his dream of peace.
Awake! ye hypocrites, and deign to scan
The actions of your "brotherhood of Man."
Could your shrill pipings in the race impair
The warlike impulse put by Nature there?
Where now the gentle maxims of the school,
The cant of preachers, and the Golden Rule?
What feeble word or doctrine now can stay
The tribe whose fathers own'd Valhalla's sway?
Too long restrain'd, the bloody tempest breaks,
And Midgard 'neath the tread of warriors shakes.
On to thy death, Berserker bold! And try
In acts of Godlike bravery to die!
Who cares to find the heaven of the priest,
When only warriors can with Woden feast?
The flesh of Sehrimnir, and the cup of mead,
Are but for him who falls in martial deed:
Yon luckless boor, that passive meets his end,
May never in Valhalla's court contend.
Slay, brothers, Slay! And bathe in crimson gore;
Let Thor, triumphant, view the sport once more!
All other thoughts are fading in the mist,

But to attack, or if attack'd, resist.
List, great Alfadur, to the clash of steel;
How like a man does each brave swordsman feel!
The cries of pain, the roars of rampant rage,
In one vast symphony our ears engage.
Strike! Strike him down! Whoever bars the way;
Let each kill many ere he die today!
Ride o'er the weak; accomplish what ye can;
The Gods are kindest to the strongest man!
Why should we fear? What greater joy than this?
Asgard alone could give us sweeter bliss!
My strength is waning; dimly can I see
The helmeted Valkyries close to me.
Ten more I slay! How strange the thought of fear,
With Woden's mounted messengers so near!
The darkness comes; I feel my spirit rise;
A kind Valkyrie bears me to the skies.
With conscience clear, I quit the earth below,
The boundless joys of Woden's halls to know.
The grove of Glasir soon shall I behold,
And on Valhalla's tablets be enroll'd:
There to remain, till Heimdall's horn shall sound,
And Ragnarok enclose creation round;
And Bifrost break beneath bold Surtur's horde,
And Gods and men fall dead beneath the sword;
When sun shall die, and sea devour the land,
And stars descend, and naught but Chaos stand.
Then shall Alfadur make his realm anew,
And Gods and men with purer life indue.
In that blest country shall Abundance reign,
Nor shall one vice or woe of earth remain.
Then, not before, shall men their battles cease,
And live at last in universal peace.
Through cloudless heavens shall the eagle soar,
And happiness prevail forevermore.

—H. P. Lovecraft

Author's Note

The writer here endeavours to trace the ruthless ferocity and
incredible bravery of the modern Teutonic soldier to the hereditary
influence of the ancient Northern Gods and Heroes. Despite the
cant of the peace-advocate, we must realise that our present

Christian civilisation, the product of an alien people, rests but lightly upon the Teuton when he is deeply aroused, and that in the heat of combat he is quite prone to revert to the mental type of his own Woden-worshipping progenitors, losing himself in that superb fighting zeal which baffled the conquering cohorts of a Caesar, and humbled the proud aspirations of a Varus. Though appearing most openly in the Prussian, whose recent acts of violence are so generally condemned, this native martial ardour is by no means peculiar to him, but is instead the common heritage of every branch of our indomitable Xanthochroic race, British and Continental alike, whose remote forefathers were for countless generations reared in the stern precepts of the virile religion of the North. Whilst we may with justice deplore the excessive militarism of the Kaiser Wilhelm and his followers, we cannot rightly agree with those effeminate preachers of universal brotherhood who deny the virtue of that manly strength which maintains our great North European family in its position of undisputed superiority over the rest of mankind, and which in its purest form is today the bulwark of Old England. It is needless to say to an educated audience that the term "Teuton" is in no way connected with the modern German Empire, but embraces the whole Northern stock, including English and Belgians.

In the Northern religion, Alfadur, or the All-Father, was a vague though supreme deity. Beneath him were among others Woden, or Odin, practically the supreme deity, and Woden's eldest son Thor, the God of War. Asgard, or heaven, was the dwelling-place of the Gods, whilst Midgard was the earth, or abode of man. The rainbow, or bridge of Bifrost, which connected the two regions, was guarded by the faithful watchman Heimdall. Woden lived in the palace of Valhalla, near the grove of Glasir, and had as messengers to earth the Valkyries, armed, mailed and mounted virgins who conveyed from the earth to Asgard such men as had fallen bravely in battle. Only those who fell thus could taste to the full the joys of paradise. These joys consisted of alternate feasting and fighting. At Woden's feasts in Valhalla was served the flesh of the boar Sehrimnir, which, though cooked and eaten at every meal, would regain its original condition the next day. The wounds of the warriors in each celestial combat were miraculously healed at the end of the fighting.

But this heaven was not to last forever. Some day would come Ragnarok, or the Twilight of the Gods, when all creation would be destroyed, and all the Gods and men save Alfadur perish. Surtur, after killing the last of these Gods, would burn up the world. Afterward the supreme Alfadur would make a new earth or paradise, creating again the Gods and men, and suffering them ever after to dwell in peace and plenty.

54

THE UNITED AMATEUR

OFFICIAL ORGAN OF THE UNITED AMATEUR PRESS ASSOCIATION

Volume XV GEORGETOWN, ILL., APRIL, 1916 Number 9

DEPARTMENT OF PUBLIC CRITICISM

The Brooklynite for January contains one of Rheinhart Kleiner's characteristic poems, entitled "A Mother's Song". Mr. Kleiner's command of good taste, harmony, and correctness requires no further panegyric amongst those who know him; but to the more recent United members who have not yet read extensively in our journals, his work may well be recommended as undoubtedly the safest of all amateur poetical models for emulation. Mr. Kleiner has a sense of musical rhythm which few amateur bards have ever possessed, and his choice of words and phrases is the result of a taste both innate and cultivated, whose quality appears to rare advantage in the present degenerate age. This remarkable young poet has not yet fully displayed in verse the variety of thoughts and images of which his fertile brain and well selected reading have made him master, but has preferred to concentrate most of his powers upon delicate amatory lyrics. While some of his readers may at times regret this limitation of endeavor, and wish he might practice to a greater extent that immense versatility which he permitted the amateur public to glimpse in the September Piper; it is perhaps not amiss that he should cultivate most diligently that type of composition most natural and easy to him, for he is obviously a successor of those polished and elegant poets of gallantry whose splendour adorned the reigns of Queen Elizabeth and King James the First.

The Conservative for January opens with Winifred Virginia Jordan's "Song of the North Wind", one of the most powerful poems lately seen in the amateur press. Mrs. Jordan is the newest addition to the United's constellation of genuine poetical luminaries; shining as an artist of lively imagination, faultless taste, and graphic expression, whose work possesses touches of genius and individualism that have already brought her renown in amateur circles. In the poem under consideration, Mrs. Jordan displays a phenomenal comprehension of the sterner aspects of Nature, producing a thoroughly virile effect. Words are chosen with care

55

and placed with remarkable force, whilst both alliteration and onomatopoeia are employed with striking success. By the same author is the shorter poem entitled "Galileo and Swammerdam", which though vastly different in aspect and rhythm, yet retains that suggestion of mysticism so frequently encountered in Mrs. Jordan's work.

James Tobey Pyke, a lyrical and philosophical poet of high scholastic attainments, contributes two poems; "Maia", and "The Poet". The latter is a stately sonnet, rich in material for reflection. Such is the quality of Mr. Pyke's work, that his occasional contributions are ever to be acclaimed with the keenest interest and appreciation.

Rheinhart Kleiner, our Laureate, is another bard twice represented in the January Conservative. His two poems, "Consolation" and "To Celia", though widely different in structure, are yet not unrelated in sentiment, being both devoted to the changing heart. One amateur critic has seen fit to frown upon so skilled an apotheosis of inconsistency, but it seems almost captious thus to analyse an innocuous bit of art so daintily and tastefully arrayed. "To Celia" is perhaps slightly the better of the two, having a very commendable stateliness of cadence, and a gravity of thought greater than that of "Consolation".

"The Horizon of Dreams", by Mrs. Renshaw, is a graphic and enthralling venture into the realm of nocturnal unreality. The free play of active imagination, the distorted and transitory conceptions and apparitions, and the strangely elusive analogies, all lend charm and color to this happy portrayal of the vague boundaries of Somnus' domain. Mrs. Renshaw's rank as a poet is of very high tone, most of her productions involving a spiritual insight and metaphysical comprehension vastly beyond that of the common mind. But this very nobility of imagination, and superiority to the popular appeal, are only too likely to render her best work continually underestimated and unappreciated by the majority. She is not a "poet of the masses", and her graver efforts must needs reach audiences more notable for cultured than numerical magnitude. Of Mrs. Renshaw's liberal metrical theories, enough is said elsewhere. This Department can neither endorse principles so radical, nor refrain from remarking that want of proper rhyme and metre has relegated to obscurity many a rich and inspired poem.

"Departed", by Maude Kingsbury Barton, is a sentimental poem of undoubted grace and sweetness, happily cast in unbroken metre.

The Coyote for January is adorned by no less than three of Mrs. Winifred V. Jordan's exquisite short poems. "The Night-Wind"

56

is a delicately beautiful fragment of dreamy metaphor. There is probably a slight misprint in the last line, since the construction there becomes somewhat obscure. "My Love's Eyes" has merit, but lacks polish. The word "azure" in the first stanza, need not be in the possessive case; whilst the use of a singular verb with a plural noun in the second stanza (smiles-beguiles) is a little less than grammatical. "Longing" exhibits the author at her best, the images and phraseology alike showing the touch of genius.

Other poetry in this issue is by Adam Dickson, a bard of pleasing manner but doubtful correctness. "Smile" needs rigorous metrical and rhetorical revision to escape puerility. "Silver Bells of Memory" is better, though marred by the ungrammatical passage "thoughts doth linger". In this passage, either the noun must be made singular, or the verb form plural.

"Prohibition in Kansas" is a well written prose article by Editor William T. Harrington, wherein he exhibits a commendably favourable attitude toward the eradication of the menace of strong drink. Mr. Harrington is an able and active amateur, and takes an intelligent interest in many public questions. His style and taste are steadily improving, so that The Coyote has already become a paper of importance among us.

The Dixie Booster for January is Mr. Raymond E. Nixon's Capital City News, transferred to the amateur world, and continued under the new name. With this number the editor's brother, Mr. Roy W. Nixon, assumes the position of Associate Editor. This neat little magazine is home-printed throughout, and may well remind the old-time amateurs of those boyish "palmy days" whose passing they lament so frequently. By means of a cut on the third page, we are properly introduced to Editor Nixon, who at present boasts but thirteen years of existence. The gifted and versatile associate editor, Mr. Roy W. Nixon, shows marked talent in three distinct departments of literature; essay-writing, fiction, and verse. "Writing as a Means of Self-Improvement" is a pure, dignified and graceful bit of prose whose thought is as commendable as its structure. "A Bottle of Carbolic Acid" is a gruesome but clever short story of the Poe type, exhibiting considerable comprehension of abnormal psychology as treated in literature. "My Valentine" is a poem of tuneful metre and well expressed sentiment, though not completely polished throughout. The third stanza, especially, might be made less like prose in its images.

Dowdell's Bearcat for December is quaint and attractive in appearance. The youthful editor has provided himself with a series of cuts of the metaphorical "Bruin" in various attitudes and various employments, these clever little pictures lending a pleasing novelty

57

to the cover and the margins. Judiciously distributed red ink, also, aids in producing a Christmas number of truly festive quality. Mr. Dowdell's "Growls from the Pit" is a series of editorials both timely and interesting, while his "Did You Hear That" is a lively page of fresh news. This issue is notable for Mrs. Winifred V. Jordan's poetical contributions, of which there are three. "Life's Sunshine and Shadows" is a tuneful moral poem whose rhythm and imagery are equally excellent. "Contentment" is brief but delightful. "When the Woods Call" is a virile, graphic piece; vibrant with the thrill of the chase, and crisp with the frosty air of the Northern Woods.

The present reviewer's lines "To Samuel Loveman" contain five misprints, as follows:

Line	3	for	**are**	read	**art**
"	5	"	**Appollo**	"	**Apollo**
"	6	"	**versus**	"	**verses**
"	15	"	**eternal**	"	**ethereal**
"	18	"	**the**	"	**thee**

"Beads from my Rosary", by Mary M. Sisson, is a collection of well written and sensible paragraphs on amateur journalism, which ought to assist in arousing enthusiasm amongst many members hitherto dormant. Editor Dowdell's pithy little epigrams at the foot of each page form an entertaining feature, many of them being of considerable cleverness. Dowdell's Bearcat will soon revert to its original newspaper form, since Mr. Dowdell intends to make newspaper work his life Profession.

The Inspiration for November is a decidedly informal though exceedingly clever personal paper issued by Miss Edna von der Heide as a reminiscence of the Rocky Mount convention. Prose and verse of whimsically humorous levity are employed with success in recording the social side of the amateur gathering.

The Looking Glass for January is composed wholly of biographical matter, introducing to the association the multitude of accomplished recruits obtained through Mrs. Renshaw and others. In these forty life stories, most of them autobiographical, the student of human nature may find material for profound reflection on the variety of mankind. The more recent members of the United, as here introduced, are in the aggregate a maturer, more serious, and more scholarly element than that which once dominated the amateur world; and if they can be properly welcomed and acclimated to the realm of amateur letters, they will be of great value indeed in building up the ideals and character of the association. For this influx of sedate, cultivated members, the United has Mrs. Renshaw to thank, since the present policy of recruiting was originated and is conducted largely by the Second Vice-President.

Ole Miss' for December is the most important of all recent additions to amateur letters, and it is with regret that we learn of the magazine's prospective discontinuance. The issue under consideration is largely local, most of the contributions being by Mississippi talent, and it must be said that the contributors all reflect credit upon their native or adopted State.

Mr. J. W. Renshaw's page of editorials is distinguished equally by good sense and good English. His attitude of disapproval toward petty political activities and fruitless feuds in the United is one which every loyal member will endorse, for nearly all of the past disasters in amateur history have been caused not by serious literary differences, but by conflicting ambitions among those seeking no more than cheap notoriety.

Mrs. Renshaw is well represented both by prose and by verse, the most interesting of her pieces being possibly the essay entitled "Poetic Spontaneity", wherein more arguments are advanced in her effort to prove the inferior importance of form and metre in poesy. According to Mrs. Renshaw, the essence of all genuine poetry is a certain spontaneous and involuntary spiritual or psychological perception and expression; incapable of rendition in any prescribed structure, and utterly destroyed by subsequent correction or alteration of any kind. That is, the bard must respond unconsciously to the noble impulse furnished by a fluttering bird, a dew-crowned flower, or a sun-blest forest glade; recording his thoughts exactly as evolved, and never revising the result, even though it be detestably cacophonous, or absolutely unintelligible to his less inspired circle of readers. To such a theory as this we must needs reply, that while compositions of the sort indicated may indeed represent poesy, they certainly represent art in its proper sense no more than do "futuristic" pictures and other modern monstrosities of a like nature. The only exact means whereby a poet may transmit his ideas to others is language, a thing both definite and intellectual. Granting that vague, chaotic, dissonant lines are the best form in which the tender suitor of the Muses may record his spiritual impressions for his own benefit and comprehension, it by no means follows that such lines are at all fitted to convey those impressions to minds other than his own. When language is used without appropriateness, harmony, or precision, it can mean but little save to the person who writes it. The soul of a poem lies not in words but in meaning; and if the author have any skill at all in recording thought through language, he will be able to refine the uncouth mass of spontaneous verbiage which first comes to him as representing his idea, but which in its original amorphous state may fail entirely to suggest the same idea to another brain. He will be able to preserve and perpetuate his idea in a style of language which the world may understand, and in a rhythm which may not offend the reader's sense of propriety with conspicuous harshness, breaks, or sudden transitions.

"Flames of the Shadow", Mrs. Renshaw's longest poetical contribution to this issue, is a powerful piece which, despite the author's theory, seems in no way injured by its commendably regular structure. "Immortality of Love" is likewise rather regular, though the plan of rhyming breaks down in the last stanza. "For You" and "Sacrament of Spirit" are short pieces, the former containing an "allowable" rhyming of "tongue" and "long", which would not meet with the approval of the Kleiner type of critic, but upon which this department forbears to frown.

James T. Pyke's two poems, "To a Butterfly" and "Life and Time" are gems of incomparable beauty. "Ole Gardens", by Winifred V. Jordan, is a haunting bit of semi-irregular verse which deserves warm applause for the cleverness of its imagery and the aptness of its phraseology. "The Reward of it All", by Emilie C. Holladay, is a potent but pathetic poem of sentiment, whose development is highly commendable, but whose metrical construction might be improved by judicious care. "A Mississippi Autumn" was written as prose by Mrs. Renshaw, and set in heroic verse without change of ideas by the present critic. The metaphor is uniformly lofty and delicate, whilst the development of the sentiment is facile and pleasing. It is to be hoped that the original thoughts of the author are not impaired or obscured by the technical turns of the less inspired versifier. "My Dear, Sweet, Southern Blossom", dedicated to Mr. and Mrs. Renshaw with Compliments of the Author, James Laurence Crowley, is a saccharine and sentimental piece of verse reminiscent of the popular ballads which flourished ten or more years ago. Triteness is the cardinal defect, for each genuine image is what our discerning private critic Mr. Moe would call a "rubber-stamp" phrase. Mr. Crowley requires a rigorous course of reading among the classic poets of our language, and a careful study of their art as a guide to the development of his taste. At present his work has about it a softness bordering on effeminacy, which leads us to believe that his conception of the poet's art is rather imperfect. It is only in caricature that we discover the poet as a sighing, long-haired scribbler of gushing flights of infantile awe or immature adoration.

Earnestness, dignity, and at times, sonorous stateliness, become a good poet; and such thoughts as are generally suggested by the confirmed use of "Oh", "Ah", "dear", "little", "pretty", "darling", "sweetest flow'ret of all", "where the morning-glory twineth", and so on, belong less to literary poetry than to the Irving Berlin song-writing industry of "Tin Pan Alley" in the Yiddish wilds of New York City. Mr. Crowley has energy of no mean sort, and if he will apply himself assiduously to the cultivation of masculine taste and technic, he can achieve a place of prominence among United bards.

W. S. Harrison deserves a word of praise for his poem of Nature, entitled "Our Milder Clime", wherein he celebrates the charms of Mississippi, his native state. The lines contain an old-fashioned grace too often wanting in contemporary verse. Other contributions to Ole Miss' are Mrs. Maude K. Barton's "Something of Natchez", a very interesting descriptive sketch in prose, and Dr. Rolfe Hunt's two negro dialect pieces, both of which are of inimitable wit and cleverness.

The Pippin for February is the first number of this important high-school journal to be issued without the supervision of Mr. Moe, and its excellence well attests the substantial independent merit of the Appleton Club. The city of Appleton forms the dominant theme in this number, and with the assistance of seven attractive half-tone illustrations, the publication well displays the beauty and advantages of the pleasant Wisconsin town. Miss Eleanor Halls cleverly weaves into conversational form much information concerning the remote history of Appleton, emphasizing the superior character resulting from the select quality of the settlers, and the early introduction of learning. Mr. Alfred Galpin surprises many readers when he reveals the fact that Appleton possessed the first of all telephone systems, a surprise quickly followed by Mr. Joseph Harriman's illustrated paragraph telling of the first street-car, also an Appleton innovation. Among other articles, that by Miss Torrey on Lawrence College is of unusual interest. "The Immortalization of the Princess", by Miss Fern Sherman, is an excellent Indian tale, whose structure and atmosphere well suggest not only the characteristic tribal legends of the red folk, but other and more classical myths as well. Though Miss Sherman is not yet a member of the United, one of such gifts would be heartily welcomed in the ranks.

The Plainsman for December is the most substantial number of his journal which Mr. Ira Cole has yet issued. First in order of importance among the contents is perhaps the editor's own prose sketch entitled "Monuments", wherein Mr. Cole reveals to particular advantage his exceptional skill in depicting and philosophizing upon the various aspects and phenomena of Nature. Mr. Cole's style is constantly improving, though not now of perfect polish, it is none the less remarkable for its grace and fluency. "To Florence Shepphird", also by Mr. Cole, is a rather long piece of blank verse, containing many beautiful passages. The author's skill in stately and sonorous poetry is far above the common level, and his work has about it an atmosphere of the polished past which that of most amateur bards lacks; yet the present poem is not without errors. The passage (lines 10-11) reading: "calm days that knoweth not dread Boreas' chilling breath" must be changed so that either the noun shall be singular or the verb plural. The double negative in line 23 might well be eliminated. Two lines whose metre could be improved are the 13th and 50th. The final quatrain is pleasing to the average ear, including that of the present critic; though the very exact taste of today, as represented by Mr. Kleiner, frowns upon such deviation from the dominant blank verse arrangement. "On the Cowboys of the West" is a brief bit of verse by this reviewer, accompanied by a note from the pen of Mr. Cole. The note is better than the verse, and exhibits Mr. Cole's vivid and imaginative prose at its best. "The Sunflower", a versified composition by James Laurence Crowley, concludes the issue. There is much attractiveness in the lines; though we may discover particularly in the second stanza, that touch of excessive softness which occasionally mars Mr. Crowley's work. No one can fail to discern the weakness of such a line as "You big giant of all the flowers".

The Providence Amateur for February is worthy of particular attention on account of Mr. Peter J. MacManus' absorbing article on "The Irish and the Fairies". Mr. MacManus firmly believes not only that fairies exist in his native Ireland, but that he has actually beheld a troop of them; facts which impart to this article a psychological as well as a literary interest. The prose style of Mr. MacManus is very good, being notable alike for fluency and freedom from slang, whilst his taste is of the best. His future work will be eagerly awaited by the amateur public. Edmund L. Shehan contributed both verse and prose to this issue. "Death" is a stately poem on a grave subject, whose sentiments are all of suitable humility and dignity. The apparently anomalous pronoun "her", in the tenth line, is a misprint for "he". The piece ends with a rhyming couplet, to which Mr. Kleiner, representing correct modern taste, takes marked exception. The present reviewer, however, finds no reason to object to any part of Mr. Shehan's poem, and attributes this concluding couplet to the influence of similar Shakespearian terminations. The prose piece by Mr. Shehan well describes a visit to a cinematograph studio, and is entitled "The Making of a Motion

Picture". In the verses entitled "A Post-Christmas Lament", Mr. John T. Dunn combines much keenness of wit with commendable regularity of metre. Mr. Dunn is among the cleverest of the United's humorous writers. "To Charlie of the Comics" is a harmless parody on our Laureate's excellent poem "To Mary of the Movies", which appeared some time ago in The Piper. In "The Bride of the Sea", Mr. Lewis Theobald, Jr., presents a rather weird piece of romantic sentimentality of the sort afforded by bards of the early nineteenth century. The metre is regular, and no flagrant violations of grammatical or rhetorical precepts are to be discerned, yet the whole effort lacks clearness, dignity, inspiration, and poetic spontaneity. The word printed "enhanc'd" in the sixth stanza is properly "entranc'd".

Tom Fool, Le Roi bears no definite date, but is a sort of pensive autumn reverie following the Rocky Mount convention of last summer. This grave and dignified journal is credited to the House of Tillery, and if typographical evidence may be accepted, it belongs most particularly to that branch now bearing the name of Renshaw and having its domain in Coffeeville, Mississippi. "Mother Gooseries from the Convention", by Emilie C. Holladay, is a long stanzaic and Pindaric ode, whose taste and technic are alike impeccable. The exalted images are sketched with artistic touch, whilst the deep underlying philosophy, skillfully clothed in well balanced lines, arouses a sympathetic reaction from every cultural intellect. "The Carnival", by Mrs. E. L. Whitehead, is an admirable example of stately descriptive prose mixed with aesthetic verse. The long and euphonious periodic sentences suggest the style of Gibbon or of Dr. Johnson, whilst the occasional metrical lines remind the reviewer of Dr. Young's solemn "Night Thoughts". "Dummheit", by Dora M. Hepner, is a grave discourse on Original Sin, describing the planning of Tom Fool, Le Roi. Elizabeth M. Ballou's article entitled "Our Absent Friend" forms a notable contribution to amateur historical annals, and displays Miss Ballou as the possessor of a keen faculty for observation, and a phenomenally analytical intellect. "Banqueters from the Styx", Mrs. Renshaw's masterly description of the convention dinner and its honoured guests from the regions of Elysium and elsewhere, reminds the reviewer of the 11th book of the Odyssey and the 6th book of the Aeneid, wherein the fraternizing of men with the shades of men is classically delineated.

Tom Fool is a memorable publication, suggesting the old "fraternal" papers, whose passing so many amateurs regret.

THE UNITED AMATEUR for November contains besides the official matter a small but select assortment of poems, prominent among which is "The Meadow Cricket", by Jas. T. Pyke. It is impossible to overestimate the beauty of thought and expression which Mr. Pyke shows in all his verses, and the United is fortunate in being able to secure specimens of his work.

"Remorse", by James Laurence Crowley, is one of the best samples of this gentleman's poesy which we have yet seen, though Mr. Crowley insists that one of the punctuation marks has been wrongfully located by the reviser. Since the present critic prepared the manuscript for publication, he is willing to assume full culpability for this crime. There is genuine poetic feeling in this short piece; and it seems an undoubted fact that Mr. Crowley with a little added restraint and dignity of expression, is capable of producing excellent work. "List to the Sea", by Winifred V. Jordan, is a delightfully musical lyric, whose dancing dactyls and facile triple rhymes captivate alike the fancy and the ear. "The Wind and the Beggar", by Maude K. Barton, is sombre and powerful. "Ambition", by William de Ryee, is regular in metre and commendable in sentiment, yet not exactly novel or striking in inspiration. "Choose ye", by Ella C. Eckert, is a moral poem of clever conception and correct construction.

The United Official Quarterly for January opens with "A Prayer for the New Year", by Frederick R. Chenault. Mr. Chenault is a poet of the first order so far as inspiration is concerned, but his work is frequently marred by irregularity of metre, and the use of assonance in place of rhyme. The metre of this poem is correct, but the two attempted rhymes "deeper-meeker" and "supremely-sincerely" are technically no more than assonant sounds. Pres. Fritter writes very powerfully on our publishing situation in this number; and his article should not only be perused with attention, but heeded with sincerity and industriousness.

"Behind the Canvas Wall", by William J. Dowdell, is one of the cleverest and most ingenious bits of fiction which the amateur press has contained for some time. That it is of a nature not exactly novel is but a trivial objection. The homely, appealing plot, and the simple, sympathetic treatment, both point to Mr. Dowdell as a possible success in the realm of short story writing, should he ever care to enter it seriously. Another excellent tale is "The Good Will of a Dog", by P. J. Campbell. The plot is of a well defined type which always pleases, whilst the incidents are graphically delineated. "The Bookstall" is a metrical monstrosity by the present reviewer. Mr. Maurice W. Moe, the distinguished Private Critic, lately gave us the following opinion of our verse. "You are," he writes, "steeped in the poetry of a certain age; an age, by the way, which cut and fit its thought with greater attention to one model than any other age before or since; and the result is that when you turn to verse as a medium of expression, it is just as if you were pressing a button liberating a perfect flood of these perfectly good but stereotyped formulae of expression. The result is very ingenious, but just because it is such a skillful mosaic of Georgian 'rubber-stamp' phrases, it must ever fall short of true art." Mr. Moe is correct. We have, in fact, heard this very criticism reiterated by various authorities ever since those prehistoric days when we began to lisp in numbers. Yet somehow we perversely continue to "mosaic" along in the same old way! But then, we have never claimed to possess "true art"; we are merely a metrical mechanic. "A New Point of View In Home Economics", a clever article by Miss Eleanor Barnhart, concludes the Official Quarterly proper.

But the New Member supplement, with its profusion of brilliant credentials, yet remains to be considered. "Dutch Courage", by Louis E. Boutwell, is a liquorish sketch whose scene is laid in a New Jersey temple of Bacchus. Being totally unacquainted with the true saloon atmosphere, we find ourself a little embarrassed as to critical procedure, yet we may justly say that the characters are all well drawn, every man in his humor.

"Ol' Man Murdock" is a quaint, and in two senses an absorbing, figure. The rest of the issue is given over to the Muses of poesy. "The Saturday Fray" is a clever piece by Daisy Vandenbank. The rhyming is a little uneven, and in one case assonance is made to answer for true rhyme. "Cream" and "mean" cannot make an artistic couplet. "The Common Soldiers", by John W. Frazer, is a poem of real merit; whilst "Little Boy Blue", by W. Hume, is likewise effective. Mr. Hume's pathetic touch is fervent and in no manner betrays that weakness bordering on the ridiculous, to which less skillful flights of pathos are prone. "The Two Springs" is a pleasant moral sermon in verse by Margaret Ellen Cooper. Concluding the issue is "The Under Dog in the Fight", a vigorous philosophical poem by Andrew Stevenson.

The Woodbee for January is distinguished by Mrs. Winifred V. Jordan's brilliant short poem entitled "Oh, Where is Springtime?" The sentiment of the piece is an universal one, and the pleasing lines will appeal to all. "Retribution", by Mrs. Ida C. Haughton, is a clever story, but the present critic's extreme fondness for cats makes it difficult to review after reading the first sentence. However, the well-approached conclusion is indeed just. The "moral" is a pathetic example of unregeneracy! Miss Edna M. Haughton's critical article is direct and discerning; the Woodbee Club is fortunate in having among its members so capable a reviewer. Editor Fritter likewise mounts the reviewer's throne in this issue, proceeding first of all to demolish our own fond dream of yesterday; The Conservative. Looking backward down the dim vista of those bygone but memory-haunted days of October, 1915, when we perpetrated the horribly plainspoken and frightfully ungentle number whereof Mr. Fritter treats, we are conscious of our manifold sins, and must beg the pardon of the liquor interests for shouting so rudely in the cause of total abstinence. Pres. Fritter's critical style is a good one, and is developing from month to month. His advocacy of lukewarmness in writing is perhaps not so complete as one might judge from this article; though his use of the cautious phrase "it is rumored" in connection with a well known statement seems hardly necessary. Rigid impartiality, the critic's greatest asset, is manifest throughout the review, and we thoroughly appreciate the favorable mention not infrequently accorded us. In passing upon the merits of Dowdell's Bearcat, Mr. Fritter shows equal penetration and perspicuity, and we are convinced that his rank amongst amateur reviewers is very high.

H. P. LOVECRAFT,
Chairman

THE UNITED AMATEUR

OFFICIAL ORGAN OF THE UNITED AMATEUR PRESS
ASSOCIATION

Volume XV GEORGETOWN, ILL., JUNE, 1916 Number 11

DEPARTMENT OF PUBLIC CRITICISM

The Coyote for July opens with Harry E. Rieseberg's verses entitled "The Sum of Life", whose structure is excellent as a whole, though defective in certain places. The word "mirage" is properly accented on the second syllable, hence is erroneously situated in the first stanza. "A mirage forever seeming" is a possible substitute line. Other defects are the attempted rhymes of "decay" with "constancy", "carried" with "hurried", and "appalled" with "all". The metre is without exception correct, and the thoughts and images in general well presented, wherefore we believe that with a little more care Mr. Rieseberg can become a very pleasing poet indeed. "The Philippine Question", by Earl Samuel Harrington, aged 15, is an excellent juvenile essay, and expresses a very sound opinion concerning our Asiatic colonies. It is difficult to be patient with the political idiots who advocate the relinquishment of the archipelago by the United States, either now or at any future time. The mongrel natives, in whose blood the Malay strain predominates, are not and never will be racially capable of maintaining a civilized condition by themselves. "How Fares the Garden Rose?" is a poem bearing the signature of Winifred Virginia Jordan, which is a sufficient guarantee of its thorough excellence. "To a Breeze", also by Mrs. Jordan, is distinguished by striking imagery, and displays in the epithet "moon-moored", that highly individualistic touch which is characteristic of its author. "Peace", by Andrew Francis Lockhart, is a poem of excellent construction, though marred by two serious misprints which destroy the harmony of the first and third lines.

The Dixie Booster for March-April is an exceedingly neat and clever paper from the House of Nixon. "Spring in the South", a poem by Maude K. Barton, opens the issue in pleasant fashion, the attractive images well atoning for certain slight mechanical deficiencies. "Dick's Success", by Gladys L. Bagg, is a short story whose phraseology exhibits considerable talent and polish. The didactic element is possibly more emphasized than the plot, though not to a tedious extent. Whether or not a rough draft of a novel may be completed in the course of a single afternoon, a feat described in this tale, we leave for the fiction-writing members of the United to decide! Of the question raised regarding the treatment of the Indian by the white man in America it is best to admit in the words of Sir Roger de Coverly, "that much might be said on both sides". Whilst the driving back of the aborigines has indeed been ruthless and high-handed, it seems the destiny of the Anglo-Saxon to sweep inferior races from his path wherever he goes. There are few who love the Indian so deeply that they would wish this continent restored to its original condition, peopled by savage nomads instead of civilized colonists. "The Deuce and Your Add", by Melvin Ryder, is a bit of light philosophy whose allegorical case is well maintained. "To a Warbler", by Roy W. Nixon, is a meritorious piece of verse whose rhythm moves with commendable sprightliness, though the first line of the first stanza might be made to correspond better with the first line of the second stanza. The word "apparent" in the last line, seems a little unsuited to the general style of the poem, being more suggestive of the formal type of composition. "Grandma", also by Mr. Roy Nixon, is a noble sonnet whose quality foreshadows real poetical distinction for its author. "You", by Dora M. Hepner, contains sublime images, but possesses metrical imperfections. The general anapaestic or dactylic rhythm is much disturbed by the iambic fourth line of the first stanza. The editorials, jokes, and jingles in this issue are all clever, and proclaim Mr. Raymond Nixon as a capable and discriminating editor.

Literary Buds for February exhibits the amateurs of Harvey, Illinois, after a long absence from the publishing arena. The present issue, edited by Mr. Caryl Wilson Dempesy, contains matter of merit and interest. "The Dells of the Wisconsin", by A. Myron Lambert, is an interesting account of an outing spent amidst scenes of natural grandeur and beauty. The author's style is fluent and pleasing, though a few slight crudities are to be discerned. On page 1, where the height of a large dam is mentioned, it is stated "that the water must raise that distance before it can fall". Of course, "rise" is the verb which should have been used. Another erroneous phrase is "nature tract". "Nature" is not an adjective, but a noun; "natural" is the correct word. However, this anomalous use of nouns for adjectives has only too much prevalence amongst all grades of writers today, and must not be too harshly censured in this case. On page 4 the word "onto" should be supplanted by "upon", and the awkward phrase: "to be convinced that we had ventured to a place that we did not know any dangers were connected with", should be changed to something like this: "to convince us that we had ventured to a seemingly dangerous place whose apparent dangers we had not then noticed". "A Song of Love", by Editor Dempesy, is cast in uniformly flowing and regular metre, but some of the words require comment. "Lover" is not generally applied by bards to adored members of the gentler sex, "love" being the conventional term. Likewise, the phrase "heart which always softly does its beating" might well be revised with greater attention to poetical precedent. Yet the whole is of really promising quality, and exhibits a metrical correctness much above the average. "The Operation" is a very witty sketch by Miss Clara I. Stalker, with a sudden turn toward the end which arouses the complete surprise and unexpected mirth of the reader. "The High Cost of Flivving", by Albert Thompson, is a bright bit of versified humour involving novel interpretations of certain technical terms of literature. The swinging dactylic rhythm is well managed except where the words "descending" and "ascending" occur, and where, in line 24, the metre becomes momentarily anapaestic.

The Looking Glass for May is the final number of Mrs. Renshaw's journal of introductions, and makes known to the association a group of 27 new members. One of the most interesting autobiographies is that of Mr. J. E. Hoag of Greenwich, New York, whose friendly sentences, written from the cumulative experience of 85 years of life, possess an elusively captivating quality. Of the non-biographical matter in this issue, Mrs. Renshaw's compilation entitled "Writing for Profit" deserves particular perusal. This is well set off by the same author's colloquial lines, "Pride O' The Pen", wherein the lethal taint of trade in literature is effectively deplored. "Something", by David H. Whittier, is a thoughtful analysis of conditions in the United, with suggestions for improvement. "One Bright Star Enough For Me", by Mr. John Hartman Oswald of Texas, is a pious poem reminding one of Mr. Addison's well known effort which begins: "The spacious firmament on high". We doubt, however, if Mr. Addison has been much improved upon, since several instances of imperfect poetical taste are to be found in Mr. Oswald's lines. But there are evidences of a great soul throughout the ten stanzas, and the metre is in the main correct. What Mr. Oswald appears to require is a thorough reading of the English classics, with minute attention to their phraseology and images. With such study we believe him capable of development into a poet of enviable force and sincerity.

Toledo Amateur for April marks the welcome reappearance of Mr. Wesley H. Porter's neat little journal after a year's absence. "A Story", by David H. Whittier, possesses a tragical plot whose interest is slightly marred by triteness and improbable situations. Of the latter we must point out the strained coincidence whereby four distinct things, proceeding from entirely unrelated causes, give rise to the final denouement. The culmination of the aged father's resolve to kill his enemy, the conditions which make possible the return of the son, the presence of the enemy's hat and coat under the wayside tree, and the storm which prompts the son to don these garments, are all independent circumstances, whose simultaneous occurrence, each at exactly the proper time to cause the catastrophe, may justly be deemed a coincidence too great for the purpose of good literature. In an artistically constructed tale, the various situations all develop naturally out of that original cause which in the end brings about the climax; a principle which, if applied to the story in question, would limit the events and their sequences to those arising either directly or indirectly from the wrong committed by the father's enemy. Since there is no causative connection between the immediate decision of the father to kill his foe, and the developments or discoveries which enable the son to return, the simultaneous occurrence of these unusual things is scarcely natural. Superadded to this coincidence are two more extraneous events; the rather strange presence of the hat and coat near the road, and the

69

timely or untimely breaking of the storm, the improbability indeed increasing in geometrical progression with each separate circumstance. It must, however, be admitted that such quadruple coincidences in stories are by no means uncommon among even the most prominent and widely advertised professional fiction-blacksmiths of the day. Mr. Whittier's style is that of a careful and sincere scholar, and we believe that his work will become notable in this and the succeeding amateur journalistic generation. The minuteness of the preceding criticism has been prompted not by a depreciatory estimate of his powers, but rather by an appreciative survey of his possibilities. "Say, Brother", by Mrs. Renshaw, is a poem describing life in the trenches of the Huns. The metre is quite regular, and the plan of rhyming but once broken. Mr. Porter's prose work; editorial, introductory, and narrative, is all pleasing, though, not wholly free from a certain slight looseness of scholarship. We should advise rigorous exercise in parsing and rhetoric. "Respite", by Edgar Ralph Cheyney, shows real poetical genius, and the iambic heptameters are very well handled, save where one redundant syllable breaks the flow of the last line. Even that would be perfect if the tongue could condense the noun and article "the music", into "th' music".

The Tornado for April constitutes the publishing debut of Mrs. Addie L. Porter, mother of Toledo Amateur's gifted young editor. Mrs. Porter's "Recollections From Childhood" are pleasant and well phrased, bringing to mind very vividly the unrivalled joys of Christmas as experienced by the young. Wesley H. Porter, in "My Vacation", tells entertainingly of his visit to the hive of the Woodbees last September. The editorial and news paragraphs are all of attractive aspect, completing a bright paper whose four pages teem with enthusiasm and personality. It is to be hoped that other comparatively new United members may follow Mr. Porter's example in entering the publishing field; for individual journals, though of no greater size than this, are ever welcome, and do more than anything else to maintain interest and promote progress in the association.

The Trail for April must by no means be confused with Alfred L. Hutchinson's professionalized magazine of identical title, for this Trail is an older and emphatically non-professional publication issued co-operatively by Dora M. Hepner and George W. Macauley. Non-professionalism, indeed, seems to dominate the entire issue to a degree unusual in the broadened and developed United. With the exception of one poem and one short story or sketch, the contents are wholly personal and social. "He Reached my Hand", by Dora M. Hepner, is an excellent piece of verse, though perhaps not of that extreme polish which is observed in the productions of very careful bards. Miss Hepner has great refinement of fancy and vigour of expression, but evidently neglects to cultivate that beautiful rhetoric and exquisite rhythmic harmony which impress us so forcibly in the work of scholars and bookmen like Rheinhart Kleiner. "A Girl of the U. S.", by George W. Macauley, is a prose piece whose nature seems to waver between that of a story and a descriptive sketch. Though description apparently preponderates, the narrative turn toward the conclusion may sanction classification as fiction. The faults are all faults of imperfect technique rather than of barren imagination, for Mr. Macauley wields a graphic pen, and adorns every subject he approaches. In considering minor points, we must remark the badly fractured infinitive "to no longer walk", and the unusual word "relieffful". We have never seen the latter expression before, and though it may possibly be a modernism in good usage, it was certainly unknown in the days when we attempted to acquire our education. Mr. Macauley, with his marked descriptive ability, is less at ease in stories of contemporary life than in historical fiction, particularly mediaeval and Oriental tales. His genius is not unlike that of Sir Walter Scott, and shows to especial advantage in annals of knights and chivalry. "Scratchings" are by the pen of Miss Hepner, and display an active wit despite the profusion of slang. It would seem, however, that so brilliant a writer could preserve the desired air of vivacity without quite so many departures from the standard idioms of our language.

Miss Hepner's remarks on the assimilation of new United members are worthy of note. The cruder amateurs should not feel discouraged by the extraordinary average scholarship of the recent element, but should rather use it as a model for improvement. They should establish correspondence with the cultivated recruits, thereby not only benefiting themselves, but helping each gifted newcomer to find a useful and congenial place amongst us. The present situation is pitifully ludicrous, for practically all young aspirants call upon only one or two sadly overburdened older members for literary aid, forgetting that there are scores of brilliant writers, teachers, and professors waiting anxiously but vainly to be of real service to their fellow-amateurs. Several of the scholarly new members have particularly inquired how they can best assist the association; yet the association, as represented by its literary novices, has failed to take advantage of most of these offers of instructions and co-operation. We are impelled here to reiterate the slogan which Mr. Daas has so frequently printed in his various journals: "Welcome the Recruits!". Such a welcome is certain to react with double felicity upon the giver.

"From the Michigan Trail" is Mr. Macauley's personal column, and contains so bitter an attack on some of the United's policies of improvement, that we are tempted to remonstrate quite loudly. The captious criticism of the Second Vice-President's invaluable activities, constructive labours which have practically regenerated the association and raised it to a higher plane in the world of educational endeavour, is positively ungenerous. To speak of the article in Ole Miss' entitled "Manuscripts and Silver" as "mercenary", is the summit of injustice, for it was nothing more or less than the absolutely gratuitous offer to the United of what is now the Symphony Literary Service. We are rather at a loss to divine Mr. Macauley's precise notion of amateur journalism. He speaks of it as a "tarn", but we cannot believe he would have it so stagnant a thing as that name implies. Surely, the United is something greater than a superficial fraternal order composed of mediocre and unambitious dabblers. Progress leads toward the outside world of letters, and to cavil at work such as Mrs. Renshaw's is to set obstacles in the path of progress. Professional literary success on the part of amateur journalists can never react unfavorably on the United, and it seems far from kind and proper to impede the development of members. Why is a professional author necessarily less desirable as an amateur journalist than a professional plumber or boiler-maker? But there is one sound principle at the base of Mr. Macauley's argument, which deserves more emphasis than the points he elaborates. Professionalism must not enter into the workings of the association, nor should the professionalized amateur take advantage of amateur connexions to create a market for writings otherwise unsalable. This applies to the now happily extinct tribe of "ten-cents-a-year" publishers, who coolly expected all amateur journalists to subscribe to their worthless misprints as a matter of fraternal obligation. Mr. Macauley is an extremist on the subject of amateur rating, a fact which explains many otherwise puzzling allusions in his current editorials.

THE UNITED AMATEUR for February is the final number of the Daas regime, and constitutes a noble valedictory indeed. We find it impossible to express with sufficient force our regret at the withdrawal of Mr. Daas from the United, and we can but hope that the retirement may prove merely temporary. The February official organ is wholly literary in contents, and in quality sustains the best traditions of amateur journalism. Miss Olive G. Owen's poem, "Give us Peace!", which opens the issue, is tasteful in imagery and phraseology, and correct in rhyme and metre, but contains the customary unrealities and substitutions of emotion for reasoning which are common to all pacific propaganda. "The Little Old Lady's

Dream", by M. Almedia Bretholl, is a short story of the almost unpleasantly "realistic" type, whose development and atmosphere exhibit much narrative talent and literary skill. "The Teuton's Battle-Song" is an attempt of the present critic to view the principles of human warfare without the hypocritical spectacles of sentimentality. "Nature in Literature", by Arthur W. Ashby, is an essay of unusual quality, revealing a depth of well assimilated scholarship and a faculty for acute observation and impartial analysis, of which few amateur writers may justly boast. "His All", is an excellent poem by Mrs. Ella Colby Eckert, distinguished equally for its noble thought and facile rhythm. "'Twixt the Red and the White", a short story by Miss Coralie Austin, displays marked skill in construction and phraseology, though its development is not without a few of the typical crudities of youthful work. There is a trifling suspicion of triteness and banality in plot and dialogue; which is, however, compensated for in the artistic passages so frequently encountered. "Romance, Mystery, and Art", an essay by Edgar Ralph Cheyney, reflects the learning and thoughtfulness of its author. The poetical fragments entitled "Songs from Walpi", by Mrs. Winifred V. Jordan, describe the hopeless affection of a Southwestern Indian prince for a maiden of the conquering white race. The atmosphere and images are cleverly wrought, whilst the rhythm is in every detail satisfactory. "Nescio Quo", by Kathleen Baldwin, is a poem of great attractiveness both in structure and sentiment. "A Crisis", by Eleanor J. Barnhart, is a short story of distinctly modern type, whose substance and development compare well with professional work. "My Heart and I", a sonnet by James T. Pyke, exhibits the skill and philosophical profundity characteristic of its author. "My Native Land", a poem by Adam Dickson, describes the Scottish Border with pleasing imagery and bounding anapaestic metre. Mr. Dickson is a poet whose progress should be carefully watched. His improvement is steady, the present piece being easily the best specimen of his work to appear in the amateur press. "Poetry and its Power", by Helen M. Woodruff, is a delightful essay containing liberal quotations from various classic bards. "A Resolution", by Harry Z. Moore, seems to be modelled after Mrs. Renshaw's well known poem, "A Symphony". The various precepts are without exception sound and commendable. Helene E. Hoffman presents a brief but pleasing critique of Sir Thomas Browne's "Hydriotaphia, Urn-Burial; or a Discourse of the Sepulchral Urns lately found in Norfolk". It is refreshing to discover a modern reader who can still appreciate the quaint literature of the seventeenth century, and Miss Hoffman is to be thanked for her sympathetic review of the pompous, Latinised phrases of the old physician. "He and She", by Margaret A. Richard, is a thoroughly meritorious poem whose two "allowable rhymes", "fair-dear", and "head-prayed", would be censured only by a critic of punctilious exactitude. "At Sea", a witty bit of vers de societe by Henry Cleveland Wood, forms an appropriately graceful conclusion to a richly enjoyable issue of the magazine.

THE UNITED AMATEUR for March brings to the fore Mr. George S. Schilling's unusual editorial talent, and makes manifest the bright future of the official organ for the balance of the present administrative year. The chief literary contribution is "Hail, Autumn!", one of Mr. Arthur Ashby's brilliant and scholarly essays on Nature. The quality of Mr. Ashby's work deserves particular attention for its reflective depth of thought, and glowing profusion of imagery. His style is remarkably mature, and escapes completely that subtle suggestion of the schoolboy's composition which seems inseparable from the average amateur's attempts at natural description and philosophizing. Mr. Schilling's editorials are forcible and straightforward, vibrant with enthusiasm for the welfare of the association. "A Representative Official Organ", by Paul J. Campbell, serves to explain the author's highly desirable constitutional amendment proposed for consideration at the coming election, which will open the columns of THE UNITED AMATEUR to the general membership at a very reasonable expense. The News Notes in the present issue are sprightly and interesting.

THE UNITED AMATEUR for April is made brilliant by the presence of Henry Clapham McGavack's terse and lucid exposure of hyphenated hypocrisy, entitled "Dr. Burgess, Propagandist". Mr. McGavack's phenomenally virile and convincing style is supported by a remarkable fund of historical and diplomatic knowledge, and the feeble fallacies of the pro-German embargo advocates collapse in speedy fashion before the polished but vigorous onslaughts of his animated pen. Another essay inspired by no superficial thinking is Edgar Ralph Cheyney's "Nietzschean Philosophy", wherein some of the basic precepts of the celebrated iconoclast are set forth in comprehensive array. "The Master Voice of Ages Calls for Peace", a poem by Mrs. Frona Scott, has fairly regular metre, though its sentiment is one of conventional and purely emotional pacifism. "A Gentle Satire on Friendship", by Freda de Larot, is a very clever piece of light prose; which could, however, be improved by the deletion of much slang, and the rectification of many loose constructions. "A Wonderful Play" is Mrs. Eloise R. Griffith's well worded review of Jerome K. Jerome's "The Passing of the Third Floor Back", as enacted by Forbes-Robertson. Mrs. Griffith has here, as in all her essays, achieved a quietly pleasing effect, and pointed a just moral. "Fire Dreams" is a graphic and commendably regular poem by Mrs. Renshaw. "The Beach", a poem by O. M. Blood, requires grammatical emendation. "How better could the hours been spent" and "When life and love true pleasure brings" cannot be excused even by the exigencies of rhyme and metre. After the second stanza, the couplet form shifts in an unwarranted manner to the quatrain arrangement. The phraseology of the entire piece displays poetical tendencies yet reveals a need for their assiduous cultivation through reading and further practice. "My Shrine", by James Laurence Crowley, exhibits real merit both in wording and metre, yet has a rather weak third stanza. The lines:

> "One day I crossed the desert sands;
> One day I ride my train;"

are obviously anticlimactic. To say that the subject is trite would be a little unjust to Mr. Crowley's Muse, for all amatory themes, having been worked over since the very dawn of poesy, are necessarily barren of possibilities save to the extremely skilled metrist. Contemporary love-lyrics can scarcely hope to shine except through brilliant and unexpected turns of wit, or extraordinarily tuneful numbers. The following lines by Margaret, Duchess of Newcastle, who died in 1673, well express the situation despite their crudeness:

> "O Love, how thou art tired out with rhyme!
> Thou art a tree whereon all poets climb;
> And from thy branches every one takes some
> Of the sweet fruit, which Fancy feeds upon.
> But now thy tree is left so bare and poor,
> That they can hardly gather one plum more!"

"Indicatory", a brilliant short sketch by Ethel Halsey, well illustrates the vanity of the fair, and completes in pleasing fashion a very creditable number of our official magazine.

THE UNITED AMATEUR for May forms still another monument to the taste and energy of our official editor, Mr. Schilling. Biography is the keynote of the current issue, Mrs. Renshaw, Mr. J. E. Hoag, and Mr. Henry Cleveland Wood each receiving mention. Miss Emilie C. Holladay displays a pleasing prose style in her account of our Second Vice-President, and arouses interest with double force through the introduction of juvenile incidents.

"Happiness Defined" is a delightful little sketch by Ida C.

Haughton, whose philosophy will awake an universal response from the breasts of the majority. "The Wind Fairies", by Jean F. Barnum, is a poem in prose which contains more of the genuine poetic essence than does the average contemporary versified effort. The grace and grandeur of the clouds and the atmosphere have in all ages been admired, and it is but natural that they figure to a great extent in the beautiful legends of primitive mythology. "The Ship that Sails Away", by J. E. Hoag, is a delicate and attractive poem whose images and phraseology are equally meritorious. Mr. Hoag's poetical attainments are such that we await with eagerness the appearance of the pieces predicted in his biography. "To Flavia", by Chester Pierce Munroe, is a sweet lyric addressed to a young child and pervaded throughout with a quaintly whimsical, almost Georgian, semblance of stately gallantry. The first word of the seventeenth line should read "small" instead of "swell". As misprinted, this line conveys a rather incongruous impression. "Mountains in Purple Robes of Mist", a vivid and powerful poem of Nature by Rev. Eugene B. Kuntz, is cast in Alexandrine quatrains, a rather uncommon measure. The only possible defect is in line thirteen, where the accent of the word "sublime" seems to impede the flow of the metre. Line nineteen apparently lacks two syllables, but the deficiency is probably secretarial or typographical rather than literary. "Man as Cook", also by Dr. Kuntz, is a clever bit of humorous verse in octosyllabic couplets. "Consolation" well exhibits Andrew Francis Lockhart's remarkable progress as a poet. His verse is increasing every day in polish, and is fast becoming one of the most pleasing and eagerly awaited features of amateur letters. "At the End of the Road", by Mary Faye Durr, is a graphic and touching description of a deserted schoolhouse. The atmosphere of pensive reminiscence is well sustained by the judiciously selected variety of images and allusions. "There's None Like Mine at Home", by James Laurence Crowley, is a characteristic bit of Crowleian sentimentality which requires revision and condensation. There is not enough thought to last out three stanzas of eight lines each. Technically we must needs shudder at the apparent incurable use of "m-n" assonance. "Own" and "known" are brazenly and repeatedly flaunted with "roam" and "home" in attempted rhyme. But the crowning splendour of impossible assonance is attained in the "Worlds-girls" atrocity. Mr. Crowley needs a long session with the late Mr. Walker's well-known Rhyming Dictionary! Metrically, Mr. Crowley is showing a decided improvement of late. The only censurable points in the measure of this piece are the redundant syllables in lines 1 and 3, which might in each case be obviated by the substitution of "I've" for "I have", and the change of form in the first half of the concluding stanza. Of the general phraseology and imagery we may only remark that Mr. Crowley has much to forget, as well as to learn, before he can compete with Mr. Kleiner or other high-grade amatory poets in the United. Such expressions as "my guiding star", "my own dear darling Kate", or "she's the sweetest girl that e'er on earth did roam", tell the whole sad story to the critical eye and ear. If Mr. Crowley would religiously eschew the popular songs and magazine "poetry" of the day, and give over all his time to a perusal of the recognized classics of English verse, the result would immediately be reflected in his own compositions. As yet, he claims to be independent of scholarly tradition, but we must remind him of the Latin epigram of Mr. Owen, which Mr. Cowper thus translated under the title of "Retaliation":

"The works of ancient bards divine,
Aulus, thou scorn'st to read;
And should posterity read thine,
It would be strange indeed!"

So energetic and prolific a writer as Mr. Crowley owes it alike to himself and to his readers to develop as best he can the talent which rests latent within him.

The Woodbee for April opens with a melodious poem by Adam Dickson, entitled "Love". While the metre might well be changed in the interests of uniformity, the general effect is not at all harsh, and the author is entitled to no small credit for his production. The only other poem in the magazine is "Alone With Him", by Mrs. Ida C. Haughton. This piece is remarkable for its rhyming arrangement, each rhyme being carried through four lines instead of the usual couplet. The sentiments are just, the images well drawn, and the technique correct; the whole forming a highly commendable addition to amateur literature. "The Melody and Colour of 'The Lady of Shalott'", by Mary Faye Durr, is a striking Tennysonian critique, whose psychological features, involving a comparison of chromatic and poetic elements, are ingenious and unusual. Miss Durr is obviously no careless student of poesy, for the minute analyses of various passages give evidence of thorough assimilation and intelligent comprehension. "On Being Good", by Newton A. Thatcher, contains sound sense and real humour, whilst its pleasingly familiar style augurs well for Mr. Thatcher's progress in this species of composition. "War Reflections", by Herbert Albing, is an apt and thoughtful epitome of the compensating benefits given to mankind by the present belligerent condition of the world. The cogent and comprehensive series of reviews by Miss

Edna M. Haughton, and the crisp and pertinent paragraphs by
Editor Fritter, combine with the rest of The Woodbee's contents to
produce an issue uniformly meritorious.

H. P. LOVECRAFT,
Chairman

THE POETRY OF THE MONTH

CONTENT

An Epistle to RHEINHART KLEINER, Esq., Poet-Laureate, and
Author of "Another Endless Day".

Beatus ille qui procul negotiis,
Ut prisca gens mortalium,
Paterna rura bobus exercet suis.

—HORACE

KLEINER! in whose quick pulses wildly beat
The youth's ambition, and the lyrist's heat,
Whose questing spirit scorns our lowly flights,
And dares the heavens for sublimer heights:
If passion's force will grant an hour's relief,
Attend a calmer song, nor nurse thy grief.
What is true bliss? Must mortals ever yearn
For stars beyond their reach, and vainly burn;
Must suff'ring man, impatient, seek to scale
Forbidden steeps, where sharper pangs prevail?
Alas for him who chafes at soothing ease,
And cries for fever'd joys and pains to please:
They please a moment, but the pleasure flies,
And the rack'd soul, a prey to passion, dies.
Away, false lures! and let my spirit roam
O'er sweet Arcadia, and the rural home;
Let my sad heart with no new sorrow bleed,
But rest content in Morven's mossy mead.
Wild thoughts and vain ambitions circle near,

78

Whilst I, at peace, the abbey chimings hear.
Loud shakes the surge of Life's unquiet sea,
Yet smooth the stream that laves the rustic lea.
Let others feel the world's destroying thrill,
As 'midst the kine I haunt the verdant hill.
Rise, radiant sun! to light the grassy glades,
Whose charms I view from grateful beechen shades;
O'er spire and peak diffuse th' expanding gleam
That gilds the grove, and sparkles on the stream.
Awake! ye sylphs of Flora's gorgeous train,
To scent the fields, and deck the rising main.
Soar, feathered flock, and carol o'er the scene,
To cheer the lonely watcher on the green.
Sweet is the song the morning meadow bears,
And with the darkness fade ambitious cares:
Above the abbey tow'r the rays ascend,
As light and peace in matchless beauty blend.
Why should I sigh for realms of toil and stress,
When now I bask in Nature's loveliness;
What thoughts so great, that they must needs expand
Beyond the hills that bound this fragrant land?
These friendly hills my infant vision knew,
And in the shelt'ring vale from birth I grew.
Yon distant spires Ambition's limit show,
For who, here born, could farther wish to go?
When sky-blest evening soothes the world and me,
Are moon and stars more distant from my lea?
No urban glare my sight of heav'n obscures,
And orbs undimm'd rise o'er the neighb'ring moors.
What priceless boon may spreading Fame impart,
When village dignity hath cheer'd the heart?
The little group that hug the tavern fire
To air their wisdom, and salute their squire,
Far kinder are, than all the courtly throng
That flatter Kings, and shield their faults in song!
And in the end; what if no man adore
My senseless ashes 'neath Westminster's floor?
May not my weary frame, at Life's dim night,
Sleep where my childhood first enjoy'd the light?
Rest were the sweeter in the sacred shade
Of that dear fane where all my fathers pray'd;
Ancestral spirits bless the air around,
And hallow'd mem'ries fill the gentle ground.
So stay, belov'd Content! nor let my soul

In fretful passion seek a farther goal.
Apollo, chasing Daphne, gain'd his prize,
But lo! she turn'd to wood before his eyes!
Our earthly prizes, though as holy sought,
Prove just as fleeting, and decay to naught.
Enduring bliss a man may only find
In virtuous living, and contented mind.

H. P. LOVECRAFT

THE UNITED AMATEUR AUGUST 1916

DEPARTMENT OF PUBLIC CRITICISM

FIRST ANNUAL REPORT 1915-1916

Following a novel idea originated by the present Columbus administration, the Department of Public Criticism will herewith submit for the first time in its history an annual report, or summary of the preceding year's literary events within the United Amateur Press Association.

The programme of improvement informally decided upon in the official year of 1913-1914 received its definite ratification at the Rocky Mount Convention, when the assembled representatives of the United pledged "Individual collective support" to Mr. Fritter, the new President, in his endeavors to raise the literary standard of our society, and when an absolutely unanimous vote invested Mrs. J. W. Renshaw, the leading spirit of progress, with the important office of Second Vice-President. Pres. Fritter has since discharged his obligations and sustained his responsibilities in a thoroughly satisfactory manner despite many trying difficulties, whilst Mrs. Renshaw, as a recruiter, has succeeded in laying the foundations of a completely broadened, elevated, and rejuvenated association. Yet all that has been accomplished is merely the prologue of that greater period of change which must bring about the final assimilation of Mrs. Renshaw's phenomenally gifted recruits, and the materialization of the still nebulous plans evolved during the past twelvemonth.

The undersigned has on several occasions advocated the

80

formation of a regular "Department of Instruction" in the United, to be conducted by professional teachers and college instructors for the purpose of guiding the more or less inexperienced members. He has communicated his idea to several high-school preceptors of great ability, and has learned that under present conditions such a department is not perfectly feasible. It has been suggested that if each experienced and educated amateur would assume a personal and sympathetic advisory position toward some one of the younger or cruder members, much actual good might result. As our list now stands, the crude and the cultured are perhaps evenly balanced, yet instant success even in this modified course can scarcely be expected. At least another year seems to be required, in which the various members may gain a closer knowledge of each other through the wider diffusion of their printed efforts. However, the need for a more uniformly educated membership is pressing, and the undersigned will welcome aid or advice of any kind from those willing to assist him in establishing some sort of scholastic Department.

Another idea which has received undeserved neglect and discouraging opposition is the Authors' Placing Bureau or "United Literary Service", as outlined by the Second Vice-President. The normal goal of the amateur writer is the outside world of letters, and the United should certainly be able to provide improved facilities for the progress of its members into the professional field. The objections offered to this plan are apparently less vital than those affecting the Department of Instruction, and it is to be hoped that the mistaken zeal of our non-professional sticklers may not serve to prevent a step so sorely needed.

Passing on to the details of Departmental work, the undersigned is pleased to report a remarkable increase in the literary value of the compositions brought forth in the United this year; an increase which may be fairly declared to constitute a true elevation of our intellectual standard, and which undoubtedly compensates for the present regrettable paucity of amateur publishing media. In verse, particularly, is the advance notable. Some of our poets are securing recognition in the outside world of letters, whilst many lesser bards show a steady upward trend in their amateur efforts. Prose continues to suffer because of the seemingly unavoidable brevity of the average amateur journal. It is impossible to crowd any really well developed piece of prose within the limits generally assigned, hence our best authors seem almost to be driven into verse as a medium of expression. Financial prosperity of sufficient extent to ensure the publication of larger papers is obviously the only remedy for this deplorable condition.

Of our poets, the Laureate Rheinhart Kleiner (also Laureate of the National for 1916-1917) continues as the foremost technician and harmonist. His accurate and tasteful lines satisfy the ear and the understanding with equal completeness, and he shows no sign of yielding to the corrupting influences of decadent modern standards. In his own journal, The Piper, he reveals a versatile and phenomenally well stocked mind. The September number, containing imitations of the work of other amateur poets, will long be remembered. Mrs. Renshaw maintains her high place as a philosophical and expressionistic bard, though hampered by unusual theories of spontaneous versification. A greater deference to the human ear and metrical sense would render her already lofty poetry as attractive as it is exalted. Miss Olive G. Owen, former Laureate, has lately returned to activity, and may well be expected to duplicate her former successes in the domain of the Muses. The poetical progress of Andrew Francis Lockhart is a notable feature of amateur letters this year. Mr. Lockhart has always possessed the true genius of the bard, writing ably and voluminously; but his recent technical care is bringing out hitherto undiscovered beauties in his verse, and placing him in the very front rank of United poets. "Benediction" and "Consolation" are vastly above the average.

Of the new poets of prime magnitude who have risen above our horizon during the past year, Mrs. Winifred Virginia Jordan of Newton Centre, Mass., deserves especial mention both for high quality and great volume of work. Mrs. Jordan's poetry is of a tunefully delicate and highly individualistic sort which has placed it in great demand amongst amateur editors, and it is not unlikely that the author may be rewarded with a Laureateship at no distant date. The work is invariably of spontaneously graceful rhythm and universally pleasing in sentiment, having frequently an elusive suggestion of the unreal. A few of Mrs. Jordan's poems are of the grimly weird and powerful variety. "The Song of the North Wind" is a remarkable contribution to amateur letters, and has won the enthusiastic admiration of the United's poetical element. Professional success has recently crowned the efforts of Mrs. Jordan. Weekly Unity for June 17 contains her lines on "The Singing Heart", whilst several other poems from her pen have been accepted by The National Magazine. Rev. James Tobey Pyke is another poet of the first order whose writings have lately enriched the literature of the United. His style is correct, and his thought deep and philosophical. "The Meadow Cricket" is a poem which deserved more than a superficial perusal. John Russell, formerly of Scotland but now of Florida, is a satirist and dialect writer of enviable talent. His favorite measure is the octosyllabic couplet, and in his skilled hands this simple metre assumes a new and sparkling lustre. Rev. Frederick Chenault is a prolific lyrical poet whose sentiments are of uniform loftiness. The substitution of exact rhyme for assonance in his lines would double the already immense merit of his work. Other new bards of established ability are W. S. Harrison, Kathleen Baldwin, Eugene B. Kuntz, Mary Evelyn Brown, Henry Cleveland Wood, John W. Frazier, William Hume, Ella Colby Eckert, J. E. Hoag, Edgar Ralph Cheyney, Margaret A. Richard, William de Ryee, Helen H. Salls, and Jeanette Aylworth.

Of the poets whom we may term "rising", none presents a more striking figure than Ira A. Cole of Bazine, Kansas. Previously well known as a prose writer and publisher, he made his debut as a metrist just a year ago, through a very beautiful piece in the heroic couplet entitled "A Dream of the Golden Age". Mr. Cole is one of the few survivors of the genuine classic school, and constitutes a legitimate successor to the late Georgian poets. His development has been of extraordinary rapidity, and he will shortly surprise the amateur public both by a poetic drama called "The Pauper and the Prince", and by a long mythological poem not unlike Moore's "Lalla Rookh". The natural and pantheistic character of Mr. Cole's philosophy adapts him with phenomenal grace to his position as a mirror of classical antiquity. Another developing poet is Mr. Roy Wesley Nixon of Florida. "Grandma", his latest published composition, is a sonnet of real merit. Adam Dickson, a Scotsman by birth, but now a resident of Los Angeles, writes tunefully and pleasantly. His pieces are not yet of perfect polish, but each exhibits improvement over the preceding. He tends to favor the anapaest and the iambic tetrameter. Mrs. Ida Cochran Haughton of Columbus is scarcely a novice, but her latest pieces are undeniably showing a great increase of technical grace. Chester Pierce Munroe of North Carolina is a delicate amatory lyrist of the Kleiner type. He has the quaint and attractive Georgian touch, particularly evident in "To Flavia" and "To Chloris". Miss M. Estella Shufelt is absolutely new to the kingdom of poesy, yet has already produced work of phenomenal sweetness and piety. Mrs. E. L. Whitehead, though formerly confined wholly to prose, has entered the poetical field with intelligent and discriminating care. Her words are thoughtfully weighed and selected, whilst her technique has rapidly assumed a scholarly exactitude. Two new poets whose work requires much technical improvement are Mrs. Agnes R. Arnold and Mr. George M. Whiteside. Mr. Whiteside has indications of qualities not far remote from genius, and would be well repaid by a rigorous course of study. Messrs. John Hartman Oswald and James Laurence Crowley are both gifted with a fluency and self-sufficiency which might prove valuable assets in a study of poesy. W. F. Booker of North Carolina possesses phenomenal grace, which greater technical care would develop into unusual power. Rev. Robert L. Selle, D. D., of Little Rock, Arkansas, is inspired by sincerest religious fervor, and has produced a voluminous quantity of verse whose orthodoxy is above dispute. Mrs. Maude K. Barton writes frequently and well, though her technical polish has not yet attained its maximum. John Osman Baldwin of Ohio is a natural poet of spontaneous grace, though requiring cultivation in correct style.

From the foregoing estimate it may easily be gathered that imperfect technique is the cardinal sin of the average amateur poet. We have among us scores of writers blest with beautiful thoughts and attractive fluency, yet the number of precise versifiers may be counted on one's fingers. Our association needs increased requirements in classic scholarship and literary exactitude. At present, it is impossible for an impartial critic to give unstinted approval to the technique of any well known United poet save Rheinhart Kleiner.

Turning to the consideration of our prose writers, the undersigned finds it difficult to render a true judgment, owing to the adverse conditions mentioned earlier in this report. Many fluent pens are doubtless cramped into feebleness through want of space.

Fiction is among us the least developed of all the branches of literature. Really good stories are rare phenomena, whilst even mediocrity is none too common. The best short stories of the year are probably those by M. Almedia Bretholl and Eleanor Barnhart; the others are mainly juvenile work. Roy W. Nixon and Miss Coralie Austin represent the extremes of excitement and tameness, with "A Bottle of Carbolic Acid" on the one hand, and with "Jane" and "'Twixt the Red and the White" on the other. Both of these authors possess substantial ability. David H. Whittier is developing along classic lines, and will be a prominent figure in the next generation of amateur journalists. Mr. Moe's pupils are all good story-tellers, the work of Miss Gladys L. Bagg standing forth quite prominently this year. Florence Brugger's "Tale of the Sea" is a graphic narrative from a youthful pen, as is William Dowdell's "Behind the Canvas Wall", in a somewhat different way. Henriette and Florenz Ziegfeld have each contributed excellent work, nor must Mary M. Sisson's "Tempora Mutantur" be forgotten.

The rather loosely defined domain of the "sketch" has thriven this year, since it elicits fluent expression from those less prolific in other branches of literature. Mr. Melvin Ryder has entertained us with an entire magazine of this sort of material, whilst Mrs. Ida C. Haughton, Irene Metzger, Benjamin Repp, Mary Faye Durr, Ethel

Halsey, Clara Inglis Stalker, Freda de Larot, Helene E. Hoffman Cole, Helen M. Woodruff, Ira A. Cole, and Eloise N. Griffith prove no less entertaining with shorter sketches.

Criticism is well represented by Leo Fritter, Edna M. Haughton, Mrs. J. W. Renshaw, and Rheinhart Kleiner. The latter is no less gifted a critic than a poet, and gives out very acute judgments in his journal, The Piper.

In viewing the formal essays of the year, one is impressed with the profusion of mere schoolboy compositions. Masters of the Addisonian art are few but those few almost atone for the general lack of polish. Henry Clapham McGavack leads the list with a clarity of style and keenness of reasoning unsurpassed in the association. His "Dr. Burgess, Propagandist" is an amateur classic. Edgar Ralph Cheyney is an extreme radical, but is none the less a masterful essayist. His articles take a very high rank both for thoughtfulness and for diction. A third writer of unusual power and analytical depth is Arthur W. Ashby, whose essays on the varied aspects of Nature command our serious attention. The two Schillings, George and Samuel, deserve more than a passing mention, whilst Pres. Fritter's Laureateship well attests his merit. Rev. E. P. Parham has produced work of attractive quality. Joseph W. Renshaw's essays and editorials command notice whenever beheld; whilst Ira A. Cole, ever versatile, will shortly display his epistolary skill in the now unpublished series of "Churchill-Tutcombie Letters". William T. Harrington has progressed by leaps and bounds to a prominent place amongst our essay-writers, his able encomiums of Old England being a delightful feature of the year. It would be gratifying to speak of Maurice W. Moe's splendid style and terse English at this point, for he is one of our very foremost essayists; but his enforced inactivity in amateur journalism this year has deprived us of any current specimens save the brief editorial in the February Pippin.

The general quality of our prose is by no means satisfactory. Too many of our authors are contaminated with modern theories which cause them to abandon grace, dignity, and precision, and to cultivate the lowest forms of slang.

Papers and magazines have been neither ample nor numerous this year; in fact, the tendency of the times appears to be a centralization of effort in THE UNITED AMATEUR; something which is for many reasons to be applauded, and for a few reasons to be deplored. Those members who feel capable of issuing individual papers should be encouraged to do so; whilst those who are ordinarily silent, should be encouraged to join the contributing staff of THE UNITED AMATEUR as provided by the Campbell amendment.

The best individual journal of the year is Ole Miss'. For frequency and regularity, The Scot, The Woodbee, The Dixie Booster, and The Coyote are to be commended. THE UNITED AMATEUR has prospered as a monthly despite adverse conditions. The elaborate September, October and February numbers put us in deep debt to Mr. Edward F. Daas, while subsequent examples of good editorship must be accredited to Mr. George Schilling. It is gratifying to note the increasing literary character of the Official Organ; purely official numbers are invariably tedious, many of the long, detailed reports being quite superfluous. It is a strong and sincere hope of the undersigned, that Mr. Daas may rejoin us at and after the present convention. The resumption of The Lake Breeze would supply a pressing need. Mr. Moitoret's Cleveland Sun, which promises to be a frequently issued paper, made its first appearance lately, and will, after much of its "loudness" has been removed, be of substantial benefit to new members. The "sporting" features should be eliminated at once, as not only being in bad taste, but exerting a noxious influence over the literary development of the younger members.

While upon the subject of papers, the undersigned would like to enter a renewed protest against the persistent use of certain distorted forms of spelling commonly called "simplified". These wretched innovations, popular amongst the less educated element during the past decade, are now becoming offensively prominent in certain periodicals of supposedly better grade, and require concerted opposition on the part of all friends of our language. The advantages claimed for the changes are almost wholly unsubstantial, whilst the inevitable disadvantages are immense. Let us see fewer "thrus" and "thoros" in the amateur press!

What the association needs above all things is a return to earlier forms in prose and verse alike; to poetry that does not pain the ear, and paragraphs that do not affront the aesthetic sense of the reader. If our writers would pay more attention to the tasteful Georgian models, they would produce work of infinitely less cacophonous quality. Almost every one of our authors who is familiar with the literature of the past, is distinguished by exceptional grace and fluency of composition.

As this report draws toward its conclusion, a few minor aims of the Department of Public Criticism are to be noted. It is now the desire of the undersigned to aid authors in rectifying the injustices to which they are subjected by the wretched typography of most amateur journals. Writers are hereby encouraged to transmit to this

Department corrected copies of all misprinted work, the corrections to be made public in THE UNITED AMATEUR. By this method it is hoped that no amateur journalist will again be forced to suffer for faults not his own, as so many have suffered in the past. Of course, the critical reports themselves are frequently misprinted, but the vast majority of mistakes may with care be eliminated.

Concerning the name of this association, which a number wish changed in a manner that will eliminate the word "amateur", the undersigned feels that the sentiment of the veteran element is too strongly against such a move to warrant its immediate adoption. The primary object is the training of young writers before they have attained the professional grade, wherefore the present title is by no means such a misnomer as might be inferred from the talents of the more cultivated members. However, the proposed alteration is certainly justified in many ways, hence the idea should be deferred rather than abandoned altogether.

The wane of interest in amateur political affairs is to be commended as a recognition of the superior importance of literary matters. Amateur journalism is rapidly progressing nearer and nearer its ideal: a device for the instruction of the young and crude, and an aid for the obscure author of any sort, rather than a playground for the aimless and the frivolous.

Last of all, the undersigned wishes to thank the membership for its kind reception of the Department's reports. It is ever the Chairman's design to render impartial judgment, and if harshness or captiousness may at any time have been noticed in the reports, it has in each case been unintentional. An ideal of sound conservatism has been followed, but in no instance has the critic sought to enforce upon others that peculiarly archaic style of which he is personally fond, and which he is accustomed to employ in his own compositions. The Department of Public Criticism aspires to be of substantial assistance to the members of the United, and hopes next year to co-operate with Mr. Lockhart in presenting reviews of truly constructive quality.

Solicitous for the approval, and confident of the indulgence of the association, the Department herewith has the honor to conclude its first annual report; in the hope that such a summary of events and estimate of conditions may be of use to the incoming administration.

H. P. LOVECRAFT,
Chairman

DEPARTMENT OF PUBLIC CRITICISM

The Amateur Special for July is a voluminous magazine of credentials and other work of new members, edited by Mrs. E. L. Whitehead, retiring Eastern Manuscript Manager, with the assistance of the Recruiting Committee. Of all papers lately issued in the United, this is without doubt among the most valuable and most significant; since it is the pioneer of the new regime, whereby the talent of all our membership is to be brought out by better publishing facilities. Mrs. Whitehead, with notable generosity, has reserved for herself but one page, on which we find a clever and correct bit of verse, and a number of graceful acknowledgments and useful suggestions. The contents in general are well calculated to display the thorough literary excellence and supremacy of the United in its present condition; for in this collection of stories, poems, and articles, taken practically at random from the manuscript bureaus, there is scarce a line unworthy of commendation.

"Tatting", by Julian J. Crump, is a fluent and graceful colloquial sketch. "Mother and Child", by J. E. Hoag, is a sombre and thoughtful poem having a certain atmosphere of mysticism. The metre, which is well handled, consists of regular iambic pentameter quatrains with a couplet at the conclusion. An annoying misprint mars the first stanza, where "sigh" is erroneously rendered as "sight". "Homesick for the Spring", a poem by Bessie Estelle Harvey, displays real merit in thought and construction alike. "Mother Earth", by Rev. E. P. Parham, is a well adorned little essay in justification of the traditional saying that "the earth is mother of us all". George M. Whiteside, a new member of the United, makes his first appearance before us as a poet in "The Little Freckled Face Kid". Mr. Whiteside's general style is not unlike that of the late James Whitcomb Riley, and its prevailing air of homely yet pleasing simplicity is well maintained. "To Chloris", by Chester Pierce Munroe, is a smooth and melodious amatory poem of the Kleiner school. The imagery is refined, and the polish of the whole amply justifies the inevitable triteness of the theme. The word "adorns", in next the last line, should read "adorn". "A Dream", by Helen Harriet Salls, is a hauntingly mystical succession of poetic images cast in appropriate metre. The natural phenomena of the morning are vividly depicted in a fashion possible only to the true poet. The printer has done injustice to this exquisite phantasy in three places. In the first stanza "wonderous" should read "wondrous", while in the seventh stanza "arient" should be "orient". "Thou'st", in the eleventh stanza, should be "Thou'rt". "Prayers", a religious poem by Rev. Robert L. Selle, D. D., displays the classic touch of the eighteenth century in its regular octosyllabic couplets, having some resemblance to the work of the celebrated Dr. Watts. "Snow of the Northland", by M. Estella Shufelt, is a religious poem of different sort, whose tuneful dactylic quatrains contain much noble and appropriate metaphor. In the final line the word "re-cleaned" should read "re-cleansed". "In Passing By", by Sophie Lea Fox, is a meritorious poem of the thoughtful, introspective type, which has been previously honoured with professional publication. "A Time to Sing", by M. B. Andrews, introduces to the United another genuine poet of worth. The lines are happy in inspiration and finished in form, having only one possible defect, the use of "heralding" as a dissyllable. "The Stately Mountains", by Rev. Eugene B. Kuntz, D. D., is a notable contribution to amateur poetic literature. Dr. Kuntz chooses as his favourite metre the stately Alexandrine; and using it in a far more flexible and ingenious manner than that of Drayton, he manages to achieve a dignified and exalted atmosphere virtually impossible in any other measure. The even caesural break so common to Alexandrines, and so often urged by critics as an objection against them, is here avoided with great ingenuity and good taste. Dr. Kuntz's sentiments and phrases are as swelling and sublime as one might expect from his metre. His conception of Nature is a broad and noble one, and his appreciation of her beauties is that of the innate poet. "An April Memory" acquaints us with W. Frank Booker, a gifted lyrist whose lines possess all the warmth, witchery and grace of his native Southland. James J. Hennessey, in his essay on "The Army in Times of Peace", exhibits very forcibly the various indispensable services so quietly and efficiently performed by the United States Army in every-day life. Mr. Hennessey makes plain the great value of having among us a body of keen, versatile, and well-trained men ready for duty of any sort, and ever alert for their country's welfare in peace or in war. The American Soldier well deserves Mr. Hennessey's tribute, and the present essay adds one more to the already incontrovertible array of arguments in favour of an adequate military system. As printed, the article is marred by a superfluous letter "s" on the very last word, which should read "citizen". "Sowing the Good", a brief bit of moralizing by Horace Fowler Goodwin, contains a serious misprint, for the final word of line 1, stanza 2, should be "say".

"Bobby's Literary Lesson", by Gladys L. Bagg, is a delightful specimen of domestic satire in prose. The handling of the conversation exhibits Miss Bagg as a writer of considerable skill and promise. "The Leaf", a clever poem of Nature by Emily Barksdale, contains some gruesome atrocities by the printer. In the second stanza "it's" should be "it", and "wonderous" should be "wondrous". In the third stanza the typographical artist has killed a pretty woodland "copse" with the letter "r", so that it reads "corpse"! In the fourth stanza "head" should read "heard". Perhaps the "r" which murdered the "copse" escaped from this sadly mutilated word! In stanza five, "Chaots" should be "chants". But why continue the painful chronicle? Mr. Kleiner said just what we would like to say about misprints over a year ago, when he wrote "The Rhyme of the Hapless Poet"! "Submission", by Eugene B. Kuntz, is a delightful bit of light prose, forming the autobiography of a much-rejected manuscript. This piece well exhibits Dr. Kuntz's remarkable versatility. The humour is keen, and nowhere overstrained. "Number 1287", a short story by Gracia Isola Yarbrough, exhibits many of the flaws of immature work, yet contains graphic touches that promise well for the author. The lack of unity in plot and development detracts somewhat from the general effect, while the unusual lapses of time and artificial working up of the later situations are also antagonistic to technical polish. Triteness is present, but that is to be expected in all amateur fiction. "A Drama of Business", by Edgar Ralph Cheyney, is a terse bit of prose which might well serve as an editorial in a liberal literary magazine. "The Schools of Yesterday and Today", a sketch by Selma Guilford, presents in pleasing fashion an interesting and optimistic contrast. In "Mother", George M. Whiteside treats a noble theme in rather skilful fashion, though the rhyming of "breezes" and "trees is" can hardly be deemed suitable in a serious poem. "When the Sea Calls", a poem by Winifred Virginia Jordan, is possibly the most striking feature of the magazine. Mrs. Jordan's style in dealing with the wilder aspects of Nature has a grim potency all its own, and we can endorse without qualification the judgment of Mr. Moe when he calls this poem "positively magnificent in dynamic effect". To Mrs. Jordan is granted a natural poetic genius which few other amateurs can hope to parallel. Not many of our literary artists can so aptly fit words to weird or unusual passages, or so happily command all the advantages of alliteration and onomatopoeia. We believe that Mrs. Jordan's amateur eminence will eventually ripen into professional recognition. "Preachers in Politics", by Rev. James Thomas Self, is a long, thoughtful, and extremely well phrased essay against the descent of the ministry to the uncertain affairs of practical legislation. Dr. Self has a just idea of the dignity of the cloth; an idea which some clergymen of less conservative habits would do well to acquire. Very painful is the sight of the slang-mouthing "evangelist" who deserts his pulpit for the stump or the circus-tent. "Peace, Germany!", a poem by Maude Kingsbury Barton, constitutes an appeal to the present outlaw among nations. We feel, however, that it is only from London that Germany will eventually be convinced of the futility of her pseudo-Napoleonic enterprise. And when peace does come to Germany, it will be British-made peace! The structure of Mrs. Barton's poem is regular, and many of the images are very well selected. The worst misprints are those in the sixth stanza, where "in" is omitted before the word "pomp", and in the seventh stanza where "come" is printed as "came". In the biographical sketch entitled "Two Lives", Helen Hamilton draws a powerful moral from the contrasting but contemporaneous careers of Florence Nightingale and the ex-Empress Eugenie. "Class-Room Spirits I Have Known", an essay by Bessie Estelle Harvey, displays a sound comprehension of pedagogical principles. Two more poems by Mrs. Jordan conclude the issue. "The Time of Peach Tree Bloom" is the fourth of the "Songs from Walpi", three of which appeared in THE UNITED AMATEUR. "In a Garden" is a gem of delightful delicacy and ethereal elegance. It is indeed not without just cause that the author has, from the very first, held the distinction of being the most frequent poetical contributor in all amateur journalism.

The Cleveland Sun for June is the first number of an amateur newspaper edited by Anthony F. Moitoret, Edwin D. Harkins, and William J. Dowdell; and remarkable for an excellent heading, drawn by a staff artist of the Cleveland Leader. The present issue is printed in close imitation of the modern professional daily, and displays some interesting examples of "newspaper English". Mr. Moitoret is an old-time United man, now reentering the sphere of activity, and he is to be commended warmly both for his generous attitude toward the new members, and for his really magnanimous offer of aid to those desirous of issuing individual papers. His editorial hostility toward the Campbell amendment is, we believe, mistaken; yet is none the less founded on a praiseworthy desire to serve what he deems the best interests of the Association. Were Mr. Moitoret more in touch with the rising ideals of the newer United, he would realize the essential childishness of our "official business" as contrasted with the substantial solidity of our developing literature. Possibly the plan of Mr. Campbell, as experimentally tried during the present year, will alter Mr. Moitoret's present opinion. Taken altogether, we are not sure whether the Sun will prove beneficial or harmful to the United. We most assuredly need some sort of stimulus to activity, yet the comparatively crude atmosphere of newspaperdom is anything but inspiring in a literary society. We cannot descend from the ideals of Homer to those of Hearst without a distinct loss of quality, for which no possible gain in mere enthusiasm can compensate. Headlines such as "Columbus Bunch Boosting Paul" or "Hep Still Shows Pep", are positive affronts to the dignity of amateur journalism. There is room for an alert and informing news sheet in the United, yet we feel certain that the Sun must become a far more sedate and scholarly publication before it can adequately supply the need. At present, its garish rays dazzle and blind more than they illuminate; in a perusal of its pages we experience more of sunstroke than of sunshine. Of "The Best Sport Page In Amateurdom" we find it difficult to speak or write. Not since perusing the delectable lines of "Tom Crib's Memorial to Congress", by jovial old "Anacreon Moore", have we beheld such an invasion of prize-fight philosophy and race-track rhetoric. We learn with interest that a former United member named "Handsome Harry" has now graduated from literature to left field, and has, through sheer genius, risen from the lowly level of the ambitious author, to the exalted eminence of the classy slugger. Too proud to push the pen, he now swats the pill. Of such doth the dizzy quality of sempiternal Fame consist! Speaking without levity, we cannot but censure Mr. Dowdell's introduction of the ringside or ball-field spirit into an Association purporting to promote culture and lettered skill. Our members can scarcely be expected to place the Stygian-hued John Arthur Johnson, Esq., on a pedestal beside his well-known namesake Samuel; or calmly to compare the stinging wit of a Sidney Smith with the stinging fist-cuffs of a "Gunboat" Smith. In a word, what is suited to the street-corner is not always suited to the library, and the taste of the United is as yet but imperfectly attuned to the lyrical liltings of the pool-room Muse. It is both hard and unwise to take the "Best Sport Page" seriously. As a copy of "yellow" models it is a work of artistic verisimilitude; indeed, were Mr. Dowdell a somewhat older man, we might justly suspect a satirical intention on his part.

We trust that The Cleveland Sun may shine on without cloud or setting, though we must needs hope that the United's atmosphere of academic refinement will temper somewhat the scorching glare with which the bright orb has risen.

The Conservative for April opens with Andrew Francis Lockhart's melodious and attractive poem entitled "Benediction".

As a whole, this is possibly the best piece of verse which Mr. Lockhart has yet written; the sentiment is apt, if not entirely novel, whilst the technical construction is well-nigh faultless. Such expressions as "pearl-scarr'd" serve to exhibit the active and original quality of Mr. Lockhart's genius. "Another Endless Day", by Rheinhart Kleiner, is a beautiful and harmonious poetical protest against monotony. Much to be regretted is the misprint in line 3 of the third stanza, where the text should read:

"A love to thrill with new delight".

"April", by Winifred Virginia Jordan, is a seasonable and extremely tuneful poem whose imagery is of that dainty, sprightly sort which only Mrs. Jordan can create. "In Morven's Mead", also by Mrs. Jordan, contains an elusive and haunting suggestion of the unreal, in the author's characteristic style. "The Night Wind Bared My Heart" completes a highly meritorious trilogy. In justice to the author, it should be stated that the last of these three poems is, as here presented, merely a rough draft. Through our own reprehensible editorial oversight, the printer received this unpolished copy instead of the finished poem. The following emendations should be observed:

Stanza I, line 4, to read: "Awak'd my anguish'd sighs".
Stanza II, line 3, to read: "But Oh, from grief were prest".

"The Best Wine", by William de Ryee, is an earnestly introspective poem, well cast in iambic pentameter quatrains. "Ye Ballade of Patrick von Flynn" is a comic delineation of the cheap pseudo-Irish, England-hating agitators who have been so offensively noisy on this side of the Atlantic ever since the European war began, and particularly since the late riots in Dublin. This class, which so sadly misrepresents the loyal Irish people, deserves but little patience from Americans. Its members stutter childishly about "breaches of neutrality" every time a real American dares speak a word in favour of the Mother Country; yet they constantly violate neutrality themselves in their clumsy attempts to use the United States as a catspaw against England. The actual German propagandists have the excuse of patriotism for their race and Vaterland, but these Hibernian hybrids, neither good Irishmen nor good Americans, have no excuse whatever when they try to subvert the functions of the country which is giving them protection and livelihood.

The Conservative for July pays a deserved tribute to one of the most lucid and acute of our amateur essayists, by devoting the entire issue to his work. Henry Clapham McGavack, in "The American Proletariat versus England", exposes with admirable fearlessness the silly Anglophobic notions which a mistaken conception of the Revolution, and an ignorant Irish population, have diffused among our lower classes. It is seldom that an author ventures to speak so frankly on this subject, for the servile tendency of the times impels most writers and publishers to play the demagogue by essaying to feed the Irish masses with the anti-English swill they desire; but Mr. McGavack wields an independent pen, and records the truth without fear of the mobile vulgus and its shallow views. In power, directness, urbanity, and impartiality, Mr. McGavack cannot be excelled. He marshals his arguments without passion, bias, or circumlocution; piling proof upon proof until none but the most stubborn England-hater can fail to blush at the equal injustice and stupidity of those who malign that mighty empire to whose earth-wide circle of civilisation we all belong.

The Coyote for April is a Special English Number, dedicated to our soldier-member, George William Stokes of Newcastle-on-Tyne. The opening poem "To England", well exhibits the versatility of Mrs. Winifred V. Jordan, who here appears as a national panegyrist of commendable dignity and unexceptionable taste. The word at the beginning of the fourth line should read "Is" instead of "To". The short yet stirring metre is particularly well selected. "Active English Amateurs I Have Met", by Ernest A. Dench, is a rather good prose piece, though not without marks of careless composition. "The Vultur", by Henry J. Winterbone of the B. A. P. A., is a remarkably good story whose development and conclusion would do credit to a professional pen. We hope Mr. Winterbone may join the United, thereby giving American readers a more ample opportunity to enjoy his work. Editor William T. Harrington, whose prose is so rapidly acquiring polish and fluency, contributes two brief but able essays: "History Repeats" and "How Great Britain Keeps Her Empire". In "History Repeats", certain parts of the second sentence might well be amended a trifle in structure, to read thus: "it must be remembered that the first half was a series of victories for the South, and that only after the Battle of Gettysburg did the strength of the North begin to assert itself". This number of The Coyote is an exceedingly timely and tasteful tribute to our Mother Country, appearing at an hour when the air of America reeks with the illiterate anti-British trash of the "Sinn Fein" simpletons and Prussian propagandists.

Invictus for July is the second number of Mr. Paul J. Campbell's personal organ, and represents the strictly individual magazine in its most tasteful and elaborate form. Unimpeachably artistic in appearance, its contents justify the exterior; the whole constituting a publication of the first rank, wherein are joined the virtues both of the old and of the new schools of amateur journalism. Since Mr. Campbell is preeminently an essayist, it is to his dissertations on "The Pursuit of Happiness" and "The Age of Accuracy" which we turn most eagerly; and which in no way disappoint our high expectations. The first of these essays is a dispassionate survey of mankind in its futile but frantic scramble after that elusive but unreal sunbeam called "happiness". The author views the grimly amusing procession of human life with the genuine objective of an impartial spectator, and with commendable freedom from the hypocritical colouring of those who permit commonplace emotions and tenuous idealizings to obscure the less roseate but more substantial vision of their intellects. "The Age of Accuracy" presents an inspiring panorama of the evolution of Intellect, and of its increasing domination over the more elemental faculties of instinct and emotion. At the same time, much material for reflection is furnished, since it is obvious that the advance is necessarily confined to a comparatively small and select part of humanity. Instinct and emotion are still forces of tremendous magnitude, against which Reason wages an upward struggle of incredible bravery. Only the strong can escape the clutch of the primitive, wherefore there can be no successful social order which does not conform in its essentials to the blind impulses of the natural man or man-ape. We are in danger of overestimating the ascendancy and stability of Reason, for it is in reality the most fragile and rudimentary element in our mortal fabric. A heavy blow on certain parts of the skull, or a bullet in certain parts of the brain, can destroy in an instant all the accumulated intellect which aeons of heredity have bestowed, depressing the victim from the zenith of culture and refinement to a condition separated only by colour and contour from that of the negro or the gorilla; yet not all the edicts of the lawgiver, devices of the educator, measures of the reformer, or skill of the surgeon, can extirpate the ingrained instincts and seated superstitions of the average human animal.

The poetry of Mr. Campbell is represented in Invictus by three specimens, whose merit speaks well for the author's progress in the art. "The Sunshine Girl" is an amatory panegyric of no small skill and polish, though not strikingly novel in sentiment or expression. "German Kultur" is a scathing and virile indictment of the present enemies of humanity. The versification is bold, and in places rugged, whilst the imagery is appropriately grim and sardonic. Points which we might criticise are the repeated use of "civilization" as a word of only four syllables, and the archaic pronunciation of "drown-ed" as a dissyllable. This latter usage would be objectionable in verse of stately or conservative cast, but here grates upon the ear as an anachronism. The trenchant wit of the piece is well sustained, and brought out with particular force in the second and fourth stanzas. "The Major Strain" is without doubt the foremost verse of the issue. This is real poetry. The sustained rhyming, whereby each stanza contains only one rhyming sound, is pleasing and unusual. Mr. Campbell's comment on "Amateur Affairs" really deserves to be classed as an essay, for its thoughtful conclusions and intelligent analyses of human nature certainly draw it within the pale of true literature. The broad comprehension and continued love of amateur journalism here exhibited, are potent justifications of the author's practically unanimous election to the Presidency of the United. Invictus is one of the very foremost journals of the amateur world, and the only possible objection which can be raised against it, is its infrequency of appearance. It is the voice of a virile and vibrant personality who unites vigour of thought with urbanity of expression.

The Scot for May marks the advent of this highly entertaining and well conducted magazine to the United, and extends the northern frontier of amateur journalism to Bonnie Dundee, in Auld Scotland, the Land of Mountain and Flood. "Hidden Beauty", a poem in blank verse by R. M. Ingersley, opens the issue with a combination of lofty conceptions, vivid imagery, and regular structure. "England's Glory", by Clyde Dane, is a stirring tale of that fearless and self-sacrificing honour which has given to the Anglo-Saxon the supremacy of the world. It would be in bad taste to cavil at slight technical imperfections or instances of triteness when considering so earnest and glowing a delineation of the British character; the noblest human type ever moulded by the Creator. "Oh Rose, Red Rose!" is a tuneful little lyric by Winifred V. Jordan, whose work is never too brief to be pleasing, or too long to be absorbing. "Clemency versus Frightfulness", by William T. Harrington, is a thoughtful and lucid exposition of the British governmental ideal of lenient justice; an ideal whose practical success has vividly demonstrated its thorough soundness. "At Last", by Muriel Wilson, is a blank verse poem of much merit. "Do You Remember?", by the late Lieut. Roy Arthur Thackara, R. N., is a delicate sketch possessing the additional interest of coming from the pen of one who has now given his life for King and Country; the author having gone down with H. M. S. India. "A Battle with the Sea", a sketch by Midshipman Ernest L. McKeag, exhibits descriptive power of no common order, yet might well have a less abrupt conclusion. "To Some One", by Margaret Trafford, is a poem in dactylic measure, dedicated to the women of Britain. The sentiment is noble, and the encomium well bestowed, though the metre could be improved in polish. "Gum", by Henry J. Winterbone, is a delightfully humorous sketch. It is evident that those who depreciate British humour must have taken pains to avoid its perusal, since it has a quietly pungent quality seldom found save among Anglo-Saxons. Personally, we believe that the summit of clumsy pseudo-jocoseness is attained by the average "comic" supplement of the Hearst Sunday papers. These, and not the British press, present the pathetic spectacle of utter inanity and repulsive grotesqueness without the faintest redeeming touch of genuine comedy, legitimate satire, or refined humour. "Life's Voyage", by Matthew Hilson, is a poem of great attractiveness, though of scarcely impeccable construction. Concerning the expression "tempests wild do roar", we must reiterate the advice of Mr. Pope, who condemned the expletive "do", "doth", or "did" as a "feeble aid". Such usage has, in fact, been in bad taste ever since the reign of Queen Anne; Dryden being the last bard in whom we need not censure the practice. Mr. McColl's editorials are brief but informing. He may well be congratulated on his work as a publisher, and he certainly deserves as hearty a welcome as the United can give.

The Scot for June is a "British Old-Timers' Number", confined wholly to the work of the senior amateur journalists of the Mother Country. Edward F. Herdman, to whom this number is dedicated, opens the issue with a religious poem entitled "Life", which compares well with the bulk of current religious verse. Mr. Herdman also contributes one of several prose essays on amateur journalism, in which the various authors view our field of endeavor from similar angles. "A Song of a Sailor", by R. D. Roosemale-Cocq, exhibits buoyant animation, and considerable ease in the handling of a rollicking measure. The internal rhymes are for the most part well introduced, though greater uniformity might have been used in their distribution. The first two lines have none. In the last stanza there are two lines whose metre seems deficient, but being conscious of the uncertainties of the secretarial and typographical arts, we suspend judgment on the author. "A Song of Cheer", by Alfred H. Pearce, is an optimistic ode of real merit. The last line furnishes a particularly pleasing example of sprightly wit. Mr. Gavin T. McColl is sensible and perspicuous in all his editorial utterances. His work in issuing one of the only two regular monthly magazines in amateurdom has already brought him to prominence, though his connexion with the press associations is still new.

THE UNITED AMATEUR for June is given over largely to critical and official matter, though two pieces of verse serve to vary

97

the monotony. "Content", from our own pen, is an answer to Mr. Rheinhart Kleiner's delightful poem in the April Conservative, entitled "Another Endless Day". The lines are notable chiefly on account of some fearful and wonderful typographical errors. In the fourth line "sublime" should read "sublimer". In the eighth line there should be no apostrophe in the word "stars". In the second column, eleventh line from the end, there should be no apostrophe in the word "fathers", and finally, in the ninth line from the end, "hollow'd" should read "hallow'd". "The Swing in the Great Oak Tree", by Mrs. Agnes Richmond Arnold, is a reminiscent poem whose measure is as swinging as its subject, and whose atmosphere is pleasantly rural. There are flaws in the metre, and irregularities in the rhyming arrangement, but the spirit of the whole rises blithesomely above such slight technical matters. Editor Schilling's column is to be praised for its dignified style, and endorsed for its sound opinions.

The Woodbee for July is an attractive and important contribution to the history of amateur journalism; since it is entirely devoted to the biographies of the gifted Columbus amateurs, and to the annals of their brilliant local organization. The Woodbees undoubtedly form the most active and representative adult club in the United; to which only the Appleton Club, representing the juvenile Muse, may justly be compared. The Woodbees are typical, in a sense, of all that is best in the entire association. They are pursuing courses of serious literary study, producing a regularly issued magazine of unfailing merit and good taste, working enthusiastically for the welfare and expansion of the United, and leading or following every worthy or progressive movement in amateur politics. They reflect credit upon themselves, their society, the Association, and amateur journalism as a whole. The delightful biographical article which occupies the major portion of the current Woodbee is unsigned; but deserves particular praise, whoever the author may be. The various characters are well displayed, and their pleasing qualities and manifold activities well exhibited.

Mr. Fritter's editorials are as usual timely, lucid, and sensible. His advocacy of the Campbell Amendment is to be applauded; and will, we trust, be justified by the year's trial which that measure is now undergoing. The present issue marks the conclusion of Mr. Fritter's term as editor. He has given the amateur public a creditable volume, and is entitled to the gratitude of every member of our Association. A final word of praise is due the excellent group photograph of the Woodbees which forms the frontispiece of the magazine. Added to the biographical matter, it completes a

thoroughly commendable introduction to a thoroughly
commendable body of literary workers.

H. P. LOVECRAFT,
Chairman

THE UNITED AMATEUR

OFFICIAL ORGAN OF THE UNITED AMATEUR PRESS ASSOCIATION

Volume XVI GEORGETOWN, ILL., NOVEMBER, 1916 Number 4

THE ALCHEMIST

High up, crowning the grassy summit of a swelling mound
whose sides are wooded near the base with the gnarled trees of the
primeval forest, stands the old chateau of my ancestors. For
centuries its lofty battlements have frowned down upon the wild
and rugged countryside about, serving as a home and stronghold for
the proud house whose honoured line is older even than the moss-
grown castle walls. These ancient turrets, stained by the storms of
generations and crumbling under the slow yet mighty pressure of
time, formed in the ages of feudalism one of the most dreaded and
formidable fortresses in all France. From its machicolated parapets
and mounted battlements Barons, Counts, and even Kings had been
defied, yet never had its spacious halls resounded to the footstep of
the invader.

But since those glorious years all is changed. A poverty but
little above the level of dire want, together with a pride of name that
forbids its alleviation by the pursuits of commercial life, have
prevented the scions of our line from maintaining their estates in
pristine splendour; and the falling stones of the walls, the
overgrown vegetation in the parks, the dry and dusty moat, the ill-
paved courtyards, and toppling towers without, as well as the
sagging floors, the worm-eaten wainscots, and the faded tapestries
within, all tell a gloomy tale of fallen grandeur. As the ages passed,
first one, then another of the four great turrets were left to ruin,

until at last but a single tower housed the sadly reduced descendants of the once mighty lords of the estate.

It was in one of the vast and gloomy chambers of this remaining tower that I, Antoine, last of the unhappy and accursed Comtes de C——, first saw the light of day, ninety long years ago. Within these walls, and amongst the dark and shadowy forests, the wild ravines and grottoes of the hillside below, were spent the first years of my troubled life. My parents I never knew. My father had been killed at the age of thirty-two, a month before I was born, by the fall of a stone somehow dislodged from one of the deserted parapets of the castle, and my mother having died at my birth, my care and education devolved solely upon one remaining servitor, an old and trusted man of considerable intelligence, whose name I remember as Pierre. I was an only child, and the lack of companionship which this fact entailed upon me was augmented by the strange care exercised by my aged guardian in excluding me from the society of the peasant children whose abodes were scattered here and there upon the plains that surround the base of the hill. At the time, Pierre said that this restriction was imposed upon me because my noble birth placed me above association with such plebeian company. Now I know that its real object was to keep from my ears the idle tales of the dread curse upon our line, that were nightly told and magnified by the simple tenantry as they conversed in hushed accents in the glow of their cottage hearths.

Thus isolated, and thrown upon my own resources, I spent the hours of my childhood in poring over the ancient tomes that filled the shadow-haunted library of the chateau, and in roaming without aim or purpose through the perpetual dusk of the spectral wood that clothes the sides of the hill near its foot. It was perhaps an effect of such surroundings that my mind early acquired a shade of melancholy. Those studies and pursuits which partake of the dark and occult in nature most strongly claimed my attention.

Of my own race I was permitted to learn singularly little, yet what small knowledge of it I was able to gain, seemed to depress me much. Perhaps it was at first only the manifest reluctance of my old preceptor to discuss with me my paternal ancestry that gave rise to the terror which I ever felt at the mention of my great house, yet as I grew out of childhood, I was able to piece together disconnected fragments of discourse, let slip from the unwilling tongue which had begun to falter in approaching senility, that had a sort of relation to a certain circumstance which I had always deemed strange, but which now became dimly terrible. The circumstance to which I allude is the early age at which all the Comtes of my line had met their end. Whilst I had hitherto considered this but a natural attribute of a family of short-lived men, I afterward pondered long upon these premature deaths, and began to connect them with the wanderings of the old man, who often spoke of a curse which for centuries had prevented the lives of the holders of my title from much exceeding the span of thirty-two years. Upon my twenty-first birthday, the aged Pierre gave to me a family document which he said had for many generations been handed down from father to son, and continued by each possessor. Its contents were of the most startling nature, and its perusal confirmed the gravest of my apprehensions. At this time, my belief in the supernatural was firm and deep-seated, else I should have dismissed with scorn the incredible narrative unfolded before my eyes.

The paper carried me back to the days of the thirteenth century, when the old castle in which I sat had been a feared and impregnable fortress. It told of a certain ancient man who had once dwelt on our estates, a person of no small accomplishments, though little above the rank of peasant; by name, Michel, usually designated by the surname of Mauvais, the Evil, on account of his sinister reputation. He had studied beyond the custom of his kind, seeking such things as the Philosopher's Stone, or the Elixir of Eternal Life, and was reputed wise in the terrible secrets of Black Magic and Alchemy. Michel Mauvais had one son, named Charles, a youth as proficient as himself in the hidden arts, and who had therefore been called Le Sorcier, or the Wizard. This pair, shunned by all honest folk, were suspected of the most hideous practices. Old Michel was said to have burnt his wife alive as a sacrifice to the Devil, and the unaccountable disappearances of many small peasant children were laid at the dreaded door of these two. Yet through the dark natures of the father and the son ran one redeeming ray of humanity; the evil old man loved his offspring with fierce intensity, whilst the youth had for his parent a more than filial affection.

One night the castle on the hill was thrown into the wildest confusion by the vanishment of young Godfrey, son to Henri, the Comte. A searching party, headed by the frantic father, invaded the cottage of the sorcerers and there came upon old Michel Mauvais, busy over a huge and violently boiling cauldron. Without certain cause, in the ungoverned madness of fury and despair, the Comte laid hands on the aged wizard, and ere he released his murderous hold his victim was no more. Meanwhile joyful servants were proclaiming aloud the finding of young Godfrey in a distant and unused chamber of the great edifice, telling too late that poor Michel had been killed in vain. As the Comte and his associates turned away from the lowly abode of the alchemists, the form of Charles Le Sorcier appeared through the trees. The excited chatter

101

of the menials standing about told him what had occurred, yet he seemed at first unmoved at his father's fate. Then, slowly advancing to meet the Comte, he pronounced in dull yet terrible accents the curse that ever afterward haunted the house of C——.

> "May ne'er a noble of thy murd'rous line
> Survive to reach a greater age than thine!"

spake he, when, suddenly leaping backwards into the black wood, he drew from his tunic a phial of colourless liquid which he threw in the face of his father's slayer as he disappeared behind the inky curtain of the night. The Comte died without utterance, and was buried the next day, but little more than two and thirty years from the hour of his birth. No trace of the assassin could be found, though relentless bands of peasants scoured the neighboring woods and the meadow-land around the hill.

Thus time and the want of a reminder dulled the memory of the curse in the minds of the late Comte's family, so that when Godfrey, innocent cause of the whole tragedy and now bearing the title, was killed by an arrow whilst hunting, at the age of thirty-two, there were no thoughts save those of grief at his demise. But when, years afterward, the next young Comte, Robert by name, was found dead in a nearby field from no apparent cause, the peasants told in whispers that their seigneur had but lately passed his thirty-second birthday when surprised by early death. Louis, son to Robert, was found drowned in the moat at the same fateful age, and thus down through the centuries ran the ominous chronicle; Henris, Roberts, Antoines, and Armands snatched from happy and virtuous lives when a little below the age of their unfortunate ancestor at his murder.

That I had left at most but eleven years of further existence was made certain to me by the words which I read. My life, previously held at small value, now became dearer to me each day, as I delved deeper and deeper into the mysteries of the hidden world of black magic. Isolated as I was, modern science had produced no impression upon me, and I laboured as in the Middle Ages, as wrapt as had been old Michel and young Charles themselves in the acquisition of demonological and alchemical learning. Yet read as I might, in no manner could I account for the strange curse upon my line. In unusually rational moments, I would even go so far as to seek a natural explanation, attributing the early deaths of my ancestors to the sinister Charles Le Sorcier and his heirs; yet having found upon careful inquiry that there were no known descendants of the alchemist, I would fall back to my occult

102

studies, and once more endeavour to find a spell that would release my house from its terrible burden. Upon one thing I was absolutely resolved. I should never wed, for since no other branches of my family were in existence, I might thus end the curse with myself.

As I drew near the age of thirty, old Pierre was called to the land beyond. Alone I buried him beneath the stones of the courtyard about which he had loved to wander in life. Thus was I left to ponder on myself as the only human creature within the great fortress, and in my utter solitude my mind began to cease its vain protest against the impending doom, to become almost reconciled to the fate which so many of my ancestors had met. Much of my time was now occupied in the exploration of the ruined and abandoned halls and towers of the old chateau, which in youth fear had caused me to shun, and some of which old Pierre had once told me had not been trodden by human foot for over four centuries. Strange and awsome were many of the objects I encountered. Furniture, covered by the dust of ages and crumbling with the rot of long dampness met my eyes. Cobwebs in a profusion never before seen by me were spun everywhere, and huge bats flapped their bony and uncanny wings on all sides of the otherwise untenanted gloom.

Of my exact age, even down to days and hours, I kept a most careful record, for each movement of the pendulum of the massive clock in the library tolled off so much more of my doomed existence. At length I approached that time which I had so long viewed with apprehension. Since most of my ancestors had been seized some little while before they reached the exact age of the Comte Henri at his end, I was every moment on the watch for the coming of the unknown death. In what strange form the curse should overtake me, I knew not; but I was resolved at least that it should not find me a cowardly or a passive victim. With new vigour I applied myself to my examination of the old chateau and its contents.

It was upon one of the longest of all my excursions of discovery in the deserted portion of the castle, less than a week before that fatal hour which I felt must mark the utmost limit of my stay on earth, beyond which I could have not even the slightest hope of continuing to draw breath, that I came upon the culminating event of my whole life. I had spent the better part of the morning in climbing up and down half ruined staircases in one of the most dilapidated of the ancient turrets. As the afternoon progressed, I sought the lower levels, descending into what appeared to be either a mediaeval place of confinement, or a more recently excavated storehouse for gunpowder. As I slowly traversed the nitre-encrusted passageway at the foot of the last staircase, the paving became very damp, and soon I saw by the light of my flickering torch that a

103

blank, water-stained wall impeded my journey. Turning to retrace my steps, my eye fell upon a small trap-door with a ring, which lay directly beneath my feet. Pausing, I succeeded with difficulty in raising it, whereupon there was revealed a black aperture, exhaling noxious fumes which caused my torch to sputter, and disclosing in the unsteady glare the top of a flight of stone steps. As soon as the torch, which I lowered into the repellent depths, burned freely and steadily, I commenced my descent. The steps were many, and led to a narrow stone-flagged passage which I knew must be far underground. This passage proved of great length, and terminated in a massive oaken door, dripping with the moisture of the place, and stoutly resisting all my attempts to open it. Ceasing after a time my efforts in this direction, I had proceeded back some distance toward the steps, when there suddenly fell to my experience one of the most profound and maddening shocks capable of reception by the human mind. Without warning, I heard the heavy door behind me creak slowly open upon its rusted hinges. My immediate sensations are incapable of analysis. To be confronted in a place as thoroughly deserted as I had deemed the old castle with evidence of the presence of man or spirit, produced in my brain a horror of the most acute description. When at last I turned and faced the seat of the sound, my eyes must have started from their orbits at the sight that they beheld. There in the ancient Gothic doorway stood a human figure. It was that of a man clad in a skull-cap and long mediaeval tunic of dark colour. His long hair and flowing beard were of a terrible and intense black hue, and of incredible profusion. His forehead, high beyond the usual dimensions; his cheeks, deep sunken and heavily lined with wrinkles; and his hands, long, claw-like and gnarled, were of such a deathly, marble-like whiteness as I have never elsewhere seen in man. His figure, lean to the proportions of a skeleton, was strangely bent and almost lost within the voluminous folds of his peculiar garment. But strangest of all were his eyes; twin caves of abysmal blackness; profound in expression of understanding, yet inhuman in degree of wickedness. These were now fixed upon me, piercing my soul with their hatred, and rooting me to the spot whereon I stood. At last the figure spoke in a rumbling voice that chilled me through with its dull hollowness and latent malevolence. The language in which the discourse was clothed was that debased form of Latin in use amongst the more learned men of the Middle Ages, and made familiar to me by my prolonged researches into the works of the old alchemists and demonologists. The apparition spoke of the curse which had hovered over my house, told me of my coming end, dwelt on the wrong perpetrated by my ancestor against old Michel Mauvais, and

104

gloated over the revenge of Charles Le Sorcier. He told me how the young Charles had escaped into the night, returning in after years to kill Godfrey the heir with an arrow just as he approached the age which had been his father's at his assassination; how he had secretly returned to the estate and established himself, unknown, in the even then deserted subterranean chamber whose doorway now framed the hideous narrator; how he had seized Robert, son of Godfrey, in a field, forced poison down his throat and left him to die at the age of thirty-two, thus maintaining the foul provisions of his vengeful curse. At this point I was left to imagine the solution of the greatest mystery of all, how the curse had been fulfilled since that time when Charles Le Sorcier must in the course of nature have died, for the man digressed into an account of the deep alchemical studies of the two wizards, father and son, speaking most particularly of the researches of Charles Le Sorcier concerning the elixir which should grant to him who partook of it eternal life and youth.

His enthusiasm had seemed for the moment to remove from his terrible eyes the hatred that had at first so haunted them, but suddenly the fiendish glare returned, and with a shocking sound like the hissing of a serpent, the stranger raised a glass phial with the evident intent of ending my life as had Charles Le Sorcier, six hundred years before, ended that of my ancestor. Prompted by some preserving instinct of self-defense, I broke through the spell that had hitherto held me immovable, and flung my now dying torch at the creature who menaced my existence. I heard the phial break harmlessly against the stones of the passage as the tunic of the strange man caught fire and lit the horrid scene with a ghastly radiance. The shriek of fright and impotent malice emitted by the would-be assassin proved too much for my already shaken nerves, and I fell prone upon the slimy floor in a total faint.

When at last my senses returned, all was frightfully dark, and my mind remembering what had occurred, shrank from the idea of beholding more; yet curiosity overmastered all. Who, I asked myself, was this man of evil, and how came he within the castle walls? Why should he seek to avenge the death of poor Michel Mauvais, and how had the curse been carried on through all the long centuries since the time of Charles Le Sorcier? The dread of years was lifted off my shoulders, for I knew that he whom I had felled was the source of all my danger from the curse; and now that I was free, I burned with the desire to learn more of the sinister thing which had haunted my line for centuries, and made of my own youth one long-continued nightmare. Determined upon further exploration, I felt in my pockets for flint and steel, and lit the unused torch which I had with me. First of all, the new light revealed the distorted and blackened form of the mysterious stranger. The hideous eyes were now closed. Disliking the sight, I turned away and entered the chamber beyond the Gothic door. Here I found what seemed much like an alchemist's laboratory. In one corner was an immense pile of a shining yellow metal that sparkled gorgeously in the light of the torch. It may have been gold, but I did not pause to examine it, for I was strangely affected by that which I had undergone. At the farther end of the apartment was an opening leading out into one of the many wild ravines of the dark hillside forest. Filled with wonder, yet now realizing how the man had obtained access to the chateau, I proceeded to return. I had intended to pass by the remains of the stranger with averted face, but as I approached the body, I seemed to hear emanating from it a faint sound, as though life were not yet wholly extinct. Aghast, I turned to examine the charred and shrivelled figure on the floor.

Then all at once the horrible eyes, blacker even than the seared face in which they were set, opened wide with an expression which I was unable to interpret. The cracked lips tried to frame words which I could not well understand. Once I caught the name of Charles Le Sorcier, and again I fancied that the words "years" and "curse" issued from the twisted mouth. Still I was at a loss to gather the purport of his disconnected speech. At my evident ignorance of his meaning, the pitchy eyes once more flashed malevolently at me, until, helpless as I saw my opponent to be, I trembled as I watched him.

Suddenly the wretch, animated with his last burst of strength, raised his hideous head from the damp and sunken pavement. Then, as I remained, paralyzed with fear, he found his voice and in his dying breath screamed forth those words which have ever afterward haunted my days and my nights. "Fool," he shrieked, "can you not guess my secret? Have you no brain whereby you may recognize the will which has through six long centuries fulfilled the dreadful curse upon your house? Have I not told you of the great elixir of eternal life? Know you not how the secret of Alchemy was solved? I tell you, it is I! I! I! that have lived for six hundred years to maintain my revenge, FOR I AM CHARLES LE SORCIER!"

H. P. LOVECRAFT

DEPARTMENT OF PUBLIC CRITICISM

The Conservative for October opens with Miss Olive G. Owen's tuneful lines on "The Mocking Bird." Of the quality of Miss Owen's poetry it is scarce necessary to speak; be it sufficient to say that the present piece ranks among her best. In the intense fervour of the sentiment, and the felicitous choice of the imagery, the touch of the born poet is alike shown. Through an almost inexcusable editorial mistake of our own, the first word of this poem is erroneously rendered. Line 1 should read:

"Where Southern moonlight softly falls."

"Old England and the Hyphen" is an attempt of the present critic to demonstrate why relations between the United States and Mother England must necessarily be closer than those between the States and any of the really foreign powers. So patent and so inevitable is the essential unity of the Anglo-Saxon world that such an essay as this ought really to be superfluous; but its practical justification is found in the silly clamour of those Anglophobes who are unfortunately permitted to reside within our borders. "Insomnia," by Winifred Virginia Jordan, is a remarkable piece of verse whose dark turns of fancy are almost worthy of a Poe. The grotesque tropes, the cleverly distorted images, the bizarre atmosphere, and ingeniously sinister repetitions all unite to produce one of the season's most notable poems. Each of the stanzas is vibrant with the hideous, racking turmoil of the insomnious mind. "Prussianism," by William Thomas Harrington, is a concise and lucid essay on a timely subject, reviewing ably the cause and responsibility of the present war. It is especially valuable at this season of incoherent peace discussion, for it explodes very effectively that vague, brainless "neutrality" which prompts certain pro-German pacifists to cry for peace before the normal and final settlement of Europe's troubles shall have been attained by the permanent annihilation of the Prussian military machine. "Twilight," by Chester Pierce Munroe, is a beautiful bit of poetic fancy and stately phraseology. Mr. Munroe, a Rhode Islander transplanted to the mountains of North Carolina, is acquiring all the grace and delicacy of the native Southern bard, while retaining that happy conservatism of expression which distinguishes his work from that of most contemporary poets. Callously modern indeed must be he who would wish Mr. Munroe's quaintly euphonious lines transmuted into the irritatingly abrupt and barren phraseology of the day. "The Bond Invincible," by David H. Whittier, is a short story of great power and skilful construction, suggesting Poe's "Ligeia" in its central theme. The plot is developed with much dexterity, and the climax comes so forcibly and unexpectedly upon the reader, that one cannot but admire Mr. Whittier's mastery of technique. Certain overnice critics may possibly object to the tale, as containing incidents which no one survives to relate; but when we reflect that Poe has similarly written a story without survivors, ("The Masque of the Red Death") we can afford to applaud without reservation. The complete absence of slang and of doubtful grammar recommends this tale as a model to other amateur fiction-writers. "Respite" is a lachrymose lament in five stanzas by the present critic. The metre is regular, which is perhaps some excuse for its creation and publication. "By the Waters of the Brook," by Rev. Eugene B. Kuntz, D. D., is one of the noblest amateur poems of the year. While the casual reader may find in the long heptameter lines a want of sing-song facility; the true lover of the Nine pauses in admiration at the deep flowing nobility of the rhyme. The quick rippling of the brook is duplicated within each line, rather than from line to line. The imagery and phraseology are of the sort which only Dr. Kuntz can fashion, and are rich in that exalted pantheism of fancy which comes to him who knows Nature in her wilder and more rugged moods and aspects. "The Pool," by Winifred Virginia Jordan, contains an elusive hint of the terrible and the supernatural which gives it high rank as poetry. Mrs. Jordan has two distinct, yet related, styles in verse. One of these mirrors all the joy and buoyant happiness of life, whilst the other reflects that undertone of grimness which is sometimes felt through the exterior of things. The kinship betwixt these styles lies in their essentially fanciful character, as distinguished from the tiresomely commonplace realism of the average modern rhymester. Another bit of sinister psychology in verse is "The Unknown," by Elizabeth Berkeley. Mrs. Berkeley's style is less restrained than that of Mrs. Jordan, and presents a picture of stark, meaningless horror, the like of which is not often seen in the amateur press. It is difficult to pass upon the actual merit of so peculiar a production, but we will venture the opinion that the use of italics, or heavy-faced type, is not desirable. The author should be able to bring out all needed emphasis by words, not printer's devices. The issue concludes with "Inspiration," a poem by Lewis Theobald, Jun. The form and rhythm of this piece are quite satisfactory, but the insipidity of the sentiment leaves much to be desired. The whole poem savours too much of the current magazine style.

The Coyote for October is made notable by Editor Harrington's thoughtful and well compiled article on "Worldwide Prohibition," wherein an extremely important step in the world's progress is truthfully chronicled. That legislation against alcohol is spreading rapidly throughout civilization, is something which not even the densest champions of "personal liberty" can deny. The utter emptiness of all arguments in behalf of strong drink is made doubly apparent by the swift prohibitory enactments of the European nations when confronted by the emergencies of war, and by the abolition of liquor in a large number of American states for purely practical reasons. All these things point to a general recognition of liquor as a foe to governmental and industrial welfare. Mr. Harrington's style in this essay is clear and in most respects commendable; though certain passages might gain force and dignity through a less colloquial manner. In particular, we must protest against the repeated use of the vulgarism booze, a word probably brought into public favour by the new school of gutter evangelism, whose chief exponent is the Reverend William Sunday. The verb to booze, boose, or bouse, meaning "to drink immoderately," and the adjective boozy, boosy, or bousy, meaning "drunken," are by no means new to our language, Dryden having written the form bousy in some of his verses; but booze as a noun signifying "liquor" is certainly too vulgar a word for constant employment in any formal literary composition. Another essay of Mr. Harrington's is "The Divine Book," a plea for the restoration of the Bible as a source of popular reading and arbiter of moral conduct. Whatever may be the opinion of the searching critic regarding the place of the Scriptures in the world of fact, it is undeniably true that a closer study of the revered volume, and a stricter adherence to its best precepts, would do much toward mending the faults of a loose age. We have yet to find a more efficacious means of imparting virtue and contentment of heart to the masses of mankind. "Pioneers of New England," an article by Alice M. Hamlet, gives much interesting information concerning the sturdy settlers of New Hampshire and Vermont. In the unyielding struggles of these unsung heroes against the sting of hardship and the asperity of primeval Nature, we may discern more than a trace of that divine fire of conquest which has made the Anglo-Saxon the empire builder of all the ages. In Mr. Harrington's editorial column there is much discussion of a proposed "International Amateur Press Association," but we fail to perceive why such an innovation is needed, now that the United has opened itself unreservedly to residents of all the countries of the globe.

Merry Minutes for November is a clever publication of semi-professional character, edited by Miss Margaret Trafford of London, and containing a pleasant variety of prose, verses, and puzzles. "King of the Nursery Realm," by Margaret Mahon, is a smooth and musical piece of juvenile verse which excels in correctness of form rather than in novelty of thought.

"Bards and Minstrels, and The Augustan Age," by Beryl Mappin, is the second of a series of articles on English literature and its classical foundations. The erudition and enthusiasm displayed in this essay speak well for the future of the authoress, though certain faults of style and construction demand correction. Careful grammatical study would eliminate from Miss Mappin's style such solecisms as the use of like for as, whilst greater attention to the precepts of rhetoric would prevent the construction of such awkward sentences as the following: "The same if one is reading an interesting book, can one not see all that is happening there as clearly with one's inner eyes as if it was all taking place before one, and viewed with one's outer ones?" This passage is not only wanting in coherence and correctness of syntax, but is exceedingly clumsy through redundancy of statement, and repetition of the word one. This word, though essential to colloquial diction, becomes very tiresome when used to excess; and should be avoided in many cases through judicious transpositions of the text. The following is a revised version of the sentence quoted above: "Thus, in reading an interesting book, can one not see with the inner eyes all that is happening there, as clearly as if it were taking place in reality before the outer eyes?" Other parts of the essay require similar revision. Concerning the development of the whole, we must needs question the unity of the topics. Whilst the connecting thread is rather evident after a second or third perusal, the cursory reader is apt to become puzzled over the skips from the Graeco-Roman world to the early Saxon kingdoms, and thence to the dawn of our language amongst the Anglo-Normans. What Miss Mappin evidently wishes to bring out, is that the sources of English literature are twofold; being on the one hand the polished classics of antiquity, inspired by Greece, amplified and diffused by Rome, preserved by France, and brought to England by the Normans; and on the other hand the crude but virile products of our Saxon ancestors, brought from the uncivilized forests of the continent or written after the settlement in Britain. From this union of Graeco-Roman classicism with native Anglo-Saxon vitality springs the unquestioned supremacy of English literature. Assiduous devotion to the mastery of rhetoric, and the habit of constructing logical synopses before writing the text of articles would enable Miss Mappin to utilise her knowledge of literary history in a manner truly worthy of its depth. "Trinidad and its People," by "F. E. M. Hercules," exhibits a somewhat maturer style, and forms a very interesting piece of geographical description. "The Pursuit of the Innocent," is a serial story by Miss Trafford, and though only a small part of it is printed in the current issue, we judge that it derives its general atmosphere from the popular "thrillers" of the day. The dialogue is not wholly awkward, but there is a noticeable want of proportion in the development of the narrative. Miss Trafford would probably profit by a more faithful study of the standard novelists, and a more complete avoidance of the type of fiction found in modern weekly periodicals such as Answers or Tit-Bits. Those who feel impelled to introduce stirring adventure into their tales, can do so without sacrifice of excitement and interest by following really classic writers like Poe and Stevenson; or semi-standard authors like Sir A. Conan Doyle. The puzzles propounded by Miss Hillman are quite interesting, though matter of this sort is scarcely to be included within the domain of pure literature. We guess airship as the answer to the first one, but have not space to record our speculations concerning the second. Merry Minutes closes with the following poem by Master Randolph Trafford, a very young author:

> "Once upon a time, there was a little boy,
>   And, if you please, he went to school;
> That little boy, he always would annoy,
>   And found at school a very nasty rule."

Without undue flattery to Master Trafford, we may conclusively state that we deem his poem a great deal better than most of the vers libre effusions which so many of his elders are perpetrating nowadays!

The Scot for July is devoted completely to the work of the feminine amateurs of the United States, and is announced by its editor as an "American 'Petticoat' Number"; a title which might possibly bear replacement by something rather less colloquial. "Over the Edge of the World," a poem by Olive G. Owen, is correct in construction and appropriate in sentiment, deriving much force from the continued repetition of the first line. "In Morven's Mead," by Winifred V. Jordan, is one of a series of fanciful poems all bearing the same title. The present verses show all the charm and delicacy which characterise the whole. "Patience—A Woman's Virtue," is one of Mrs. Eloise N. Griffith's thoughtful moral essays, and is as commendable for its precepts as for its pure style. "His Flapper," by Edna von der Heide, is a clever piece of trochaic verse in Cockney dialect, which seems, so far as an American critic can judge, to possess a very vivid touch of local colour. "An Eye for an Eye," by the same authoress, seems vaguely familiar, having possibly been published in the amateur press before. If so, it is well worthy of republication. "Women and Snakes," a sketch by Eleanor J. Barnhart, is not a misogynistical attempt at comparison, but a theory regarding the particular fear with which the former are popularly supposed to regard the latter. Whilst Miss Barnhart writes with the bravery of the true scientist, we are constrained to remark that a certain dislike of snakes, mice, and insects is a very real thing; not only amongst the fair, but equally amongst those sterner masculine souls who would stoutly deny it if questioned. It is an atavistical fear, surviving from primitive ages when the venomous qualities of reptiles, insects, and the like, made their quick avoidance necessary to uninstructed man. "Be Tolerant," by Winifred V. Jordan, is a didactic poem of the sort formerly published in The Symphony. While it does not possess in fullest measure the grace and facility observed in Mrs. Jordan's more characteristic work; it is nevertheless correct and melodious, easily equalling most poetry of its kind. Mr. McColl's editorial column, the only masculine feature of the issue, contains a very noble tribute to the two soldier cousins of Miss von der Heide, who have laid down their lives for the cause of England and the right. From such men springs the glory of Britannia.

The Scot for August opens with Winifred V. Jordan's tuneful lines, "If You but Smile," whose inspiration and construction are alike of no mean order. "Hoary Kent," by Benjamin Winskill, is an exquisite sketch of a region where the past still lives. In an age of turmoil and unrest, it is a comfort to think that in one spot, at least, the destroying claws of Time have left no scars. There lie the scenes dear to every son and grandson of Britain; there are bodied forth the eternal and unchanging traditions that place above the rest of the world

"This precious stone set in the silver sea—
This blessed plot, this earth, this realm, this England."

"Meditation of a Scottish Queen on Imprisonment," a poem by Margaret Trafford, contains noble passages, but is marred by defective technique. Passing over the use of the expletives do and doth as legitimate archaisms in this case, we must call attention to some awkward phraseology, and to the roughness of certain lines, which have either too few or too many syllables. The very first line of the poem requires contraction, which might be accomplished by substituting hapless for unhappy. Line 8 would read better if thus amended:

"I would that death might come and me release."

The final line of the first stanza lacks a syllable, which might be supplied by replacing vile with hateful. The second stanza will pass as it is, but the entire remainder of the poem requires alteration, since but two of the lines are of normal decasyllabic length. The following is rough revision, though we have not attempted to build the poetry anew:

Oh! could I breathe again dear Scotland's air;
Behold once more her stately mountains high,
Thence view the wide expanse of azure sky,
Instead of these perpetual walls so bare!

Could I but see the grouse upon the moor,
Or pluck again the beauteous heather bell!
Freedom I know not in this dismal cell,
As I my anguish from my heart outpour.

My Scotland! know'st thou thy poor Queen's distress,
And canst thou hear my wailing and my woe?
May the soft wind that o'er thy hills doth blow
Waft thee these thoughts, that I cannot suppress!

"Six Cylinder Happiness," a brief essay by William J. Dowdell, presents in ingeniously pleasing style a precept not entirely new amongst philosophers. Mr. Dowdell's skill with the pen is very considerable, particularly when he ventures outside the domain of slang. We should like to suggest a slightly less colloquial title for this piece, such as "Real Happiness." "For Right and Liberty," a poem by Matthew Hilson, is commendable in sentiment and clever in construction, but lacks perfection in several details of phraseology. In the third line of the third stanza the word ruinous must be replaced by a true dissyllable, preferably ruin'd. "For Their Country," a short story by Margaret Trafford, is vivid in plot and truly heroic in moral, but somewhat deficient in technique, particularly at the beginning. Miss Trafford should use care in moulding long sentences, and should avoid the employment of abbreviations like etc. in the midst of narrative text. "That Sunny Smile," by John Russell, is a cleverly optimistic bit of verse whose rhythm is very facile, but which would be improved by the addition of two syllables to the third and sixth lines of each stanza. The

113

rhyme of round you and found true is incorrect, since the second syllables of double rhymes must be identical. "The Evil One," by Narcissus Blanchfield, is announced as "A Prose-poem, after Oscar Wilde—a long way after." As an allegory it is true to the facts of the case; though one cannot but feel that there is room for a freer play of the poetic imagination in so great a subject.

Toledo Amateur for October is a literary publication which reflects much credit upon its young editor, Mr. Wesley Hilon Porter, and upon the several contributors. "Twilight," a correct and graceful poem by Miss von der Heide opens the issue. "A Sabbath," by Mary Margaret Sisson, is a sketch of great merit, though not wholly novel in subject. The hypocrisy of many self-satisfied "pillars of the church" is only too well known both in life and in literature. At the very close of the piece, the word epithet is used in a slightly incorrect sense, meaning "motto." Epithet, as its Greek derivation shows, signifies an adjective or descriptive expression. "The Workers of the World," by Dora M. Hepner, is another sociological sketch of no small merit, pleasantly distinguished by the absence of slang. "Not All," by Olive G. Owen, is a poem of much fervour, albeit having a somewhat too free use of italics. The words and rhythm of a poet should be able to convey his images without the more artificial devices of typographical variation. Another questionable point is the manner of using archaic pronouns and verb forms. Miss Owen seems to use both ancient and modern conjugations of the verb indifferently with such subjects as thou. "A Day at Our Summer Home," by Emma Marie Voigt, is a descriptive sketch of considerable promise, and "My First Amateur Convention," by Mrs. Addie L. Porter, is a well written chronicle of events. "The Wild Rose," by Marguerite Allen, is a poem of no little grace, though beset with many of the usual crudities of youthful work. In the first place, the quatrains should have their rhymes regularly recurring; either in both first and third, and second and fourth lines; or only in second and fourth. A rhyme occurring only in first and third lines gives an unmusical cast, since it causes the stanza to end unrhymed. Secondly, the words fence and scent do not form a legitimate rhyme. The easy correctness of the metre is an encouraging sign, and indicates a poetic talent which Miss Allen would do well to cultivate. Mr. Porter's article on amateur journalism is interesting and quite just, though we hope that the United has not quite so "little to offer" the devotee of "so-called high-class literature" as the author believes. If we are to retain our cultivated members, or our younger members after they acquire cultivation, we must necessarily cater to the better grade of taste; though of course without neglecting the succeeding generation of novices. The editorial column of this issue is bright and fluent, concluding one of the best amateur journals of the season.

THE UNITED AMATEUR for September contains something only too seldom found in the amateur press; a really meritorious short story. "The Shadow on the Trail," by Eleanor J. Barnhart, possesses every element of good fiction; a substantial and really interesting plot, a logical development from beginning to conclusion, an adequate amount of suspense, a climax which does not disappoint, and a praiseworthy degree of local colour. Besides all of which it is fluent in language and correct in syntax. The rest of the literary department in this issue is devoted to verse. "To a Friend," by Alice M. Hamlet, is particularly pleasing through the hint of old-school technique which its well ordered phrases convey. The one weak point is the employment of thy, a singular expression, in connexion with several objects; namely, "paper, pen, and ready hand." Your should have been used. The metre is excellent throughout, and the whole piece displays a gratifying skill on its author's part. "The Path Along the Sea," by Rev. Eugene B. Kuntz, is a flawless and beautiful bit of sentimental poetry, cast in fluent and felicitous heptameter. "Dad," by Horace Fowler Goodwin, is decidedly the best of this writer's pieces yet to appear in the amateur press. The defects are mostly technical, including the bad rhyme of engaged and dismayed, and the overweighted seventh line of the final stanza. The latter might be rectified by substituting blest, or some other monosyllable, for lucky. "Li'l Baby Mine," by W. Frank Booker, is a quaint and captivating darky lullaby, whose accuracy of dialect and atmosphere comes from that first-hand knowledge of the negroes which only a Southern writer can possess. Mr. Booker is one of our most promising bards, and will be doubly notable when his style shall have received its final polish. "When I Gaze on Thee," by Kathleen Foster Smith, is an amatory poem of much grace and fluency.

THE UNITED AMATEUR for October furnishes us with a species of composition not frequently encountered in amateurdom; an official report which is also a literary classic. Pres. Campbell's message is really an essay on contemporary amateur journalism, and contains a multitude of well stated truths which every member of the fraternity would do well to peruse. "The Wanderer's Return," by Andrew Francis Lockhart, is a beautiful piece of anapaestic verse whose flow is as pleasing as its sentiment.

The Woodbee for October is edited by Mrs. Ida C. Haughton, and though not of large size, does credit both to her and to the Columbus Club. "To the Woodbees," a witty parody of Poe's "Annabel Lee," exhibits Miss Irene Metzger as the possessor of no little skill in numbers; and incidentally suggests that other young bards might well improve their styles by judicious exercises of this sort. Much of the spirit of metre may be absorbed through copying the works of the standard poets. "Louise's Letter," a short story by Norma Sanger, contains some of the defects of early composition, notably an undue hastening of the action immediately after the letter quoted in the text. The plot involves a rather unusual coincidence, yet is probably no more overstrained than that of the average piece of light fiction. "The Ruling Passion," by Edna M. Haughton, is a story of phenomenal power and interest, forming a psychological study worthy of more than one perusal. All the requirements of good fiction, both inspirational and technical, are complied with to the satisfaction of even the most exacting critic. Miss Haughton's work is of a very high grade, and would be welcomed in larger quantities by the amateur world. Miss Harwood's interesting News Notes and Mrs. Haughton's thoughtful editorial conclude an issue whose every feature deserves commendation.

H. P. LOVECRAFT,
Chairman

THE UNITED AMATEUR MAY 1917

DEPARTMENT OF PUBLIC CRITICISM

The Conservative for January deserved distinction for its opening poem, "The Vagrant," which proceeds from the thrice-gifted pen of Mrs. W. V. Jordan. The piece is one well worthy of close attention, since it contains to a marked degree those elements of charm which render its author so prominent among amateur bards. Bold and discriminating choice of words and phrases, apt and unique images and personifications, and a carefully sustained atmosphere of delicate unreality, all unite to impart a characteristic beauty to the lines. This beauty, searchingly analysed, reveals itself as something more sylvan and spontaneous than studied and bookish; indeed, all of Mrs. Jordan's verse is born rather than built.

"The Unbreakable Link," a prose sketch by Arthur W. Ashby, is smooth and graphic in its delineation of a dream or vision of the past. The ancient heritage of Old England and its hoary edifices is here vividly set forth. Mr. Ashby's work, always notable for its command and intelligent interpretation of detail, is welcome wherever encountered.

"When New-Year Comes," a poem by Rev. Eugene B. Kuntz, exhibits its brilliant author in a most felicitous though decidedly novel vein. Turning from his usual Alexandrines and heptameters, and laying aside his characteristically stately and sonorous vocabulary, Dr. Kuntz has produced a gem of brevity and simplicity in octosyllabic couplets. The ease and naturalness of the language are so great that the reader feels no other words or constructions could have been used with equal effect. The remainder of The Conservative, being the work of the present critic, deserves no particular mention.

The Coyote for January bears an attractive cover design illustrating the gentle beast after which the publication is named. The opening piece, an alleged poem by the present critic, contains an humiliating error for which none but the author is responsible. The impossible word supremest in line 16, should read sublimest. The author is likewise responsible for the omission of the following couplet after line 26:

> "Around his greatness pour disheart'ning woes,
> But still he tow'rs above his conquering foes."

The rest of the magazine is devoted to prose of practical nature, containing suggestions by Editor Harrington and Rev. Graeme Davis for the resuscitation of one of the dormant press associations.

The Coyote for April, home-printed and reduced to the conventional 5×7 page, opens with Mrs. Jordan's pleasant lines on "The Duty." While the general sentiment of this piece is by no means novel, the powerful and distinctive touch of the authoress is revealed by such highly original passages as the following:

> "And black-wing'd, clucking shadows
> Brought out their broods of fears."

A poet of rather different type is displayed in "The Five-Minute School," by Lovell Leland Massie. Mr. Massie is said to have "an unlimited supply of poems on hand which he desires to publish," but it is evident that some preliminary alterations would not be undesirable. In the first place, the metre requires correction; though it is remarkably good for beginner's work. Particularly weak lines are the second in stanza four, and the second in stanza six. The phraseology is stiff but by no means hopeless, and proclaims nothing more serious than the need of greater poetic familiarity on the author's part. The rhymes are good with two exceptions; past and class, and jewel and school. Mr. Massie, however, is not the first bard to reduce jew-el to "jool!" "The Coyote," by Obert O. Bakken, is a worthy and interesting composition upon a well known animal. "A Soul," by Olive G. Owen, is reprinted from the professional press, and amply merits the honour. The poem is of unexceptionable technique and adequate sentiment. Miss Owen's brilliant, fruitful, and long-continued poetical career has few parallels in the amateur world. "The Amateur Christian," a brief prose essay by Benjamin Winskill, presents more than one valuable truth; though we wish the word "par," near the close, might be expanded to proper fulness. We presume that it is intended to stand for paragraph.

The Crazyquilt for December is a highly entertaining illustrated publication whose exact classification is a matter of some difficulty. We might perhaps best describe it as a bubbling over of youthful spirits, with here and there a touch of unobtrusive seriousness. The editor, Mr. Melvin Ryder, is to be commended upon his enterprise; which consists in approximately equal parts of prose, verse, and whimsical vers libre. It is the last named product which most absorbs our attention, since the given specimens afford a very brilliant satire on the absurd medium in which they are set. The choicest selections are due to the fertile pen of Mr. William S. Wabnitz, assisted by that not unknown classic called "Mother Goose," whose ideas accord well with the thought of the new "poetry." "A Futuresk Romance," by Mr. Wabnitz alone, is of exceeding cleverness. Among the genuine poems, we may give particular commendation to "Bluebirds are Flying Over," by Mrs. Dora Hepner Moitoret; "Longin' and Yearnin'," "Spring," "Verses," and "Dreaming," by J. H. Gavin; and "Stars After Rain," by William S. Wabnitz. Mr. Gavin's "Dreaming" is a hauntingly pretty piece, though marred by an imperfect line (the twelfth) and by an incorrect accentuation of the word romance. This word should be accented on the final syllable.

"Odd Patches and Even" is the title of the editorial column, which contains many words of wisdom (though not too grave) by Mr. Ryder. We hope to behold future issues of The Crazyquilt.

Dowdell's Bearcat for October, partly compiled and financed by the United's official board in lieu of the missing Official Quarterly, comes to us unbound and without a cover; yet contains, aside from the inexcusable editorials, a rich array of meritorious material. Mr. Dowdell's comment on radical eccentrics and malcontents is apt and clever, showing how bright this young writer can be when he avoids bad taste and personalities.

"A Little Lovely Lyric," by Mrs. Dora H. Moitoret, is one of the choicest of this author's poems, having a spirit and cadence of rare quality. In "The Real Amateur Spirit," Pres. Campbell presents in vigorous prose many important truths and principles of amateur journalism. The concluding sentence forms a definition of our animating impulse which deserves repeated publication as a motto and inspiration. "An American To Mother England," by the present critic, is an expression of cultural and ancestral ties which have now, through the fortunes of war, grown doubly strong. The word Saxon, in the last line, should begin with a capital. "Dream Life" is a vivid piece of prose mysticism by our versatile and gifted Vice-President, Mr. Ira A. Cole. Defying precise grouping either as a sketch or a story, this enigmatical bit of fancy deserves highest praise for its fluent diction, rich imagination, potent atmosphere, and graphic colouring. Mr. Cole has a bright future in prose as well as in verse for in both of these media he is a genuine and spontaneous poet. "United Impressions," by Mrs. E. L. Whitehead, is clear, interesting, and well-written, as is also the sketch by Mary M. Sisson entitled "Passion versus Calm." "The Elm Tree," by James Tobey Pyke, is a poem of remarkable sweetness and nobility, through whose lofty sentiment shines the true splendour of the inspired bard. There is a master touch in the passage referring to

> "——a sweet heaven
> Of singing birds and whispering leaves."

Mrs. Winifred Virginia Jordan, without one of whose delightful verses no amateur publication can really compete, contributes a sparkling succession of amatory anapaests entitled "Dear." The middle stanza rises to great lyric heights, and should prove especially captivating to such discriminating critics of lyricism as our colleague Mr. Kleiner.

The Enthusiast for February is a hectographed publication issued by our latest young recruit, Mr. James Mather Mosely of Westfield, Mass. Mr. Mosely is a youth of sterling ability and great promise, whose work is already worthy of notice and encouragement. The editor's leading article, "The Secret Inspiration of a Man Who Made Good," shows unusual fluency and literary assurance, though we might wish for a more dignified title. The expression to make good is pure slang, and should be supplanted by one of the many legitimate English words and phrases which convey the same meaning. Mr. Mosely's editorials are likewise open to criticism on the ground of colloquialism, though the natural exuberance of youth excuses much. "The Birds," by Harold Gordon Hawkins, is a truly excellent specimen of juvenile verse, which contains much promise for the author's efforts. Increased familiarity with standard literary models will remove all evidences of stiffness now perceptible. "How Men Go Wrong," a conventional moral homily by Edgar Holmes Plummer, shows a slight want of original ideas and a tendency to commonplaces; though having much merit in construction. Another subject might display Mr. Plummer's talent to better advantage. The use of the word habitat for inhabitant or denizen is incorrect, for its true meaning is a natural locality or place of habitation. "Blueberry Time," by Ruth Foster, is obviously a schoolgirl composition, albeit a pleasing one.

F. R. Starr's cartoon scarcely comes within the province of a literary critic, but is doubtless an excellent example of elementary art. We question, however, the place of popular cartoons in serious papers; the "funny picture" habit is essentially a plebeian one, and alien to journalism of the highest grade. All things considered, The Enthusiast is a creditable exponent of junior letters, which deserves the encouragement and support of the United.

Excelsior for March is in many respects the most notable of the season's amateur magazines edited by our brilliant Laureate Recorder, Miss Verna McGeoch, it contains a surprisingly ample and impressive collection of prose and verse by our best writers; including the delectable lyricist Perrin Holmes Lowrey, whose work has hitherto been unrepresented in the press of the United. The issue opens with Mr. Jonathan E. Hoag's stately "Ode to Old Ocean," whose appropriate imagery and smooth couplets are exceedingly pleasant to the mind and ear alike. Mr. Hoag's unique charm is no less apparent in the longer reminiscent piece entitled "The Old Farm Home," which describes the author's boyhood scenes at Valley Falls, New York, where he was born more than eighty-six years ago. This piece has attracted much favorable notice in the professional world, having been reprinted in The Troy Times. Perrin Holmes Lowrey contributes a cycle of three poems touching on the beauties of the month of April; one of which, "April in Killarney," will this summer be set to music by Leopold Godowsky. The style of Mr. Lowrey possesses an attractive individuality and delicacy which is already bringing him celebrity in the larger literary sphere. What could be more thoroughly enchanting than such a stanza as the following?

> "Oh, it's April in Killarney,
> Early April in Killarney,

Where the Irish lanes are merry
And the lyric breezes blow;
And the scented snows of cherry
Drift across the fields of Kerry—
Oh, it's April in Killarney
And she loves the April so."

"Treasure Trove," by Henry Cleveland Wood, is a pleasant and urbane bit of light verse; while "Percival Lowell," by Howard Phillips Lovecraft, is an abominably dull elegiac piece of heavy verse. Edwin Gibson's "Sonnet to Acyion" deserves keen attention as the work of a capable and rapidly developing young bard. "Real versus Ideal" is a bright metrical divertissement by John Russell, which suffers through the omission of the opening line by the printer. This line is:

"For sale—a cottage by the sea."

We recommend the final line to the attention of those careless bards who pronounce real as reel, and ideal as ideel. The correct quantities, as there given, will serve as examples. Verse of deeper quality is furnished by amateurdom's foremost expressionist, Anne Tillery Renshaw, two of whose poems appear. "The Singing Sea" contains an error of technique, hope and note being placed in attempted rhyme; but the structure is in general very regular, considering the author's radical theories. Of the merit of the sentiment it is unnecessary to speak. "A Wish" is cast in less fluent metre, but is so replete with aptness, grandeur and refinement of ideas, that the sternest critic must needs view its form with lenient glance. The prose contents of Excelsior are worthy company for the verse. Paul J. Campbell is represented by a very brief though characteristic essay entitled "The Price of Freedom," wherein appears the sound reasoning and courageous philosophy for which Mr. Campbell has always been distinguished. Another notable essay or review is "English History," by Henry Clapham McGavack. Mr. McGavack here ably employs his keen analysis and lucid style in dissecting Prof. Meyer's absurdly biased but diabolically clever pro-German History of England.

"The Association," by David H. Whittier, teems with good advice concerning the proper management of the United. Mr. Whittier's style is smooth and dignified, exhibiting a sober maturity unusual for a young author. "Tonio's Salvation," a short story by Edna von der Heide, is the only bit of fiction in the magazine. This brief glimpse of the cosmopolitan child life of a modern city is marked equally by naturalness of plot and facility of technic, forming a piece quite professional in quality and atmosphere. Excelsior has done much to sustain the best traditions of the United, and we hope its future appearance will be frequent and regular. The editorial column reveals the genius and exquisite taste of its gifted publisher.

Merry Minutes for December-January is an interesting number of an interesting publication, opening with some extremely clever cartoons by the United's soldier-member, George William Stokes. "Merry Minutes," a poem in trochaic measure by Olive G. Owen, is distinguished by the touch of beauty characteristic of all its author's work; but has a singular sort of rhyming in the first and third lines of the stanzas. The cadence seems to call for double rhymes, yet only the final syllables agree. The last word of the first stanza is unfortunately shorn by the printer of its final s. "The Dancing Tiger" is an excellent short story by Raymond Blathwayt, which might, however, be improved in style by a slightly closer attention to punctuation and structure of sentences. "Home," by Margaret Mahon, is a poem in that rather popular modern measure which seems to waver betwixt the iambus and anapaest. The imagery is pleasing, and the sentiment, though not novel, is acceptable. "The Choice," a serial story by Beryl Mappin, exhibits the same immaturities of style which mark the didactic articles of this author; yet so active is the imagination shown in some of the passages, that we believe Miss Mappin requires only time and harder study in order to become a very meritorious writer. The syntactical structure of this story is, on the average, smoother than that of Miss Mappin's essays; indeed, there is reason to believe that fiction is the better suited to her pen. "Absence," by Winifred Virginia Jordan, is a brief poem of faultless harmony whose quaintly sparkling imagery gives to an old theme a new lustre. "Education in Trinidad" is another of F. E. Hercules' terse and informing descriptive sketches. "Alley," by Mrs. Jordan, is a light pulsing lyric of almost Elizabethan quality, one of whose rhymes is of a type which has caused much discussion in the United's critical circles. The native pronunciation of New England makes of scarf and laugh an absolutely perfect rhyme; this perfection depending upon the curtailed phonetic value of the letter r; which in a place such as this is silent, save as it modifies the quality of the preceding vowel. In the London of Walker's day the same condition existed. But the tongue and ear of the American West have become accustomed to a certain roll which causes scarf to be enunciated as scarrf, thus throwing it out of rhyme with words of similar sound which lack the r. The Westerner would have to write scahf, in order to express to his own mind the New-England sound of scarf. Hitherto, the present critic has called no notice to rhymes of this type; and has, indeed, frequently employed them himself; but recognition of etymological principles involved will hereafter impel him to abandon and discourage the practice, which was not followed by the older classicists. To the New-England author this renunciation means relinquishment of many rhymes which are to his ear perfect, yet in the interests of tradition and universality it seems desirable that the sacrifice be made. "Why Mourn Thy Soldier Dead," is a poem of brave sorrow by Olive G. Owen. The fervour of the lines is deep, and the sentiments are of great nobility. Structurally the piece is flawless. "Chaucer, the Father of English Poetry," is the third of Miss Mappin's series of articles on literary history. An unfortunate misprint relegates to the bottom of the footnote a line which should immediately follow the specimen verse. The style is decidedly clearer and better than that of the preceding instalment of the series. "When You Went," by Mrs. Jordan, is an engagingly pathetic poem; with just that touch of the unseen which lends so particular a charm to Jordanian verse. Miss Trafford's appealing lines on "A Girl to Her Dead Lover" form a vividly pathetic glimpse into low life. The poetic form is quite satisfactory. As a whole, Merry Minutes constitutes a rather remarkable enterprise, sustaining through troubled times the spark of activity which will kindle anew the fires of British amateur journalism after the victorious close of the war. May America, in her new crisis, do as well!

Merry Minutes for February opens with Margaret Mahon's poem "God's Solace," a smooth and restful bit of versification. "Spencer and the Beginning of the Elizabethan Era" is the current article of Beryl Mappin's series on English Literature, and contains some very promising passages, especially the almost poetic introduction. Miss Mappin has an unusual fund of knowledge, and a pleasing gift of expression; but these advantages are as yet not fully systematised or marshalled to best effect. Miss Trafford's serial, "The Pursuit of the Innocent," concludes in this number. This story bears many of the signs of juvenile workmanship, the present instalment being so hurried in action that it almost attains the brevity of a synopsis. Careful and analytical perusal of standard fiction would assist greatly in maturing and perfecting the author's style. "Religion and Superstition" is the current article in F. E. M. Hercules' interesting series on Trinidad; and exhibits all the polish, lucidity and conciseness of its predecessors. "His Photo," by Master Randolph Trafford, is a very promising poem by a youthful bard. Every rhyme is correct, which is more than can be claimed for a great deal of the poesy perpetrated by older and more pretentious versifiers on this side of the Atlantic. The present instalment of "The

Choice," by Beryl Mappin, is marked by considerable fluency and animation, though possessed of certain limitations previously mentioned.

Merry Minutes for March commences with the present critic's dull lines "On Receiving a Picture of the Marshes at Ipswich." Passing to more meritorious matter, we encounter Miss Mappin's latest literary article, "Shakespeare," which interests even whilst it reveals deficiencies of prose technique. "Jimmy's Little Girl," by Joseph Parks, is a vivid transcript of military life by a military author. While the tale is not one of vast originality, it nevertheless recommends itself through simplicity and verisimilitude. Miss Mappin's serial "The Choice," concludes in this issue. It is very praiseworthy for its many colourful passages, but mildly censurable for its melodramatic atmosphere and rhetorical lapses. The opening sentence of this instalment contains instances of both of these faults: "A terrible foreboding gripped Christabel's heart in bands of steel, as if for a moment to cleave her tongue to the roof of her mouth." This is the last number of the publication to appear under the present name. Beginning with the April issue it will be known as The Little Budget; and will contain, on the average, a rather higher grade of reading matter than heretofore. But in forming a judgment of any kind, it is well to recognize that the magazine's appeal is frankly popular.

Pep for February is the first number of a somewhat extraordinary enterprise conducted by George W. Macauley with the laudable object of waking up a sleeping amateurdom. The editor very justly takes the press associations to task for their manifold sins, particularly the dubious circumstances surrounding a recent convention, in which it is needless to say the United had no part. Mr. Macauley's literary attainments are very considerable, but as yet unperfected. Possessed of rare charm in descriptive prose, he needs to exercise a greater nicety of construction in order to develop fully the riches which are his. Gifted with a large, facile, and ingenious vocabulary, he is not sufficiently precise and discriminating in his employment of words according to their finer shades of meaning. This carelessness makes faults of his very virtues; for his vigour of expression tends to take the form of outre and inadmissible rhetoric, whilst his talent for word-painting tends to degenerate into word-coining. It would be quite possible for an acute critic to compile a dictionary of peculiarly Macaulian words and phrases, to which the current Pep might contribute such terms as probverb (proverb?). Spelling and punctuation also should claim more of Mr. Macauley's time and attention; for he might easily avoid such slips as believeing, it's (for its), thots, and the like. In short, Mr. Macauley

124

is at present a gifted writer and brilliant editor labouring under the disadvantages of haste, carelessness, and perhaps a dash of radicalism.

The Phoenician for Spring is the first number of an enthusiastically conducted semi-professional venture of juvenile nature, whose connexion with the United hinges on the associate editorship of our clever recruit, Mr. James Mather Mosely. Like Merry Minutes, this publication is of the popular rather than conservative sort; being obviously designed primarily to please, secondarily to instruct. We deplore the use of commonplace and sensational topics, colloquial expressions, and malformed spelling; but make due concessions to the youth of the editorial staff and the nascent state of the periodical. So promising are the young publishers that time cannot fail to refine and mature their efforts. "An Hour with a Lunatic," by Harry B. Sadik, is a very short and very thrilling tale of the "dime novel" variety. Mr. Sadik has a commendable sense of the dramatic, which would serve him well should he choose a less sensational field of endeavour. "Our Soldiers," a Canadian mother's war song by Mrs. Minnie E. Taylor, exhibits merit, though having many signs of imperfect technic. In line 2 of the first stanza bid should be replaced by bade. The final rhyme of the poem, that of gain and name, is false and inadmissible. Metrically there is much roughness, which careful study and diligent reading of good verse can in time correct. "Candy and Health," and "If You Were Down and Out," by James Mather Mosely, are two typical newspaper interviews with representative men. Mr. Mosely shows much aptitude as a reporter, having an almost professional ease and fluency. This is not literature, but it is good journalism. "The Dinner Never Paid For," by Viola Jameson, is a piece of characteristic light fiction; commendably innocuous, and not at all overburdened with philosophical complexity. "The Secret of Success," by Edith L. Clark, is a promising bit of didactic prose. "The End of the Road," by Pearl K. Merritt, is a brief essay of substantial worth. "The Toll of the Sea," a poem by Harold Gordon Hawkins, shows considerable merit despite irregularities. "Memories," by Arthur Goodenough, well sustains the high poetical reputation of its author, though it is cruelly marred by the illogical and censurable "simplified" spelling which the young editors see fit to employ. One line affords a silent but striking instance of the utter senselessness and confusion of the new orthographical fad. This line reads:

"Of human thot might well be wrought."

Now in the first place, thot does not express the true pronunciation of thought. The word, thus written, tends to acquire the vocal quality of shot or blot, as distinguished from taught or brought. Secondly, in this place it is out of accord with wrought, which is correctly spelled. If Messrs. Plummer and Mosely would be logical, let them write wrought as wrot—or perhaps plain rot would be still more correct and phonetic, besides furnishing a laconic punning commentary on simple spelling in general. The Phoenician's editorial column is conducted with laudable seriousness, the item of "The Power of Books" being well worthy of perusal. What could best be spared from the magazine are the vague jokes and cartoons, purposeless "fillers" of miscellaneous nature, and columns of idle gossip about things in general. Some of the moving picture items are greatly suggestive of what a newspaper man would dub "press agent stuff." The magazine represents a degree of purpose and energy quite rare amongst the anaemic youth of today, and should receive corresponding encouragement from the members of the United. Those who are inclined to censure its professional aspect would do well to remember the much-vaunted beginnings of amateur journalism, when the most highly respected sheets were of this selfsame variety.

THE UNITED AMATEUR for November is heavily burdened with a sombre and sinister short story from our own pen, entitled "The Alchemist." This is our long unpublished credential to the United, and constitutes the first and only piece of fiction we have ever laid before a critical and discerning public wherefore we must needs beg all the charitable indulgence the Association can extend to an humble though ambitious tyro. A more interesting feature of the magazine is the biography of Mr. Fritter, written by our brilliant Official Editor, Andrew Francis Lockhart. Mr. Lockhart's quaint and friendly prose style is here displayed at its best, giving a vivid and sympathetic portrayal of his prominent subject. "Beyond the Law," by Mary Faye Durr, is a light short story of excellent idea and construction, whose only censurable point is the use of "simplified" spelling. We believe that some procedure of quite drastic nature should be taken against the spread of this empty innovation before our settled orthography shall have become completely disorganized. Even in the United we can "do our bit." Our editors should band together in an effort to exclude the new forms from their publications, and our manuscript managers should see that every piece passing through their hands is duly purged of these radical distortions. At the same time, a series of articles explaining and analysing the spelling problem should be given wide publicity. The poetry in this issue is of encouraging quality. George M. Whiteside, in "Dream of the Ideal," gives indications of real genius; at the same time displaying a little of the technical infelicity which has marked his earlier verse. Mr. Whiteside's greatest weakness is in the domain of rhyme, a noticeable error in the present poem being the attempted rhyming of hours with bars and stars. "I Know a Garden," by Agnes Richmond Arnold, is a tuneful and beautiful lyric of a somewhat Elizabethan type. The metre, as the lines are rendered, appears to be quite unusual; but scansion reveals the fact that it is none other than the octosyllabic couplet, disguised by the printer's art.

THE UNITED AMATEUR for December begins with "A Girl's Ambition," a poem by Margaret Trafford. The general idea of the piece is both ingenious and appropriate, but the language and technical development leave considerable to be desired. In the first place, the rhyming plan is unfortunate; the opening and concluding couplets of each stanza being unrhymed. In the second place, the metre is irregular; departing very widely in places from the iambic heptameter which appears to be the dominant measure. Miss Trafford should cultivate an ear for rhythm, at the same time counting very carefully the syllables in each line she composes. A third point requiring mention is the occasional awkwardness of expression, a juvenile fault which will doubtless amend itself in time. Just now we will call attention to only one defect—the exceedingly forced abbreviation "dresses'd" for dresses would. "To My Physician," by M. Estella Shufelt, is a smooth, graceful, and serious poem whose only possible fault is the infrequency of rhyme. This is not a technical defect, since the plan of construction is well maintained throughout; but we believe a poem of this type requires more than one rhyme to each stanza of eight lines. "The Old Inn," a stirring short story by Gertrude L. Merkle, is a very promising piece of work, albeit somewhat conventional and melodramatic. The alliterative romance of Harry Henders and Hazel Hansen has a genuinely mid-Victorian flavour. "Dead Men Tell No Tales," a short story by Ida Cochran Haughton, is a ghastly and gruesome anecdote of the untenanted clay; related by a village dressmaker. The author reveals much comprehension of rural psychology in her handling of the theme; an incident which might easily shake the reason of a sensitive and imaginative person, merely "unnerves" the two quaint and prim maiden ladies. Poe would have made of this tale a thing to gasp and tremble at; Mrs. Haughton, with the same material, constructs genuine though grim comedy!

THE UNITED AMATEUR for January contains Editor Lockhart's captivatingly graceful retrospect of the older amateur journalism, concluding with a just and eloquent appeal for the

127

revival of our ancient enthusiasm. "Who Pays," by Helene H. Cole, is a brief and tragic story of considerable sociological significance. We deplore the use of the false verbal form alright; for while the expression all right may well occur in conversation of the character uttering it, the two words should be written out in full. "To a Babe," by Olive G. Owen, embodies in impeccable verse a highly clever and pleasing array of poetical conceits; and deserves to be ranked amongst the choicest of recent amateur offerings. "Girls are Like Gold," by Paul J. Campbell, is a striking and witty adaptation of Thomas Hood's celebrated lines on

"Gold! Gold! Gold! Gold!
Bright and yellow, hard and cold."

Mr. Campbell exhibits both ingenuity and metrical ability in this facile jeu d'esprit.

THE UNITED AMATEUR for March contains "Love's Scarlet Roses," an exquisite piece of lyric verse by Mary Henrietta Lehr of California. Miss Lehr, a scholar and poetic genius of high order, is a prominent amateur of a few years ago, lately returned to activity after a period of endeavour in other fields. Her verse is uniformly distinguished by depth of inspiration, delicacy of sentiment, and grace of structure; occupying a place amongst the rarest products of amateurdom. Another poem of remarkable merit in this issue is "The Gods' Return," by Olive G. Owen. Inspired by a recent article from the pen of Richard Le Gallienne, these well-wrought lines interpret one of the subtlest yet most potent of the varied moods created in the human breast by the momentous occurrences of the age. Looking over the file of THE UNITED AMATEUR for the present administrative year, one may discover a diverse and meritorious array of poetry and prose, which amply proves the contention of Pres. Campbell that a literary official organ is not only feasible but eminently desirable.

The Woodbee for January introduces to amateurdom a new bard, Mr. J. Morris Widdows, Hoosier exponent of rural simplicity. Mr. Widdows has enjoyed considerable success in the professional world as a poet, song-writer, and musical composer; hence it is no untried or faltering quill which he brings within our midst. "Stringtown on the Pike," which adorns the first page of the magazine, is a very pleasing bit of dialect verse whose accent and cadences suggest the work of the late James Whitcomb Riley. The metre is gratifyingly correct, and the rusticisms exceedingly colourful; though the average reader might find it somewhat difficult to associate the name Miko with Yankee countryside. Such a praenomen carries with it suggestions of a rich brogue rather than a nasal drawl. "Personal Liberty," a brilliant short essay by Leo Fritter, ably and sensibly explodes one of the characteristically specious arguments of the liquor advocates. Mr. Fritter's legal training aids him in presenting a clear, polished, and logical arraignment of anti-prohibition hypocrisy. "Just a Little Love Tale," by Elizabeth M. Ballou, is a smoothly constructed bit of very light fiction. Mrs. Haughton's editorial, "A Review of Reviews," is concise and sensible; giving a merited rebuke to those who seek to create unrest and dissatisfaction in amateur journalism.

The Woodbee for April is an ample and attractive number, opening with Dora H. Moitoret's excellent poem in the heroic couplet, "The April Maiden." The metre of this piece follows the fashion of the nineteenth rather than of the eighteenth century, having very few "end-stopt" lines or sense-limiting couplets. The final rhyme of caprice and these is somewhat imperfect, the effect being that of an attempted rhyme of s and z. "Her Fateful Day," a short story by Maude Dolby, is pleasing and ingenious despite certain improbabilities. "Ashes of Roses," by Frieda M. Sanger, belongs to that abnormal and lamentable type of pseudo-literature known as vers libre, and is the first serious specimen of its kind ever inflicted upon the United. We are sincerely sorry that one so gifted as Miss Sanger should descend to this hybrid, makeshift medium, when she could so well express her thoughts either in legitimate prose or legitimate verse. "Free Verse" has neither the flow of real verse nor the dignity of real prose. It tends to develop obnoxious eccentricities of expression, and is closely associated with bizarre and radical vagaries of thought. It is in nine cases out of ten a mere refuge of the obtuse, hurried, indolent, ignorant, or negligent bard who cannot or will not take the time and pains to compose genuine poetry or even passable verse. It has absolutely no justification for existence, and should be shunned by every real aspirant to literary excellence, no matter how many glittering inducements it seems to hold out. True, a person of very little knowledge or ability can make himself appear extremely cultured, aesthetic, and aristocratic by juggling a few empty words in the current fashion; scribbling several lines of unequal length, each beginning with a capital letter. It is an admirably easy way to acquire a literary reputation without much effort. As the late W. S. Gilbert once wrote of a kindred fad:

> "The meaning doesn't matter
> If it's only idle chatter
> Of a transcendental kind."

But we believe that the members of the United are more earnest and solid in their ambition, hence we advise Miss Sanger to turn her undoubted talent into more substantial channels. That she possesses genuine poetic genius is amply evident, even from the specimen of vers libre before us. The labour of real versification will be more arduous, but the fruits will prove richer in proportion. It is better to glean a little gold than much fools' gold. Miss Sanger's nephew, Mr. Norman Sanger, is more conservative in his tastes, and is creditably represented by his lines on "The Ol' Fishin' Hole." This piece contains many of the rhythmical defects common to juvenile composition, but is pervaded by a naturalness and pastoral simplicity which promise well for its young author. Wider reading and closer rhetorical study will supply all that Mr. Sanger now lacks. At present we should advise him to seek metrical regularity by taking some one well defined line as a model, and moulding all the others to it by counting the syllables and intoning the accents in each. In the case of the present poem, the very first line will serve as a perfect guide; its conformity to the iambic heptameter plan being absolute. The alternating stresses of the fourteen syllables should be noted and copied:

"The days are get-tin' balm-y now, and first-est thing you know."

Two defects of rhyme are to be noted. By and lullaby cannot properly be rhymed, since the rhyming syllables are identical, instead of merely similar. "Rapcher" and laughter do not rhyme at all. Miss Haughton's essay "Is a Lie Ever Justifiable?" forms a prominent feature of the magazine, and presents some very ingenious though dogmatic reasoning. Mrs. Haughton's editorial, "United We Stand," is an exceedingly timely appeal for genuine amateur activity, and should be of much value in stimulating a renaissance of the Association. The passage reading "Who has been the latest victim of Cupid? Whom of Hymen?" arouses a query as to the grammatical status of whom. We fear this is what Franklin P. Adams of the New York Tribune playfully calls a "Cyrilization." It is, as all readers of "The Conning Tower" can testify, a remarkably common error; and one into which many of the leading authors of the age frequently fall. The jingle "A Soldier's Delight," by George William Stokes, concludes the current issue in tuneful manner.

Amidst the present dearth of amateur magazines it is ever a delight to behold The Woodbee; meritorious in contents and regular in issuance. The debt of the United to the Columbus Club is indeed a heavy one.

H. P. LOVECRAFT,
Chairman

THE UNITED AMATEUR

OFFICIAL ORGAN OF THE UNITED AMATEUR PRESS ASSOCIATION

Volume XVI GEORGETOWN, ILL., JULY, 1917 Number 9

ODE FOR JULY FOURTH, 1917

As Columbia's brave scions, in anger array'd,
Once defy'd a proud monarch and built a new nation;
'Gainst their brothers of Britain unsheath'd the sharp blade
That hath ne'er met defeat nor endur'd desecration;
So must we in this hour
Show our valour and pow'r,
And dispel the black perils that over us low'r:
Whilst the sons of Britannia, no longer our foes,
Will rejoice in our triumphs and strengthen our blows!

See the banners of Liberty float in the breeze
That plays light o'er the regions our fathers defended;
Hear the voice of the million resound o'er the leas,
As the deeds of the past are proclaim'd and commended;
And in splendour on high
Where our flags proudly fly,
See the folds we tore down flung again to the sky:
For the Emblem of England, in kinship unfurl'd,
Shall divide with Old Glory the praise of the world!

Bury'd now are the hatreds of subject and King,
And the strife that once sunder'd an Empire hath vanish'd.
With the fame of the Saxon the heavens shall ring
As the vultures of darkness are baffled and banish'd:
And the broad British sea,
Of her enemies free,
Shall in tribute bow gladly, Columbia, to thee:
For the friends of the Right, in the field side by side,
Form a fabric of Freedom no hand can divide!

H. P. LOVECRAFT

DEPARTMENT OF PUBLIC CRITICISM

The Conservative for July opens with Ira A. Cole's delightful and melodious lines "In Vita Elysium" (Heaven in Life), which present a strong arraignment of those conventional theologians who deem all things beautiful reserved for a vague existence after death. While the orthodox reader may deem the flight of the imagination too free, the rational and appreciative litterateur will delight in the vigour of imagination and delicacy of fancy displayed. The metrical structure is beyond reproach in taste and fluency, the regular and spirited heroic couplets affording a refreshing contrast to the harsh and languid measures of the day. Mr. Cole's poetical future is bright indeed, for he possesses an innate conception of fitness and poetic values which too few of his contemporaries can boast. We wish to emphasize to those readers who are familiar with The Conservative's editorial policy, that the lines appear practically without revision; every bold conception and stroke of genius being Mr. Cole's own. Two couplets in particular delight the ear and the imagination, proving the author's claim to distinction as a poet of the purest classical type:

> "Go! Go! vain man, to those unbounded fanes
> Where God's one proven priest—fair Nature—reigns."

> "Uplifted, glad, thy spirit then shall know
> That life is light, and heaven's here below!"

"The Genesis of the Revolutionary War," by Henry Clapham McGavack, is one of those searchingly keen bits of iconoclastic analysis which have made Mr. McGavack so famous as an essayist since his advent to the United. Our author here explodes conclusively a large body of bombastic legend which false textbooks have inflicted upon successive generations of innocent American youth. We are shown beyond a doubt that the Revolution of 1776 was no such one-sided affair as the petty political "historians" would have us believe, and that our Mother Country indeed had a strong case before the bar of International justice. It is an article which makes us doubly proud of our racial and cultural affiliations.

"Sweet Frailty," a poem by Mary Henrietta Lehr, contains all those elements of charm, delicacy, and ingenuity which mark its author as one of amateurdom's most cultivated and gifted members. Of the editorial column modesty forbids us to speak, but we hope the amateur public may be duly charitable with our shortcomings as therein displayed.

The Inspiration for April is a "Tribute Number," dedicated to the amateur journalists of Great Britain and Canada who have devoted their lives and fortunes to the cause of civilisation and the Empire. With so wonderfully inspiring a subject, it is small wonder that the magazine lives gloriously up to its name. Miss von der Heide shows extreme skill and sympathy in the editorship of the publication, and in the verses which she contributes; proving herself worthy indeed of the high place she has occupied in amateurdom for so many years.

"The Lion's Brood," by Henry Clapham McGavack, exhibits the versatility of this brilliant writer; for though he is by preference a concise essayist, he here rises to great heights in the domain of rhetorical panegyric. His stirring encomium is ingeniously continued by Mr. William T. Harrington, who adds many merited words of praise for our kindred across the seas. The present critic's lines are as full of heartfelt love of England as they are wanting in merit; while the lines of Olive G. Owen possess both deep fervour and conspicuous merit. Mrs. Griffith's tribute, "He Conquers who Endures," breathes out the true spirit of the American nation today, anticipating the official action of a cautious and slow-moving government. The "Open Letters" of Messrs. Macauley, Stokes and Martin, speak the brave spirit of the age, and make us the more sharply regretful of our own rejection for military service. "Treasure," by Miss von der Heide, is an appealing bit of sentiment, whose interest is timely indeed.

Viewed as a whole, The Inspiration takes first rank amongst the amateur papers published since March.

The Little Budget for May opens with Paul J. Campbell's meritorious poem entitled "Signals." Mr. Campbell, always facile in metre, exhibits increasing power in the realm of poetical imagination, and is entitled to a substantial place on the slopes of Parnassus. A misprint in the present version of "Signals" gives look when looked should appear.

"The Adventures of 'Dido' Plum," by Joseph Parks, is a pleasing story of military life by one who is himself a soldier. Mr. Parks' brief sketches form a pleasing feature of the contemporary amateur press, being distinguished by a naturalness which intensifies their interest as literal transcripts of the army atmosphere. "Road Song," a tuneful lyric by Eleanor J. Barnhart, marks the first appearance of that brilliant author as a poet. Her inexperience in this art, however, is not at all to be suspected from this fervent and finished composition; which might well do credit to

133

some of our veteran bards. "Impulse," by Norah Sloane Stanley, is described as "A Parisian Fragment," and exhibits much ingenuity in spirit and atmosphere. "Keep a Cheerful Countenance," by Eugene B. Kuntz, is a poem of great merit despite the doubtful rhyme of way and quality in the last stanza. Miss Mappin, in her article on Milton, displays her ample knowledge of literary history, and even more than her customary fluency. "The Contented Robin," a poem by Margaret Mahon, is apt, pleasing and harmonious; whilst Miss Trafford's brief jingle is quaint and clever. "Spring," by Randolph Trafford (aetat 10) is full of the exuberant vigour of youth, and speaks well for the future of this bright young bard.

The Little Budget for June gains distinction from Henry Clapham McGavack's brilliant essay on American Anglophobia, entitled "Blood is not Thicker Than Water." This acute analysis of anti-British sentiment among certain classes in the States reveals a lamentable result of bigotry and historical ignorance; which may, we hope, be cured by the new bonds of alliance betwixt the Old and the New Englands. As Mr. McGavack well demonstrates, most of our Anglophobia is manufactured by the alleged "historians" who poison the minds of the young through mendacious textbooks. This species of false teaching, an evil potently fostered by the Fenians and Sinn Feiners who lurk serpent-like in our midst, is one which cannot too soon be eradicated; for the cultural identity and moral unity of the States and the Empire make such sources of unintelligent prejudice increasingly nauseous and detrimental. We may add that the textbook treatment of our War between the States is almost equally unfair, the Northern cause being ridiculously exalted above the brave and incredibly high-minded attitude of the Confederacy.

Another delightful prose contribution is "Back to Blighty," by Joseph Parks, a vivid vignette of one phase of military life. "Trinidad and its Forests," by F. E. M. Hercules, is marked by its author's customary ease of expression and felicity of diction; presenting many facts of general interest. The poetry in this issue includes work from the pens of J. E. Hoag, H. P. Lovecraft, Rev. Eugene B. Kuntz, Beryl Mappin, and the Editor. Dr. Kuntz's lines to the memory of Phillips Gamwell are animated with a nobility which well befits their subject, though the rhyme of day and melody is not strictly correct. Few amateur poets are able to achieve the sonorous dignity which Dr. Kuntz imparts to his flowing Alexandrines, or to select with equal appropriateness the vivid and musical words that so irresistibly delight the ear and impress the imagination. Miss Mappin's metrical effort, entitled "Only a Thought," betrays some of the crudities of youth; including the attempted rhyme of alone and home. The metre, phraseology, and plan of rhyming demand extensive revision, the following being a possible amended version of the piece:

As sad and alone in a distant land
I sat by the dismal shore,
My chin laid pensively in my hand,
And my dreams all of home once more;
I watch'd and mus'd o'er the sunless sea,
And study'd the cruel foam;
For the waves bore an exile's woe to me,
From my kindred forc'd to roam.

But lo! floating light upon the wind
And murm'ing o'er ocean crest,
Come the thoughts of those I left behind,
Bringing comfort and love and rest.
Only a word—aye, only a thought!
Each speeds like a heav'n-sent dart;
Who can measure the gladness and aid they've brought—
These thoughts—to the breaking heart?

The first line of the original, "Far away in a distant land," is lamentably pleonastic; whilst the identity or intended identity of the second and fourth rhymes is undesirable. In a verse of this type, it is not well to repeat a rhyme immediately. In the second stanza the first and third lines and the fifth and seventh are unrhymed, a variation from the original design which is not sanctioned by custom. Once a poet decides on his metre and plan of rhyme, he should maintain them unchanged throughout the poem. In the foregoing revised version, all these defects have been remedied. Miss Trafford's poem, "After a Dream," shows much promise both technically and in the thought. The final line of the first stanza, "And the joy it contains is much," is very weak; and should be changed to read: "And of joy it contains so much." In writing the definite article, Miss Trafford mistakenly uses the contracted form th' when full syllabic value is to be given. This contraction is employed only when the article is metrically placed as a proclitic before another word, and is thereby shorn of its separate pronunciation as follows:

Th' ambitious bard a nobler theme essays.

The illustrated bit of humor by George William Stokes deserves mention as presenting one of the cleverest drawings to

135

appear lately in the amateur press. It is difficult to decide in which domain Mr. Stokes shines the more brightly, literature or pictorial art. His heading for The Little Budget is a masterpiece of its kind.

The Pippin for May brings once more to our notice amateurdom's foremost high-school club, the Appleton aggregation, whose existence is due to Mr. Maurice W. Moe's untiring efforts. "Doings of the Pippins," by Joseph Harriman, is a terse and informing chronicle of recent activity. "Once Upon a Time," by Florence A. Miller, is a bit of humorous verse whose metre might be improved by the use of greater care. "Some Cloth!," by John Ingold, is an exceedingly clever piece of wit; which, though avowedly Irish, bears the characteristic hall-mark of native American humor. The delightful exaggerations recall some of the brightest spots in American light literature. "Speed," by Matilda Harriman, is an interesting sketch recalling Poe's "Mellonta Tauta," in its imaginative flights. "From Over the Threshold," by Ruth Ryan, shows much promise in the realm of fiction. "Once an Amateur, Always an Amateur" is one of those rare bits of prose with which our distinguished Critical member, Mr. Moe, favours us. We are proud of the unshaken amateur allegiance of so brilliant a personality, and trust that some day he may realise his dream of "an attic or basement printshop." "The Press Club," by Ruth Schumaker, is a pleasing sketch, as is also Miss Kelly's "Our Club and the United." We trust that the Appleton Club may safely weather the hard times of which Miss Kelly complains.

THE UNITED AMATEUR for May contains a captivating and graceful sketch by W. Edwin Gibson, entitled "Beauty." Mr. Gibson is one of our younger members who bids fair to become prominent in the coming amateur generation. Of the month's poetry, we may mention with particular commendation Miss von der Heide's "Worship," though through some error, possibly typographical, the final line of the second stanza seems to lack two syllables. "When Dreams Come True," by Kathleen Foster Smith, is likewise of more than common merit, though the word hear in the second line of the second stanza is probably a misprint for heard. "Smile," by O. M. Blood, is ingenious though scarcely novel. Its chief defects are inequalities in the lines, which care should be able to correct. The first line contains two superfluous syllables, while the fourth line contains one too many. The ninth line of the final section contains two syllables too many, as do the tenth and eleventh lines as well. The rhyme of appear and disappear is incorrect, since syllables in rhyme should be merely similar—not the same. Mr. Blood requires much practice in poetry, but undoubtedly possesses the germ of success. "To the U. A. P. A.," by Matthew Hilson, is acceptable in construction and delightful in sentiment, laying strata on the new Anglo-American unity—the one redeeming feature of the present international crisis. THE UNITED AMATEUR closes with a quotation from Euripides, which we will not attempt to review here, since the author has been receiving critical attention from far abler men for many centuries!

H. P. LOVECRAFT,
Chairman

NEWS NOTES

Maurice W. Moe, Chief of our Department of Private Criticism, is trying a novel experiment this summer for the sake of his health. He has undertaken a labourer's work on one of the new buildings of Lawrence College, lifting planks, shovelling mud, and wheeling bags of cement like a seasoned workingman. While painful at first, the regimen is proving actually beneficial, and Mr. Moe is proud of the physical prowess he is beginning to exhibit. One of our amateur poetasters recently perpetrated the following four lines on the unusual occurrence of a learned instructor working manually upon a college building:

To M. W. M.

Behold the labourer, who builds the walls
That soon shall shine as Learning's sacred halls;
A man so apt at ev'ry art and trade,
He well might govern what his hands have made!

137

THE UNITED AMATEUR

OFFICIAL ORGAN OF THE UNITED AMATEUR PRESS ASSOCIATION

Volume XVII ATHOL, MASS., NOVEMBER, 1917 Number 2

A REMINISCENCE OF DR. SAMUEL JOHNSON

Humphry Littlewit, Esq.

The Privilege of Reminiscence, however rambling or tiresome, is one generally allow'd to the very aged; indeed, 'tis frequently by means of such Recollections that the obscure occurrences of History, and the lesser Anecdotes of the Great, are transmitted to Posterity.

Tho' many of my readers have at times observ'd and remark'd a Sort of antique Flow in my Stile of Writing, it hath pleased me to pass amongst the Members of this Generation as a young Man, giving out the Fiction that I was born in 1890, in America. I am now, however, resolv'd to unburthen myself of a secret which I have hitherto kept thro' Dread of Incredulity; and to impart to the Publick a true knowledge of my long years, in order to gratifie their taste for authentick Information of an Age with whose famous Personages I was on familiar Terms. Be it then known that I was born on the family Estate in Devonshire, of the 10th day of August, 1690, (or in the new Gregorian Stile of Reckoning, the 20th of August) being therefore now in my 228th year. Coming early to London, I saw as a Child many of the celebrated Men of King William's Reign, including the lamented Mr. Dryden, who sat much at the Tables of Will's Coffee-House. With Mr. Addison and Dr. Swift I later became very well acquainted, and was an even more familiar Friend to Mr. Pope, whom I knew and respected till the Day of his Death. But since it is of my more recent Associate, the late Dr. Johnson, that I am at this time desir'd to write; I will pass over my Youth for the present.

I had first Knowledge of the Doctor in May of the year 1738, tho' I did not at that Time meet him. Mr. Pope had just compleated his Epilogue to his Satires, (the Piece beginning: "Not twice a Twelvemonth you appear in Print.") and had arrang'd for its Publication. On the very Day it appear'd, there was also publish'd a Satire in Imitation of Juvenal, entituled "London," by the then unknown Johnson; and this so struck the Town, that many Gentlemen of Taste declared, it was the Work of a greater Poet than Mr. Pope. Notwithstanding what some Detractors have said of Mr. Pope's petty Jealousy, he gave the Verses of his new Rival no small Praise; and having learnt thro' Mr. Richardson who the Poet was, told me, "that Mr. Johnson wou'd soon be deterre."

I had no personal Acquaintances with the Doctor till 1763, when I was presented to him at the Mitre Tavern by Mr. James Boswell, a young Scotchman of excellent Family and great Learning, but small Wit, whose metrical Effusions I had sometimes revis'd.

Dr. Johnson, as I beheld him, was a full, pursy Man, very ill drest, and of slovenly Aspect. I recall him to have worn a bushy Bob-Wig, untyed and without Powder, and much too small for his Head. His Cloaths were of rusty brown, much wrinkled, and with more than one Button missing. His Face, too full to be handsom, was likewise marred by the Effects of some scrofulous Disorder; and his Head was continually rolling about in a sort of convulsive way. Of this Infirmity, indeed, I had known before; having heard of it from Mr. Pope, who took the Trouble to make particular Inquiries.

Being nearly seventy-three, full nineteen Years older than Dr. Johnson, (I say Doctor, tho' his Degree came not till two Years afterward) I naturally expected him to have some Regard for my Age; and was therefore not in that Fear of him, which others confess'd. On my asking him what he thought of my favourable Notice of his Dictionary in The Londoner, my periodical Paper, he said: "Sir, I possess no Recollection of having perus'd your Paper, and have not a great Interest in the Opinions of the less thoughtful Part of Mankind." Being more than a little piqued at the Incivility of one whose Celebrity made me solicitous of his Approbation, I ventur'd to retaliate in kind, and told him, I was surpris'd that a Man of Sense shou'd judge the Thoughtfulness of one whose Productions he admitted never having read. "Why, Sir," reply'd Johnson, "I do not require to become familiar with a Man's Writings in order to estimate the Superficiality of his Attainments, when he plainly shews it by his Eagerness to mention his own Productions in the first Question he puts to me." Having thus become Friends, we convers'd on many Matters. When, to agree with him, I said I was distrustful of the Authenticity of Ossian's Poems, Mr. Johnson said: "That, Sir, does not do your Understanding particular Credit; for what all the Town is sensible of, is no great Discovery for a Grub-Street Crick to make. You might as well say, you have a strong Suspicion that Milton wrote 'Paradise Lost!'"

I thereafter saw Johnson very frequently, most often at Meetings of THE LITERARY CLUB, which was founded the next

Year by the Doctor, together with Mr. Burke, the parliamentary Orator, Mr. Beauclerk, a Gentleman of Fashion, Mr. Langton, a pious Man and Captain of Militia, Sir J. Reynolds, the widely known Painter, Dr. Goldsmith, the Prose and poetick Writer, Dr. Nugent, father-in-law to Mr. Burke, Sir John Hawkins, Mr. Anthony Chamier, and my self. We assembled generally at seven o'clock of an Evening, once a Week, at the Turk's-Head, in Gerrard-Street, Soho, till that Tavern was sold and made into a private Dwelling; after which Event we mov'd our Gatherings successively to Prince's in Sackville-Street, Le Tellier's in Dover-Street, and Parsloe's and the Thatched House in St. James's-Street. In these Meetings we preserv'd a remarkable Degree of Amity and Tranquillity, which contrasts very favourably with some of the Dissensions and Disruptions I observe in the literary and amateur Press Associations of today. This Tranquillity was the more remarkable, because we had amongst us Gentlemen of very opposed Opinions. Dr. Johnson and I, as well as many others, were high Tories; whilst Mr. Burke was a Whig, and against the American War, many of his Speeches on that Subject having been widely publish'd. The least congenial Member was one of the Founders, Sir John Hawkins, who hath since written many misrepresentations of our Society. Sir John, an eccentrick Fellow, once declin'd to pay his part of the Reckoning for Supper, because 'twas his Custom at Home to eat no Supper. Later he insulted Mr. Burke in so intolerable a Manner, that we all took Pains to shew our Disapproval; after which Incident he came no more to our Meetings. However, he never openly fell out with the Doctor, and was the Executor of his Will; tho' Mr. Boswell and others have Reason to question the genuineness of his Attachment. Other and later Members of the CLUB were Mr. David Garrick, the Actor and early Friend of Dr. Johnson, Messieurs Tho. and Jos. Warton, Dr. Adam Smith, Dr. Percy, Author of the "Reliques," Mr. Edw. Gibbon, the Historian, Dr. Burney, the Musician, Mr. Malone, the Critick, and Mr. Boswell. Mr. Garrick obtain'd Admittance only with Difficulty; for the Doctor, notwithstanding his great Friendship, was for ever affecting to decry the Stage and all Things connected with it. Johnson, indeed, had a most singular Habit of speaking for Davy when others were against him, and of arguing against him, when others were for him. I have no Doubt but that he sincerely lov'd Mr. Garrick, for he never alluded to him as he did to Foote, who was a very coarse Fellow despite his comick Genius. Mr. Gibbon was none too well lik'd, for he had an odious sneering Way which offended even those of us who most admir'd his historical Productions. Mr. Goldsmith, a little Man very vain of his Dress and very deficient in Brilliancy of Conversation, was my particular

Favourite; since I was equally unable to shine in the Discourse. He was vastly jealous of Dr. Johnson, tho' none the less liking and respecting him. I remember that once a Foreigner, a German, I think, was in our Company; and that whilst Goldsmith was speaking, he observ'd the Doctor preparing to utter something. Unconsciously looking upon Goldsmith as a meer Encumbrance when compar'd to the greater Man, the Foreigner bluntly interrupted him and incurr'd his lasting Hostility by crying, "Hush, Toctor Shonson iss going to speak!"

In this luminous Company I was tolerated more because of my Years than for my Wit or Learning; being no Match at all for the rest. My Friendship for the celebrated Monsieur Voltaire was ever a Cause of Annoyance to the Doctor; who was deeply orthodox, and who us'd to say of the French Philosopher: "Vir est acerrimi Ingenii et paucarum Literarum."

Mr. Boswell, a little teazing Fellow whom I had known for some Time previously, us'd to make Sport of my aukward Manners and old-fashion'd Wig and Cloaths. Once coming in a little the worse for Wine (to which he was addicted) he endeavour'd to lampoon me by means of an Impromptu in verse, writ on the Surface of the Table; but lacking the Aid he usually had in his Composition, he made a bad grammatical Blunder. I told him, he shou'd not try to pasquinade the Source of his Poesy. At another Time Bozzy (as we us'd to call him) complain'd of my Harshness toward new Writers in the Articles I prepar'd for The Monthly Review. He said, I push'd every Aspirant off the Slopes of Parnassus. "Sir," I reply'd, "you are mistaken. They who lose their Hold do so from their own Want of Strength; but desiring to conceal their Weakness, they attribute the absence of Success to the first Critick that mentions them." I am glad to recall that Dr. Johnson upheld me in this Matter.

Dr. Johnson was second to no Man in the Pains he took to revise the bad Verses of others; indeed, 'tis said that in the book of poor blind old Mrs. Williams, there are scarce two lines which are not the Doctor's. At one Time Johnson recited to me some lines by a Servant to the Duke of Leeds, which had so amus'd him, that he had got them by Heart. They are on the Duke's Wedding, and so much resemble in Quality the Work of other and more recent poetick Dunces, that I cannot forbear copying them:

> "When the Duke of Leeds shall marry'd be
> To a fine young Lady of high Quality
> How happy will that Gentlewoman be
> In his Grace of Leeds' good Company."

I ask'd the Doctor, if he had ever try'd making Sense of this Piece; and upon his saying he had not, I amus'd myself with the following Amendment of it:

> When Gallant LEEDS auspiciously shall wed
> The virtuous Fair, of antient Lineage bred,
> How must the Maid rejoice with conscious Pride
> To win so great an Husband to her Side!

On shewing this to Dr. Johnson, he said, "Sir, you have straightened out the Feet, but you have put neither Wit nor Poetry into the Lines."

It wou'd afford me Gratification to tell more of my Experiences with Dr. Johnson and his circle of Wits; but I am an old Man, and easily fatigued. I seem to ramble along without much Logick or Continuity when I endeavour to recall the Past; and fear I light upon but few Incidents which others have not before discuss'd. Shou'd my present Recollections meet with Favour, I might later set down some further Anecdotes of old Times of which I am the only Survivor. I recall many Things of Sam Johnson and his Club, having kept up my Membership in the Latter long after the Doctor's Death, at which I sincerely mourn'd. I remember how John Burgoyne, Esq., the General, whose Dramatick and Poetical Works were printed after his Death, was blackballed by three Votes; probably because of his unfortunate Defeat in the American War, at Saratoga. Poor John! His Son fared better, I think, and was made a Baronet. But I am very tired. I am old, very old; it is Time for my Afternoon Nap.

DEPARTMENT OF PUBLIC CRITICISM

The Dabbler, for September, in the entire unexpectedness and splendor of its appearance, must be counted as one of the most effective of recent rebukes to the pessimists. There have been several such rebukes, and those who had already prepared themselves for another barren year in amateur journalism are beginning to realize that even history cannot be relied upon to repeat itself indefinitely. The Dabbler is issued by H. L. Lindquist of Chicago, and contains 16 pages, exclusive of the covers. The initial letters and a few incidental adornments are printed in green, and

142

the title-page, with its harmonious arrangement of type and decoration, is a delight to the eye. The typography, throughout, is almost flawless, and the contents, in general, are worthy of the care with which they have been presented to the reader. Paul J. Campbell, in his article, "What Does Amateur Journalism Mean to You?" once again defines the peculiar benefits and pleasures to be derived from our hobby, and warns away all those who come to it because of an idle curiosity, or a vain desire for self-glorification, or any motive other than a true impulse toward mental development and literary culture. "A Critical Review," by Frank C. Reighter, is devoted to the July Brooklynite, and subjects that publication to a well-nigh exhaustive analysis and criticism. The article is both interesting and instructive and reveals Mr. Reighter as an acute and capable critic. The verses with which he concludes his remarks are particularly clever and melodious, and furnish an excellent example of light verse when it is written by one possessing a natural aptitude for that form of expression. Jennie M. Kendall, in her fragment, "The One Thing Needful," makes a modern business woman give her opinion of idle wives, which she does in forceful, although not always accurate, English. "U. A. P. A. Convention Echoes," by Litta Voelchert; "The Old-Timer's Comeback," by L. J. Cohen; and "The Only Hope of A. J.," by W. E. Mellinger, consist of reminiscence, assurance and advice, from three well-known amateur journalists. The articles were obviously written somewhat hastily but are, nevertheless, very interesting and suggestive. H. L. Lindquist, in "At It Again," tells how he severed his connection with amateur journalism six years ago—being occupied with several professional ventures—only to find that the old passion would not die and finally compelled him to return to his early love. Those who have seen the result of Mr. Lindquist's acquiescence in his Fate will gain some idea of what his activity must have meant in other days.

The Dabbler, for October, follows hard upon its predecessor and, in all essentials, is of equal merit. "Hiking in the Rocky Mountain National Park," by Louis H. Kerber, Jr., is a well-written account of a tour through some of America's most wonderful scenery, and reflects great credit on Mr. Kerber's powers of observation. "Day-Dreams," by Frank C. Reighter, is a didactic poem and so labors under an initial handicap in attempting to hold the attention of the reader. The technique of the poet, however, is deserving of praise, and if a fault must be pointed out, it is in the forced pronunciation of the word "idea" in the last line, which seems too cheap a device to appear in poetry, even when, as in the present case, it is used intentionally. "Dominion Day in Winnipeg," by W. B. Stoddard, is an account of a patriotic celebration in Canada and was evidently witnessed by the writer on his recent—and somewhat protracted—travels. "Ecstasy," a poem, by Eleanor J. Barnhart, begins rather promisingly but we do not proceed very far before detecting various crudities of craftsmanship. Lines like the following:

"The changing fire splendor of sky opals, rare,"

and

"Like sea gulls swift soaring in tireless sky flight,"

and, once again,

"Till star gleams bright glittering high in mid-sky,"

contain the germ of true poetry, but when we read them we are aware not only of a harsh and difficult combination of consonants but also of an entire absence of metrical swing and grace. In fact, we get an impression from the above lines that an excessive number of important words have been crowded hap-hazard upon a metrical pattern which was not intended to hold so many, and it is not surprising that the fabric should show signs of being subjected to a severe strain. But care and practise may yet awaken that poet's instinct within Miss Barnhart which will enable her to detect and reject, instantly, all such blemishes in what should be the rounded beauty of her song.

Thomas Curtis Clark is indeed a poet of "Ring and Swing," as an editorial note to his poems declares him to be. "The Dawn of Liberty" and "America's Men" must be read in their entirety to be appreciated, but a quotation from the latter poem may not be amiss.

We are America's men,
Brave, dauntless and true;
We are America's men,
Ready to dare and do;
Ready to wield the sword with might,
Ready the tyrant's brow to smite—
And ready to sheath the sword—for Right!
We are America's Men.

The unsigned story entitled, "The Man Out of Work," is very brief, but apparently not the effort of a tyro. It would probably hold the attention even if it were much longer and we are almost inclined to regret its extreme abruptness. Nevertheless, it is complete as it stands and an artistic whole. "Still At It," by Mr. Lindquist, gives us

144

interesting information regarding the editor and also some sound advice as to finding congenial employment. Mr. Lindquist seems to be a philosopher whose practise will bear comparison with his theory.

The Olympian for October, awakens much of the old-time thrill with which amateurs were wont to receive the once frequent issues of that justly known and esteemed publication. The present number is not so ambitious in some respects as many of its predecessors, but it must be said that within a somewhat smaller scope it accomplishes quite as much as a more pretentious issue could hope to do. Nor is the latest Olympian at all in need of any apologies for shortcomings in the way of size, appearance, or general literary quality. Indeed, publications that consist of 12 pages and cover are always certain of a hearty welcome, while the present production of Mr. and Mrs. Cole has qualifications in addition to those just mentioned that recommend it warmly to all readers. The poem, "Motherhood," by Ethelwyn Dithridge is a truly noble and inspired effort. Amateur journalism is fortunate to number a poet of Miss Dithridge's attainments in its ranks. In "Retrospect and Prospect," Edward H. Cole sums up the three years of amateur history which have just passed and comes to the conclusion that "the best hope for amateur journalism in these days of stress and strain ... is in the peaceful co-operation of the surviving associations in a campaign of expansion of a practicable nature." "Here and Now," by Helene Hoffman Cole, consists of suggestions for the practical co-operation proposed by Mr. Cole, and should be a stimulus to increased activity in some positive form among present-day amateurs. "The Reviewers' Club" is quite as authoritative and sound in its criticisms as in the past and must always be considered one of the most delightful and instructive features of The Olympian.

The National Amateur Press Association could hardly inaugurate a year of promised activity more auspiciously than it has by the sterling issue of its president's Sprite. It is just about everything that one could ask for in amateur journalism. The modest grey of the cover, the excellence of the paper stock, the flawlessness of the typography, the exquisite taste with which the component parts are blended—all these strike the eye at the first glance. When one comes to read the contents, he finds each contribution well worth the setting. For a leading article we have something that is well nigh unique in literature, either amateur or professional, an attempted reconstruction of a scene supposedly excised from "King Lear." This is so unusual, in fact, that it might well be called a "stunt," but certainly it is a successful stunt. In the not overly long scene presented, which pictures the ruthless hanging of Cordelia and the Fool before the eyes of the aged Lear, we can discern no quality that is not strictly Shakespearian. The language has been purged of every trace of modernism and flows with that semi-solemn, archaic, Elizabethan cadence that almost makes it hard to believe that it was written in this century. But all this might be done without achieving the supreme Shakespearian touch. The triumph of the scene is that the character delineation is carried on with such a mastery of its intricacies that this scene might be interpolated in a new edition of the play and fool the higher critics of the future. The author, Samuel Loveman, is an amateur of former days who celebrates his return to the hobby with this feat so characteristic of his peculiar genius. The United has its Lovecraft, a belated Georgian who says he is nowhere so much at home today as he would be in the coffee-houses of Pope or Johnson. The National once more after a lapse of years has its Loveman, a belated Elizabethan who could have walked into the Mermaid Tavern and proved a congenial soul to Kit Marlowe and friend Will. The United welcomes him back.

Harry Martin, the editor, follows with an essay on the elements of the classic Greek tragedy to be found in "King Lear," which in depth, tone, and general literary quality are strongly reminiscent of the best work that appears in the Atlantic Monthly. As an essay it is perfect in form, its thesis is stated clearly and developed with forceful logic, and the wealth of material brought to bear upon the subject displays a knowledge of Shakespeare and the classic drama worthy of Truman Spencer, of beloved amateur memory.

The editorial section is only to be criticized in that Mr. Martin has cut us off with so few of his readable "Views Martinique," but we shall live in hopes of another excellent Sprite with a longer editorial department. George Cribbs' "History" is just a little poem used for a filler, but this must not be taken in derogation, for it is filler chosen with the good taste that characterizes the choice of all the other contributions. In spite of its simplicity and its brevity, it plays with the deft touch of mastery on that chord of pathos that always vibrates to the thought of Time's ceaseless and inevitable surge. From every point of view the whole journal is a symphony of excellence.

The Yerma, for October, is edited by John H. D. Smith of Orondo, Washington, and, aside from the fact that it is an attractive and well-printed publication, may be considered as being rather in the nature of a promise of future achievement. The dedicatory verses "To the Yerma," by Alice M. Hamlet are fairly good so far as rhyme and metre are concerned. They run smoothly and are really graceful in sentiment. They contain one or two grammatical inversions, however, such as

"I would a little jingle write,"

and

"I'd love to be a poet great,"

which have no more right to appear in verse than in prose. Then, too, they betray an occasional inelegance of expression like the following:

"I find that I am stuck."

But Miss Hamlet should by all means persist in her versifying, since there can be no doubt that she owns an instinctive grasp of the basic laws of rhyme and rhythm. If she will read and study the lighter efforts to be found in any standard anthology of poetry and then, with such models ever before her, strive sincerely to overcome her present defects by unremitting practise, Miss Hamlet may yet become a truly clever and accomplished versifier. "The Reform Spirit—Its Mission," by P. A. Spain, M. D., is an exceedingly able and thought provoking essay. It is to be hoped that in future issues Mr. Smith will give us an inkling of his own ideas on various subjects. The chief defect in The Yerma is the entire absence of editorial comment.

REPORTS OF OFFICERS

PRESIDENT'S MESSAGE

Fellow-Amateurs:—

The fourth month of the United's official year opens with the organization still nearer completion; Mrs. Helene Hoffman Cole, former President and thoroughly active and capable amateur, having accepted appointment as Supervisor of Amendments. The Fourth Vice-Presidency has been accepted by Alfred Galpin, Jr., 779 Kimball St., Appleton, Wisconsin.

The Official Editor is to be commended for the excellence of the September United Amateur, as is also the printer, Mr. W. Paul Cook. The Association will be gratified to hear that Mr. Cook has accepted the position of Official Publisher for the year; but the members must remember that only by their liberality in replenishing the Official Organ Fund, can regular issuance be ensured.

The 1916-1917 Year-Book of the Association, having been completed by the Committee, is now undergoing critical inspection and condensation by the expert judgment of Messrs. Paul J. Campbell and Edward F. Daas. Here again we appeal to the generosity of the members, especially the veteran members, to make possible the publication in full of this epitome of amateur history. Unless the Year-Book Fund is materially swelled, the volume cannot possibly be printed in its unabridged form of sixty-three closely typed manuscript pages.

The amateur press is now showing signs of a gradual recovery from the late period of minimum activity. Mr. Martin's remarkable production, The Sprite, Mr. Lindquist's two numbers of The Dabbler, Mr. and Mrs. Cole's welcome Olympian, Mr. Cook's wonderfully ample Vagrant, and Mr. John H. D. Smith's small but enterprising Yerma, all attest the reality of this awakening. Within the next few months many more papers are to be expected; including an excellent one from Miss Lehr, a scholarly Piper from Mr. Kleiner, a brilliant first venture, The Arcadian, from Mrs. Jordan, and both a Vagrant and a Monadnock from Mr. Cook. Mr. Cook makes a truly philanthropic offer to print small papers at reasonable rates, and it is to be hoped that a large number of members will avail themselves of it, communicating with Mr. Cook regarding particulars. His address is 451 Main St., Athol, Mass.

Recruiting proceeds steadily if not with meteoric rapidity, some excellent material having been obtained since the beginning of the year's campaign. The most serious defect in our system is the lack of a general welcome shown the new members, particularly as regards the distribution of papers. One of our most important recruits of last July, now a responsible officer, declares he has seen but a fraction of the papers issued since his entrance; a fact indicating a censurable but easily remediable condition. Let us impress it upon ourselves, that if we would do our full share toward maintaining the Association and its literary life, we must see that all our respective publications reach every member new or old. A considerable part of our yearly losses in membership are undoubtedly due to the indifferent reception which so many gifted newcomers receive.

The general signs of the times are bright and encouraging. A renascent amateur press, a closer co-operation between members, an influx of interested recruits, and an improved state of relations with our contemporaries, are but a few of the good omens which promise to make the coming year a pleasing and profitable one.

H. P. LOVECRAFT, President.
October 28, 1917

THE UNITED AMATEUR JANUARY 1918

REPORTS OF OFFICERS

PRESIDENT'S MESSAGE

Fellow-Amateurs:—
The dawn of the new year discovers the United in what may, considering the general condition of the times, be called a very enviable position. With a full complement of officers, and with the recruiting machinery fairly under way, our course seems clear and our voyage propitious.

The November Official Organ deserves praise of the highest sort; and will remain as a lasting monument to the editorial ability of Miss McGeoch and the mechanical good taste of Mr. Cook. It has set a standard beneath which it should not fall, but to maintain which a well-supplied Official Organ Fund is absolutely necessary. If each member of the Association would send a dollar, or even less, to Custodian McGeoch, this Fund might be certain of continuance at a level which would ensure a large and regularly published UNITED AMATEUR.

The publication of lists of new and prospective members should arouse every amateur to recruiting activity, and cause each newcomer to receive a goodly number of letters, papers, and postcards. It would be well if the line of demarcation between Recruiting Committees and the general amateur public were not so sharply drawn; for whilst it is the duty of the official recruiter to approach these new names, any other members confer no less a favour on the United by doing so unofficially. We must remedy the condition which permits able writers to join and pass out of the

149

Association almost without a realization of the fact of their membership. How few of these gifted amateurs who entered in 1915-1916 are now with us!

Publishing activity is strikingly exemplified by the appearance of Spindrift, a regularly issued monthly from the able pen of Sub-Lieut. Ernest Lionel McKeag of the Royal Navy. When a busy naval officer in active service can edit so excellent a magazine as this, no civilian should complain that the present war has made amateur journalism an impossibility! The number of papers expected in the near future has been increased by a plan of the Second Vice-President to unite the members of the Recruiting Committee in a co-operative editorial venture. It is to be hoped that this enterprise may succeed as well as similar papers conducted during former administrations. Of great interest to the literary element will be Mr. Cook's contemplated volume of laureate poetry, containing the winning pieces of all our competitions from the establishment of Laureateships to the present time.

The Association extends its heartiest congratulations, individually and collectively, to ex-Pres. Campbell and Treasurer Barnhart, who were most auspiciously joined in wedlock on Thanksgiving Day. Its heartfelt sympathy is transmitted to relatives of the late Rev. W. S. Harrison, whose death on December 3d left a vacancy in the ranks of stately and spiritual poets which cannot be filled.

A final word of commendation should be given to those more than generous teachers, professors, and scholars who are making "The Reading Table" so pleasing and successful a feature of the United's literary life. The idea, originated by Miss McGeoch, has been ably developed by Messrs. Moe and Lowrey, and is likely to redeem many of the promises of real progress which have pervaded the Association during the past few years.

H. P. LOVECRAFT, President.
January 2, 1918

REPORTS OF OFFICERS

PRESIDENT'S MESSAGE

Fellow-Amateurs:—

As the second half of the official year progresses, we behold the United in excellent condition, though not marked by as great a degree of activity as might be desired. The official organ faithfully maintains its phenomenally high standard, the January issue indeed eclipsing all precedents; but a larger number of other papers must be published, if we are to make the present term as memorable quantitatively as it is qualitatively. An excellent example is set by Mrs. Jordan, whose newly established Eurus comes so opportunely. May this publication prove permanent, and of frequent appearance! Besides this, we are indebted to Miss Trafford, Lieut. McKeag, and Mr. Martin for a Little Budget, Spindrift, and Sprite, respectively. Several other papers are reported in press, including what promises to be a very remarkable Vagrant.

In order to increase the publishing activity of the Association, the administration will endeavour to arrange for the publication of one or more co-operative papers. Any United member able to contribute $1.50 or more to such an enterprise should communicate with the undersigned, who will attend to the details of issuance if a sufficient number of contributing editors can be obtained. $1.50 will pay for one page, 7×10, and each contributor is at liberty to take as many pages as he desires at that rate. Contributors may utilise their space according to their own wishes, and all will be equally credited with editorship. This plan, successfully practiced four years ago, should enable many hitherto silent members to appear in the editorial field to great advantage, in a journal whose contents and appearance will alike be creditable.

The comparative scarcity of entries makes imperative a second warning regarding the new conditions in the Laureateship department. Ten persons must compete in any class before an award in that particular division can be granted, and at present no class contains an adequate variety of entries. Again it is urged that the members lose no time in submitting their printed literary productions to Mr. Hoag for entry.

A careful study of the four proposed constitutional amendments is necessary to ensure intelligent voting next July. The undersigned, as their author, naturally favours their passage; but the one providing for an abolition of the officers' activity requirements should not be adopted without ample opportunity for debate and interchange of views.

The congratulations of the Association are extended to Mr. and Mrs. Edward H. Cole upon the advent of a son, Edward Sherman Cole, on February 14. With equal sincerity the United felicitates Ex-President Leo Fritter, on his marriage to Miss Frances P. Hepner, March 6.

The United's 22nd annual convention will be held on July 22nd, 23d and 24th, at the Dells of the Wisconsin River. Under the direction of Mr. Daas this event cannot fail to be of interest and pleasure to all delegates, and every member who finds attendance possible is urged to be present.

To commend the official board for its generous, harmonious, and industrious co-operation this year, seems but a reiteration of needless panegyric; yet it would not be just to conclude this message without some such expression of grateful appreciation. The enthusiastic and unswerving loyalty of all our leaders has been a constant shield against the adversity of these gloomy times, and has been wonderfully successful in maintaining the United at a high cultural level.

H. P. LOVECRAFT, President.
March 8, 1918

THE UNITED AMATEUR MAY 1918

SUNSET

Howard Phillips Lovecraft

The cloudless day is richer at its close;
A golden glory settles on the lea;
Soft stealing shadows hint of cool repose
To mellowing landscape, and to calming sea.

And in that nobler, gentler, lovelier light,
The soul to sweeter, loftier bliss inclines;

152

Freed from the noonday glare, the favour'd sight
Increasing grace in earth and sky divines.

But ere the purest radiance crowns the green,
Or fairest lustre fills th' expectant grove,
The twilight thickens, and the fleeting scene
Leaves but a hallow'd memory of love!

DEPARTMENT OF PUBLIC CRITICISM

Eurus for February serves a double purpose; to introduce to the United in an editorial capacity the gifted poetess, Mrs. W. V. Jordan, and to commemorate the 87th natal anniversary of amateurdom's best beloved bard, Jonathan E. Hoag. The dedication to Mr. Hoag is both worthy and well merited. There are few whose qualities could evoke so sincere an encomium, and few encomiasts who could render so felicitous an expression of esteem. The entire production sustains the best traditions of Mrs. Jordan's work, and forms the most creditable individual paper to appear in the United since the dawn of the new year.

The issue opens with Mr. Hoag's stately and beautiful poem, "To the Falls of Dionondawa," which describes in an exquisite way the supposed history of a delightful cascade in Greenwich, New York. The lines, which are cast in the heroic couplet, have all the pleasing pomp and fire of the Augustan age of English verse; and form a refreshing contrast to the harsh or languid measures characteristic of the present day. Mr. Hoag brings down to our time the urbane arts of a better literary period.

"An Appreciation," by Verna McGeoch, is a prose-poetical tribute to Mr. Hoag, whose literary merit is of such a quality that we must needs lament the infrequency with which the author contributes to the amateur press. Of this piece a reader of broad culture lately said: "I have never read a production of this kind, more finely phrased, more comprehensive, more effective, and withal, so terse, and throughout, in such excellent taste." Eurus has good reason for self-congratulation on carrying this remarkable bit of composition.

"Chores," by Winifred Virginia Jordan, displays this versatile writer in a very singular vein; that of sombre, repellent, rustic

153

tragedy. It has all the compelling power which marks Mrs. Jordan's darker productions, and is conveyed in an arresting, staccato measure which emphasizes the homely horror of the theme. The phraseology, with its large proportion of rural and archaic words and constructions, adds vastly to the general effect and atmosphere. We believe that Mrs. Jordan analyses the New-England rustic mind more keenly and accurately than any other amateur writer; interpreting rural moods and sentiments, be they bright or dark, with unvarnished simplicity and absolute verisimilitude, notwithstanding the fact that most of her verse is of a much more polished and classical character. In "Chores" we are brought vividly face to face with the bleakest aspect of rusticity; the dull, commonplace couple, dwelling so far from the rest of mankind that they have become almost primitive in thought and feelings, losing all the complex refinements and humanities of social existence. The poem intensifies that feeling of hidden terror and tragedy which sometimes strikes us on beholding a lonely farmer, enigmatical of face and sparing of words, or on spying, through the twilight, some grey, unpainted, ramshackle, cottage, perched upon a wind-swept hill or propped up against the jutting boulders of some deserted slope, miles from the town and remote from the nearest neighbour.

"Young Clare," by Edith Miniter, is a narrative poem of that power and polish which might be expected of its celebrated author. The only considerable objection which could possibly be brought against it is a technical one, applying to the fourth line of the opening stanza:

"To work a cabaret show."

Here we must needs wonder at the use of work as a transitive verb when the intransitive sense is so clearly demanded, and at the evident accentuation of cabaret. We believe that the correct pronunciation of cabaret is trisyllabic, with the accent on the final syllable, thus: "cab-a-ray." We will not be quite so dogmatic about artiste in line 2 of the last stanza, though we think the best usage would demand the accent on the final syllable.

"Gentle Gusts," the quaintly named editorial section, contains much matter of merit, clothed in a pleasantly smooth style. The classical name of the publication is here ingeniously explained, and its dedication formally made. The tribute to Mr. Hoag is as well rendered as it is merited. The editorial note on amateur criticism is sound and kindly; the author voicing her protests in a manner which disarms them of malice, and putting us in a receptive attitude. Personally, the present critic is in complete agreement with the remarks on poetical elision and inversions; but we are confident that those of our board who hold different views, will accept the dicta in the friendly spirit intended.

"Someone—Somewhere," by Jennie E. T. Dowe, is a delightful lyric by an authoress too well known in amateurdom to need an introduction. Mrs. Dowe writes with the polish of long experience and genuine culture, displaying an enviable poetic genius.

Eurus closes with some commendatory lines to Mr. Hoag from the pen of H. P. Lovecraft. They are in heroics, and redolent of the spirit of two centuries ago. We discern no striking violations of good taste or metre, nor do we find any remarkable poetic power or elevation of thought.

The Little Budget for February and March is a double number, whose size and quality are alike encouraging. The issue opens with an ornate and felicitous Nature-poem by Rev. Eugene B. Kuntz, entitled "Above the Clouds," in which the author for once breaks away from his favourite Alexandrines and heptameters, presenting us with an ideally beautiful specimen of the heroic quatrain. Despite the strong reasons which impel Dr. Kuntz to adhere to long measures, we believe he should compose more in pentameter. That his chosen metres have peculiar advantages, none will deny; but it seems plain that the standard shorter line has other advantages which amply outweigh them. It was not by chance that the line of five iambuses became the dominant metre of our language. In the present poem we discern a grace and flow far greater than any which could pervade an Alexandrine piece; a condition well shown by parallel perusal of this and one of the same author's more characteristic efforts. As a creator of graphic, lofty, and majestic images, Dr. Kuntz has no peer in amateurdom. His sense of colour and of music weaves a rich and gorgeous element into the fabric of his work, and his sensitive literary faculty gives birth to happy combinations of words and phrases which not only please the imagination with their aptness, but delight the ear with their intrinsic euphony.

"The Drama as a Medium of Education," by Lieut. Ernest L. McKeag, is a short but terse essay on a neglected factor in liberal culture. It is true that our ordinary curricula lay all too little stress on dramatic art; and that as a result, this branch of æsthetic expression is grossly and consistently undervalued. The low estimate of the dramatic profession entertained by Dr. Johnson is a sad illustration of the one-sided state of mind prevailing even amongst scholars, concerning an art which is certainly not inferior to painting and sculpture, and probably much superior to music, in the æsthetic and intellectual scale.

"The Wizard of the North," an essay on Sir Walter Scott, is the

155

current instalment of Miss Mappin's Modern Literature Series. It is marred by a seeming hiatus, discernible not so much in the flow of words as in the flow of the narrative, which leads us to believe that a considerable portion has been left out, either through accident, or through an attempt at abridgment.

"My Books," by Alfred H. Pearce is a sonnet of apt idea and perfect construction.

"On Self-Sacrifice," by W. Townsend Ericson, is one of the "Essays of a Dreamer" which are regularly appearing in the Budget. The effort is marked by much sincerity and idealism, though in grammar and practicability it is less distinguished. We might mention the erroneous use of whom for who (a not uncommon defect amongst amateur writers), the faulty use of the word usurping where depriving is meant, and the split infinitive "to at least make;" all three of which mistakes occur on page 138. Mr. Ericson should drill himself more thoroughly in the principles of syntax. Other essays of this series are included in the present issue. "On Contentment" gives an illustration which we fear will injure Mr. Ericson's contention more than it will aid it. It is the reductio ad absurdum of the typical "Pollyanna" school of philosophy.

"Down an' Out," by Ernest L. McKeag, is a very clever ballad of the "rough and ready" school; picturesque in atmosphere, but somewhat defective in technique. Lieut. McKeag should pay a trifle more attention to his rhymes; which are not, however, worse than many of the rhymes in "Hudibras" and other comic pieces.

"Why Roses are White," a children's story, by Margaret Mahon, is marked by much grace and ingenuity; the central idea being quite original so far as we know. Further contributions to the children's department are made by Miss Birkmyre, whose woodland sketches will be appreciated by older readers as well.

"Selfish Ambition," a poem, by Nell Hilliard, is as correct and fluent in metre as we might expect from the author, though the expletive does in the final line of the first stanza is not to be commended. The sentiment is not precisely novel, but is well presented.

"The Flying Dutchman," a Romance of the Sea, by Joseph Parks, is more replete with nautical verisimilitude than with literary force. As compared with many of Mr. Parks' other tales, its plot is distinctly weak and lacking in symmetry. We must, however, praise the generally salty atmosphere. The picture of seafaring life is vivid and realistic.

The current Budget concludes with a summary of the year just closed, displaying a record of achievement of which the editress may well be proud.

The Silver Clarion for March is the publication of John Milton Samples, of Macon, Ga., a new member of the United. In tone the paper is quite serious and strongly inclined toward the religious; but so able are the majority of the contributions, that it lacks nothing in interest.

"Singing on the Way," a poem by James Larkin Pearson, opens the issue in attractive fashion. The lines are tuneful and felicitous, the triple rhymes giving an especially pleasing effect; though we must criticise the line

"Will certainly provide for us"

as being a trifle prosaic. We should recommend "plenteously provide," or something of that nature, as more poetic. Mr. Pearson is a poet of ability and experience, with a volume of published verse to his credit, whose work never falls below a high standard of merit.

"Just Icicles," by Sarah Story Duffee, is a sort of fairy tale with a juvenile exterior; which contains, however, more than a slight hint of the vanity of human wishes and fruitlessness of human endeavour. Whilst it exhibits no little cleverness in construction, we must own that it possesses certain looseness, insipidity, and almost rambling quality, which detract from its merit as a piece of literature. Mrs. Duffee would profit from a closer study of classical models, and a slighter attention to the more ordinary folk tales.

"The Blessings of Thorns," by Sallie M. Adams, is a religious poem of considerable excellence, containing a pious and worthy sentiment well expressed. The chief defects are technical. In the first stanza, line 3 lacks a syllable, whilst line 4 has one too many. Also, the day-way rhyme is repeated too closely. To have but one rhyming sound through two rhymes is a fault hard to excuse. All the defects above enumerated might be removed with ease, as the following revised version of the opening lines illustrates:

When we thank our Heav'nly Father
For the boons each day bestow'd;
For the flowers that are scatter'd
O'er the roughness of the road.

In the third stanza we find the day-way rhyme again repeated, also a superfluity of syllables in the sixth line. The latter might be cut down by the omission of the second the.

"Springtime in Dixieland," by John Milton Samples, is a tuneful pastoral which justifies the author's right to his first two names. But one or two defects mar the general delightful effect. The phrase "zephyr breeze," in the opening stanza, strikes us as a trifle

157

pleonastic; since a zephyr is itself a breeze; not a quality of a breeze. The syntax of the latter part of this stanza is somewhat obscure, but might be cleared up if the seventh line were thus amended:

"And save when cloud-ships cross their track."

The sixth and seventh lines of the last stanza each have a syllable too many, and in line 6 the word raise is used incorrectly; rise being the word needed. This, of course, would necessitate a change of rhyme.

"One Face is Passing," by Mamie Knight Samples, is a timely and excellent sketch concerning soldiers.

"Co-ee," a poem by Harry E. Rieseberg, contains much genuine pathos, and is generally smooth and commendable in technique.

"The Likeness of the Deity," by Arthur H. Goodenough, is one of the characteristically excellent products of its author, who holds the proud rank of "Literatus" in the United. The amount and quality of Mr. Goodenough's work is very unusual; few other amateurs producing so much verse of the first order. As a religious poet, he stands alone; resembling the celebrated Dr. Watts. He invests every theme he touches with an atmosphere truly and richly poetic.

"Astral Nights," by John Milton Samples, is a genuinely poetic piece of prose arranged in lines resembling those of verse. We believe that the loftiness and excellence of this composition would justify its metamorphosis into real verse.

Also by Editor Samples is the prose sketch entitled "The Present War: A Blessing in Disguise." From the title, one would expect Mr. Samples' point of view to be akin to that of the esteemed Gen. von Bernhardi; but such is not the case, since Mr. Samples means to say that he considers the conflict a just Divine Punishment for a sinful world—a punishment which will bring about a sinless and exemplary future. We wish it were so.

"Lord, Keep My Spirit Sweet," by Mr. Samples, is a religious lyric of substantial charm and grace.

The Editorials in this issue consist mainly of critical notes on previous numbers, and in general show a gratifying soundness of opinion.

Spindrift for January opens with "Mater Dolorosa," a poem, by Vere M. Murphy, whose sentiment and technique are alike deserving of praise.

"The Spirit of January," a sketch by Jean Birkmyre, runs into the February issue, and is quite acceptable from every point of view, though not distinguished by that highly imaginative colouring which we find in many of Miss Birkmyre's similar pieces.

"The Mystery of Murdor Grange" this month falls into the hands of Editor McKeag, who furnishes one of the best chapters we have so far perused; possibly the very best. It is exasperating to be cut off abruptly in the midst of the exciting narrative, with the admonition to wait for page 47!

Spindrift for February has as its leading feature an essay on "Heredity or Environment," by the Editor. In this brief article many truths are stated, though we fear Lieut. McKeag slightly underestimates the force of heredity. We might remind him of the Darwin family, beginning with the poet and physician, Erasmus Darwin. The grandson of this celebrated man was the immortal Charles Darwin, whilst the sons of Charles have all occupied places of eminence in the world of intellect.

"To the Enlisted men of the United States," by Edna Hyde, is an ode of admirable spirit and faultless construction.

"A Fragment," by S. L. (whose identity is now known to us!) shows much poetical ability, though the metre would move much more smoothly if judiciously touched up here and there. The description of the crescent moon sinking in the morning, is astronomically erroneous.

"The Estates of Authors," by Albert E. Bramwell, is a brief but informative article. As the late Dr. Johnson said of the Ordinary of Newgate's account, "it contains strong facts."

Spindrift for March very appropriately commences with a poem on that blustering month, from the pen of Annie Pearce. Apparently the piece is a juvenile effort, since despite a commendably poetic atmosphere there are some striking errors of construction. In the third line of the first stanza there is a very awkward use of the impersonal pronoun one. This pronoun has no place in good poetry, and should always be avoided by means of some equivalent arrangement. In the second stanza it appears that the authoress, through the exigencies of versification, has fallen into the paradox of calling the "fair green shoots" "roots!" Perhaps we are mistaken, but our confusion is evidence of the lack of perspicuity in this passage. A rather more obvious error is the evidently transitive use of the verb abound in the last line of this stanza. Be it known, that abound is strictly an intransitive verb!

"The Soul of Newcastle," an historical article by John M'Quillen, begins in this number; and describes the Roman period. We regret the misprint whereby the name Aelii becomes Aelu. The presence of a Hunnish umlaut over the u adds insult to injury! Mr. M'Quillen writes in an attractive style, and we shall look forward to the remainder of the present article.

159

"Heart Thirst," by Vere M. Murphy, is a very meritorious lyric, containing an ingenious conceit worthy of a more classical age.

As the literary contributions to the UNITED AMATEUR for January are mainly in the form of verse, I shall devote most of my attention to them. Poetry, like the poor, we have always with us; but the critic is moved to remark, as he casts back in his mind over the last twenty years of amateur publishing activity, that on the whole the tone of amateur poetry is distinctly higher than it used to be. Banal verse we still have in larger amounts than we should; but the amateur journals of a decade or two ago had reams of it. On the other hand, they contained not a few poems with more than a passing spark of the divine fire. The promising fact is that in the poetry of today's journals we get much more frequent glimpses of this true inspiration. In passing, the critic cannot forbear calling attention to Mr. Kleiner's "Ruth" in the February Brooklynite, which attains the highest levels of lyric expression, although only the simplest of figure and diction are employed. It is not often that one runs across a poem so simple and yet so pregnant with sincere emotion.

The first poem in the UNITED AMATEUR arouses mixed feelings. "Give Aid," by Julia R. Johnson, presents a thought that cannot be too often or too strongly stressed in this gloomy old world. Mrs. Johnson, furthermore, has carved out her own poetic medium, alternating two tetrameter lines with a single heptameter, a most unusual combination. It is always a promising sign to find a new poet experimenting with unhackneyed verse forms, although the experiments may not always be happy ones. But a word about the thought of this poem. It is one of those "recipe" poems, so-called because it can be produced in almost unlimited quantities by any writer clever enough to follow the formula. Some day the critic is going to take enough time off to write a book of poetic recipes, and already he has his subject so well blocked out that he is sure his book will contain the fundamental ingredients of a great majority of the amateur poems now appearing. The poem under consideration belongs to the "glad" recipe, an off-shoot of the Pollyanna school of fiction, and true to type it contains its quota of "glad" ingredients such as "cheer," "merry song," "troubles," and "sorrows," the last two, of course, for the sake of contrast.

"Astrophobos," by Ward Phillips, is another recipe poem; although his recipe is so much more intricate that it is not to be recommended for the Freshman. The critic would denominate a poem composed according to this recipe, a ulalumish poem, as it has so many earmarks of Poe. True to type, it is ulaluminated with gorgeous reds and crimsons, vistas of stupendous distances, coined phrases, unusual words, and general touches of either mysticism or purposeless obscurity. Such a poem is a feast for epicures who delight in intellectual caviar, but is not half so satisfying to the average poetic taste as Mr. Kleiner's "Ruth."

Theodore Gottlieb's "Contentment" is a clever and readable working out in verse of Mr. Ruskin's theme in his "King's Treasures"; namely, the satisfying companionship of great books. Mr. Gottlieb shows commendable control of the felicitous phrase, while the literary allusions with which his lines bristle mark a catholicity of taste entirely beyond the ordinary.

Metrical versions of the Psalms are not at all new; they are used, in fact, in Scotch Presbyterian churches in place of regular hymns. The poetic paraphrase of the first Psalm by Wilson Tylor is well done, and only in a few such phrases as "winds that blow" and "perish and shall not be blest," does he get dangerously near redundancy for the sake of rhyme and metre.

"A Thought," by Dorothy Downs, is a pretty little thought indeed, and prettily expressed, although the term "holiness divine" is strained when applied to a rose, and "we will be surprised" is frankly ungrammatical as a simple future in the first person. The sine qua non of all poetry is absolutely correct grammar and freedom from redundancy.

The bit of verse heading the War Items written by F. G. Morris, is quite adequate except for the lack of a rhyme in the last line, where the form of the stanza leads the reader to expect a rhyme for "part."

Matthew Hilson's rhymed greeting to the United from across the water, is on the whole, graceful and well done, and the United acknowledges its receipt with thanks.

One other piece of work in this number deserves especial mention. Alfred Galpin's "Mystery" introduces to the association a thinker more gifted for his years than probably any other recruit within recent years. This judgment is not based alone on the short article under consideration, but even this little piece of thought, if carefully analysed, is enough to stamp him as one who thinks with extreme facility in the deepest of abstractions, and who for expression of that thought commands a vocabulary of remarkable range. Mr. Galpin is going far in this world, and we hope that he will sojourn long enough with us so that we can feel that whatever glory he may attain will cast some of its rays upon the Association.

The editorial remarks in this issue of the UNITED AMATEUR are worthy of close perusal on account of their graceful literary quality. Seldom has the critic seen the subject of the New Year so felicitously treated as in this brief study by Miss McGeoch. The

161

author's mastery of appropriate words, phrases, and images, and her intuitive perception of the most delicate elements of literary harmony, combine to make the reader wish she were more frequently before the Association as a writer, as well as in an editorial capacity.

REPORTS OF OFFICERS

PRESIDENT'S MESSAGE

Fellow-Amateurs:—

According to indications, the last few weeks of the United's administrative year will exceed their predecessors in general activity and work accomplished. The college recruiting campaign, delayed through an unavoidable combination of circumstances, is now taking definite form; and may be expected to show some actual results even before the close of the present term, though its greatest fruits must necessarily be reaped by the next administration. General recruiting is on the increase, and a more satisfactory number of renewals and reinstatements is noted.

One of the greatest obstacles to be combated during this unsettled era, is the mistaken notion that amateur journalism is a non-essential and a luxury, unworthy of attention or support amidst the national stress. The prevalence of this opinion is difficult to account for, since its logic is so feeble. It is universally recognised that in times like these, some form of relaxation is absolutely indispensable if the poise and sanity of the people are to be preserved. Amusements of a lighter sort are patronised with increased frequency, and have risen to the dignity of essentials in the maintenance of the national morale. If, then, the flimsiest of pleasures be accorded the respect and favour of the public, what may we not say for amateur journalism, whose function is not only to entertain and relieve the mind, but to uplift and instruct as well? Mr. Edward H. Cole has ably treated this matter in his recent Bema, and no one who thoughtfully reviews the situation can dispute the force and verity of his conclusions. As Mr. Cole points out in a later communication, war-time amateur effort must of course be less elaborate than in pre-war days; but amateurdom itself is now worthy of double encouragement, rather than discouragement, since by its soothing and steadying influence it becomes a source of calm and strength, and therefore an active factor in the winning of the war. Let us on this side of the Atlantic view the rejuvenescence of British amateurdom after four years of warfare, as exhibited in the formation of the prosperous Amateur Press Club by Messrs. Winskill and Parks. The moral is not hard to deduce.

Of the new publications of the season it is hard to speak without using superlatives, since Mr. Cook's epoch-making June Vagrant is among their number. This veritable book of 148 pages and cover constitutes the greatest achievement of contemporary amateurdom, and may legitimately be considered as one of the outstanding features in the recent history of the institution. It is the one product of our day which will bear actual comparison with the publications of the departed "Halcyon" period. A July Vagrant, of equal quality though lesser size, may be expected in the near future. A newcomer to our list of journals is The Silver Clarion, issued by Mr. John Milton Samples of Macon, Ga., a promising poet, essayist, and editor, who has just entered the Association. The Clarion, whose contents are distinguished for their wholesome tone and pleasing literary quality, is a regularly issued monthly, and forms a substantial addition to the literature of the United. Another welcome paper is The Roamer, published by Mr. Louis H. Kerber, Jr., of Chicago. This journal, devoted exclusively to travel articles, will occupy a unique place in the United. Among the papers to be expected before the close of the official year are a Dabbler from Mr. Lindquist and a Yerma from Mr. J. H. D. Smith, now a soldier in the service of his country at Camp Laurel, Md.

Responses to the proposal for a co-operative paper have been slow in coming in. Let the members once more reflect upon the advantages of the plan, and unite in an effort to increase the literary output of the Association.

The annual convention, to be held on the 22nd, 23d and 24th of next July at the Dells of the Wisconsin River, may well be expected to stimulate interest to an unusually high pitch. A large attendance is urged, and since Mr. Daas is in charge of arrangements, the gathering will undoubtedly prove a bright spot in the year's programme.

H. P. LOVECRAFT, President.
May 6, 1918

ASTROPHOBOS

Ward Phillips

In the midnight heavens burning
Through ethereal deeps afar,
Once I watch'd with restless yearning
An alluring, aureate star;
Ev'ry eve aloft returning,
Gleaming nigh the Arctic car.

Mystic waves of beauty blended
With the gorgeous golden rays;
Phantasies of bliss descended
In a myrrh'd Elysian haze;
And in lyre-born chords extended
Harmonies of Lydian lays.

There (thought I) lie scenes of pleasure,
Where the free and blessed dwell,
And each moment bears a treasure,
Freighted with the lotus-spell,
And there floats a liquid measure
From the lute of Israfel.

There (I told myself) were shining
Worlds of happiness unknown,
Peace and Innocence entwining
By the Crowned Virtue's throne;
Men of light, their thoughts refining
Purer, fairer, than our own.

Thus I mus'd, when o'er the vision
Crept a red delirious change;
Hope dissolving to derision,
Beauty to distortion strange;
Hymnic chords in weird collision,
Spectral sights in endless range.

Crimson burn'd the star of sadness
As behind the beams I peer'd;

All was woe that seem'd but gladness
Ere my gaze with truth was sear'd;
Cacodaemons, mir'd with madness,
Through the fever'd flick'ring leer'd.

Now I know the fiendish fable
That the golden glitter bore;
Now I shun the spangled sable
That I watch'd and lov'd before;
But the horror, set and stable,
Haunts my soul forevermore.

THE UNITED AMATEUR JULY 1918

AT THE ROOT

H. P. Lovecraft
(Editor Laureate)

To those who look beneath the surface, the present universal war drives home more than one anthropological truth in striking fashion; and of these verities none is more profound than that relating to the essential immutability of mankind and its instincts.

Four years ago a large part of the civilised world laboured under certain biological fallacies which may, in a sense, be held responsible for the extent and duration of the present conflict. These fallacies, which were the foundation of pacifism and other pernicious forms of social and political radicalism, dealt with the capability of man to evolve mentally beyond his former state of subservience to primitive instinct and pugnacity, and to conduct his affairs and international or inter-racial relations on a basis of reason and good-will. That belief in such capability is unscientific and childishly naive, is beside the question. The fact remains, that the most civilised part of the world, including our own Anglo-Saxondom, did entertain enough of these notions to relax military vigilance, lay stress on points of honour, place trust in treaties, and permit a powerful and unscrupulous nation to indulge unchecked

165

and unsuspected in nearly fifty years of preparation for world-wide robbery and slaughter. We are reaping the result of our simplicity.

The past is over. Our former follies we can but regret, and expiate as best we may by a crusade to the death against the Trans-Rhenane monster which we allowed to grow and flourish beneath our very eyes. But the future holds more of responsibility, and we must prepare to guard against any renascence of the benevolent delusions that four years of blood have barely been able to dispel. In a word, we must learn to discard forever the sentimental standpoint, and to view our species through the cold eyes of science alone. We must recognise the essential underlying savagery in the animal called man, and return to older and sounder principles of national life and defence. We must realise that man's nature will remain the same so long as he remains man; that civilisation is but a slight coverlet beneath which the dominant beast sleeps lightly and ever ready to awake. To preserve civilisation, we must deal scientifically with the brute element, using only genuine biological principles. In considering ourselves, we think too much of ethics and sociology—too little of plain natural history. We should perceive that man's period of historical existence, a period so short that his physical constitution has not been altered in the slightest degree, is insufficient to allow of any considerable mental change. The instincts that governed the Egyptians and the Assyrians of old, govern us as well; and as the ancients thought, grasped, struggled, and deceived, so shall we moderns continue to think, grasp, struggle, and deceive in our inmost hearts. Change is only superficial and apparent.

Man's respect for the imponderables varies according to his mental constitution and environment. Through certain modes of thought and training it can be elevated tremendously, yet there is always a limit. The man or nation of high culture may acknowledge to great lengths the restraints imposed by conventions and honour, but beyond a certain point primitive will or desire cannot be curbed. Denied anything ardently desired, the individual or state will argue and parley just so long—then, if the impelling motive be sufficiently great, will cast aside every rule and break down every acquired inhibition, plunging viciously after the object wished; all the more fantastically savage because of previous repression. The sole ultimate factor in human decisions is physical force. This we must learn, however repugnant the idea may seem, if we are to protect ourselves and our institutions. Reliance on anything else is fallacious and ruinous. Dangerous beyond description are the voices sometimes heard today, decrying the continuance of armament after the close of the present hostilities.

166

The specific application of the scientific truth regarding man's native instincts will be found in the adoption of a post-bellum international programme. Obviously, we must take into account the primordial substructure and arrange for the upholding of culture by methods which will stand the acid test of stress and conflicting ambitions. In disillusioned diplomacy, ample armament, and universal military training alone will be found the solution of the world's difficulties. It will not be a perfect solution, because humanity is not perfect. It will not abolish war, because war is the expression of a natural human tendency. But it will at least produce an approximate stability of social and political conditions, and prevent the menace of the entire world by the greed of any one of its constituent parts.

REPORTS OF OFFICERS

PRESIDENT'S MESSAGE

Fellow-Amateurs:—

The conclusion of an administrative year is naturally a time for retrospection rather than for announcement and planning, and seldom may we derive more satisfaction from such a backward glance than at the present period.

The United has just completed a twelvemonth which, though not notable for numerousness of publications or expansion of the membership list, will nevertheless be long remembered for the tone and quality of its literature, and the uniformly smooth maintenance of its executive programme. The virtual extirpation of petty politics, and the elimination of all considerations save development of literary taste and encouragement of literary talent, have raised our Association to a new level of poise, harmony, dignity, and usefulness to the serious aspirant.

Prime honours must be awarded to our Official Editor and Official Publisher, who have given us an official organ unequalled and unapproached in the history of amateur journalism. The somewhat altered nature of contents, and radically elevated standard of editorship, mark an era in the progress of the Association; since the UNITED AMATEUR is really the nucleus of our activity and a reflection of the best in our current thought and ideals. We have this year helped to shatter the foolish fetichism which restricts the average official organ to a boresome and needless display of facts and figures, relating to the political mechanism of amateurdom. The organ has been a literary one, as befits a literary association; and has been conducted with a sounder sense of relative values than in times when amateurs seemed to place elections and annual banquets above art, taste, and rhetoric.

The publications of the year have been distinguished for their merit, general polish, and scholarly editorship. The percentage of crude matter appearing in print has been reduced to a minimum through the careful and conscientious critical service rendered both by the official bureau and by private individuals. The artistic standard of the United has evolved to a point where no aims short of excellence can win unqualified approval. The classics have become our sole models, and whilst even the most glaring faults of the sincere beginner receive liberal consideration and sympathetically constructive attention, there is no longer a seat of honour for complacent crudity. Genuine aspiration is our criterion of worth. The spirit of this newer amateur journalism is splendidly shown by such magazines of the year as Eurus, Spindrift, The Vagrant, and the official organ.

Just before the close of the present term, several new publications have appeared, amongst them a Vagrant, a Conservative, and Mr. Moloney's splendid first venture, The Voice From the Mountains. Early in the next fiscal year will appear The United Co-Operative, the fruit of this year's planning, edited by Mrs. Jordan, Miss Lehr, Mr. J. Clinton Pryor, and the undersigned. A revival of manuscript magazines, inaugurated by the appearance of Sub-Lieut. McKeag's Northumbrian, is in a measure solving the problems created by the high price of printing. Next month the undersigned will put into circulation Hesperia, a typewritten magazine designed to foster a closer relationship between British and American amateurdom.

Judges of Award for the Laureateship contests have been appointed as follows: Poetry, Mr. Nixon Waterman, a New England bard who needs no introduction to the lover of lofty and graceful expression. Verse, Dr. Henry T. Schnittkind of the Stratford Publishing Co. Essay, Prof. Lewis P. Shanks of the University of Pennsylvania. Study, Mr. J. Lee Robinson, Editor of the Cambridge Tribune. Story, Mr. William R. Murphy of the Philadelphia Evening Ledger, a former United man of the highest attainments. Editorial, Hon. Oliver Wayne Stewart, Associate Editor of The National Enquirer.

In doffing the official mantle after a year of executive endeavour, the undersigned must express regret at his inability to serve in as vigorous a manner as would the ideal President. He is acutely conscious of his shortcomings in a position which demands constant care and exertion, and which imposes a strain that only the robust are perfectly qualified to bear. It would be impossible for him fully to express his gratitude to his faithful and capable colleagues, to whose unremitting and faultlessly co-ordinated efforts all the successes of the present year must in justice be attributed. Valete!

H. P. LOVECRAFT, President.
June 26, 1918

THE UNITED AMATEUR

OFFICIAL ORGAN OF THE UNITED AMATEUR PRESS
ASSOCIATION

Volume XVIII ATHOL, MASS., NOVEMBER, 1918 Number 2

DEPARTMENT OF LITERATURE

The Literature of Rome

H. P. Lovecraft

The centre of our studies, the goal of our thoughts, the point to which all paths lead and the point from which all paths start again, is to be found in Rome and her abiding power.—Freeman.

Few students of mankind, if truly impartial, can fail to select as the greatest of human institutions that mighty and enduring civilisation which, first appearing on the banks of the Tiber, spread throughout the known world and became the direct parent of our own. If to Greece is due the existence of all modern thought, so to Rome is due its survival and our possession of it; for it was the majesty of the Eternal City which, reducing all Western Europe to a single government, made possible the wide and uniform diffusion of the high culture borrowed from Greece, and thereby laid the foundation of European enlightenment. To this day the remnants of the Roman world exhibit a superiority over those parts which never came beneath the sway of the Imperial Mother; a superiority strikingly manifest when we contemplate the savage code and ideals of the Germans, aliens to the priceless heritage of Latin justice, humanity, and philosophy. The study of Roman literature, then, needs no plea to recommend it. It is ours by intellectual descent; our bridge to all antiquity and to those Grecian stores of art and thought which are the fountain head of existing culture.

In considering Rome and her artistic history, we are conscious of a subjectivity impossible in the case of Greece or any other ancient nation. Whilst the Hellenes, with their strange beauty-worship and defective moral ideals, are to be admired and pitied at once, as luminous but remote phantoms; the Romans, with their greater practical sense, ancient virtue, and love of law and order, seem like our own people. It is with personal pride that we read of the valour and conquests of this mighty race, who used the alphabet we use, spoke and wrote with but little difference many of the words we speak and write, and with divine creative power evolved virtually all the forms of law which govern us today. To the Greek, art and literature were inextricably involved in daily life and thought; to the Roman, as to us, they were a separate unit in a many-sided civilisation. Undoubtedly this circumstance proves the inferiority of the Roman culture to the Greek; but it is an inferiority shared by our own culture, and therefore a bond of sympathy.

The race whose genius gave rise to the glories of Rome is, unhappily, not now in existence. Centuries of devastating wars, and foreign immigration into Italy, left but few real Latins after the early Imperial æra. The original Romans were a blend of closely related dolichocephalic Mediterranean tribes, whose racial affinities with the Greeks could not have been very remote, plus a slight Etruscan element of doubtful classification. The latter stock is an object of much mystery to ethnologists, being at present described by most authorities as of the brachycephalic Alpine variety. Many Roman customs and habits of thought are traceable to this problematical people.

It is a singular circumstance, that classic Latin literature is, save in the case of satire, almost wholly unrelated to the crude effusions of the primitive Latins; being borrowed as to form and subject from the Greeks, at a comparatively late date in Rome's political history. That this borrowing assisted greatly in Latin cultural advancement, none may deny; but it is also true that the new Hellenised literature exerted a malign influence on the nation's ancient austerity, introducing lax Grecian notions which contributed to moral and material decadence. The counter-currents, however, were strong; and the virile Roman spirit shone nobly through the Athenian dress in almost every instance, imparting to the literature a distinctively national cast, and displaying the peculiar characteristics of the Italian mind. On the whole, Roman life moulded Roman literature more than the literature moulded the life.

The earliest writings of the Latins are, save for a fragment or two, lost to posterity; though a few of their qualities are known. They were for the most part crude ballads in an odd "Saturnian" metre copied from the Etruscans, primitive religious chants and dirges, rough medleys of comic verse forming the prototype of satire, and awkward "Fescennine" dialogues or dramatic farces enacted by the lively peasantry. All doubtless reflected the simple, happy and virtuous, if stern, life of the home-loving agricultural race which was destined later to conquer the world. In B. C. 364 the medleys or "Saturæ" were enacted upon the Roman stage, the words supplemented by the pantomime and dancing of Etruscan performers who spoke no Latin. Another early form of dramatic art was the "fabula Atellana," which was adapted from the neighbouring tribe of Oscans, and which possessed a simple plot and stock characters. While this early literature embodied Oscan and Etruscan as well as Latin elements, it was truly Roman; for the Roman was himself formed of just such a mixture. All Italy contributed to the Latin stream, but at no time did any non-Roman dialect rise to the distinction of a real literature. We have here no parallel for the Æolic, Ionic, and Doric phases of Greek literature.

Classical Latin literature dates from the beginning of Rome's free intercourse with Greece, a thing brought about by the conquest of the Hellenic colonies in Southern Italy. When Tarentum fell to the Romans in B. C. 272, there was brought to Rome as a captive and slave a young man of great attainments, by name Andronicus. His master, M. Livius Salinator, was quick to perceive his genius, and soon gave him his liberty, investing him according to custom with his own nomen of Livius, so that the freedman was afterward known as Livius Andronicus. The erstwhile slave, having established a school, commenced his literary career by translating the Odyssey into Latin Saturnian verse for the use of his pupils. This feat was followed by the translation of a Greek drama, which was enacted in B. C. 240, and formed the first genuinely classic piece beheld by the Roman public. The success of Livius Andronicus was very considerable, and he wrote many more plays, in which he himself acted, besides attempting lyric and religious poetry. His

171

work, of which but 41 lines remain in existence, was pronounced inferior by Cicero; yet must ever be accorded respect as the very commenecent of a great literature.

Latin verse continued to depend largely on Greek models, but in prose the Romans were more original, and the first celebrated prose writer was that stern old Greek hater, M. Porcius Cato (234-149 B. C.), who prepared orations and wrote on history, agriculture, and other subjects. His style was clear, though by no means perfect, and it is a source of regret that his historical work, the "Origines," is lost. Other prose writers, all orators, extending from Cato's time down to the polished period, are Lælius, Scipio, the Gracchi, Antonius, Crassus, and the celebrated Q. Hortensius, early opponent of Cicero.

Satire, that one absolutely native product of Italy, first found independent expression in C. Lucilius (180-103 B. C.), though the great Roman inclination toward that form of expression had already found an outlet in satirical passages in other sorts of writing. There is perhaps no better weapon for the scourging of vice and folly than this potent literary embodiment of wit and irony, and certainly no author ever wielded that weapon more nobly than Lucilius. His æra was characterised by great degeneracy, due to Greek influences, and the manner in which he upheld failing Virtue won him the unmeasured regard of his contemporaries and successors. Horace, Persius, and Juvenal all owe much to him, and it is melancholy to reflect that all his work, save a fragment or two, is lost to the world. Lucilius, sometimes called "The Father of Satire," was a man of equestrian rank, and fought with Scipio at Numantia.

With the age of M. Tullius Cicero (106-43 B. C.)—the Golden Age—opens the period of highest perfection in Roman literature. It is hardly necessary to describe Cicero himself—his luminous talents have made him synonymous with the height of Attic elegance in wit, forensic art, and prose composition. Born of equestrian rank, he was educated with care, and embarked on his career at the age of twenty-five. His orations against L. Sergius Catilina during his consulship broke up one of the most dastardly plots in history, and gained for him the title of "Father of His Country." Philosophy claimed much of his time, and his delightful treatises "De Amicitia" and "De Senectute" will be read as long as friendship endures on earth, or men grow old. Near the end of his life Cicero, opposing the usurpations of M. Antonius, delivered his masterpieces of oratory, the "Philippics," modelled after the similar orations of the Greek Demosthenes against Philip of Macedonia. His murder, demanded by the vengeful Antonius in the proscription of the second triumvirate, was the direct result of these Philippics. Contemporary with Cicero was M. Terentius Varro, styled "most learned of the Romans," though ungraceful in style. Of his works, embracing many diverse subjects, only one agricultural treatise survives.

In this survey we need allot but little space to Caius Julius Cæsar, probably the greatest human being so far to appear on this globe. His Commentaries on the Gallic and Civil Wars are models of pure and perspicuous prose, and his other work, voluminous but now lost, was doubtless of equal merit. At the present time, passages of Cæsar's Gallic War are of especial interest on account of their allusions to battles against those perpetual enemies of civilisation, the Germans. How familiar, for instance, do we find the following passage from Book Six, describing German notions of honour:

"Latrocinia nullam habent infamiam, quæ extra fines cujusque civitatis fiunt, atque ea juventutis exercendæ ac desidiæ minuendæ causa fieri prædicant!"

The next generation of authors fall within what has been termed the "Augustan Age," the period during which Octavianus, having become Emperor, encouraged letters to a degree hitherto unknown; not only personally, but through his famous minister Mæcenas (73-8 B. C.). The literature of this period is immortal through the genius of Virgil, Horace, and Ovid, and has made the name "Augustan" an universal synonyme for classic elegance and urbanity. Thus in our own literary history, Queen Anne's reign is known as the "Augustan Age" on account of the brilliant wits and poets then at their zenith. Mæcenas, whose name must ever typify the ideal of munificent literary patronage, was himself a scholar and poet, as was indeed Augustus. Both, however, are overshadowed by the titanic geniuses who gathered around them.

Succeeding the Golden Age, and extending down to the time of the Antonines, is the so-called "Silver Age" of Latin literature, in which are included several writers of the highest genius, despite a general decadence and artificiality of style. In the reign of Tiberius we note the annalists C. Velleius Paterculus and Valerius Maximus, the medical writer, A. Cornelius Celsus, and the fabulist Phædrus, the latter a freedman from Thrace who imitated his more celebrated predecessor Æsop.

The satirist, A. Persius Flaccus (34-62 A. D.), is the first eminent poet to appear after the death of Ovid. Born at Volaterræ of an equestrian family, carefully reared by his gifted mother, and educated at Rome by the Stoic philosopher Cornutus, he became famous not only as a moralist of the greatest power and urbanity, but as one whose life accorded perfectly with his precepts; a character of unblemished virtue and delicacy in an age of unprecedented evil. His work, which attacked only the less repulsive follies of the day, contains passages of the highest nobility. His early death terminated a career of infinite promise.

In the person of D. Junius Juvenalis (57-128 A. D.), commonly called Juvenal, we behold the foremost satirist in literary history. Born at Aquinum of humble but comfortably situated parents, he came to Rome as a rhetorician; though upon discovering his natural bent, turned to poetical satire. With a fierceness and moral seriousness unprecedented in literature, Juvenal attacked the darkest vices of his age; writing as a relentless enemy rather than as a man of the world like Horace, or as a detached spectator like Persius. The oft repeated accusation that his minute descriptions of vice shew a morbid interest therein, may fairly be refuted when one considers the almost unthinkable depths to which the republic had fallen. Only a tolerant or a secluded observer could avoid attacking openly and bitterly the evil conditions which obtruded themselves on every hand; and Juvenal, a genuine Roman of the active and virtuous old school, was neither tolerant nor secluded. Juvenal wrote sixteen satires in all, the most famous of which are the third and tenth, both imitated in modern times with great success by Dr. Johnson. Contemporary with Juvenal was the Spaniard, M. Valerius Martialis (43-117 A. D.), commonly called Martial, master of the classic epigram. Unsurpassed in compact, scintillant wit, his works present a subjective and familiar picture of that society which Juvenal so bitterly attacked from without.

We come now upon one of the most distressing spectacles of human history. The mighty empire of Rome; its morals corrupted through Eastern influences, its spirit depressed through despotic government, and its people reduced to mongrel degeneracy through unrestrained immigration and foreign admixture; suddenly ceases to be an abode of creative thought, and sinks into a mental lethargy which dries up the very fountains of art and literature. The Emperor Constantinus, desirous of embellishing his new capital with the most magnificent decorations, can find no artist capable of fashioning them; and is obliged to strip ancient Greece of her choicest sculptures to fulfil his needs. Plainly, the days of Roman glory are over; and only a few and mainly mediocre geniuses are to be expected in the years preceding the actual downfall of Latin civilisation.

It is interesting, in a melancholy way, to trace the course of Roman poetry down to its very close, when it is lost amidst the darkness of the Middle Ages. Claudius Rutilius Namatianus, who flourished in the 5th century, was a Gaul, and wrote a very fair piece culled the "Itinerarium," describing a voyage from Rome to his native province. Though inferior to his contemporary, Claudian, in genius, Rutilius excels him in purity of diction and refinement of taste. At this period, pure Latin was probably confined to the highest circles, the masses already using that eloquium vulgare which later on formed the several modern Romance Languages; hence Rutilius must have been in a sense a classical antiquarian.

The end draws near. Compilers, grammarians, critics, commentators, and encyclopædists; summarising the past and quibbling over technical minutiæ; are the last survivors of a dying literature from whence inspiration has already fled. Macrobius, a critic and grammarian of celebrity, flourished in the fourth or fifth century, and interests us as being one through knowledge of whose works Samuel Johnson first attracted notice at Oxford. Priscian, conceded to be one of the principal grammatical authorities of the Roman world, flourished about the year 500. Isidorus Hispalensis, Bishop of Seville, grammarian, historian and theologian, was the most celebrated and influential literary character of the crumbling Roman fabric, save the philosopher Boetius and the historian Cassiodorus, and was highly esteemed during the Middle Ages, of which, indeed, he was as much a part, as he was a part of expiring classicism.

Now falls the curtain. Roma fuit. At the time of Isidorus' death in A. D. 636, the beginnings of mediævalism were fully under way. Authorship had disappeared in the broader sense; learning, such as it was, had retired into the monasteries; whilst the populace of the erstwhile Empire, living side by side with the invading barbarians, no longer spoke a language justly to be called classical Latin. With the revival of letters we shall see more Latin writings, but they will not be Roman; for their authors will have new and strange idioms for their mother-tongues, and will view life in a somewhat different manner. The link of continuity will have been irreparably broken, and these revivers will be Romans only in an artificial and antiquarian sense. He who calls himself "Pomponius Lætus" will be found to have been baptised Pomponio Leto. Classical antiquity, with its simple magnificence, can never return.

In glancing back over the literature we have examined, we are impressed by its distinctiveness, despite its Greek form. It is truly characteristic of the Roman people, and expresses Rome's majestic mind in a multitude of ways. Law, order, justice, and supremacy; "these things, O Roman, shall to you be arts!" All through the works of Latin authors runs this love of fame, power, order, and permanence. Art is not a prime phase of life or entirely an intrinsic pleasure, but a means of personal or national glorification; the true Roman poet writes his own epitaph for posterity, and exults in the lasting celebrity his memory will receive. Despite his debt to Hellas, he detests the foreign influence, and can find no term of satirical opprobrium more biting than "Græculus." The sense of rigid virtue, so deficient in the Greek, blossoms forth nobly in the Roman; making moral satire the greatest of native growths. Naturally, the Roman mind is most perfectly expressed in those voluminous works of law, extending all the way down to the Byzantine age of Justinianus, which have given the modern world its entire foundation of jurisprudence; but of these, lack of space forbids us to treat. They are not, strictly speaking, a part of literature proper.

The influence of the Latin classics upon modern literature has been tremendous. They are today, and will ever be, vital sources of inspiration and guidance. Our own most correct age, that of Queen Anne and the first three Georges, was saturated with their spirit; and there is scarce a writer of note who does not visibly reflect their immediate influence. Each classic English author has, after a fashion, his Latin counterpart. Mr. Pope was a Horace; Dr. Johnson a Juvenal. The early Elizabethan tragedy was a reincarnation of Seneca, as comedy was of Plautus. English literature teems with Latin quotations and allusions to such a degree that no reader can extract full benefit if he have not at least a superficial knowledge of Roman letters.

Wherefore it is enjoined upon the reader not to neglect cultivation of this rich field; a field which offers as much of pure interest and enjoyment of necessary cultural training and wholesome intellectual discipline.

TO ALAN SEEGER

Howard Phillips Lovecraft

(In National Enquirer)

SEEGER, whose soul, with animated lyre
Wak'd the dull dreamer to a manlier fire;
Whose martial voice, by martial deeds sustain'd,
Denounc'd the age when shameful peace remain'd;
Let thy brave spirit yet among us dwell,

And linger where thy form in valour fell:
Proudly before th' invader's fury mass'd,
Behold thy country's cohorts, rous'd at last!
It was not for thy mortal eye to see
Columbia arm'd for right and liberty;
Thine was the finer heart, that could not stay
To wait for laggards in the vital fray,
And ere the millions felt thy sacred heat,
Thou hadst thy gift to Freedom made complete.
But while thou sleepest in an honour'd grave
Beneath the Gallic sod thou bledst to save,
May thy soul's vision scan the ravag'd plain,
And tell thee that thou didst not fall in vain:
Here, as though pray'dst, a million men advance,
To prove Columbia one with flaming France,
And heeding now the long-forgotten debt,
Pay with their blood the gen'rous LAFAYETTE!
Thy ringing odes to prophecies are turn'd,
Whilst legions feel the blaze that in thee burn'd.
Not as a lonely stranger dost thou lie,
Thy form forsaken 'neath a foreign sky,
On Gallic tongues thy name forever lives,
First of the mighty host thy country gives:
All that thou dreamt'st in life shall come to be,
And proud Columbia find her voice in thee!

(Alan Seeger fell in the Cause of Civilisation at Belloy-en-
Santerre, July 4, 1916.)

THE UNITED AMATEUR JANUARY 1919

THEODORE ROOSEVELT
1858-1919

Last of the giants, in whose soul shone clear
The sacred torch of greatness and of right,
A stricken world, that cannot boast thy peer,
Mourns o'er thy grave amidst the new-born night.

Sage, seer and statesman, wise in ev'ry art;
First to behold, and first to preach, the truth;
Soldier and patriot, in whose mighty heart
Throbb'd the high valour of eternal youth.

Foremost of citizens and best of chiefs,
Within thy mind no weak inaction lay;
Leal to thy standards, firm in thy beliefs;
As quick to do, as others are to say.

Freeman and gentleman, whose spirit glow'd
With kindness' and with goodness' warmest fire;
To prince and peasant thy broad friendship flow'd,
Each proud to take, and eager to admire.

Within thy book of life each spotless page
Lies open for a world's respecting view;
Thou stand'st the first and purest of our age,
To private, as to public virtue true.

In thee did such transcendent greatness gleam,
That none might grudge thee an Imperial place;
Yet such thy modesty, thou need'st must seem
The leader, not the monarch, of thy race.

Courage and pow'r, to wit and learning join'd,
With energy that sham'd the envious sun;
The ablest, bravest, noblest of mankind—
A Caesar and Aurelius mixt in one.

At thy stern gaze Dishonour bow'd its head;
Oppression slunk ingloriously away;
The virtuous follow'd where thy footsteps led,
And Freedom bless'd thy uncorrupted sway.

When from the East invading Vandals pour'd,
And selfish ignorance restrain'd our hand,
Thy voice was first to bid us draw the sword
To guard our liberties and save our land.

Envy deny'd thee what thy spirit sought,
And held thee from the battle-seething plain;
Yet thy proud blood in filial bodies fought,
And poppies blossom o'er thy QUENTIN slain.

'Twas thine to see the triumph of thy cause;
Thy grateful eyes beheld a world redeem'd;
Would that thy wisdom might have shap'd the laws
Of the new age, and led to heights undream'd!

Yet art thou gone? Will not thy presence cling
Like that of all the great who liv'd before?
Will not new wonders of thy fashioning
Rise from thy words, as potent as of yore?

Absent in flesh, thou with a brighter flame
Shin'st as the beacon of the brave and free;
Thou art our country's soul—our loftiest aim
Is but to honour and to follow thee!

H. P. LOVECRAFT
January 13, 1919

THE UNITED AMATEUR MARCH 1919

A NOTE ON HOWARD P. LOVECRAFT'S VERSE

Rheinhart Kleiner

Comment occasioned by the verse of Mr. Howard P. Lovecraft, who is a more or less frequent contributor to the amateur press, has not consisted of unmixed praise.

Certain critics have regarded his efforts as too obviously imitative of a style that has long been discredited. Others have accepted his work with admiration and have even gone so far as to imitate the couplets which he produces with such apparent ease.

Between these two opinions there is a critical neutral ground, the holders of which realise how large an element of conscious parody enters into many of Mr. Lovecraft's longer and more serious productions, and who are capable of appreciating the cleverness and literary charm of these pastoral echoes without being dominated by them to the extent of indiscriminate praise and second-hand imitation.

179

Those who would beguile Mr. Lovecraft from his chosen path are probably unaware of the attitude which he consistently maintains toward hostile criticism. Mr. Lovecraft contends that it gives him pleasure to write as the Augustans did, and that those who do not relish his excursions into classic fields need not follow him. He tries to conciliate no one, and is content to be his own sole reader! What critic, with these facts before him, will think it worthwhile to break a lance with the poet?

But even Mr. Lovecraft is willing to be original, at times. He has written verse of a distinctly modern atmosphere, and where his imagery is not too obtrusively artificial—according to the modern idea—many of his quatrains possess genuine poetic value.

Many who cannot read his longer and more ambitious productions find Mr. Lovecraft's light or humorous verse decidedly refreshing. As a satirist along familiar lines, particularly those laid down by Butler, Swift and Pope, he is most himself—paradoxical though it seems. In reading his satires one cannot help but feel the zest with which the author has composed them. They are admirable for the way in which they reveal the depth and intensity of Mr. Lovecraft's convictions, while the wit, irony, sarcasm and humour to be found in them serve as an indication of his powers as a controversialist. The almost relentless ferocity of his satires is constantly relieved by an attendant broad humour which has the merit of causing the reader to chuckle more than once in the perusal of some attack levelled against the particular person or policy which may have incurred Mr. Lovecraft's displeasure.

OFFICIAL REPORTS

DEPARTMENT OF PUBLIC CRITICISM

The Coyote for October-January is a "Special War Number," dedicated to Cpl. Raymond Wesley Harrington, the editor's valiant soldier brother, and having a general martial atmosphere throughout. Among the contents are two bits of verse by the gallant overseas warrior to whom the issue is inscribed, both of which speak well for the poetic sentiment of their heroic author.

"Lord Love You, Lad," a poem by Winifred V. Jordan, is the

opening contribution; and deserves highest commendation both for its spirit and for its construction.

"The Paramount Issue," by William T. Harrington, is a somewhat ambitious attempt to trace the responsibility for the great war to alcoholic liquor and its degenerative effect on mankind. The author even goes so far as to say that "had man been represented in his true and noble form, then war would have been impossible." Now although the present critic is and always has been an ardent prohibitionist, he must protest at this extravagant theory. Vast and far-reaching as are the known evil effects of drink, it is surely transcending fact to accuse it of causing mankind's natural greed, pride, and combative instincts, which lie at the base of all warfare. It may, however, be justly suggested that much of the peculiar bestiality of the Huns is derived from their swinish addiction to beer. Technically, Mr. Harrington's essay is marked by few crudities, and displays an encouraging fluency. Other pieces by Mr. Harrington are "A Bit of My Diary," wherein the author relates his regrettably brief military experience at Camp Dodge, and "Victory," a stirring editorial.

"Black Sheep," by Edna Hyde, is an excellent specimen of blank verse by our gifted laureate. Line 14 seems to lack a syllable, but this deficiency is probably the result of a typographical error.

A word of praise is due the general appearance of the magazine. The cover presents a refreshing bit of home-made pictorial art, whilst the photograph of Corporal Harrington makes a most attractive frontispiece.

The Pathfinder for January is easily the best issue yet put forth by its enterprising young editor. "Hope," which adorns the cover, is a poem of much merit by Annie Pearce. The apparent lack of a syllable in line 2 of the third stanza is probably due to a printer's error whereby the word us is omitted immediately after the word for.

"How and Why Roses Are White," by Margaret Mahon, is a fairy legend of much charm and decided originality, which argues eloquently for its author's imaginative scope and literary ability.

"Happiness in a Glove" is a very facile and pleasing rendering of a bit of Spanish dialogue. Through a mistake, the authorship is credited to the translator, Miss Ella M. Miller, though her own manuscript fully proclaimed the text as a translation.

"Welcome, 1919," is a brief contemplative essay by Editor Glause; in spirit admirable, but in phraseology showing some of the uncertainty of youthful work. Mr. Glause might well pay more attention to compact precision in his prose, using as few and as forceful words as possible to express his meaning. For instance, his opening words would gain greatly in strength if contracted to the following: "Now that a new year is beginning." Farther down the page we find the word namely in a place which impels us to question its use. Its total omission would strengthen the sentence which contains it. Another point we must mention is the excessive punctuation, especially the needless hyphenation of amateurdom and therefore, and the apostrophe in the possessive pronoun its. The form it's is restricted to the colloquial contraction of "it is"; the similarly spelled pronoun is written solidly without an apostrophe. Additional notes by Mr. Glause are of equal merit, and his reply to a recent article on travel is highly sensible and commendable. He is a writer and thinker of much power, and needs only technical training in order to develop into an essayist of the first rank. As an editor he cannot be praised too highly for his faithfulness in publishing his welcome and attractive quarterly.

Pine Cones for February well maintains the high standard set by Mr. Pryor in his opening number. "Life, Death and Immortality," by Jonathan E. Hoag, is a brief but appealing piece from the pen of a gifted and venerable bard, and thoroughly deserves its place of honour on the cover. On the next page occurs a metrical tribute to this sweet singer on his 88th birthday, written by H. P. Lovecraft in the latter's typical heroic strain.

"The Helpful Twins," a clever child story by Editor Pryor, is the prose treat of the issue. It would, indeed, be hard to find more than one or two equally interesting, human, and well-developed bits of fiction in any current amateur periodicals. Not only are the characters drawn with delightful naturalness, but there is real humour present; and the plot moves on to its climax without a single instance of awkwardness or a single intrusive or extraneous episode. In short, the story is almost a model of its kind; one which ought to prove a success in a professional as well as an amateur magazine. Mr. Pryor's humour is more broadly shown in the smile-producing pseudo-anecdotes of "The Boy Washington."

The bit of unsigned verse, "A New Year Wish," is excellent, though we question the advisability of having an Alexandrine for the final line.

"Comment Pryoristic" is always interesting, and that in the current Pine Cones forms no exception to the rule. The appearance of this vigorously alive and intelligently edited publication is proving a great and gratifying factor in amateurdom's post-bellum renaissance.

The Recruiter for January marks the advent to amateurdom of a new paper, which easily takes its place among the very best of recent editorial enterprises. Edited by Misses Mary Faye Durr and

L. Evelyn Schump in the interest of the United recruits whom they are securing, its thoroughly meritorious quality speaks well for the new members thus added to our circle.

The issue opens auspiciously with a lyric poem of distinguished excellence by Helen McFarland, entitled "A Casualty." In depth of sentiment, fervour of expression, and correctness of construction, these melodious lines leave little to be desired; and seem to indicate that the United has acquired one more poet of the first rank.

"Billy," a character sketch by L. Evelyn Schump, introduces to the Association a light essayist of unusual power and grace, whose work is vividly natural through keen insight, apt and fluent expression, and mastery of homely and familiar detail. The present sketch is captivatingly lifelike and thoroughly well-written, arousing a response from every lover of children.

"Winter," a brief poem by Hettie Murdock, celebrates in a pleasant way an unpleasant season. The lines are notable for correctness, spontaneity and vitality, though not in the least ambitious in scope.

Martha Charlotte Macatee's "Song of Nature" reveals its 12-year-old creator as a genuine "Galpiness" (if we may coin a word which only amateurs and Appletonians will understand). Mistress Macatee has succeeded in infusing more than a modicum of really poetic atmosphere and imagery into her short lyric, and may be relied upon to produce important work in the coming years of greater maturity. The chief defect of her present piece is the absence of rhyme, which should always occur in a short stanzaic poem. Rhyming is not at all difficult after a little practice, and we trust that the young writer will employ it in later verses.

"Tarrytown," by Florence Fitzgerald, is a reminiscent poem of phenomenal strength, marred only by a pair of false rhymes in the opening stanza. Assonance must never be mistaken for true rhyme, and combinations like boats-float or them-brim should be avoided. The imagery of this piece is especially appealing, and testifies to its author's fertility of fancy.

"Shades of Adam," by Mary Faye Durr, is an interesting and humorously written account of the social side of our 1918 convention. Miss Durr is exceptionally gifted in the field of apt, quiet, and laconic wit, and in this informal chronicle neglects no opportunity for dryly amusing comment on persons and events.

"Spring," by L. Evelyn Schump, is a refreshingly original poem in blank verse, on a somewhat familiar subject. For inspiration and technique alike, the piece merits enthusiastic commendation; though we may vindicate our reputation as a fault-finding critic by asking why alternate lines are indented despite the non-existence of alternate rhymes.

The Recruiter's editorial column is brief and businesslike, introducing the magazine as a whole, and its contributors individually. Amateurdom is deeply indebted to the publishers of this delightful newcomer, and it is to be hoped that they may continue their efforts; both toward seeking recruits as high in quality as those here represented, and toward issuing their admirable journal as frequently as is feasible.

The Silver Clarion for January comes well up to the usual standard, containing a number of pieces of considerable power. In "The Temple of the Holy Ghost," Mr. Arthur Goodenough achieves his accustomed success as a religious poet, presenting a variety of apt images, and clothing them in facile metre. The only defect is a lack of uniformity in rhyming plan. The poet, in commencing a piece like this, should decide whether or not to rhyme the first and third lines of quatrains; and having decided, should adhere to his decision. Instead, Mr. Goodenough omits these optional rhymes in the first stanza and in the first half of the third and fourth stanzas; elsewhere employing them. The result, while not flagrantly inharmonious, nevertheless gives an impression of imperfection, and tends to alienate the fastidious critic. Mr. Goodenough possesses so great a degree of inspiration, and so wide an array of allusions and imagery; that he owes it to himself to complete the excellence of his vivid work with an unexceptionable technique.

"The Cross," a sonnet by Captain Theodore Draper Gottlieb, is dedicated to the Red Cross, with which the author is serving so valiantly. In thought and form this piece deserves unqualified praise.

"Death," by Andrew Francis Lockhart, exhibits our versatile Western bard in sober mood. The poem contains that unmistakable stamp of genuine emotion which we have come to associate with Mr. Lockhart's work, and is technically faultless.

"Destiny," by W. F. Pelton, is a sonnet of smooth construction and thorough excellence by one whom we know better as "Wilfrid Kemble."

The lines "To My Pal, Fred" present Mr. Harry E. Rieseberg, a new member of the United who has for some time been a regular Clarion contributor. In this piece Mr. Rieseberg falls somewhat below his usual standard; for though the sentiment is appropriate, the metre is sadly irregular. Mr. Rieseberg should count the syllables in his lines, for he is a young poet of much promise, and should allow his technique to keep pace with his genius.

"Faith," by Winifred V. Jordan, enunciates a familiar doctrine in melodious and original metaphor, and well sustains the poetical reputation of its celebrated author.

"The Song Unsung," by W. F. Booker, is a war poem in minor key, which deserves much praise.

"You're Like a Willow," by Eugene B. Kuntz, is marked by that warmth of fancy and wealth of imagery for which its author is noted.

"Thoughts," a courtly offering from the quill of James Laurence Crowley, winds up the poetical part of the magazine; this month a very ample part. In rhyme and metre this sentimental gem is quite satisfactory.

The only prose in this issue is Mr. Samples' well-written editorial on "The Passing Year." Herein we find some really excellent passages, savouring somewhat of the oratorical in style.

The Silver Clarion for February is of ample size and ample merit. Opening the issue is an excellent poem in heroic couplets by Mrs. Stella L. Tully of Mountmellick, Ireland, a new member of the United. Mrs. Tully, whose best work is in a lyric and religious vein, is one endowed with hereditary or family genius; as the Association no doubt appreciated when reading the poetry of her gifted sister, Mrs. S. Lilian McMullen of Newton Centre, in the preceding issue of THE UNITED AMATEUR. The present piece by Mrs. Tully, "The Greatest of These is Love," is based upon a Biblical text, and sets forth its ideas very effectively, despite a few passages whose stiff construction betrays a slight inexperience in the traditions of heroic verse.

"The Two Crosses," by Capt. Theodore Gottlieb, is also in heroics, and graphically compares the most holy symbols of today and of nineteen hundred years ago.

More of the religious atmosphere is furnished by John Milton Samples' trochaic composition entitled "The Millennium"—from whose title, by the way, one of the necessary n's is missing. In this pleasing picture of an impossible age we note but three things requiring critical attention. (1) The term "super-race" in stanza 5, is too technically philosophical to be really poetic. (2) The rhyme of victory and eternally is not very desirable, because both the rhyming syllables bear only a secondary accent. (3) There is something grotesque and unconsciously comic in the prophecy "Then the lamb shall kiss the lion." Such grotesqueness is not to be found in the original words of Mr. Samples' predecessor and source of inspiration, the well-known prophet Isaiah. (Vide Isaiah, xi: 6-7.)

"Nature Worship," by Arthur Goodenough, is one of the most meritorious poems in the issue, despite some dubious grammar in the first stanza, and an internal rhyme in the final stanza which has no counterpart in the lines preceding. The first named error consists of a disagreement in number betwixt subject and verb: "faith and form and ... mazes which ... perplexes, dazes."

"The New Order," an essay by John Milton Samples, is an eloquent but fantastically idealistic bit of speculation concerning the wonderful future which dreamers picture as arising out of the recent war. To us, there is a sort of pathos in these vain hopes and mirage-like visions of an Utopia which can never be; yet if they can cheer anyone, they are doubtless not altogether futile. Indeed, after the successive menaces of the Huns and the Bolsheviki, we can call almost any future Utopian, if it will but afford the comparative calm of pre-1914 days!

"No Night So Dark, No Day So Drear," by Mamie Knight Samples, is a poem which reveals merit despite many crudities. The outstanding fault is defective metre—Mrs. Samples should carefully count her syllables, and repeat her lines aloud, to make sure of perfect scansion. Since the intended metre appears to be iambic tetrameter, we shall here give a revised rendering of the first stanza; showing how it can be made to conform to that measure:

> "No night so dark, no day so drear,
> But we may sing our songs of cheer."
> These words, borne from the world without,
> Cheer'd a heart sick with grief and doubt.
> O doubting soul, bow'd down so low,
> If thou couldst feel, and only know
> The darkness is in thee alone,
> For grief and tears it would atone.
> "No night so dark, no day so drear,
> But we may sing our songs of cheer."

Let the authoress note that each line must have eight syllables—no more, no less. For the trite ideas and hackneyed rhymes, nothing can be recommended save a more observant and discriminating perusal of standard poets. It must be kept in mind that the verse found in current family magazines and popular hymn-books is seldom, if ever, true poetry. The only authors suitable as models, are those whose names are praised in histories of English literature.

W. F. Booker's "Song" is a delightful short lyric whose sentiment and technique deserve naught but praise.

"When I Am Gone," a poem in pentameter quatrains by James Laurence Crowley, contains the customary allotment of sweet sentiment, together with some really commendable imagery. Mr. Crowley's genius will shine brightly before long.

"The Path to Glory," by Andrew Francis Lockhart, is perhaps the poetic gem of the issue. In this virile anapæstic piece Mr. Lockhart sums up all the horrors of the trenches in such a way that the reader may guess at the extent of the sacrifice undergone by those who have given all for their country.

In "Coconino Jim, Lumberjack," Mr. Harry E. Rieseberg shows himself a true and powerful poet of the rugged, virile school of Kipling, Service, Knibbs, and their analogues. The present piece is entirely correct in rhyme and well-developed in thought, wanting only good metre to make it perfect. This latter accomplishment Mr. Rieseberg should strive hard to attain, for his poetry surely deserves as good a form as he can give it.

A word of praise should be given Mr. Samples' editorial, "The Professional in Amateur Journalism," in which he shows the fallacy of the plea for a cruder, more juvenile amateurdom, which often emanates from members of the older and less progressive associations. As the editor contends, intellectual evolution must occur; and the whole recent career of the United demonstrates the value of a purely literary society for genuine literary aspirants of every age and every stage of mental development.

THE UNITED AMATEUR MAY 1919

HELENE HOFFMAN COLE—LITTERATEUR

Howard Phillips Lovecraft

Of the various authors who have contributed to the fame of our Association, few can be compared in sustained ability and breadth of interests to the late Helene Hoffman Cole. Represented in the press as a poet, critic, essayist, and fiction-writer, Mrs. Cole achieved distinction in all of these departments; rising during recent years to an almost unique prominence in the field of book-reviewing. Her compositions display a diversity of attainments and catholicity of taste highly remarkable in one of so relatively slight an age, familiar knowledge of foreign and archaic literature supplying a mature background too seldom possessed by amateur authors.

It is as a poet that Mrs. Cole has been least known, since her verse was not of frequent occurrence in the amateur press. A glance at the few existing specimens, however, demonstrates conclusively that her poetical gifts were by no means inconsiderable; and that had she chosen such a course, she might easily have become one of the leading bards of the United. Verse like the unnamed autumn pieces in Leaflets and The Hellenian possess an aptness and cleverness of fancy which bespeak the true poet despite trivial technical imperfections.

In fiction the extent of Mrs. Cole's genius was still further revealed, nearly all her narratives moving along with impeccable grace and fluency. Her plots were for the most part light and popular in nature, and would have reflected credit on any professional writer of modern magazine tales. Of her stories, "The Picture," appearing in Leaflets for October, 1913, is an excellent example. More dramatic in quality is "Her Wish," in the August, 1914, Olympian. This brief tragedy of a Serbian and his bride is perhaps one of the very first tales written around the World War.

But it is in the domain of the literary essay that this authoress rose to loftiest altitude. Of wide and profound reading, and of keen and discriminating mind, Mrs. Cole presented in a style of admirable grace and lucidity her reactions to the best works of numerous standard authors, ancient and modern, English and foreign. The value of such work in amateurdom, extending the cultural outlook and displaying the outside world as seen through the eyes of a gifted, respected, and representative member, scarce needs the emphasis of the commentator. He who can link the amateur and larger spheres in a pleasing and acceptable fashion, deserves the highest approbation and panegyric that the United can bestow. Notable indeed are Mrs. Cole's sound reviews of Sir Thomas Browne's "Hydriotaphia" in THE UNITED AMATEUR, of "Pelle, the Conqueror" in The Tryout, and of numerous South American works but little known to Northern readers. Of equal merit are such terse and delightful essays as "M. Tullius Cicero, Pater Patriae," where the essayist invests a classical theme with all the living charm of well-restrained subjectivity. The style of these writings is in itself captivating; the vocabulary containing enough words of Latin derivation to rescue it from the Boeotian harshness typical of this age. All that has been said of Mrs. Cole's broader reviews may be said of her amateur criticism, much of which graced the columns of The Olympian and other magazines.

The exclusively journalistic skill of Mrs. Cole now remains to be considered, and this we find as brilliant as her other attainments. As the editor of numerous papers during every stage of her career, she exhibited phenomenal taste and enterprise; never failing to create enthusiasm and evoke encomium with her ventures both individual and co-operative. Her gift for gathering, selecting and writing news was quite unexampled. As the reporter par excellence of both associations, she was the main reliance of other editors for convention reports and general items; all of which were phrased with an ease, urbanity, and personality that lent them distinctiveness. Not the least of her qualities was a gentle and unobtrusive humour which enlivened her lighter productions. Amateurdom will long remember the quaint piquancy of the issues of The Martian which she cleverly published in the name of her infant son.

During these latter days nearly every amateur has expressed a kind of incredulity that Mrs. Cole can indeed be no more, and in this the present writer must needs share. To realise that her gifted pen has ceased to enrich our small literary world requires a painful effort on the part of everyone who has followed her brilliant progress in the field of letters. The United loses more by her sudden and untimely demise than can well be reckoned at this moment.

THE UNITED AMATEUR JULY 1919

AMERICANISM

Howard Phillips Lovecraft

Laureate

It is easy to sentimentalise on the subject of "the American spirit"—what it is, may be, or should be. Exponents of various novel political and social theories are particularly given to this practice, nearly always concluding that "true Americanism" is nothing more or less than a national application of their respective individual doctrines.

Slightly less superficial observers hit upon the abstract principle of "Liberty" as the keynote of Americanism, interpreting this justly esteemed principle as anything from Bolshevism to the right to drink 2.75 per cent. beer. "Opportunity" is another favourite byword, and one which is certainly not without real significance.

The synonymousness of "America" and "opportunity" has been inculcated into many a young head of the present generation by Emerson via Montgomery's "Leading Facts of American History." But it is worthy of note that nearly all would-be definers of "Americanism" fail through their prejudiced unwillingness to trace the quality to its European source. They cannot bring themselves to see that abiogenesis is as rare in the realm of ideas as it is in the kingdom of organic life; and consequently waste their efforts in trying to treat America as if it were an isolated phenomenon without ancestry.

"Americanism" is expanded Anglo-Saxonism. It is the spirit of England, transplanted to a soil of vast extent and diversity, and nourished for a time under pioneer conditions calculated to increase its democratic aspects without impairing its fundamental virtues. It is the spirit of truth, honour, justice, morality, moderation, individualism, conservative liberty, magnanimity, toleration, enterprise, industriousness, and progress—which is England—plus the element of equality and opportunity caused by pioneer settlement. It is the expression of the world's highest race under the most favourable social, political, and geographical conditions. Those who endeavour to belittle the importance of our British ancestry, are invited to consider the other nations of this continent. All these are equally "American" in every particular, differing only in race-stock and heritage; yet of them all, none save British Canada will even bear comparison with us. We are great because we are a part of the great Anglo-Saxon cultural sphere; a section detached only after a century and a half of heavy colonisation and English rule, which gave to our land the ineradicable stamp of British civilisation.

Most dangerous and fallacious of the several misconceptions of Americanism is that of the so-called "melting-pot" of races and traditions. It is true that this country has received a vast influx of non-English immigrants who come hither to enjoy without hardship the liberties which our British ancestors carved out in toil and bloodshed. It is also true that such of them as belong to the Teutonic and Celtic races are capable of assimilation to our English type and of becoming valuable acquisitions to the population. But, from this it does not follow that a mixture of really alien blood or ideas has accomplished or can accomplish anything but harm. Observation of Europe shows us the relative status and capability of the several races, and we see that the melting together of English gold and alien brass is not very likely to produce any alloy superior or even equal to the original gold. Immigration cannot, perhaps, be cut off altogether, but it should be understood that aliens who choose America as their residence must accept the prevailing language and

190

culture as their own; and neither try to modify our institutions, nor to keep alive their own in our midst. We must not, as the greatest man of our age declared, suffer this nation to become a "polyglot boarding house."

The greatest foe to rational Americanism is that dislike for our parent nation which holds sway amongst the ignorant and bigoted, and which is kept alive largely by certain elements of the population who seem to consider the sentiments of Southern and Western Ireland more important than those of the United States. In spite of the plain fact that a separate Ireland would weaken civilisation and menace the world's peace by introducing a hostile and undependable wedge betwixt the two major parts of Saxondom, these irresponsible elements continue to encourage rebellion in the Green Isle; and in so doing tend to place this nation in a distressingly anomalous position as an abettor of crime and sedition against the Mother Land. Disgusting beyond words are the public honours paid to political criminals like Edward, alias Eamonn, de Valera, whose very presence at large among us is an affront to our dignity and heritage. Never may we appreciate or even fully comprehend our own place and mission in the world, till we can banish those clouds of misunderstanding which float between us and the source of our culture.

But the features of Americanism peculiar to this continent must not be belittled. In the abolition of fixed and rigid class lines a distinct sociological advance is made, permitting a steady and progressive recruiting of the upper levels from the fresh and vigorous body of the people beneath. Thus opportunities of the choicest sort await every citizen alike, whilst the biological quality of the cultivated classes is improved by the cessation of that narrow inbreeding which characterises European aristocracy.

Total separation of civil and religious affairs, the greatest political and intellectual advance since the Renaissance, is also a local American—and more particularly a Rhode Island—triumph. Agencies are today subtly at work to undermine this principle, and to impose upon us through devious political influences the Papal chains which Henry VIII first struck from our limbs; chains unfelt since the bloody reign of Mary, and infinitely worse than the ecclesiastical machinery which Roger Williams rejected. But when the vital relation of intellectual freedom to genuine Americanism shall be fully impressed upon the people, it is likely that such sinister undercurrents will subside.

The main struggle which awaits Americanism is not with reaction, but with radicalism. Our age is one of restless and unintelligent iconoclasm, and abounds with shrewd sophists who use the name "Americanism" to cover attacks on that institution itself. Such familiar terms and phrases as "democracy," "liberty," or "freedom of speech" are being distorted to cover the wildest forms of anarchy, whilst our old representative institutions are being attacked as "un-American" by foreign immigrants who are incapable both of understanding them or of devising anything better.

This country would benefit from a wider practice of sound Americanism, with its accompanying recognition of an Anglo-Saxon source. Americanism implies freedom, progress, and independence; but it does not imply a rejection of the past, nor a renunciation of traditions and experience. Let us view the term in its real, practical, and unsentimental meaning.

THE UNITED AMATEUR NOVEMBER 1919

THE WHITE SHIP

Howard Phillips Lovecraft

I am Basil Elton, keeper of the North Point light that my father and grandfather kept before me. Far from the shore stands the grey lighthouse, above sunken slimy rocks that are seen when the tide is low, but unseen when the tide is high. Past that beacon for a century have swept the majestic barques of the seven seas. In the days of my grandfather there were many; in the days of my father not so many; and now there are so few that I sometimes feel strangely alone, as though I were the last man on our planet.

From far shores came those white-sailed argosies of old; from far Eastern shores where warm suns shine and sweet odours linger about strange gardens and gay temples. The old captains of the sea came often to my grandfather and told him of these things, which in turn he told to my father, and my father told to me in the long autumn evenings when the wind howled eerily from the East. And I have read more of these things, and of many things besides, in the books men gave me when I was young and filled with wonder.

But more wonderful than the lore of old men and the lore of books is the secret lore of ocean. Blue, green, grey, white or black; smooth, ruffled, or mountainous; that ocean is not silent. All my days have I watched it and listened to it, and I know it well. At first it told to me only the plain little tales of calm beaches and near ports, but with the years it grew more friendly and spoke of other things; of things more strange and more distant in space and in time. Sometimes at twilight the grey vapours of the horizon have parted to grant me glimpses of the ways beyond; and sometimes at night the deep waters of the sea have grown clear and phosphorescent, to grant me glimpses of the ways beneath. And these glimpses have been as often of the ways that were and the ways that might be, as of the ways that are; for ocean is more ancient than the mountains, and freighted with the memories and the dreams of Time.

Out of the South it was that the White Ship used to come when the moon was full and high in the heavens. Out of the South it would glide very smoothly and silently over the sea. And whether the sea was rough or calm, and whether the wind was friendly or adverse, it would always glide smoothly and silently, its sails distent and its long strange tiers of oars moving rhythmically. One night I espied upon the deck a man, bearded and robed, and he seemed to beckon me to embark for fair unknown shores. Many times afterward I saw him under the full moon, and ever did he beckon me.

Very brightly did the moon shine on the night I answered the call, and I walked out over the waters to the White Ship on a bridge of moonbeams. The man who had beckoned now spoke a welcome to me in a soft language I seemed to know well, and the hours were filled with soft songs of the oarsmen as we glided away into a mysterious South, golden with the glow of that full, mellow moon.

And when the day dawned, rosy and effulgent, I beheld the green shore of far lands, bright and beautiful, and to me unknown. Up from the sea rose lordly terraces of verdure, tree-studded, and shewing here and there the gleaming white roofs and colonnades of strange temples. As we drew nearer the green shore the bearded man told me of that land, the Land of Zar, where dwell all the dreams and thoughts of beauty that come to men once and then are forgotten. And when I looked upon the terraces again I saw that what he said was true, for among the sights before me were many things I had once seen through the mists beyond the horizon in the phosphorescent depths of ocean. There too were forms and fantasies more splendid than I had ever known; the visions of young poets who died in want before the world could learn of what they had seen and dreamed. But we did not set foot upon the sloping meadows of Zar, for it is told that he who treads them may nevermore return to his native shore.

As the White Ship sailed silently away from the templed terraces of Zar, we beheld on the distant horizon ahead the spires of a mighty city; and the bearded man said to me, "This is Thalarion, the City of a Thousand Wonders, wherein reside all those mysteries that man has striven in vain to fathom." And I looked again, at closer range, and saw that the city was greater than any city I had known or dreamed of before. Into the sky the spires of its temples reached, so that no man might behold their peaks; and far back beyond the horizon stretched the grim, grey walls, over which one might spy only a few roofs, weird and ominous, yet adorned with rich friezes and alluring sculptures. I yearned mightily to enter this fascinating yet repellent city, and beseeched the bearded man to land me at the stone pier by the huge carven gate Akariel; but he gently denied my wish, saying, "Into Thalarion, the City of a Thousand Wonders, many have passed but none returned. Therein walk only dæmons and mad things that are no longer men, and the streets are white with the unburied bones of those who have looked upon the eidolon Lathi, that reigns over the city." So the White Ship sailed on past the walls of Thalarion, and followed for many days a southward-flying bird, whose glossy plumage matched the sky out of which it had appeared.

Then came we to a pleasant coast gay with blossoms of every hue, where as far inland as we could see basked lovely groves and radiant arbours beneath a meridian sun. From bowers beyond our view came bursts of song and snatches of lyric harmony, interspersed with faint laughter so delicious that I urged the rowers onward in my eagerness to reach the scene. And the bearded man spoke no word, but watched me as we approached the lily-lined shore. Suddenly a wind blowing from over the flowery meadows and leafy woods brought a scent at which I trembled. The wind grew stronger, and the air was filled with the lethal, charnel odour of plague-stricken towns and uncovered cemeteries. And as we sailed madly away from that damnable coast the bearded man spoke at last, saying, "This is Xura, the Land of Pleasures Unattained."

So once more the White Ship followed the bird of heaven, over warm blessed seas fanned by caressing, aromatic breezes. Day after day and night after night did we sail, and when the moon was full we would listen to soft songs of the oarsmen, sweet as on that distant night when we sailed away from my far native land. And it was by moonlight that we anchored at last in the harbour of Sona-Nyl, which is guarded by twin headlands of crystal that rise from the sea and meet in a resplendent arch. This is the Land of Fancy, and we walked to the verdant shore upon a golden bridge of moonbeams.

In the Land of Sona-Nyl there is neither time nor space, neither suffering nor death; and there I dwelt for many æons. Green are the groves and pastures, bright and fragrant the flowers, blue and musical the streams, clear and cool the fountains, and stately and gorgeous the temples, castles, and cities of Sona-Nyl. Of that land there is no bound, for beyond each vista of beauty rises another more beautiful. Over the countryside and amidst the splendour of cities can move at will the happy folk, of whom all are gifted with unmarred grace and unalloyed happiness. For the æons that I dwelt there I wandered blissfully through gardens where quaint pagodas peep from pleasing clumps of bushes, and where the white walks are bordered with delicate blossoms. I climbed gentle hills from whose summits I could see entrancing panoramas of loveliness, with steepled towns nestling in verdant valleys, and with the golden domes of gigantic cities glittering on the infinitely distant horizon. And I viewed by moonlight the sparkling sea, the crystal headlands, and the placid harbour wherein lay anchored the White Ship.

It was against the full moon one night in the immemorial year of Tharp that I saw outlined the beckoning form of the celestial bird, and felt the first stirrings of unrest. Then I spoke with the bearded man, and told him of my new yearning to depart for remote Cathuria, which no man hath seen, but which all believe to lie beyond the basalt pillars of the West. It is the Land of Hope, and in it shine the perfect ideals of all that we know elsewhere; or at least so men relate. But the bearded man said to me, "Beware of those perilous seas wherein men say Cathuria lies. In Sona-Nyl there is no pain nor death, but who can tell what lies beyond the basalt pillars of the West?" Natheless at the next full moon I boarded the White Ship, and with the reluctant bearded man left the happy harbour for untravelled seas.

And the bird of heaven flew before, and led us toward the basalt pillars of the West, but this time the oarsmen sang no soft songs under the full moon. In my mind I would often picture the unknown Land of Cathuria with its splendid groves and palaces, and would wonder what new delights there awaited me. "Cathuria," I would say to myself, "is the abode of gods and the land of unnumbered cities of gold. Its forests are of aloe and sandalwood, even as the fragrant groves of Camorin, and among the trees flutter gay birds sweet with song. On the green and flowery mountains of Cathuria stand temples of pink marble, rich with carven and painted glories, and having in their courtyards cool fountains of silver, where purl with ravishing music the scented waters that come from the grotto-born river Narg. And the cities of Cathuria are cinctured with golden walls, and their pavements are also of gold. In

195

the gardens of these cities are strange orchids, and perfumed lakes whose beds are of coral and amber. At night the streets and the gardens are lit with gay lanthorns fashioned from three-coloured shell of the tortoise, and here resound the soft notes of the singer and the lutanist. And the houses of the cities of Cathuria are all palaces, each built over a fragrant canal bearing the waters of the sacred Narg. Of marble and porphyry are the houses, and roofed with glittering gold that reflects the rays of the sun and enhances the splendour of the cities as blissful gods view them from the distant peaks. Fairest of all is the palace of the great monarch Dorieb, whom some say to be a demigod and others a god. High is the palace of Dorieb, and many are the turrets of marble upon its walls. In its wide halls may multitudes assemble, and here hang the trophies of the ages. And the roof is of pure gold, set upon tall pillars of ruby and azure, and having such carven figures of gods and heroes that he who looks up to those heights seem to gaze upon the living Olympus. And the floor of the palace is of glass, under which flow the cunningly lighted waters of the Narg, gay with gaudy fish not known beyond the bounds of lovely Cathuria."

Thus would I speak to myself of Cathuria, but ever would the bearded man warn me to turn back to the happy shores of Sona-Nyl; for Sona-Nyl is known of men, while none hath ever beheld Cathuria.

And on the thirty-first day that we followed the bird, we beheld the basalt pillars of the West. Shrouded in mist they were, so that no man might peer beyond them or see their summits—which indeed some say reach even to the heavens. And the bearded man again implored me to turn back, but I heeded him not; for from the mists beyond the basalt pillars I fancied there came the notes of singer and lutanist; sweeter than the sweetest songs of Sona-Nyl, and sounding mine own praises; the praises of me, who had voyaged far under the full moon and dwelt in the Land of Fancy.

So to the sound of melody the White Ship sailed into the mist betwixt the basalt pillars of the West. And when the music ceased and the mist lifted, we beheld not the Land of Cathuria, but a swift-rushing resistless sea, over which our helpless barque was borne toward some unknown goal. Soon to our ears came the distant thunder of falling waters, and to our eyes appeared on the far horizon ahead the titanic spray of a monstrous cataract, wherein the oceans of the world drop down to abysmal nothingness. Then did the bearded man say to me with tears on his cheek, "We have rejected the beautiful Land of Sona-Nyl, which we may never behold again. The gods are greater than men, and they have conquered." And I closed my eyes before the crash that I knew would come,

196

shutting out the sight of the celestial bird which flapped its mocking blue wings over the brink of the torrent.

Out of that crash came darkness, and I heard the shrieking of men and of things which were not men. From the East tempestuous winds arose, and chilled me as I crouched on the slab of damp stone which had risen beneath my feet. Then as I heard another crash I opened my eyes and beheld myself upon the platform of that lighthouse from whence I had sailed so many æons ago. In the darkness below there loomed the vast blurred outlines of a vessel breaking up on the cruel rocks, and as I glanced out over the waste I saw that the light had failed for the first time since my grandfather had assumed its care.

And in the later watches of the night, when I went within the tower, I saw on the wall a calendar which still remained as when I had left it at the hour I sailed away. With the dawn I descended the tower and looked for wreckage upon the rocks, but what I found was only this: a strange dead bird whose hue was as of the azure sky, and a single shattered spar, of a whiteness greater than that of the wave-tips or of the mountain snow.

And thereafter the ocean told me its secrets no more; and though many times since has the moon shone full and high in the heavens, the White Ship from the South came never again.

TO MISTRESS SOPHIA SIMPLE, QUEEN OF THE CINEMA

(With humblest apologies to Randolph St. John, Gent.)

L. Theobald, Jun

Before our sight your mobile face
Depicts your joys or woes distracting;
We marvel at your winsome grace—
And wish you'd learn the art of acting!

Your eyes, we vow, surpass the stars;
Your mouth is like the bow of Cupid;

Your rose-ting'd cheeks no wrinkle mars—
Yet why are you so sweetly stupid?

The hero views you with delight,
To win your hand forever working;
We pity him—the witless wight—
To fall a victim to your smirking!

And yet, why should we wail in rhyme
Because so crudely you dissemble?
We can't expect for one small dime,
To see a Woffington or Kemble!

THE UNITED AMATEUR JANUARY 1920

LITERARY COMPOSITION

H. P. Lovecraft

In a former article our readers have been shewn the fundamental sources of literary inspiration, and the leading prerequisites to expression. It remains to furnish hints concerning expression itself; its forms, customs, and technicalities, in order that the young writer may lose nothing of force or charm in presenting his ideas to the public.

Grammar

A review of the elements of English grammar would be foreign to the purpose of this department. The subject is one taught in all common schools, and may be presumed to be understood by every aspirant to authorship. It is necessary, however, to caution the beginner to keep a reliable grammar and dictionary always beside him, that he may avoid in his compositions the frequent errors which imperceptibly corrupt even the purest ordinary speech. As a general rule, it is well to give close critical scrutiny to all colloquial phrases and expressions of doubtful parsing, as well as to all words and usages which have a strained or unfamiliar sound. The human memory is not to be trusted too far, and most minds harbour a considerable number of slight linguistic faults and inelegancies picked up from random discourse or from the pages of newspapers, magazines, and popular modern books.

Types of Mistakes

Most of the mistakes of young authors, aside from those gross violations of syntax which ordinary education corrects, may perhaps be enumerated as follows.

(1) Erroneous plurals of nouns, as vallies or echos.

(2) Barbarous compound nouns, as viewpoint or upkeep.

(3) Want of correspondence in number between noun and verb where the two are widely separated or the construction involved.

(4) Ambiguous use of pronouns.

(5) Erroneous case of pronouns, as whom for who, and vice versa, or phrases like "between you and I," or "Let we who are loyal, act promptly."

(6) Erroneous use of shall and will, and of other auxiliary verbs.

(7) Use of intransitive for transitive verbs, as "he was graduated from college," or vice versa, as "he ingratiated with the tyrant."

(8) Use of nouns for verbs, as "he motored to Boston," or "he voiced a protest."

(9) Errors in moods and tenses of verbs, as "If I was he, I should do otherwise," or "He said the earth was round."

(10) The split infinitive, as "to calmly glide."

(11) The erroneous perfect infinitive, as "Last week I expected to have met you."

(12) False verb-forms, as "I pled with him."

(13) Use of like for as, as "I strive to write like Pope wrote."

(14) Misuse of prepositions, as "The gift was bestowed to an unworthy object," or "The gold was divided between the five men."

(15) The superfluous conjunction, as "I wish for you to do this."

(16) Use of words in wrong senses, as "The book greatly intrigued me," "Leave me take this," "He was obsessed with the idea," or "He is a meticulous writer."

199

(17) Erroneous use of non-Anglicised foreign forms, as "a strange phenomena," or "two stratas of clouds."

(18) Use of false or unauthorized words, as burglarize or supremest.

(19) Errors of taste, including vulgarisms, pompousness, repetition, vagueness, ambiguousness, colloquialism, bathos, bombast, pleonasm, tautology, harshness, mixed metaphor, and every sort of rhetorical awkwardness.

(20) Errors of spelling and punctuation, and confusion of forms such as that which leads many to place an apostrophe in the possessive pronoun its.

Of all blunders, there is hardly one which might not be avoided through diligent study of simple textbooks on grammar and rhetoric, intelligent perusal of the best authors, and care and forethought in composition. Almost no excuse exists for their persistent occurrence, since the sources of correction are so numerous and so available. Many of the popular manuals of good English are extremely useful, especially to persons whose reading is not as yet extensive; but such works sometimes err in being too pedantically precise and formal. For correct writing, the cultivation of patience and mental accuracy is essential. Throughout the young author's period of apprenticeship, he must keep reliable dictionaries and textbooks at his elbow; eschewing as far as possible that hasty extemporaneous manner of writing which is the privilege of more advanced students. He must take no popular usage for granted, nor must he ever hesitate, in case of doubt, to fall back on the authority of his books.

Reading

No aspiring author should content himself with a mere acquisition of technical rules. As Mrs. Renshaw remarked in the preceding article, "Impression should ever precede and be stronger than expression." All attempts at gaining literary polish must begin with judicious reading, and the learner must never cease to hold this phase uppermost. In many cases, the usage of good authors will be found a more effective guide than any amount of precept. A page of Addison or of Irving will teach more of style than a whole manual of rules, whilst a story of Poe's will impress upon the mind a more vivid notion of powerful and correct description and narration than will ten dry chapters of a bulky textbook. Let every student read unceasingly the best writers, guided by the admirable Reading Table which has adorned the UNITED AMATEUR during the past two years.

It is also important that cheaper types of reading, if hitherto followed, be dropped. Popular magazines inculcate a careless and deplorable style which is hard to unlearn, and which impedes the acquisition of a purer style. If such things must be read, let them be skimmed over as lightly as possible. An excellent habit to cultivate is the analytical study of the King James Bible. For simple yet rich and forceful English, this masterly production is hard to equal; and even though its Saxon vocabulary and poetic rhythm be unsuited to general composition, it is an invaluable model for writers on quaint or imaginative themes. Lord Dunsany, perhaps the greatest living prose artist, derived nearly all of his stylistic tendencies from the Scriptures; and the contemporary critic Boyd points out very acutely the loss sustained by most Catholic Irish writers through their unfamiliarity with the historic volume and its traditions.

Vocabulary

One superlatively important effect of wide reading is the enlargement of vocabulary which always accompanies it. The average student is gravely impeded by the narrow range of words from which he must choose, and he soon discovers that in long compositions he cannot avoid monotony. In reading, the novice should note the varied mode of expression practiced by good authors, and should keep in his mind for future use the many appropriate synonymes he encounters. Never should an unfamiliar word be passed over without elucidation; for with a little conscientious research we may each day add to our conquests in the realm of philology, and become more and more ready for graceful independent expression.

But in enlarging the vocabulary, we must beware lest we misuse our new possessions. We must remember that there are fine distinctions betwixt apparently similar words, and that language must ever be selected with intelligent care. As the learned Dr. Blair points out in his Lectures, "Hardly in any language are there two words that convey precisely the same idea; a person thoroughly conversant in the propriety of language will always be able to observe something that distinguishes them."

Elemental Phases

Before considering the various formal classes of composition, it is well to note certain elements common to them all. Upon analysis, every piece of writing will be found to contain one or more of the following basic principles: Description, or an account of the appearance of things; Narration, or an account of the actions of things; Exposition, which defines and explains with precision and

201

lucidity; Argument, which discovers truth and rejects error; and Persuasion, which urges to certain thoughts or acts. The first two are the bases of fiction; the third didactic, scientific, historical and editorial writings. The fourth and fifth are mostly employed in conjunction with the third, in scientific, philosophical, and partisan literature. All these principles, however, are usually mingled with one another. The work of fiction may have its scientific, historical, or argumentative side; whilst the textbook or treatise may be embellished with descriptions and anecdotes.

Description

Description, in order to be effective, calls upon two mental qualities; observation and discrimination. Many descriptions depend for their vividness upon the accurate reproduction of details; others upon the judicious selection of salient, typical, or significant points.

One cannot be too careful in the selection of adjectives for descriptions. Words or compounds which describe precisely, and which convey exactly the right suggestions to the mind of the reader, are essential. As an example, let us consider the following list of epithets applicable to a fountain, taken from Richard Green Parker's admirable work on composition.

Crystal, gushing, rustling, silver, gently-gliding, parting, pearly, weeping, bubbling, gurgling, chiding, clear, grass-fringed, moss-fringed, pebble-paved, verdant, sacred, grass margined, moss-margined, trickling, soft, dew-sprinkled, fast-flowing, delicate, delicious, clean, straggling, dancing, vaulting, deep-embosomed, leaping, murmuring, muttering, whispering, prattling, twaddling, swelling, sweet-rolling, gently-flowing, rising, sparkling, flowing, frothy, dew-distilling, dew-born, exhaustless, inexhaustible, never-decreasing, never-failing, heaven-born, earth-born, deep-divulging, drought-dispelling, thirst-allaying, refreshing, soul-refreshing, earth-refreshing, laving, lavish, plant-nourishing.

For the purpose of securing epithets at once accurate and felicitous, the young author should familiarize himself thoroughly with the general aspect and phenomena of Nature, as well as with the ideas and associations which these things produce in the human mind.

Descriptions may be of objects, of places, of animals, and of persons. The complete description of an object may be said to consist of the following elements:

202

1. When, where, and how seen; when made or found; how affected by time.
2. History and traditional associations.
3. Substance and manner of origin.
4. Size, shape, and appearance.
5. Analogies with similar objects.
6. Sensations produced by contemplating it.
7. Its purpose or function.
8. Its effects—the results of its existence.

Descriptions of places must of course vary with the type of the place. Of natural scenery, the following elements are notable:

1. How beheld—at dawn, noon, evening, or night; by starlight or moonlight.
2. Natural features—flat or hilly; barren or thickly grown; kind of vegetation; trees, mountains, and rivers.
3. Works of man—cultivation, edifices, bridges; modifications of scenery produced by man.
4. Inhabitants and other forms of animal life.
5. Local customs and traditions.
6. Sounds—of water; forest; leaves; birds; barnyards; human beings; machinery.
7. View—prospect on every side, and the place itself as seen from afar.
8. Analogies to other scenes, especially famous scenes.
9. History and associations.
10. Sensations produced by contemplating it.

Descriptions of animals may be analyzed thus:

1. Species and size.
2. Covering.
3. Parts.
4. Abode.
5. Characteristics and habits.
6. Food.
7. Utility or harmfulness.
8. History and associations.

Descriptions of persons can be infinitely varied. Sometimes a single felicitous touch brings out the whole type and character, as when the modern author Leonard Merrick hints at shabby gentility by mentioning the combination of a frock coat with the trousers of a tweed suit. Suggestion is very powerful in this field, especially when mental qualities are to be delineated. Treatment should vary with the author's object; whether to portray a mere personified idea, or to give a quasi photographic view, mental and physical, of some vividly living character. In a general description, the following elements may be found:

1. Appearance, stature, complexion, proportions, features.
2. Most conspicuous feature.
3. Expression.
4. Grace or ugliness.
5. Attire—nature, taste, quality.
6. Habits, attainments, graces, or awkwardnesses.
7. Character—moral and intellectual—place in the community.
8. Notable special qualities.

In considering the preceding synopses, the reader must remember that they are only suggestions, and not for literal use. The extent of any description is to be determined by its place in the composition; by taste and fitness. It should be added, that in fiction description must not be carried to excess. A plethora of it leads to dulness, so that it must ever be balanced by a brisk flow of Narration, which we are about to consider.

Narration

Narration is an account of action, or of successive events, either real or imagined; and is therefore the basis both of history and of fiction. To be felicitous and successful, it demands an intelligent exercise of taste and discrimination; salient points must be selected, and the order of time and of circumstances must be well maintained. It is deemed wisest in most cases to give narratives a climactic form; leading from lesser to greater events, and culminating in that chief incident upon which the story is primarily founded, or which makes the other parts important through its own importance. This principle, of course, cannot be literally followed in all historical and biographical narratives.

Fictional Narration

The essential point of fictional narration is plot, which may be defined as a sequence of incidents designed to awaken the reader's interest and curiosity as to the result. Plots may be simple or complex; but suspense, and climactic progress from one incident to another, are essential. Every incident in a fictional work should have some bearing on the climax or denouement, and any denouement which is not the inevitable result of the preceding incidents is awkward and unliterary. No formal course in fiction-writing can equal a close and observant perusal of the stories of Edgar Allan Poe or Ambrose Bierce. In these masterpieces one may find that unbroken sequence and linkage of incident and result which mark the ideal tale. Observe how, in "The Fall of the House of Usher," each separate event foreshadows and leads up to the tremendous catastrophe and its hideous suggestion. Poe was an absolute master of the mechanics of his craft. Observe also how Bierce can attain the most stirring denouements from a few simple happenings; denouements which develop purely from these preceding circumstances.

In fictional narration, verisimilitude is absolutely essential. A story must be consistent and must contain no event glaringly removed from the usual order of things, unless that event is the main incident, and is approached with the most careful preparation. In real life, odd and erratic things do occasionally happen; but they are out of place in an ordinary story, since fiction is a sort of idealization of the average. Development should be as lifelike as possible, and a weak, trickling conclusion should be assiduously avoided. The end of a story must be stronger rather than weaker than the beginning; since it is the end which contains the denouement or culmination, and which will leave the strongest impression upon the reader. It would not be amiss for the novice to write the last paragraph of his story first, once a synopsis of the plot has been carefully prepared—as it always should be. In this way he will be able to concentrate his freshest mental vigour upon the most important part of his narrative; and if any changes be later found needful, they can easily be made. In no part of a narrative should a grand or emphatic thought or passage be followed by one of tame or prosaic quality. This is anticlimax, and exposes a writer to much ridicule. Notice the absurd effect of the following couplet—which was, however, written by no less a person than Waller:

"Under the tropic is our language spoke,
And part of Flanders hath receiv'd our yoke."

Unity, Mass, Coherence

In developing a theme, whether descriptive or narrative, it is necessary that three structural qualities be present: Unity, Mass, and Coherence. Unity is that principle whereby every part of a composition must have some bearing on the central theme. It is the principle which excludes all extraneous matter, and demands that all threads converge toward the climax. Classical violations of Unity may be found in the episodes of Homer and other epic poets of antiquity, as well as in the digressions of Fielding and other celebrated novelists; but no beginner should venture to emulate such liberties. Unity is the quality we have lately noted and praised in Poe and Bierce.

Mass is that principle which requires the more important parts of a composition to occupy correspondingly important places in the whole composition, the paragraph, and the sentence. It is that law of taste which insists that emphasis be placed where emphasis is due, and is most strikingly embodied in the previously mentioned necessity for an emphatic ending. According to this law, the end of a composition is its most important part, with the beginning next in importance.

Coherence is that principle which groups related parts together and keeps unrelated parts removed from one another. It applies, like Mass, to the whole composition, the paragraph, or the sentence. It demands that kindred events be narrated without interruption, effect following cause in a steady flow.

Forms of Composition

Few writers succeed equally in all the various branches of literature. Each type of thought has its own particular form of expression, based on natural appropriateness; and the average author tends to settle into that form which best fits his particular personality. Many, however, follow more than one form; and some writers change from one form to another as advancing years produce alterations in their mental processes or points of view.

It is well, in the interests of breadth and discipline, for the beginner to exercise himself to some degree in every form of literary art. He may thus discover that which best fits his mind, and develop hitherto unsuspected potentialities.

We have so far surveyed only those simpler phases of writing which centre in prose fiction and descriptive essays. Hereafter we hope to touch upon didactic, argumentative, and persuasive writing; to investigate to some extent the sources of rhetorical strength and elegance; and to consider a few major aspects of versification.

FOR WHAT DOES THE UNITED STAND?

It is easy to comply in 500 words with a request for an article on what the United represents. An amateur journalistic association is generally too democratic to have any one object for long; it is rather a battle-ground between the proponents of opposed ideas.

I think, however, that since the dawn of the Hoffman administration, when the best elements were automatically sifted out through the secession of most of the confirmed politicians, we have been gradually acquiring a policy and a tradition which will endure. The printing-press, political and frivolous phases have been passed through; and our aspirations seem to be crystallising into a form more worthy than any of our past aspirations.

Judging from the majority of our truly active members, the United now aims at the development of its adherents in the direction of purely artistic literary perception and expression; to be effected by the encouragement of writing, the giving of constructive criticism, and the cultivation of correspondence friendships among scholars and aspirants capable of stimulating and aiding one another's efforts. It aims at the revival of the uncommercial spirit; the real creative thought which modern conditions have done their worst to suppress and eradicate. It seeks to banish mediocrity as a goal and standard; to place before its members the classical and the universal and to draw their minds from the commonplace to the beautiful.

The United aims to assist those whom other forms of literary influence cannot reach. The non-university man, the dwellers in distant places, the recluse, the invalid, the very young, the elderly; all these are included within our scope. And beside our novices stand persons of mature cultivation and experience, ready to assist for the sheer joy of assisting. In no other society does wealth or previous learning count for so little. Merit and aspiration form the only criterion we apply to our members, nor has poverty or primitive crudity ever retarded the steady progress of any determined aspirant among us. We ask only that the goal be high; that the souls of our band be seeking the antique legacy of verdant Helicon.

Practically, we are aware of many obstacles; yet we think we are in the main fulfilling our functions. Naturally, we do not expect to make a Shelley or Swinburne of every rhymer who joins us, or a

Poe or Dunsany of every teller of tales; but if we enable these persons to appreciate Shelley and Swinburne and Poe and Dunsany, and teach them how to shed their dominant faults and use words correctly and expressively, we cannot call ourselves unsuccessful and only genius can lead to the heights; it is our province merely to point the way and assist on the gentler, lower slopes.

The United, then, stands for education in the eternal truths of literary art, and for personal aid in the realisation of its members' literary potentialities. It is a university, stripped of every artificiality and conventionality, and thrown open to all without distinction. Here may every man shine according to his genius, and here may the small as well as the great writer know the bliss of appreciation and the glory of recognised achievement.

H. P. LOVECRAFT

THE UNITED AMATEUR

Official Organ of the United Amateur Press Association

Volume XX Elroy, Wis., September, 1920 Number 1

POETRY AND THE GODS

Anna Helen Crofts and Henry Paget-Lowe

A damp, gloomy evening in April it was, just after the close of the Great War, when Marcia found herself alone with strange thoughts and wishes; unheard-of yearnings which floated out of the spacious twentieth-century drawing-room, up the misty deeps of the air, and Eastward to far olive-groves in Arcady which she had seen only in her dreams. She had entered the room in abstraction, turned off the glaring chandeliers, and now reclined on a soft divan by a solitary lamp which shed over the reading table a green glow as soothing and delicious as moonlight through the foliage about an antique shrine. Attired simply, in a low-cut evening dress of black, she appeared outwardly a typical product of modern civilisation; but tonight she felt the immeasurable gulf that separated her soul from all her prosaic surroundings. Was it because of the strange home in which she lived; that abode of coldness where relations were always strained and the inmates scarcely more than strangers? Was it that, or was it some greater and less explicable misplacement in Time and Space, whereby she had been born too late, too early, or too far away from the haunts of her spirit ever to harmonise with the unbeautiful things of contemporary reality? To dispel the mood which was engulfing her more deeply each moment, she took a magazine from the table and searched for some healing bit of poetry. Poetry had always relieved her troubled mind better than anything else, though many things in the poetry she had seen detracted from the influence. Over parts of even the sublimest verses hung a chill vapour of sterile ugliness and restraint, like dust on a window-pane through which one views a magnificent sunset.

Listlessly turning the magazine's pages, as if searching for an elusive treasure, she suddenly came upon something which dispelled her languor. An observer could have read her thoughts and told that she had discovered some image or dream which brought her nearer to her unattained goal than any image or dream she had seen before. It was only a bit of vers libre, that pitiful compromise of the poet who overleaps prose yet falls short of the divine melody of numbers; but it had in it all the unstudied music of a bard who lives and feels, and who gropes ecstatically for unveiled beauty. Devoid of regularity, it yet had the wild harmony of winged, spontaneous words; a harmony missing from the formal, convention-bound verse she had known. As she read on, her surroundings gradually faded, and soon there lay about her only the mists of dream; the purple, star-strown mists beyond Time, where only gods and dreamers walk.

"Moon over Japan,
White butterfly moon!
Where the heavy-lidded Buddhas dream
To the sound of the cuckoo's call....
The white wings of moon-butterflies
Flicker down the streets of the city,
Blushing into darkness the useless wicks of round lanterns
in the hands of girls.

"Moon over the tropics,
A white-curved bud
Opening its petals slowly in the warmth of heaven....
The air is full of odours
And languorous warm sounds....

209

A flute drones its insect music to the night
Below the curving moon-petal of the heavens.

"Moon over China,
Weary moon on the river of the sky,
The stir of light in the willows is like the flashing of a
thousand silver minnows
Through dark shoals;
The tiles on graves and rotting temples flash like ripples,
The sky is flecked with clouds like the scales of a dragon."

Amid the mists of dream the reader cried to the rhythmical
stars of her delight at the coming of a new age of song, a rebirth of
Pan. Half closing her eyes, she repeated words whose melody lay hid
like crystals at the bottom of a stream before the dawn; hidden but
to gleam effulgently at the birth of day.

"Moon over Japan,
White butterfly moon!

"Moon over the tropics,
A white-curved bud
Opening its petals slowly in the warmth of heaven.
The air is full of odours
And languorous warm sounds ... languorous warm sounds.

"Moon over China,
Weary moon on the river of the sky ... weary moon!"

Out of the mists gleamed godlike the figure of a youth in
winged helmet and sandals, caduceus-bearing, and of a beauty like
to nothing on earth. Before the face of the sleeper he thrice waved
the rod which Apollo had given him in trade for the nine-corded
shell of melody, and upon her brow he placed a wreath of myrtle
and roses. Then, adoring, Hermes spoke:
"O Nymph more fair than the golden-haired sisters of Cyane
or the sky-inhabiting Atlantides, beloved of Aphrodite and blessed
of Pallas, thou hast indeed discovered the secret of the Gods, which
lieth in beauty and song. O Prophetess more lovely than the Sybil of
Cumae when Apollo first knew her, thou hast truly spoken of the
new age, for even now on Maenalus, Pan sighs and stretches in his
sleep, wishful to awake and behold about him the little rose-
crowned Fauns and the antique Satyrs. In thy yearning hast thou
divined what no mortal else, saving only a few whom the world

210

reject, remembereth; that the Gods were never dead, but only sleeping the sleep and dreaming the dreams of Gods in lotos-filled Hesperian gardens beyond the golden sunset. And now draweth nigh the time of their awaking, when coldness and ugliness shall perish, and Zeus sit once more on Olympus. Already the sea about Paphos trembleth into a foam which only ancient skies have looked on before, and at night on Helicon the shepherds hear strange murmurings and half-remembered notes. Woods and fields are tremulous at twilight with the shimmering of white saltant forms, and immemorial Ocean yields up curious sights beneath thin moons. The Gods are patient, and have slept long, but neither man nor giant shall defy the Gods forever. In Tartarus the Titans writhe, and beneath the fiery Aetna groan the children of Uranus and Gaea. The day now dawns when man must answer for his centuries of denial, but in sleeping the Gods have grown kind, and will not hurl him to the gulf made for deniers of Gods. Instead will their vengeance smite the darkness, fallacy and ugliness which have turned the mind of man; and under the sway of bearded Saturnus shall mortals, once more sacrificing unto him, dwell in beauty and delight. This night shalt thou know the favour of the Gods, and behold on Parnassus those dreams which the Gods have through ages sent to Earth to show that they are not dead. For poets are the dreams of the Gods, and in each age someone hath sung unknowing the message and the promise from the lotos-gardens beyond the sunset."

Then in his arms Hermes bore the dreaming maiden through the skies. Gentle breezes from the tower of Aiolos wafted them high above warm, scented seas, till suddenly they came upon Zeus holding court on the double-headed Parnassus; his golden throne flanked by Apollo and the Muses on the right hand, and by ivy-wreathed Dionysus and pleasure-flushed Bacchae on the left hand. So much of splendour Marcia had never seen before, either awake or in dreams, but its radiance did her no injury, as would have the radiance of lofty Olympus; for in this lesser court the Father of Gods had tempered his glories for the sight of mortals. Before the laurel-draped mouth of the Corycian cave sat in a row six noble forms with the aspect of mortals, but the countenances of Gods. These the dreamer recognised from images of them which she had beheld, and she knew that they were none else than the divine Maeonides, the Avernian Dante, the more than mortal Shakespeare, the chaos-exploring Milton, the cosmic Goethe, and the Musaean Keats. These were those messengers whom the Gods had sent to tell men that Pan had passed not away, but only slept; for it is in poetry that Gods speak to men. Then spake the Thunderer:

"O daughter, for, being one of my endless line, thou art indeed my daughter, behold upon ivory thrones of honour the august messengers that Gods have sent down, that in the words and the writings of men there may still be some trace of divine beauty. Other bards have men justly crowned with enduring laurels, but these hath Apollo crowned, and these have I set in places apart, as mortals who have spoken the language of the Gods. Long have we dreamed in lotos-gardens beyond the West, and spoken only through our dreams; but the time approaches when our voices shall not be silent. It is a time of awaking and of change. Once more hath Phaeton ridden low, searing the fields and drying the streams. In Gaul lone nymphs with disordered hair weep beside fountains that are no more, and pine over rivers turned red with the blood of mortals. Ares and his train have gone forth with the madness of Gods, and have returned, Deimos and Phobos glutted with unnatural delight. Tellus moans with grief, and the faces of men are as the faces of the Erinyes, even as when Astraea fled to the skies, and the waves of our bidding encompassed all the land saving this high peak alone. Amidst this chaos, prepared to herald his coming yet to conceal his arrival, even now toileth our latest-born messenger, in whose dreams are all the images which other messengers have dreamed before him. He it is that we have chosen to blend into one glorious whole all the beauty that the world hath known before, and to write words wherein shall echo all the wisdom and the loveliness of the past. He it is who shall proclaim our return, and sing of the days to come when Fauns and Dryads shall haunt their accustomed groves in beauty. Guided was our choice by those who now sit before the Corycian grotto on thrones of ivory, and in whose songs thou shalt hear notes of sublimity by which years hence thou shall know the greater messenger when he cometh. Attend their voices as one by one they sing to thee here. Each note shalt thou hear again in the poetry which is to come; the poetry which shall bring peace and pleasure to thy soul, though search for it through bleak years thou must. Attend with diligence, for each chord that vibrates away into hiding shall appear again to thee after thou hast returned to earth, as Alpheus, sinking his waters into the soil of Hellas, appears as the crystal Arethusa in remote Sicilia."

Then arose Homeros, the ancient among bards, who took his lyre and chaunted his hymn to Aphrodite. No word of Greek did Marcia know, yet did the message fall not vainly upon her ears; for in the cryptic rhythm was that which spake to all mortals and Gods, and needed no interpreter.

So too the songs of Dante and Goethe, whose unknown words clave the ether with melodies easy to read and to adore. But at last remembered accents rebounded before the listener. It was the Swan of Avon, once a God among men, and still a God among Gods:

> "Write, write, that from the bloody course of war,
> My dearest master, your dear son, may hie;
> Bless him at home in peace, whilst I from far,
> His name with zealous fervour sanctify."

Accents still more familiar arose as Milton, blind no more, declaimed immortal harmony:

> "Or let my lamp at midnight hour
> Be seen in some high lonely tower,
> Where I might oft outwatch the Bear
> With thrice-great Hermes, or unsphere
> The spirit of Plato, to unfold
> What worlds or what vast regions hold
> Th' immortal mind, that hath forsook
> Her mansion in this fleshy nook.
> ....
> Sometime let gorgeous Tragedy
> In sceptred pall come sweeping by,
> Presenting Thebes, or Pelops' line,
> Or the tale of Troy divine."

Last of all came the young voice of Keats, closest of all the messengers to the beauteous faun-folk.

> "Heard melodies are sweet, but those unheard
> Are sweeter: therefore, ye soft pipes, play on....
> ....
> When old age shall this generation waste,
> Thou shalt remain, in midst of other woe
> Than ours, a friend to man, to whom thou say'st,
> 'Beauty is truth, truth beauty'—that is all
> Ye know on earth, and all ye need to know."

As the singer ceased, there came a sound in the wind blowing from far Egypt, where at night Aurora mourns by the Nile for her slain son Memnon. To the feet of the Thunderer flew the rosy-fingered Goddess, and kneeling, cried, "Master, it is time I unlocked the gates of the East." And Phoebus, handing his lyre to Calliope, his bride among the Muses, prepared to depart for the jewelled and column-raised Palace of the Sun, where fretted the steeds already harnessed to the golden car of day. So Zeus descended from his carven throne and placed his hand upon the head of Marcia, saying:

"Daughter, the dawn is nigh, and it is well that thou shouldst return before the awaking of mortals to thy home. Weep not at the bleakness of thy life, for the shadow of false faiths will soon be gone, and the Gods shall once more walk among men. Search thou unceasingly for our messenger, for in him wilt thou find peace and comfort. By his word shall thy steps be guided to happiness, and in his dreams of beauty shall thy spirit find all that it craveth." As Zeus ceased, the young Hermes gently seized the maiden and bore her up toward the fading stars; up, and westward over unseen seas.

Many years have passed since Marcia dreamt of the Gods and of their Parnassian conclave. Tonight she sits in the same spacious drawing-room, but she is not alone. Gone is the old spirit of unrest, for beside her is one whose name is luminous with celebrity; the young poet of poets at whose feet sits all the world. He is reading from a manuscript words which none has ever heard before, but which when heard will bring to men the dreams and fancies they lost so many centuries ago, when Pan lay down to doze in Arcady, and the greater Gods withdrew to sleep in lotos-gardens beyond the lands of the Hesperides. In the subtle cadences and hidden melodies of the bard the spirit of the maiden has found rest at last, for there echo the divinest notes of Thracian Orpheus; notes that moved the very rocks and trees by Hebrus' banks. The singer ceases, and with eagerness asks a verdict, yet what can Marcia say but that the strain is "fit for the Gods"?

And as she speaks there comes again a vision of Parnassus and the far-off sound of a mighty voice saying, "By his word shall thy steps be guided to happiness, and in his dreams of beauty shall thy spirit find all that it craveth."

Mr. Paul J. Campbell deserves the most unstinted thanks of the United this year, for besides serving as First Vice-President he has furnished free of charge a supply of recruiting booklets and application blanks, thus relieving us of one of our most onerous burdens. Mr. Campbell's eighteen years of undiminished devotion to amateurdom form a thing worthy of emulation.

214

NYARLATHOTEP

H. P. Lovecraft

Nyarlathotep ... the crawling chaos ... I am the last ... I will tell the audient void....

I do not recall distinctly when it began, but it was months ago. The general tension was horrible. To a season of political and social upheaval was added a strange and brooding apprehension of hideous physical danger; a danger widespread and all-embracing, such a danger as may be imagined only in the most terrible phantasms of the night. I recall that the people went about with pale and worried faces, and whispered warnings and prophecies which no one dared consciously repeat or acknowledge to himself that he had heard. A sense of monstrous guilt was upon the land, and out of the abysses between the stars swept chill currents that made men shiver in dark and lonely places. There was a demoniac alteration in the sequence of the seasons—the autumn heat lingered fearsomely, and everyone felt that the world and perhaps the universe had passed from the control of known gods or forces to that of gods or forces which were unknown.

And it was then that Nyarlathotep came out of Egypt. Who he was, none could tell, but he was of the old native blood and looked like a Pharaoh. The fellahin knelt when they saw him, yet could not say why. He said he had risen up out of the blackness of twenty-seven centuries, and that he had heard messages from places not on this planet. Into the lands of civilisation came Nyarlathotep, swarthy, slender, and sinister, always buying strange instruments of glass and metal and combining them into instruments yet stranger. He spoke much of the sciences—of electricity and psychology—and gave exhibitions of power which sent his spectators away speechless, yet which swelled his fame to exceeding magnitude. Men advised one another to see Nyarlathotep, and shuddered. And where Nyarlathotep went, rest vanished; for the small hours were rent with the screams of nightmare. Never before had the screams of nightmare been such a public problem; now the wise men almost wished they could forbid sleep in the small hours, that the shrieks of cities might less horribly disturb the pale, pitying moon as it glimmered on green waters gliding under bridges, and old steeples crumbling against a sickly sky.

I remember when Nyarlathotep came to my city—the great, the old, the terrible city of unnumbered crimes. My friend had told me of him, and of the impelling fascination and allurement of his revelations, and I burned with eagerness to explore his uttermost mysteries. My friend said they were horrible and impressive beyond my most fevered imaginings; that what was thrown on a screen in the darkened room prophesied things none but Nyarlathotep dare prophesy, and that in the sputter of his sparks there was taken from men that which had never been taken before yet which shewed only in the eyes. And I heard it hinted abroad that those who knew Nyarlathotep looked on sights which others saw not.

It was in the hot autumn that I went through the night with the restless crowds to see Nyarlathotep; through the stifling night and up the endless stairs into the choking room. And shadowed on a screen, I saw hooded forms amidst ruins, and yellow evil faces peering from behind fallen monuments. And I saw the world battling against blackness; against the waves of destruction from ultimate space; whirling, churning; struggling around the dimming, cooling sun. Then the sparks played amazingly around the heads of the spectators, and hair stood up on end whilst shadows more grotesque than I can tell came out and squatted on the heads. And when I, who was colder and more scientific than the rest, mumbled a trembling protest about "imposture" and "static electricity," Nyarlathotep drave us all out, down the dizzy stairs into the damp, hot, deserted midnight streets. I screamed aloud that I was not afraid; that I never could be afraid; and others screamed with me for solace. We sware to one another that the city was exactly the same, and still alive; and when the electric lights began to fade we cursed the company over and over again, and laughed at the queer faces we made.

I believe we felt something coming down from the greenish moon, for when we began to depend on its light we drifted into curious involuntary marching formations and seemed to know our destinations though we dared not think of them. Once we looked at the pavement and found the blocks loose and displaced by grass, with scarce a line of rusted metal to show where the tramways had run. And again we saw a tram-car, lone, windowless, dilapidated, and almost on its side. When we gazed around the horizon, we could not find the third tower by the river, and noticed that the silhouette of the second tower was ragged at the top. Then we split up into narrow columns, each of which seemed drawn in a different direction. One disappeared in a narrow alley to the left, leaving only the echo of a shocking moan. Another filed down a weed-choked subway entrance, howling with a laughter that was mad. My own

216

column was sucked toward the open country, and presently felt a chill which was not of the hot autumn: for as we stalked out on the dark moor, we beheld around us the hellish moon-glitter of evil snows. Trackless, inexplicable snows, swept asunder in one direction only, where lay a gulf all the blacker for its glittering walls. The column seemed very thin indeed as it plodded dreamily into the gulf. I lingered behind, for the black rift in the green-litten snow was frightful, and I thought I had heard the reverberations of a disquieting wail as my companions vanished; but my power to linger was slight. As if beckoned by those who had gone before, I half-floated between the titanic snowdrifts, quivering and afraid, into the sightless vortex of the unimaginable.

Screamingly sentient, dumbly delirious, only the gods that were can tell. A sickened, sensitive shadow writhing in hands that are not hands, and whirled blindly past ghastly midnights of rotting creation, corpses of dead worlds with sores that were cities, charnel winds that brush the pallid stars and make them flicker low. Beyond the worlds vague ghosts of monstrous things; half-seen columns of unsanctified temples that rest on nameless rocks beneath space and reach up to dizzy vacua above the spheres of light and darkness. And through this revolving graveyard of the universe the muffled, maddening beating of drums, and thin, monotonous whine of blasphemous flutes from inconceivable, unlighted chambers beyond Time; the detestable pounding and piping whereunto dance slowly, awkwardly and absurdly the gigantic, tenebrous ultimate gods—the blind, voiceless, mindless gargoyles whose soul is Nyarlathotep.

EDITORIAL

Editorial comment upon amateur journalism generally falls within one of two classes; complacent self-congratulation upon a mythical perfection, or hectic urging toward impossible achievements. It is our purpose this month to indulge in neither of these rhetorical recreations, but to make one very prosaic and practical appeal which springs solely from realistic observation.

This appeal concerns the official situation in the United. For several years our foes have reproached us for excessive centralisation of authority: asserting that the control of our society

217

is anything from oligarchical to monarchial, and pointing to the large amount of influence wielded by a very few leaders. Denials on our part, prompted by the conspicuous absence of any dictatorial ambitions in the minds of our executives, have been largely nullified by the fact that while power has not been autocratically usurped and arbitrarily exercised, the burden of administrative work has certainly been thrust by common consent on a small number of reluctant though loyal shoulders. A few persons have been forced to retain authority because no others have arisen to relieve them of their burdens, until official nominations have come to mean no more than a campaign by one or two active spirits to persuade certain patient drudges to "carry on" another year. Nor does the formal official situation reflect all of the prevailing condition. Much of the Association's most important activity, such as recruiting, welcoming and criticism, verges into the field of unorganised effort; and here the tendency to leave everything to a narrow group is overwhelming.

Obviously, this condition demands a remedy; and that remedy lies in one direction only—an acceptance of potential official responsibility by all of those members who possess the time and experience to act as leaders. As the fiscal year progresses, the season for candidacies draws near; and amateurs who feel competent to sustain their share of the administrative burden should come forward as nominees, or at least should respond when approached by their friends. That office-holding involves tedious work, all admit, but this tedium is a small enough price to pay for the varied boons of amateurdom. In unofficial labour an equal willingness should be shown. Why is it that all the private revision in the United is performed by about three men at most, despite the presence in our ranks of a full score of scholars abundantly capable of rendering such service? If the literati as a whole will not awaken to the needs of the day, one of two things will occur. The United will stagnate quietly under the perpetual dictatorship of a limited group of unwilling but benevolent autocrats, or it will succumb to the onslaught of some political clique of vigorous barbarians who will destroy in a month what it has taken the United over ten years to build up. Memories of 1919 should prove to us the reality of such a danger of sudden relapse.

Our appeal, then, is for responsible candidates for high office, and for volunteers in the work of maintaining interest and lending literary aid. We know that executive energy and enthusiasm tend to be more abundant in the Goth than in the Greek; that those best qualified to serve are generally least moved by political ambition.

218

But we are sure that the needs of our society should arouse enough sense of duty among its cultivated membership to draw to the front a new generation of leaders. We ask for new presidential and editorial candidates who are prepared to serve faithfully and independently if elected; for new critics and recruiters who understand our traditions and are willing to expend energy in upholding and diffusing them. Shall 1921 bring them to light?

—H. P. Lovecraft

OFFICIAL ORGAN FUND

RECEIPTS

Woodbee Press Club	$25.00
From Treasurer, up to October 15	23.00
Susan Nelson Furgerson	6.00
Jonathan E. Hoag	5.00
Verna McGeoch (for each issue)	5.00
Howard R. Conover	3.00
Victor O. Schwab	3.00
Mr. and Mrs. Fritter (for each issue)	2.00
Rev. Eugene B. Kuntz	1.50
Anne Tillery Renshaw	1.50
Anonymous	.25
One dollar each: Margaret Abraham, Agnes R. Arnold, Elizabeth Barnhart, Grace M. Bromley, Mary Faye Durr, Alice M. Hamlet, Hester Harper.	
Total on hand, November 6, 1920	$82.25

REMARKS

The doubling of printing rates makes large contributions imperative if the Organ is to approach its customary standard. Acknowledgments are due the Woodbee Press Club for its exceedingly generous contribution, and ex-Editor Renshaw for the mailing of an appeal which has proved most effective in the campaign for funds. Emulation of the Woodbees' generosity by other clubs would save a situation which is very threatening.

H. P. Lovecraft,
Custodian

THE UNITED AMATEUR JANUARY 1921

OFFICIAL ORGAN FUND

Providence, R. I., April 1, 1921

RECEIPTS SINCE NOVEMBER 6, 1920

From Treasurer, up to April 1, 1921	$21.50
Verna McGeoch (3 instalments)	15.00
E. Edward Ericson	10.00
Edward F. Daas	6.00
Howard R. Conover	2.00
Anna H. Crofts	1.00
Ernest L. McKeag	1.00
John Milton Samples	1.00
Anonymous	.75
Balance on Hand, November 6, 1920	$82.25
Received, November 6, 1920, to April 1, 1921	58.25
Total Receipts	$140.50

EXPENDITURES

To E. E. Ericson, for September U. A.	$48.00
To E. E. Ericson, for November U. A.	48.00
To E. E. Ericson, for January U. A.	36.00
Total Expenditures	$132.00
Balance on Hand, April 1, 1921	$8.50

H. P. Lovecraft,
Custodian

WINIFRED VIRGINIA JACKSON: A "DIFFERENT" POETESS

H. P. Lovecraft

In these days of unrestrained license in poetry, it would at first sight seem difficult to single out any one bard as the possessor of ideas and modes of expression so unique and original that the overworked adjective "different" is merited. Every poetaster of the modern school claims to be "different," and bases his claim to celebrity upon this "difference"; an effect usually achieved by the adoption of a harsh, amorphous style, and a tone of analytical, introspective subjectivity so individual that all the common and universal elements of beauty and poetry are excluded. Indeed, eccentricity has come so completely into fashion, that he who follows up the wildest vagaries is actually the least different from the hectic scribbling throng about him.

But notwithstanding this malady of the times, there does remain among us an ample field for genius and artistic distinctiveness. The laws of human thought are unchangeable, and whenever there is born a soul attuned to real harmony, and inspired by that rare sensitiveness which enables it to feel and express the latent beauty and hidden relationships of Nature, the world receives a new poet. Such an one will of necessity break through the decadent customs of the period; and falling back to the forms of true melody, sing a spontaneous song which can not help being original, because it represents the unforced reaction of a keen and delicate mind to the panorama of life. And when this reaction is enabled to bring out in the simplest and most beautiful style fancies and images which the world has not received or noted before, we are justified in claiming that the bard is "different."

Such a bard is Winifred Virginia Jackson, whose poetry has for six years been the pride of the United Amateur Press Association. Born in Maine, and through childhood accustomed to the mystical spell of the ancient New-England countryside, Miss Jackson for a long period quietly and unconsciously absorbed a prodigious store of beauty and phantasy from life. Having no design to become a poet, she accepted these ethereal gifts as a matter of course; until about a decade ago they manifested themselves in a burst of spontaneous melody which can best be described as a sheer overflowing of delightful dreams and pictures from a mind filled to the brim with poetic loveliness. Since that time Miss Jackson has written vast quantities of verse; always rich and musical, and if one may speak in paradox, always artless with supreme art. None of these poems is in any sense premeditated or consciously composed; they are more like visions of the fancy, instantaneously photographed for the perception of others, and unerringly framed in the most appropriate metrical medium.

When we peruse the poetry of Miss Jackson we are impressed first by its amazing variety, and almost as quickly by a certain distinctive quality which gives all the varied specimens a kind of homogeneity. As we analyse our impressions, we find that both of these qualities have a common source—the complete objectivity and almost magical imagination of supreme genius. Objectivity and imagination, the gifts of the epic bards of classical antiquity, are today the rarest of blessings. We live in an age of morbid emotion and introspectiveness; wherein the poets, such as they are, have sunk to the level of mere pathologists engaged in the dissection of their own ultra-sophisticated spirits. The fresh touch of Nature is lost to the majority, and rhymesters rant endlessly and realistically about the relation of man to his fellows and to himself; overlooking the real foundations of art and beauty—wonder, and man's relation to the unknown cosmos. But Miss Jackson is not of the majority, and has not overlooked these things. In her the ancient and unspoiled bard is refulgently reincarnated; and with an amazing universality and freedom from self-consciousness she suppresses the ego completely, delineating Nature's diverse moods and aspects with an impersonal fidelity and delicacy which form the delight of the discriminating reader, and the despair of the stupid critic who works by rule and formula rather than by brain. There is no medium which the spirit of Miss Jackson can not inhabit. The same mind which reflects the daintiest and most gorgeous phantasies of the faery world, or furnishes the most finely wrought pictures or refined pathos and sentiment, can abruptly take up its abode in some remote Maine timber region and pour out such a wild, virile chantey of the woods and the river that we seem to glimpse the singer as the huskiest of a tangle-bearded, fight-scarred, loud-shouting logging crew sprawling about a pine campfire.

A critic has grouped the poetical work of Miss Jackson into six classes: Lyrics of ideal beauty, including delightful Nature-poems replete with local colour; delicate amatory lyrics; rural dialect lyrics and vigorous colloquial pieces; poems of sparkling optimism; child verse; and poems of potent terror and dark suggestion. "With her," he adds, "sordid realism has no place; and her poems glow with a

222

subtle touch of the fanciful and the supernatural which is well sustained by tasteful and unusual word-combinations, images, and onomatopoetic effects." This estimate is confirmed by the latest productions of the poetess, as we shall endeavour to show by certain specimens lately published or about to be published, selected almost at random:

"The Bonnet" is a characteristic bit of Jacksonian delicacy and originality. We here behold a sustained metaphor of that striking type which the author so frequently creates; a metaphor which draws on all Nature and the unseen world for its basis, and whose analogies are just the ones which please us most, yet which our own minds are never finely attuned enough to conceive unaided. The swain in the poem tells of his intention to make a bonnet for his chosen nymph to wear. He will fashion it with "golden thimble, scissors, needle, thread"; taking velvet from the April sky as a groundwork, stars for trimming, moonlight for banding, and a web of dreams for lining. He will scent it with the perfume of "the reddest rose that the singing wind finds sweetest where it farthest blows," and "will take it at the twilight for his love to wear." Here we have nothing of the bizarre or the conspicuous, yet in the six little stanzas of quaintly regular metre there is suggested all of that world of faery beauty which the eye can glimpse beyond the leaden clouds of reality; a world which exists because it can be dreamed of. The poem is "different" in the truest way; it is original because it conveys beauty originally in an inconspicuous and harmonious vehicle.

But turn now to "Ellsworth to Great Pond" and marvel! True, we still find the vivid delineation of human feelings, but what a distance we have travelled! Gone is the young dreamer with his world of moonshine, for here roars the Maine lumberjack with all the uncouth vigour and rude natural expressiveness of the living satyr. It is life; primal, uncovered, and unpolished—the ebullient, shouting vitality of healthy animalism.

> "Drink hard cider, swig hard cider,
> Swill hard cider, Boys!
> Throw yer spikers, throw yer peavies,
> Beller out yer noise!"

We have drifted from the aether of Keats to the earth of Fielding, yet under the guidance of the same author. Greater proof of Miss Jackson's absolute objectivity and marvellous imagination could not be produced or asked.

Yet who shall say that the Jackson pendulum is powerful only at the extremes of its sweeping arc? In "Workin' Out" we discover a pastoral love-lyric which for quaintness and graphic humanness could not well be surpassed. Here the distinctive and spontaneous inventiveness of Miss Jackson's fancy is displayed with especial vividness. The rural youth, "workin' out" far from his loved Molly, enumerates the prosaic chores he can perform with easy heart; but mentions in each case some more poetic thing which stirs his emotions and gives him loneliness for the absent fair. He can cut and husk corn, but the golden-rod reminds him of his Molly's golden hair. He can milk cows, but the gentian reminds him of his Molly's blue eyes. Aside from their intrinsic ingeniousness, these images possess an unconscious lesson for the poet who can read it. They expose with concrete illustrations the fallacy of the so-called "new poetry," which disregards the natural division between beautiful and unbeautiful things and rhapsodises as effusively over a sewer-pipe as over the crescent moon.

"The Token" exhibits Miss Jackson in her airiest lyrical mood; a mood original because it possesses the rare lyrism of pure music and fancy rather than the common lyrism of unsubtilised emotion. There is bounding music in thought and medium alike, whilst the naive plunge into the theme without introduction or explanation is a stroke savouring of the simplicity of genius. Equally effective is the simple metrical transition whereby the chorus assumes the trochaic measure of a childhood chant or carol:

> "Lightly O, brightly O,
> Down the long lane she will go!
> Dancing she, glancing she,
> Down the lane with eyes aglow!"

In "Assurance" and "It's Lovetime," the author displays a lyrical fervour of more conventional type; adding the touch of originality by means of melodious simplicity and reiteration in the one case, and pure lyric ecstasy in the other.

The metrical originality of Miss Jackson, displayed in all classes of her work, should not be slighted amidst the enthusiasm one entertains for her magical mastery of thoughts and images. No other conservative poet of the period is more versatile and individual in choice of numbers, or in adaptation of measure to mood. "Driftwood," a wonderfully original poem of imagination describing the fancies which arise from the smoke of logs wafted from far mysterious lands where once the trees grew under strange suns, moons, and rainbows, is as remarkable in form as in idea. One may judge by a sample pair of stanzas:

224

"You warm your hands
And smile
Before the fire of driftwood.

"I feel old lands'
Wan guile
That writhes in fire of driftwood."

We have so far viewed poetry which would lead us to classify Miss Jackson as a delineator of moods rather than of character; yet knowing her versatility, we naturally expect to find among her works some potent character studies. Nor are we disappointed. "Joe," a song of the Maine woods, describes in admirably appropriate verbiage—as simple and as nearly monosyllabic as possible—the typical Anglo-Saxon stoic of far places, who faces comfort and disaster, life and death, with the same unemotional attitude which Miss Jackson sums up so skilfully in the one ejaculatory bit of colloquial indifference—"Dunno!"

"The Song of Jonny Laughlin" is a highly unusual ballad relating the history of a peculiarly good and self-sacrificing river character. The story is simple, but the piece gains distinctiveness from its absolutely faithful reproduction of the spirit of frontier balladry. In words, swing, and weird refrain, there exists every internal evidence of traditional authenticity; and that such a bit of Nature could be composed by a cultivated feminine author is an overwhelming testimonial to Miss Jackson's unique gifts.

That Miss Jackson can reflect the spirit of the most dissimilar characters is further proved by the two immensely powerful studies of the vagabond type entitled "The Call" and "John Worthington Speaks." These things are masterpieces of their kind; the self-revealing narratives of restless wanderers by land and sea, crammed to repletion with details and local colour which no one but their author could command without actual experience as a derelict of five continents and as many oceans. They leave the reader veritably breathless with wonder at the objectivity and imagination which can enable a New-England poetess to mirror with such compelling vividness in thought and language the sentiments of so utterly opposite a type. Not even the narrowly specialised genius of such rough-and-ready writers as Service and Knibbs, working in their own peculiar field, can surpass this one slight phase of Miss Jackson's universal genius.

It remains to speak of the singular power of Miss Jackson in the realm of the gruesome and the terrible. With that same sensitiveness to the unseen and the unreal which lends witchery to her gayer productions, she has achieved in darker fields of verse results inviting comparison with the best prose work of Ambrose Bierce or Maurice Level. Among her older poems the ghastly and colourful phantasy "Insomnia" and the grimly realistic rustic tragedy "Chores" excited especial praise, a critic referring as follows to the latter piece:

> "It has all the compelling power which marks Miss Jackson's darker productions, and is conveyed in an arresting staccato measure which emphasises the homely horror of the theme. The phraseology, with its large proportion of rural and archaic words and constructions, adds vastly to the general effect and atmosphere."

This reference to Miss Jackson's unusual vocabulary deserves elaboration, for one of the secrets of her effective poetry is the wide and diverse array of words and word-combinations which she commands. Recondite archaisms and ruralisms, together with marvellously apt and original descriptive compounds, are things which perpetually astonish and delight her readers. Of recent specimens of Miss Jackson's darker verse, "Finality," "The Song" and "Fallen Fences" deserve especial praise. The horrible picture conjured up in the closing lines of the first named piece is one well calculated to haunt the dreams of the imaginative.

As we conclude this survey of rich and varied poetry, our dominant impression aside from admiration is that of wonder at the tardiness with which the author has been recognised by the non-amateur public. As yet the name of Jackson is a comparative novelty to the literary world, a thing explainable only by the reluctance of its possessor to adopt that species of trumpeting which helps less modest and less genuine poets into the glare of celebrity. But genius such as Miss Jackson's can not remain forever hidden, however slight be her striving for fame; so that we may reasonably expect the next few years to witness her establishment among the leading literary figures, as one of the ablest, broadest and most original of contemporary bards.

226

EX OBLIVIONE

Ward Phillips

When the last days were upon me, and the ugly trifles of existence began to drive me to madness like the small drops of water that torturers let fall ceaselessly upon one spot of their victim's body, I loved the irradiate refuge of sleep. In my dreams I found a little of the beauty I had vainly sought in life, and wandered through old gardens and enchanted woods.

Once when the wind was soft and scented I heard the south calling, and sailed endlessly and languorously under strange stars.

Once when the gentle rain fell I glided in a barge down a sunless stream under the earth till I reached another world of purple twilight, iridescent arbours and undying roses.

And once I walked through a golden valley that led to shadowy groves and ruins, and ended in a mighty wall green with antique vines, and pierced by a little gate of bronze.

Many times I walked through that valley, and longer and longer would I pause in the spectral half-light where the giant trees squirmed and twisted grotesquely, and the grey ground stretched damply from trunk to trunk, sometimes disclosing the mould-stained stones of buried temples. And always the goal of my fancies was the mighty vine-grown wall with the little gate of bronze therein.

After a while, as the days of waking became less and less bearable from their greyness and sameness, I would often drift in opiate peace through the valley and the shadowy groves, and wonder how I might seize them for my eternal dwelling-place, so that I need no more crawl back to a dull world stript of interest and new colours. And as I looked upon the little gate in the mighty wall, I felt that beyond it lay a dream-country from which, once it was entered, there would be no return.

So each night in sleep I strove to find the hidden latch of the gate in the ivied antique wall, though it was exceedingly well-hidden. And I would tell myself that the realm beyond the wall was not more lasting merely, but more lovely and radiant as well.

Then one night in the dream-city of Zakarion I found a yellowed papyrus filled with the thoughts of dream-sages who dwelt of old in that city, and who were too wise ever to be born in the waking world. Therein were written many things concerning the world of dream, and among them was lore of a golden valley and a sacred grove with temples, and a high wall pierced by a little bronze

227

gate. When I saw this lore, I knew that it touched on the scenes I had haunted, and I therefore read long in the yellowed papyrus.

Some of the dream-sages wrote gorgeously of the wonders beyond the irrepassable gate, but others told of horror and disappointment. I knew not which to believe, yet longed more and more to cross forever into the unknown land; for doubt and secrecy are the lure of lures, and no new horror can be more terrible than the daily torture of the commonplace. So when I learned of the drug which would unlock the gate and drive me through, I resolved to take it when next I awaked.

Last night I swallowed the drug and floated dreamily into the golden valley and the shadowy groves; and when I came this time to the antique wall, I saw that the small gate of bronze was ajar. From beyond came a glow that weirdly lit the giant twisted trees and tops of the buried temples, and I drifted on songfully, expectant of the glories of the land from whence I should never return.

But as the gate swung wider and the sorcery of drug and dream pushed me through, I knew that all sights and glories were at an end; for in that new realm was neither land nor sea, but only the white void of unpeopled and illimitable space. So, happier than I had ever dared hope to be, I dissolved again into that native infinity of crystal oblivion from which the daemon Life had called me for one brief and desolate hour.

OFFICIAL ORGAN FUND

Providence, R. I., July 1, 1921.

RECEIPTS SINCE APRIL 1, 1921

From Treasurer, up to July 1, 1921	$18.50
Verna McGeoch (2 instalments)	10.00
E. Edward Ericson	10.00
Mr. and Mrs. Leo Fritter	2.00
John Milton Samples	1.00
Balance on Hand, April 1, 1921	8.50
Total Receipts	$50.00

228

EXPENDITURES

To E. E. Ericson, for March U. A. $46.00

Balance on Hand, July 1, 1921 $4.00

H. P. Lovecraft,
Custodian

THE UNITED AMATEUR SEPTEMBER 1921

THE UNITED AMATEUR

Official Organ
of the
United Amateur Press Association

H. P. Lovecraft   *Official Editor*
E. Edward Ericson   *Official Publisher*
Issued bi-monthly by the United Amateur Press
Association.
Subscription Price, 50 cents per year.
Published at Elroy, Wisconsin.
Entered as second-class mail matter at the post office at
Elroy, Wis.

SEPTEMBER 1921

OFFICIAL BOARD

Official Publisher—E. Edward Ericson, Elroy, Wis.
Laureate Recorder—Howard R. Conover, Route 1, Cozaddale, Ohio.
Manuscript Manager—Grace M. Bromley, 1432 R St., N. W., Washington, D. C.
Historian—Myrta Alice Little, Westville, N. H.
Supervisor of Amendments—(To be appointed.)
Directors—Paul J. Campbell, Route 2, Ridgefarm, Ill.; Anne T. Renshaw, 2109 F St., N. W., Washington, D. C.; Jay Fuller Spoerri, 304 House Office Bldg., Washington, D. C.
Department of Public Criticism—Alfred Galpin, Jr., Chairman, 830 W. Johnson St., Madison, Wis.
Department of Private Criticism—Maurice W. Moe, Chairman, 2812 Chestnut St., Milwaukee, Wis.
Recruiting Committee—Frank Belknap Long, Jr., Chairman, Paul J. Campbell, Leo Fritter, Alfred L. Hutchinson, Gavin T. McColl, Maurice W. Moe.
Ladies' Auxiliary Committee—Eleanor Beryl North, Chairman, Mary Faye Durr, Jennie Eva Harris, Winifred Virginia Jackson, Margaret Mahon, Anne T. Renshaw.

LAUREATE TITLES

Poetry—S. Lilian McMullen; Honourable Mention, Mary Carver Williams.
Story—H. P. Lovecraft; Honourable Mention, Alfred Galpin, Jr.
Essay—Anna Helen Crofts and H. P. Lovecraft; Honourable Mention, Alfred Galpin, Jr.
Editorial—(To be awarded.)

LITERATI

Poetry—Arthur Goodenough, Olive G. Owen (deceased).
Story—Eleanor Barnhart Campbell.
Editorial—H. P. Lovecraft.

INFORMATION

"Amateur Journalism is for those who cultivate literature from taste or attachment, for those who write for the love of writing, for those who pursue the art of letters for its own sake. They may or may not be engaged (or aspire to be engaged) in authorship as a business, but those who are members of that profession will undoubtedly find in Amateur Journalism the air of freedom which develops personality in writing. They will find every encouragement to self-development, amid an environment of art. Amateur Journalism is for all those who do literary work for the love of it."

"The privileges of the United Amateur Press Association are: The use of the Manuscript Bureau and the columns of the papers connected with the Association; the Official Organ; attendance at Conventions; proxy representation at elections; laureate competitions, etc."

"Any person who edits or contributes prose or poetry to any amateur paper is eligible to membership."

"Application for membership must be accompanied by one dollar dues and a printed or written credential.... If rejected, dues will be returned."

"Renewal or reinstatement fee is two dollars."

"Applicants for membership should address their applications, with credential and dues, to the Secretary, Miss Alma B. Sanger, 667 Lilley Ave., Columbus, Ohio."

"Any person wishing to become connected with the Association without furnishing a credential or becoming active, may upon payment of two dollars be enrolled as a sustaining member for one year. A sustaining member shall be entitled to all the privileges of active membership except the right to vote or hold office."

"Laureate entries shall be poem, story, essay and editorial."

"Entries must be printed in an amateur paper, and a marked copy sent to the Laureate Recorder by June 1."

Anyone desiring application blanks for recruiting may receive them by applying to the Secretary.

IMPORTANT

Members are urged to remember the recent doubling of dues, whereby all renewals became Two Dollars each.

The fullest of apologies is due the membership for the lateness of this issue of The United Amateur. A prostrating and overwhelming flood of professional duties, coupled with a state of health permitting only the shortest of working hours, has forced the editor to delay transmission of this copy to the publisher until November 4: a date which should be remembered in justice to the latter official, who is equally handicapped in the matter of conflicting duties.

The Editor

EDITORIAL

In the excellent October Woodbee, Mr. Leo Fritter criticises with much force the attempt of the present editor to conduct The United Amateur on a tolerably civilised plane. He points out that the appearance of a journal representing a fairly uniform maturity of thought and artistic development may perhaps tend to discourage those newer aspirants who have not yet attained their full literary stature, and thus defeat the educational ends of the Association.

Mr. Fritter gathers his material for complaint from the opinions of certain amateurs with whom he has held communication, and on this basis alleges a "wide-spreading dissatisfaction" with the present editorial policy. We have ourselves received numerous and enthusiastic assurances of an opposite nature, especially since the Fritter attack, so that we must rebut at least his charge that we are ignoring the membership's wishes and "trying to conform them to a mould we have arbitrarily cast according to ideas of our own." To adopt a lower standard would, indeed, be affronting a more influential element than that which may at present be dissatisfied; an element which has possibly gained higher claims to consideration through the continuous nature of its services to the Association during trying times when others were silent and inactive.

But in determining the question of editorial policy, the abstract merits of the case are more important than the act of pleasing this or that person or group. Were we convinced that the existing order hampered the sincere novice, we would abandon it without pride or ceremony. That we do not, is because we are certain that retrogression and decadence would constitute a fatal mistake. The public we serve is assumed to be a genuinely progressive one, a group bent upon attaining some measure of proficiency in that sincere self-expression which is art. If it were not, it would have joined some other association of different purposes—the defiantly crude Erford pseudo-United or the complacently social and stationary National. What justifies the separate existence and support of the United is its higher aesthetic and intellectual cast; its demand for the unqualified best as a goal—which demand, by the way, must not be construed as discriminating against even the crudest beginner who honestly cherishes that goal. With these objects in mind, it will be seen that the self-satisfied exultation of the superficial, the obvious, the commonplace, and the conventional, would form the greatest possible tactical error. The goal would be unjustifiably obscured, and the aspiration of the

232

membership stunted, through the enshrining of a false and inferior goal—a literary Golden Calf. We must envisage a genuine scale of values, and possess a model of genuine excellence toward which to strive. It would pay better to work toward a high standard oneself, than to seek to drag the standard down to fit whatever particular grade of ignorance one may happen to have at a given moment. With proper effort any member may eventually produce work of the United Amateur grade, and such work will be certain of a cordial welcome in this office. The official organ is not so narrow as it seems; if more of our capable members would favour it with their literary contributions, the range of authors represented would not be so restricted. It is not the editor but the body of our literati who must bear responsibility for the constant reappearance of certain names. This issue is headed by the same poet who headed the last two—but only because another eminent amateur, so far unrepresented during the present regime, utterly ignored our repeated requests for a contribution.

Mr. Fritter—who, I fear, wrongs etymology in his acceptance of the word amateur as meaning a tyro rather than a genuine and disinterested artist—forgets that a relapse to cruder standards would totally unfit the United for serving that staunch element which has contributed most to its present welfare. Many would find a society of the lower grade intolerable; certainly it could not hope to hold the very ones who have given this organization its existing distinctiveness and pre-eminence.

Yet in the arguments of Mr. Fritter there is an underlying soundness which misapplication should not obscure to the analytical reader. He is right in lamenting, as we believe he does, the absence of a suitable publishing medium for the work of our younger writers. It is not in a spirit of affront to him that we give preference to the plan of President Haughton, as outlined in her opening message, for the re-establishment of a special magazine for credentials. We should be glad to curtail the official organ in the interest of such a magazine, as indeed we offered to do at the beginning of the term.

Frustra laborat, says the old proverb, qui omnibus placere studet. We regret that any one policy must of necessity displease a few members, yet do not see how any improvement could be effected by making a change which would merely shift the displeasure to another and even more continuously industrious group. It is significant that the Gothic party have no editorial candidate of their own to offer, so that the thankless and toilsome office has been forced upon one whose indifferent health makes it an almost unbearable burden to him. The question is one which should ultimately be decided at the polls, each party putting forward a nominee who can be depended upon to fulfil its mandates. Meanwhile the present editor, whose sincere beliefs and policies were fully known long before his unopposed election, stands ready to resign most cheerfully whenever a suitable successor can be found. Bitterness, division and personalities must be avoided at any cost, and we may be reckoned as a supporter of The United Amateur under any editor and policy.

THE UNITED AMATEUR NOVEMBER 1921

THE UNITED AMATEUR

Official Organ
of the
United Amateur Press Association

H. P. Lovecraft   *Official Editor*
E. Edward Ericson   *Official Publisher*
Issued bi-monthly by the United Amateur Press Association.
Subscription Price, 50 cents per year.
Published at Elroy, Wisconsin.
Entered as second-class mail matter at the post office at Elroy, Wis.

Members who criticised the present editor for severity during the chairmanship of the critical department are invited to take a vicarious revenge this month, observing the uncensored remarks of the present juvenile chairman concerning our pathetic ignorance. Of us Master Galpin says: "when the author approaches involved or technical subjects, he shows clearly the unfortunate circumstance that he has never profited by an advanced education." This certainly should purge us of all suspicion of conducting The United Amateur on too Olympian a level, although the critic qualifies his dictum by conceding that we realise our own crudity and are striving in our old age to acquire at least the rudiments of an elementary education. In the course of a few years we hope to guarantee our readers an official organ practically free from the grosser errors of spelling and grammar: meanwhile, vivat Galpinius parvulus!

Myrta Alice Little, Eugene B. Kuntz, Leo G. Schussman, Margaret Richard, Daisy Crump Whitehead, Clara L. Bell, John O. Baldwin, and the Editor.

The Tryout. October 1921. Uniform size. Contributions by H. P. Lovecraft, Margaret Richard, Beth Cheney Nichols, Arthur Goodenough, K. Leyson Brown, Horace L. Lawson, John Milton Samples, Washington Van Dusen, Leo G. Schussman, Lilian Middleton, Anita Roberta Kirksey, and the Editor.

The United Amateur. March 1921. Official Organ of the United Amateur Press Association. 14 Pages and cover. 7×10. Contributions by Winifred Virginia Jackson, Lilian Middleton, Frank Belknap Long, Jr., J. E. Hoag, Anna H. Crofts, Eleanor Beryl North, Ward Phillips, and the Editor, H. P. Lovecraft.

The United Amateur. May 1921. 8 pages. 7×10. Contributions by Lilian Middleton, Alfred Galpin, Jr., Eugene B. Kuntz, Margaret Mahon, Winifred Virginia Jackson, and Adam Harold Brown.

The United Amateur. July 1921. 6 pages. 7×10. Contributions by Lilian Middleton and Myrta Alice Little.

The United Co-Operative. April 1921. 16 pages. 6×9. Contributions by Lilian Middleton, Elizabeth Berkeley and Lewis Theobald, Jr., W. Edwin Gibson, John C. Pryor, H. P. Lovecraft, Samuel Loveman, Eugene B. Kuntz. Published under the auspices of the U. A. P. A. by the following members: Anne Tillery Renshaw, Rev. John Clinton Pryor, W. Edwin Gibson, H. P. Lovecraft.

The Woodbee. October 1921. 16 pages and cover. 5×7. Contributions by Bess Ballou, Alma B. Sanger, Norma Helena Marie Sanger, Leo Fritter, Edna M. Haughton, Peggy Hepner Fritter, Henriette Ziegfeld, and the President, Ida C. Haughton. Official Organ of the Woodbee Press Club, Columbus, Ohio.

Ziegfeld's Follies. September 1921. 1 page. 5½×8½. Contributions by the Editor, Arthur F. Ziegfeld.

Ziegfeld's Follies. October 1921. 4 pages. Uniform

size. Contributions by Ida C. Haughton, Leo Fritter, and the Editor, Arthur F. Ziegfeld.

Myrta Alice Little,
Historian

OFFICIAL ORGAN FUND

Providence, R. I., December 29, 1921

On Hand, July 1, 1921 $4.00
RECEIPTS SINCE JULY 1

Sonia H. Greene	$50.00
From Treasury, up to Dec. 29, 1921	41.60
H. P. Lovecraft	15.40
Mr. and Mrs. Leo Fritter	6.00
Howard R. Conover	5.00
Woodbee Press Club	5.00
Theodore D. Gottlieb	1.00
Ida C. Haughton	1.00
Total Receipts	$129.00

EXPENDITURES

To E. E. Ericson, for May U. A.	$24.00
To E. E. Ericson, for July U. A.	18.00
To E. E. Ericson, for Sept. U. A.	36.00
To E. E. Ericson, for Nov. U. A.	36.00
Total Expenditures	$114.00
Balance on Hand, December 29, 1921	$15.00

H. P. Lovecraft,
Custodian.

THE UNITED AMATEUR

Official Organ
of the
United Amateur Press Association

H. P. Lovecraft Official Editor
E. Edward Ericson Official Publisher
Issued bi-monthly by the United Amateur Press
Association.
Subscription Price, 50 cents per year.
Published at Elroy, Wisconsin.
Entered as second-class mail matter at the post office
at Elroy, Wis.

EDITORIAL

Amidst the prevailing efforts of a small but pugnacious group to "liven" up the United through attacks on the Official Organ, a few basic principles should be remembered by those who stand in bewilderment.

Our constitution does not define the functions of The United Amateur beyond making imperative the publication of certain official documents. The rest is left to an unwritten combination of tradition and editorial judgment. Any editor, once elected, is absolutely in control of the magazine aside from the essential official matter; his only external obligation being a tacit recognition of the prevailing objects of the Association. In the present case a narrow circle of agitators seems to be seeking political capital by accusing the editor of placing too high an estimate on the membership and purposes of the United.

Since the whole development of the Association is involved in this matter, it is important that a prompt and perfect understanding be reached. The opinions of all members should be known, and if the editor finds that he has been in error, he will be glad to arrange for the accommodation of the Organ to the wishes of the majority.

237

Up to the present time, despite the florid overstatements of the few who are trying to work up a new and wholly artificial dissatisfaction, this office has received not so much as one complaint as to policy save from the two politicians who are seeking to lower the United's standards. Endorsements as to the existing policy have been many, and as long as these remain so tremendously in the Majority, it would be a betrayal of trust to make a change to please a tiny group. If there are those who differ, why do they not speak?

Since truth is the only perfect clarifier when politics seeks to becloud, it is necessary that the editor state his policy here and now with the utmost candour. Shorn of all irrelevant things, that policy is simply the maintenance of those standards established in the United by the departure of the chronically political element in 1912. Prior to that time the Official Organ was mainly a bulletin of reports: not, as the present agitators would imply, a repository for indiscriminate amateur writings. The standard developed since then is the creation of no one person, but a logical outgrowth of the rising calibre of a vital and progressive society. It is neither one of favouritism nor one of autocracy; but merely one of stimulation. It is an embodiment of the United's desire to let the Official Organ exemplify the members' progress by using the best available material. No genuine aspirant has ever been frowned upon, or so far as we know given any ground for discouragement. The Organ is a beckoner and encourager, designed to inspire the members to renewed efforts to produce work worthy of symbolising the United. Would anyone so far insult the Association as to wish its official exponent to cater to that type of mediocrity which neither improves nor wishes to improve? Our columns are open to all who toil for the fruits of art, and statements to the contrary cannot be interpreted as other than irresponsibly ignorant or craftily misrepresentative. While insistence on a certain degree of merit is of course necessary, it is not true that The United Amateur makes any arbitrary restrictions. The Organ was not designed for the publication of various members' work, nor is access to its columns one of the special objects of membership, as certain agitators are artfully intimating. But notwithstanding those technical points, all proficient writers are welcome. It is illuminating, in view of the prevalent loose statements, to reflect that throughout the present editor's service not more than three manuscripts have been rejected; and that even these three were or will be elsewhere placed. Those seeking an Associational disturbance will not scruple to take advantage of every outward appearance which seems to favour them—unavoidable delays, spatial limitations, and other things interfering with prompt publication of all matter offered to this

238

office. The present editor will be denounced as a "tyrant" by elements attempting to degrade standards which he did not establish!

The life and well-being of the United are at stake, and it is imperative that the membership exercise the most careful and independent reflection before accepting the views of radicals bent on retrogressive experiments.

THE UNITED AMATEUR MARCH 1922

OFFICIAL ORGAN FUND

Providence, R. I., April 25, 1922.

On Hand, December 29, 1921 $15.00

RECEIPTS SINCE DECEMBER 29

From Treasury, up to April 25	$31.00
Woodbee Press Club	10.00
H. P. Lovecraft	7.00
Anonymous	5.00
Mr. and Mrs. Leo Fritter	2.00
Ida C. Haughton	2.00
Total Receipts	$72.00

EXPENDITURES

To E. E. Ericson, for January U. A.	$36.00
To E. E. Ericson, for March U. A.	36.00
Total Expenditures	$72.00
Balance on Hand, April 25, 1922	None

H. P. Lovecraft,
Custodian.

239

THE UNITED AMATEUR MAY 1922

OFFICIAL ORGAN FUND

Providence, R. I., June 23, 1922.

On Hand, April 25, 1922 None

Receipts Since April 25

From Treasury, up to June 23	$28.00
Alfred Galpin, Jr.	6.00
Woodbee Press Club	5.00
Mr. and Mrs. Leo Fritter	2.00
Total Receipts	$41.00

Expenditures

To E. E. Ericson, for May U. A. $24.00
Balance on Hand, June 23, 1922 $17.00
H. P. Lovecraft,
Custodian

AT THE HOME OF POE

A Poem in Prose
To H. P. Lovecraft

Frank Belknap Long, Jr.

The home of Poe! It is like a fairy dwelling, a gnomic palace built of the aether of dreams. It is tiny and delicate and lovely, and replete with memories of sere leaves in November and of lilies in April. It is a castle of vanished hopes, of dimly-remembered dreams, of sad memories older than the deluge. The dead years circle slowly and solemnly around its low white walls, and clothe it in a mystic veil of unseen tears. And many marvellous stories could this quaint little old house tell, many weird and cryptic stories of him of the Raven hair, and high, pallid brow, and sad, sweet face, and melancholy mien; and of the beloved Virginia, that sweet child of a thousand magic visions, child of the lonesome, pale-gray latter years, child of the soft and happy South. And how the dreamer of the spheres must have loved this strange little house. Every night the hollow boards of its porch must have echoed to his footfall, and every morn the great rising sun must have sent its rays through the little window, and bathed the lovely tresses of the dream-child in mystical yellow. And perhaps there was laughter within the walls of that house—laughter and merriment and singing. But we know that the Evil One came at last, the grim humourless spectre who loves not beauty, and is not of this world. And we know that the house of youth and of love became a house of death, and that memories bitter as the tears of a beautiful woman assailed the dreamer within. And at last he himself left that house of mourning and sought solace among the stars. But the house remains a vision out of a magical book; a thing seen darkly as in a looking-glass; but lovely beyond the dreams of mortals, and ineffably sad.